All the Wrong Reasons

Jerilee Kaye

All the Wrong Reasons

This book is a work of fiction. Names, places, events, characters, situations and incidents mentioned in this book are products of the author's imagination and/or used in a fictitious manner. Any resemblance to real or actual people, living or dead, places, brands, or events are purely coincidental and not intended by the author. Reference to public figures or brands are purely for the sake of fiction. The opinion of the characters does not reflect the opinion of the author.

Cover Design by Sir Alfred Java III, Print Vault ME
Book Trailer by Print Vault ME
Cover Illustration Copyright @ Kiuikson
Editing by Lisa Kazmier, Kathleen Consuelo Antic
and Yukta Kharbanda
Beta Readers: Fatematuz Zohra, Nha-thi Luu, Keshavi Kharbanda

Copyright 2018 Jerilee Kaye
All Rights Reserved
ISBN: 9781720201304

This book is licensed for your private use only. Any other use of the whole or part of this book (including, but not limited to, adaptation, translation, copying, issuing copies, unauthorized lending and rental, broadcasting or making available to the internet, social media, wireless technology and application) is strictly prohibited. Thank you for respecting the hard work of the author.

Acknowledgements

Big hugs and kisses to the following wonderful people who made this book a possibility:

My parents, Angel and Norma, you are the reason why I strive to go after my dreams.

My sisters, brother-in-law, aunts and uncles, you are the reason why I keep my feet on the ground.

My little angels, MarQuise, Maui and Keon, you're the reason why I stay young and happy every day.

To my Sam, my loving husband, my best friend, the love of my life, you are the reason why I sleep and wake up with a smile on my face each day. Thank you for the steamy book cover and trailer.

To my Chapters family at Crazy Maple Studio, you are the reason why more people fell in love with Justin Adams.

To my editor, Lisa K and KC Antic and Yukta Kharbanda, thanks for a wonderful job.

To my beta readers, my proofreaders, Fatematuz Zohra, Nha-thi Luu, Keshavi Kharbanda, thank you very much. You guys are amazing!

To my Wattpad friends, you are the reason why I rewrote this story and made it better than ever. Thank you for contributing to the word translations. You are the reason for the unique and cool chapter titles of this book. This will always be special because of you.

To my Readers, you are the reason why I keep writing fairy tale endings, book boyfriends and happily ever afters

1.
Heroina
Latin. Etymology of the word: Heroine.

*A*drienne Miller sat in her balcony, one October afternoon. She just finished unpacking her clothes and putting all her furniture in place. Her new apartment reflected every bit of her personality. Every vase, every painting and every jar showcased her style.

She felt very tired, having spent the rest of the day tidying up and decorating her new haven, but she was happy. She employed the services of an interior design team. She paid a fortune, but as she admired her white, gray and pink minimalist-designed haven, she thought that it was all worth it.

Her apartment stood on the middle floor of a luxurious building in a high-end area in Manhattan, just five blocks away from her office. It was a two bedroom that had two en-suite baths, a huge balcony, and walk-in closets. She placed a glass table with matching white steel chairs on her balcony which had a breathtaking view of Manhattan.

The moment her broker showed her the apartment, she immediately fell in love with it. It was expensive, but it was one of her dreams. She never indulged in other expensive material things. For quite some time now, she had been saving for this apartment, a place where she would spend the rest of her life. According to her friends, this is where she will wile away her virgin years.

Yes. She was twenty-five years old. Never been touched and infrequently kissed.

Her boyfriend, Troy Williams, lived a thousand miles away from her. They had been together for three years now, but he lived in Massachusetts. While he went to medical school, she worked as an editor in Manhattan.

Troy was old-fashioned. Traditional and quite a gentleman. He never suggested they go to bed together and she was thankful about it. Adrienne had been fantasizing about her first time all her life. She wanted it to be an intense experience. The man, the time and the place…every single thing had to be perfect.

She wanted no regrets. It had to be unforgettable. She didn't hold on to it for so long only to be disappointed. She wouldn't have sex just for the sake of losing her virginity. She wanted it to be electrifying and memorable, so that when her hair turned gray, she'd go back to that particular moment and remember it only with a smile on her face, nothing less.

Maybe she'd do it with Troy someday, but until they're both ready, Adrienne felt satisfied given the way things were.

She met Troy at a party she attended with her family. His parents were friends with hers. Adrienne thought he was cute and comfortable to be with, but not exactly her type. She usually preferred guys with a dangerous edge, cool façade and a devil-may-care attitude. But she knew too well that there's a high price to pay to be with a guy like that. There's too much risk involved and Adrienne didn't see herself as a risk taker. The last thing she wanted was to lose herself to a guy who would easily fool around with other girls. So, she settled for safe, cute and comfortable. And Troy, with his dark blonde hair and dark brown eyes, tan skin and deep dimples was as secure as a security blanket.

She recalled one of the many conversations she had with her friends about Troy.

Her best friend, Yuan Davis, once told her, "You should really think better of yourself. I think there are better fish in the ocean."

She met Yuan in college and they've been BFFs ever since. He was half-Japanese, half-American and full-on fabulous.

Her friends thought of Troy as too prim, too proper. In other words, too boring for her. They believed she deserved somebody way cuter than him. Someone who could make her laugh, challenge her mind, and encourage her to explore her wilder side.

Adrienne could understand them perfectly well. She never heard Troy tell a joke or laugh at one. And he couldn't seem to tolerate simple foibles in human behavior, even temporary things like getting wasted, occasional smoking, miniskirts or highlighted hair irked him. He was unaware that Adrienne herself had found refuge with a cigarette once in a while.

"He's like the fireman who will always water your fire!" Her other best friend, Jill Durmont said. "You have a wilder spirit than you'd like to admit. Having a guy who puts a stopper on all your flair won't help you spread your wings."

Like Yuan, Adrienne met Jill in college too. She's a petite blonde who writes gossip columns for the magazine Adrienne works for.

Troy hoped to be a doctor one day, just like his parents. Adrienne's sister, Kimberly, goes to the same medical school as Troy.

Adrienne could never be a doctor, no matter how smart she was. She couldn't stand the sight and smell of blood. She was the odd one out in a family of doctors. Well, maybe if you can't be one then marry one. And maybe that was the reason why she dated Troy in the first place.

She had a broken relationship with her mother. Somehow, she felt that her mother never loved her the way she loved her sister. And all her life, she tried her best to win her over. But she never did. Not even when she got accepted by the best universities in the country. Not even when she graduated with honors.

Instead of being proud, her mother said, "It's a very easy program!"

Adrienne earned a dual degree in journalism and mass communications. She possessed a talent for writing. She was the only one in her family who had a knack for it. Her sister couldn't put a paragraph together, her mother couldn't understand the context of metaphors and her father never showed interest in any form of literature. But no matter how good she was, her family brushed off her achievements like they were insignificant.

At the party where she met Troy, her mother introduced him to her sister first. But Troy couldn't take his eyes off her. He tried to strike up a conversation with her every chance he got.

Her mother must have really liked Troy for it not to matter which daughter he asked out. At first, she didn't know what her mother saw in him. But she became too engrossed in pleasing her that she eventually found herself enjoying Troy's company too.

But she lived in New York and he was in medical school in Massachusetts. Her odd working hours and his heavy load made it impossible for them to see each other often.

They often spoke on the phone, but they only saw each other once a month, sometimes less than that. However, she got used to their setup and thought that the phone calls and video chats were enough to keep her secure with their relationship.

What else could she ask for? He loved her. She loved him. Her mother strongly approved of their relationship. When the time felt right, maybe he'd propose to her and she'd lose her virginity on their wedding night. What else could be more perfect?

Maybe she wasn't like Jill or the other women who enjoyed sex and sleeping with their boyfriends. She accepted feeling old-fashioned and would rather wait for the right guy or for marriage. Her friends might argue that she just said this because Troy never triggered sexual feelings in her, but what if she wasn't a sexual person? What if she just felt incapable of succumbing to intense passion? Moreover, her conversations with Troy always drifted into topics like HIV, teenage pregnancy and abortion. If those weren't mood-killers for sex, she didn't know what might be.

Like her parents, Troy didn't approve of her job. Getting this apartment offered a way for her to show them that she could manage well on her own, even though she wasn't a doctor. She found a way to assert her independence and stand up for herself, regardless of what they wanted her to do or who they wanted her to be.

Suddenly, Adrienne felt glum. Ten minutes ago, she was happy and content with her life, but now, she couldn't help but feel disappointed. Thinking about Troy and her parents had that effect on her. No matter how posh this apartment seemed, her mother wouldn't approve of it. She would think Adrienne wasted her money. True, it put a huge dent in her savings, and she would require years to pay off a sizable mortgage, but when did she ever do anything risky in her life?

Her eyes drifted off her neighbors' balcony. She hadn't seen them yet, and she hoped they'd be nice or at the very least, trustworthy. She shared a bedroom wall with them. Not only that, her bedroom window ran parallel to theirs and a wide platform connected them, the kind that would allow them to break into her apartment through her bedroom window. This was the only thing she didn't like about her place. Every day she prayed that she hadn't become neighbors with mobsters.

She scanned the steel chairs and glass table on the balcony beside hers. They seemed almost the same as hers, only theirs were black. Good to know that she and her neighbors had the same taste.

She noticed an abandoned bottle of Heineken and an ashtray with cigarette butts. She guessed that at least one male lived in that family. And most likely, no babies. She believed either she lived next to a couple or a bachelor. It's comforting to know no one would complain if she held parties or let her friends sleepover and Yuan decided to play "Bette Davis Eyes" over and over again.

She turned around and started going back into her living room. Just before she could completely go inside, she caught something out of the corner of her eye.

Her neighbor stepped out to his balcony. He wore only a pair of jeans. She stared at his perfectly tanned torso. His biceps were well-toned and she figured he had at least a six pack.

He lit a cigarette and stared at their gorgeous city view, lost in his thoughts. His jet-black hair was disheveled and even from afar, she could make out his long, dark eyelashes.

As she stared at his profile, a sense of familiarity filled her.

Ohmigod! It can't be!

Her heart pounded loudly inside her rib cage.

She knew him. He was… NYC's most wanted bachelor… a.k.a. the City's most notorious playboy.

Justin Adams.

Her mind raced with information about him, she didn't even know she had.

Prodigal heir of Adams Industries, son of a steel and mining magnate. Filthy rich. But instead of living in the shadows of his father, he desired to draw his own map, his own future. He graduated with a double degree from Harvard, straight As, high distinction, but he made his father quite angry when he announced that he wouldn't work for their company right away. Instead, he chose to play in the stock market and opted to use his hobby, photography, for gainful employment.

He worked as a freelance photographer for *Blush*, the magazine that also employed her. He was a celebrity in her office. Every single girl there fancied herself in love with him. Even Jill couldn't stop talking about him like he was God's gift to women, or finally one guy deserved being called one.

Adrienne was probably the only one who didn't want to go to bed with him. She found him intriguing, yes. But she didn't really understand the fuss about him.

She hid behind her curtain and continued to watch him.

Okay. He isn't bad. No! Who am I kidding? He looked as handsome as the devil himself!

She sighed to herself. *Maybe he's worth the fuss, after all!*

He fished his phone out of his pocket and made some calls while standing in his balcony. After a few minutes, he put out his light and went inside. She continued watching him through her window. He put on a white shirt, grabbed his leather jacket and left.

Adrienne couldn't help smiling to herself.

My apartment just got even more interesting!

* * *

A few weeks later, Adrienne rushed through a deadline Monday evening. Part of her job was to write reviews about establishments around the city. Today, she needed to write an article about a newly-opened restaurant on Fifth Avenue. The food wasn't so great, the prices not so cheap, and the service a bit unorganized. She ordered a Piña Colada, and twice she received a Margarita.

She didn't want to be known around the block as the bitch who could shut down a decent restaurant, but she didn't want to compromise her professional point of view, either.

She couldn't concentrate on her work. The music from her neighbor's residence was far too loud. Moreover, the fact that she knew he sat on the balcony, playing poker with his friends, and that she could hear him laugh made it even harder for her.

She went out to the balcony to light a cigarette. She badly needed a smoke and she didn't want to light up inside her apartment. The minute she stepped out, she noticed that the guys in the other balcony all fell silent. She suddenly felt self-conscious.

Deep breaths. Deep breaths.

She needed to calm herself. She's a confident woman and she has a boyfriend. Her knees shouldn't turn to jelly just because she thought that Manhattan's playboys had started to survey her long legs.

Just then, her phone rang.

Thank God!

She needed a distraction. She craved thinking about anything other than her devilishly handsome neighbor.

"Hi honey, how are you? It's Troy."

"I'm *grood...*" She replied, unable to decide whether to say 'good' or 'great'.

"What?"

Damn it!

"I'm good. I meant I'm good. How about you? How are you?"

"Not too bad. I was out with Kim last night. She's my designated tutor now," he said with a chuckle.

"She'll be happy to help you. Our mom likes you."

"And I'm a lucky guy, aren't I?"

"Hmmm…"

Troy went on about his study date with Kimberly and she couldn't quite concentrate on what he was saying. She's hearing medical terms that she didn't need to know. She's got too much in her head… the awful food, the restaurant whose existence she was about to end in a few hours, and damn! She can't seem to get a certain dark-haired devil out of her mind.

Absent-mindedly, she let out a groan.

"What?" Troy asked. Apparently, he didn't think that his monologue on chlamydia deserved a groan. "What are you doing? Are you with someone?"

"I'm alone!" she replied. She must have sounded too defensive because Troy didn't believe her…but she hadn't even lied. She was alone. Yet the closest living, breathing human beings sat about ten feet away from her.

"You sound distracted. It didn't seem like you were listening to me at all."

"Troy, please, give me a break. I just remembered this restaurant I likely will close down in a few hours because of an awful review I'm thinking of writing and I don't want to do it. That's why I groaned."

Troy fell silent for a few seconds. Then he added, "Are you sure?"

She let out a frustrated sigh. Then she put out her cigarette and managed to walk back to her living room. By putting herself beyond anyone who could see her, she found her focus.

"Yes, I'm sure. Come on. You're my first ever boyfriend. I didn't even date anybody seriously before I met you. When did I ever give you a reason to doubt me?"

She always felt that Troy didn't trust her enough. Like she had this reputation of being a slut that everybody knew about except for him.

Whenever she went out with her friends and he could hear the background music, he would ask her who she was with, short of asking Jill and Yuan as well to swear on their dead relatives' graves that only the three of them were together. No one else.

At first, she considered it rather sweet that he felt possessive or jealous. After all, that could signal just how much he didn't want to lose her. Recently, however, she decided that it had become too much for her to handle. She needed to tell him where she was at all times, and do headcounts of the friends. It had started getting under her skin.

"It's not that…I just…I miss you. And you're beautiful, Adrienne. I'm sure plenty of guys would be hitting on you."

"And that means, I would sleep with every guy who actually shows interest in me?"

"No. I know you're not like that. And that's what I liked about you. You're…old-fashioned," Then he went on with his medical monologue again. She thought she actually fell asleep on the couch after thirty seconds. Then, finally, he said goodbye.

"Love you, sweetheart," he said.

"Love you, too."

After she hung up the phone, she thought, *"Troy is good for me. He's going to make a good husband someday. We're going to be happy. We've been together for three years, he's not getting any, but he didn't cheat on me and didn't break up with me."*

By the end of the night, she managed to write a not-so-bad review of the restaurant. She highlighted their strengths, the great ambiance and the expensive china. However, she had no choice but to mention that they could do better to lay low on soy sauce and a smile from the waiters would go a long way. She finished the one-thousand-word article amidst Collective Soul's music blasting from Justin Adams's bedroom, like he didn't know he had any neighbors.

The next day, she had lunch with her best friends. Yuan worked at the building next to hers and Jill's, and all of them worked flexible hours that they could get together for lunch and coffee breaks quite easily.

"How's Troy?" Jill asked.

She shrugged. "Having study dates with Kim."

Jill raised her brow at her.

"They deserve each other, you know," Yuan said blatantly.

"Yuan!" Jill hissed.

"What?" he asked nonchalantly. "Come on, Yen. It's not that I want you to be jealous. I just think you deserve a more exciting love life than dating a guy who spends more time with your sister. How long are you going to keep this up?"

"Yuan has a point, Yen. I think you deserve better, too. And you are in dire need of a makeover! You could use some makeup and better fitting clothes. And for God's sake, haven't you heard of contact lenses? Or lasik?" Jill flicked on her eyeglasses.

"Ouch!" Adrienne gave Jill an annoyed look. She had started to get annoyed with them telling her that she's beautiful, but she could be way prettier if she only put more effort in her looks.

She thought she wasn't butt-ugly, but she wasn't supermodel-pretty, either. She had dark brown hair with some reddish highlights. She looked like those girls who went to the salon to get red highlights, only hers were natural. She had expressive green eyes. She didn't diet or exercise regularly, but she possessed curves in the right places. She was all right, and that's how she wanted it.

She gave up hope trying to look pretty. After puberty, she did make some effort, but according to her mother, *"Adrienne is not really ugly, but Kimberly has the real beauty and brains in the family."*

Well, if your own mother didn't think you're pretty, who else would?

In fact, the only person who ever made her feel beautiful at all was Troy, when her mother introduced him to Kimberly, hoping they'd hit it off. Yet he asked for Adrienne's number because, he said, he couldn't get her beautiful face out of his mind. When she started dating Troy, she made her mother proud – for the first and last time.

Maybe Adrienne couldn't break up with Troy for this very reason, no matter how many times her friends told her to do so. No matter how many times she felt that they may actually be right. Troy seemed like the only achievement she'd ever had, as far as her mother believed.

"By the way, guys, I saw Justin Adams in the office this morning. What a snob that guy is! I tried to look him in the eye as we passed each other in the hallway, and it was like he didn't see me at all. But God! Did he look delish!" Jill said dreamily.

"How could you ever look him in the eye? Doesn't he always have that pair of shades on?" Adrienne asked her matter-of-factly.

Yuan laughed and Jill glared at him. Adrienne smiled at her guiltily. "I'm sorry. Go on with your story."

"Well, there's nothing more to it. I'm just saying that I saw him this morning. That's it."

"Well, I'm sure, you can faint in front of him, and he still wouldn't look at you," Adrienne said. "Gods don't mingle with us mere mortals. And Justin Adams thinks he's a god."

"Well, he's not the only one who thinks that," Yuan grinned proudly. "There's many of us who wouldn't disagree."

Adrienne rolled her eyes and groaned. She wanted to tell her friends about her new next-door neighbor. But after hearing how obsessed they were with him, she decided not to inform them. At least not yet. She knew the minute she told them, they would have a stakeout in her apartment. Not that she minded having them over. She didn't want Justin Adams to realize that his neighbor and her friends watched him in his own private refuge like he was a goldfish in a fish tank.

She didn't want him to be aware of her presence, the way that she had become so aware of his. And she hated feeling this way. She had a boyfriend. He loves her. Their relationship was safe and smooth-sailing. The last thing she wanted was to fall prey into a player's web and risk him breaking her heart in the process.

But somehow she found herself watching him whenever they're both home. Even if she hated to admit it, she found it exciting. She reminded herself that there was a thin line between watching and stalking...curious versus crazy.

Within a few weeks, she realized that Justin slept until twelve noon on weekends. On weekdays, he'd be busy on his cellphone long before she'd be up, and he'd return home by seven in the evening. Sometimes he would have friends over, playing poker or drinking on his balcony. Other times, he would be out by nine p.m. and return at around one a.m. Either way, he would take a shower and then go to bed. Justin probably showered three times a day and Adrienne found that too adorable. She wondered what he smelled like.

After her lunch with Yuan and Jill, she returned to her desk feeling inspired. She started typing on her laptop and found herself composing a plot. She drew a picture with words. She created a dark-haired rebel with a gorgeous body, well-sculpted like a marble statue masterpiece. She made her heroine a green-eyed, copper brown-haired princess with an evil queen stepmother and a charming but vile stepsister.

Adrienne felt excited about her new project. It had been a while since she wrote a story. When she was younger, she'd written several romance novels. That's how she knew she would be a writer and make a career out of it.

She juggled between writing her novel and meeting her deadlines for *Blush*. She skipped coffee breaks with Jill and other girls in the office. All they talked about was Justin Adams anyway. And she didn't need to hear about him. All the information she needed at that time could be found next door to her.

"Come on, Yen. Let's go out for lunch. We're celebrating!"

"Why?"

"Jada's sick! And that lady's endured flu, cough, fever and all sorts of things. She's a tough one. And now, finally, she filed for a sick leave."

"I'm sorry. I don't like Jada as much as you do, but no, I don't feel like having a party just because she's under the weather. But you girls have fun, okay?"

Jill rolled her eyes. "You're no fun," she said. "All right. I'll bring you back a waffle."

As soon as Jill left, Adrienne started working on her novel once again. There was a scene in her head she couldn't wait to put into words.

Soon, her eyes fell tired of staring too long at her screen. She stood up from her seat to stretch her arms. Just then, she caught a figure walking from the graphic artists' room towards the corridor in front of her. He was wearing a pair of shades and a leather jacket over a white shirt. He turned towards her and an eyebrow shot up. Then the corner of his lips slightly turned up. Adrienne blinked. When she opened her eyes again, he was gone.

Did he actually smile at her?

Adrienne looked around her once again. She seemed pretty sure she was alone. No one occupied any of the other cubicles around her.

His mouth turned up when he looked at her. *That's a smile, right?*

She groaned.

So, what if he smiled?

The last thing she wanted was to be obsessed with a guy half of Manhattan already fawned over. She's already writing a character inspired by him, for Christ's sake!

Later that night, she met Yuan and Jill for dinner. She needed a break from writing and waited for more ideas to come into her head and the inspiration to write to strike again.

"How come Justin Adams doesn't have a girlfriend?" She popped the question during dessert.

Jill shrugged. "He's playing the field?"

"He's too snobby," Yuan suggested. "Nobody's worth committing to—unless she's royalty, of course."

"Then what is he doing in New York? He must go to Europe if he wanted to meet some noble girl." Adrienne said.

"Well, we know he makes himself constantly available. He's dating around. He has been rumored to date models, and some members of the elite class. But his name won't be linked with these girls for more than two weeks. After that, he walks away. Gone. Then after a few weeks of being single, he'll be seen hanging out with another woman, usually prettier or richer, and the cycle starts all over again," Yuan said.

"He's a playboy," Jill began. "He can't commit. Like he would dump these women after two or three dates. Then he would move on to higher mortals."

Adrienne paid attention to what they said. She wanted to pick up some ideas to use in her novel.

"What if he's not really a player?" Adrienne asked, thinking out loud. "What if he doesn't commit because…he *can't* commit."

She cannot make her male character sleep with everything that walks in a skirt because he couldn't control his urges. One, because, *hello herpes!* And two, what woman would actually fall in love with a guy who sleeps with a woman and then forget about her after a few humps? And who would buy a book if the male protagonist feels like a hopeless case? If there is no hope for him to ever fall in love, the plot cannot lead anywhere good, can it?

"You know, maybe you're right," Yuan reflected. "Maybe it's not Justin's fault he didn't have a steady relationship. Maybe he's secretly engaged to an heiress. You know those business arrangements. I think the rich and powerful still do that."

An idea popped in Adrienne's head. What if her male character had already been previously engaged via a marriage arranged by his parents? A marriage for convenience designed to merge two empires and keep the fortune within their families.

Adrienne's smile went wider. She couldn't wait to go home and start writing again.

She went home at midnight. She went inside the elevator and pressed her floor. The door closed but after a split second, it opened again. Then a dark-haired guy entered the elevator. Her breath caught in her throat.

He smelled of aftershave. Masculine and fresh. He wore a pair of stylish yellow-tinted glasses. Justin always wore shades even at night time, like he intended to keep his eyes a secret to the world. The ones he donned tonight appeared lightly yellow-tinted, designed to reduce glare during night driving. Still, they successfully hid his eye color.

Adrienne desperately wanted to know what his eye color was. She had drawn out her rebel after Justin's physical appearance. She left out her character's eye color because she had no idea what color his eyes were. Even now, she couldn't see what's under those tinted shades.

As the elevator ascended to their floor, Justin didn't even turn towards her or acknowledge her presence in any way. He stared ahead like he was alone the whole time. She must have imagined that he smiled at her at *Blush* earlier that day.

When the elevator door opened though, he held it and motioned for her to go before him, but she doubted he was even aware of her presence.

Well, at least he is a gentleman.

Adrienne walked fast ahead of him and never looked back.

***

After two weeks of acting like a psychotic stalker, Adrienne had progressed halfway through her novel. She found time to write in between the pieces she had to submit for *Blush*.

She was writing a steamy scene between her rebel and her heroine when Jada, who recently returned to work, asked her to come to her office.

She groaned as she stood up from her seat.

What does the Devil in Prada want now?

"You called?" She asked as soon as she stepped into her boss's room.

Jada handed her a ticket.

Gypsys: An enlightening. Grand Opening.

"What is this?"

"A bar?" Jada said, looking at her like she was out of her mind.

"O-kay. What do you want me to do?"

"Since you're in-charge of features and events, I want you to go and write about them in our next issue. Or… is that not what you do?"

"Do you think I have something to compare this to? Do I look like I go to clubs?"

Jada stared at her long skirt and knitted blouse. Then she shook her head, "No, sweetheart. You look like somebody who would *never* be allowed to enter clubs."

Adrienne bit back a venomous response. What was the point, anyway? There was no arguing with Jada once she puts her mind to something. Adrienne stared at the ticket on her hand.

The caption read, *Exclusive Gathering*.

"And I have to go alone?"

Jada raised her brow. "Well, I only got one ticket."

"You don't expect me to dance, do you?"

Jada shrugged her long straight hair off her shoulder. "Well, I expect you to say something about the dance floor, the lights, the music, the crowd. If you could write about that standing beside the bouncer, then knock yourself out."

Adrienne let out a frustrated sigh, "You mean, you want me to go to some club and write a very accurate review of my experience, and for me to do that, I should dance…alone, since you only gave me one ticket?"

"There you go. You were always one of my brighter employees. Now, off you go," Jada said.

Adrienne rolled her eyes and turned to leave.

"Adrienne, dear..." Jada called.

"Yes?"

"If you dress up tonight the way you usually do…" she looked at her from head to feet and added, "You *will* be dancing alone."

Adrienne looked down at her clothes. Her long skirt and knitted blouse looked very business-like. Her hair was tidily tied up in a ponytail and she wore her glasses. What's wrong with looking smart and serious?

"What type of club is this anyway? It's not a strip club, is it?"

Jada let out a sultry laugh. "Of course not, darling. And no worries. I will have Jacob send something for you to wear tonight."

"It's not necessary," she argued.

Jada shook her head. "Come on, Adrienne. I don't want you to look like you just went there to write an article about them."

"But I am going there just so I could write about them."

Jada shook her head. "I want you to blend in. You have to trust Jacob's taste, darling."

She rolled her eyes again and dashed out of Jada's office, shaking her head in disbelief. In her haste, she ran straight into a hard surface that smelled like fresh, masculine aftershave.

"Take it easy, hon," a male voice said, and Adrienne felt a strong pair of arms wrap around her waist to balance her.

His brows shot up and then slowly he gave her a crooked smile. "So-sorry." She said curtly and then she pulled away from him and walked towards her desk.

She felt thankful that she could still walk a straight line. She started shaking and she realized that all her nerves had sprung to life the moment her body touched his and his arms went around her.

She suddenly felt heady. That had never happened to her before. Like she'd been electrically charged. Her pulse was racing and her heart pounded inside of her chest. But at the same time, the memory of his arms around her seemed warm and comfortable.

She couldn't explain the feeling, but somehow, something suddenly came alive within her.

2.
Cimarrón
Spanish. Meaning Wild or Untamed.

"Hi Adrienne, it's Mom." Adrienne's mother said on the phone.

"Hi Mom. How are you?" She asked cheerfully. Every time she got a call from her mother, she tried her best to sound her most cheerful. It was probably a defense mechanism because she knew how these conversations always ended. In misery.

"I'm wonderful, darling! I just received the best news. Kimmy got into Massachusetts General," Adrienne could tell her mother was over the moon. "It's not easy, you know. You have to be very smart to be accepted there. I'm so proud of your sister."

"That's great! That will be a nice credential for her." Adrienne agreed.

"I know," her mother said. "But I'm worried about you, Adrienne. Kimmy is going to be set for life. She's got everything going for her. But you…you should start rethinking your career path. Writing is not really a cash cow."

Here we go again!

"Just because Kimmy was the smart one, doesn't mean she was going to be the only one to have a bright future. Why don't you start out as a secretary in a big firm? Or you could look into broadcasting.

Adrienne fell silent.

"Every time my friends ask me what you do, I don't know what to say. I mean, I can't really tell them you go around Manhattan fast foods and bars, and write essays to get paid per word."

"Mom, I'm not being paid per word. I'm actually doing fine. I think I'm one of the highest paid magazine writers in the world!" She rolled her eyes. She wasn't sure if that was true though. But she was paid quite well and she loved her job, even with Jada being her boss. Unfortunately, her family didn't see it that way.

"And what's this I heard about you buying an apartment? Kimmy said you got something located in a high-end street? What were you thinking? Do you think you can pay off the mortgage being paid per word for it? Your career's not stable. You're not even working for a top newspaper. You have to pray that enough vain women stay in Manhattan so you could keep your job. That's not something I'd be proud to talk about with Troy's mom."

A tear rolled down Adrienne's cheek.

"Mom," she swallowed hard, trying her best to calm her voice, like she wasn't affected by what her mother just said. "I'm running late for a meeting. But it was nice talking to you."

"All right, dear. Call Kimmy one of these days. Congratulate her. I'm sure Troy will get into a good hospital as well since he's spending time with Kimberly. She'll give him a lot of pointers. Okay, bye."

It was pointless to fight back the tears as soon as she hung up the phone. She's had tried her whole life to win the love and respect of her mother. But no matter what she said or did, Kimberly was all she saw. She didn't want to compete with her sister. But was it too much to ask for just a little bit of approval from the woman, who should have counted as her biggest fan?

She dialed Troy's number.

"Hi, Yen. Have you heard the news? Kimberly just got into Massachusetts General. That's so wonderful! I'm so proud of her."

"Yeah, I heard."

"My parents seemed so surprised. They didn't know how smart she really was until now. They kept telling me what a lucky guy her boyfriend was going to be."

Adrienne took a sharp breath. She felt like it was a mistake to call Troy. Now, she felt even smaller than she did a minute ago.

"Troy, do you wish that she was your girlfriend instead of me?" She couldn't help asking. After all, her mother introduced Troy to Kim first, hoping they would hit it off.

Troy didn't answer right away.

Ooopppsss! That wasn't a good time to take a deep breath and think, was it, Troy?

Finally, he asked, "What are you talking about, Adrienne? Are you jealous of Kimberly? Is it because she's getting a lot of attention and you're not? Well, don't let it out on me. It's not my fault your sister's doing great and that her future's going to be brighter than yours."

"Fuck, Troy! I was just asking. I just don't particularly feel that you see the best in me! You don't make me feel like you appreciate me. News flash! That's what boyfriends do!"

"I love you, Yen. But if you want my honest opinion, yes, I'm not particularly proud of your chosen career. I think you could do better. All right? Is that what you wanted to hear?"

Adrienne couldn't respond even if she wanted to. Tears were streaming down her cheeks. She expected him to apologize and take back what he said. But instead, he said, "Let's talk when you're in the proper frame of mind!"

Then he hung up.

Adrienne stood in the middle of her living room, speechless. She felt the need to throw stuff across the floor, starting with the cordless phone.

Nobody appreciated her, and yet she had done nothing but please them. She had always been a goody-two-shoes because she thought that would make her mother proud.

She dated Troy because it made her mother happy. Now, she began to ask herself, did she really agree to go out with Troy because she found him interesting? Did she really fancy herself in love with him? Or was she in love with the idea of being in love with a guy that her mother totally approved of? Was Troy her boyfriend because he fitted the whole make-your-mama-proud charade she'd staged for over a decade?

Has she ever done anything to make herself happy? Or had she wasted away years of her life trying to please the people around her, who had no idea who she was and didn't care at all about what would make her happy?

She looked at herself in the mirror. Her eyes appeared swollen and she had tear marks on her cheeks. She still wore a pair of skintight jeans and a white Sabrina blouse.

Jacob arranged for an outfit for her to wear to the Gypsys opening but she hadn't even opened the bag he gave her.

She replayed the conversations she had with Troy and her mother. She thought she felt sad, but more and more, she found herself angry.

She was angry at her mother for not treating her fairly. She was angry at her father for not standing up for her. She was angry at Kimberly for competing with her all the time. She was angry at Troy for not being supportive, for not seeing the good in what she was and what she did.

She was mad at herself for tolerating all of them…for letting herself down…for putting up with this crap for more than half her life.

When will I start putting up a fight?

She closed her eyes for a moment.

Enough!

She clenched her fists and thought, *I've had enough!*

She stripped off her pants and blouse right there in the middle of the living room. Then she opened the bag that Jacob gave her. She took out the pair of white Armani pants and the red halter top that Jacob prepared for her. The jeans hugged her hips to perfection and the top clung to her body snugly, yet comfortably. The back of the halter top was made of crisscross strings, giving a teasing hint of her bare back. The blouse didn't allow for a bra, but the material was thick enough to make her feel comfortable. Finally, she wore a pair of red high-heeled sandals.

She stared at herself in the mirror. She looked different. She had to admit that Jacob had flair.

She got rid of her pony tail and combed her long straight hair. She put on black eye shadow and mascara and then accented her high cheekbones with a rosy pink blush and put on red lipstick. She wore the gold hoop earrings, glittery bracelet and matching necklace that Jacob arranged to compliment the outfit.

Once finished, she smiled at herself. She looked like a she-devil out on a hunt for blood. She realized that she could be hot if she chose to.

She took a cab to Gypsys. She decided that she didn't care anymore. She tried her best and so far, her mother and Troy never looked at her differently. She would never be as great as Kimberly, and they would never respect her as much, so why die trying?

For now, she wanted to feel free. She wanted to do something adventurous for herself. She remembered that when she was younger, she carried this angst-ridden, haunted spirit within her. Her mother quickly dampened down any fire within her. Now, she wanted that spirit inside to come out. Even for just one night.

Just for tonight, she didn't want to be the prim, proper, boring Adrienne her mother created. She wanted to explore. Be free, be wild! She would unleash that spirit that was screaming to come out.

Just for tonight, she would live in a way as farthest from Kimberly as possible. Because tonight, she would exist as her own woman. And she was hot enough, great enough being just herself.

She went to Gypsys on a mission. She silently thanked Jada for insisting that she come here and wear something daring. She wanted to kiss Jacob for having the perfect timing and the perfect outfit for her little rebellion.

She secured a place on the bar. Then she danced and drank. She didn't care that she was alone. She felt free. She felt beautiful. She no longer acted just for the sake of writing an article about Gypsys. She did this for herself. And she didn't care about what other people would say or think.

She ordered another shot of tequila.

"That drink is on me," she heard somebody beside her say to the bartender.

"I can pay for my own drink, chief," she responded in an annoyed voice, looking up at the guy beside her.

Suddenly, the world stood still.

The guy looked down at her with the most mesmerizing pair of crystal blue eyes that she'd ever seen.

"I know. But still, that won't stop me from buying you a drink," he asserted confidently.

She didn't reply. She just sat there and…stared.

He grinned at her, "You don't look like the tequila type."

She shook herself back to reality. "I'm not really. Besides, who are you to care?" She turned away from him and pretended not to know him.

His lips curved into a crooked smile. He extended his hand to her. "Justin Adams."

She just stared at his extended hand. "Nice to meet you, Justin Adams." She turned away to drink her tequila straight up. The world shook, but she held herself together. She didn't want to make a fool of herself in front of the City's most eligible bachelor.

He pulled back his hand and motioned the waiter to get him a beer. Amusement seemed written all over his face. Then he asked, "Aren't you going to tell me your name?"

Would she? More importantly, was he going to remember it? Guys like Justin Adams often pretended to be interested in a girl only to get into their pants. She felt a hundred percent sure he would never remember her or her name in the morning. So, it didn't really matter what name she gave him.

"Jamila McBride," she said. "You can call me... Jam."

She was laughing at her own personal joke. He stared at her for a moment and then he smiled.

"It's nice to meet you, Beautiful," he said.

"What?"

"Jamila. It means beautiful in Arabic."

"Whatever. Like I said, I prefer Jam, which means trouble or chaos in English." She took another tequila shot straight up.

He raised a brow at her in amusement. She could see that his eyes practically danced with laughter. He must have realized that she had become a bit drunk.

He took one gulp of his beer. Then he asked, "Wanna dance?"

First, he introduced himself to her and now, he just asked her to dance. Any ordinary day, she would fan-girl scream, even if she didn't want to. But she would die first before she admitted to him or herself that she was interested in him after all.

Without replying, she stood up from her seat and went to the dance floor.

He followed her. She thought that her night of freedom couldn't be more exciting. What could provide a better addition to her rebellion than flirting with the City's most eligible and sought-after bachelor?

She swayed her body to the music and let the beat take over. She didn't touch him, she didn't even look at him. It was as if she couldn't care less that he existed even as he danced beside her.

When she turned around and faced him, she noted that he was staring at her intensely. Slowly, he put his hands on her hips and gently pulled her to him. The dance became sexier. They lost all need for words. Before she knew it, she had her arms around his neck and her body close to him the way it has never been close to any stranger before.

She was drunk and feeling rebellious. She didn't care when he put his hands on her almost naked back. The minute his skin touched hers, she could barely contain the electrifying thrill that radiated from his fingertips to her spine.

How could I feel like this?

She'd never felt anything like this with Troy. She made out with him, they'd hugged a hundred times, but she never felt this electrifying intensity before. Not even once.

Before she could make a fool of herself, she pulled away from him and walked back to the bar, leaving him on the dance floor. She motioned for the bartender to give her another shot.

Justin appeared beside her and ordered another beer. She drank her tequila without taking her eyes off him. He took a gulp of his beer staring at her like she was his latest prey.

Now, she realized why her friends had told her that flirting was a mind game. They sat there staring at each other. Their eyes held out unspoken challenges.

He reached out for her hand and gently pulled her to him. She stood up from her seat and stood between his legs as he sat on the bar stool. He put his hands on her waist and pulled her even closer. She put her arms around his neck. Her world seemed to be reeling. He leaned his face towards hers and stopped to see if she would meet him halfway.

Oh, what the hell!

She would have her night of fun, her night of assuming an identity that wasn't hers. The fact that Justin Adams began flirting with her on the night that she decided to explore other territories unknown to her made everything perfect.

So she met him halfway.

He kissed her gently. She wasn't expecting that. He was a rogue. A playboy. He wasn't known to be gentle. But his lips were soft against hers. For the first time that night, he took her by surprise. When he pulled away from her, he looked deep into her eyes, drowning her in those blue depths, while his hands gently caressed her spine.

Before she could fully burn, she pulled away from him and went back to the dance floor without looking back at him. He was hot on her heels like a predator stalking his latest prey.

This time, he made sure she danced with him. His arms encircled her and he would give her neck and shoulders butterfly kisses.

Adrienne never did anything like this before in her entire life. But she allowed him to flirt with her on the dance floor. She came alone, but now, there was no doubt about it. She couldn't call herself alone anymore.

"I need to go to the ladies' room," she said to him and then she strode away, leaving him on the dance floor again. She walked away without a backward glance. She didn't want him to feel that she had become eager for his attention. She didn't want him to think that she was one of those girls pining for his attention.

She stared back at herself on the mirror. Her eyes were glittering. Her lips were red and her cheeks seemed to have acquired a permanent blush. She didn't recognize the girl staring back at her, but she liked her a lot. She's hot! And Justin Adams just kissed her.

For the first time in her life, she felt sexy, like she had unleased her spirits and colors. She glowed and she found herself capable of catching

Justin Adams's attention.

When she left the bathroom, she discovered Justin standing outside. He was leaning on the wall, with his arms crossed on his chest.

"What are you doing?" she asked him.

"Waiting for you," he replied.

"Why?"

"Just wanna make sure you make it back." He smiled almost innocently.

"To the bar? I got here by myself, chief. Of course I can make it back!" she barked in the haughtiest tone she could manage.

He shrugged and said, "Then I wanna make sure you make your way back to me."

Major flirt!

But when she turned away from him, she couldn't help the smile on her face. She was a novice in this game. But nevertheless, she could even win this.

They went back to the dance floor. This time, they were hugging and kissing more than dancing.

He brushed his lips to hers, provoking…teasing. Then finally, she gave in and he gave her one deep kiss.

All night, she didn't think about her mother or Troy. She began to relax in his company. There was something about him that made her feel like it was okay to lose herself in him, that she could trust him. And she felt glad she decided to let go, even if it was for just one night. Someday, she'll remember this, and it would always put a smile on her face.

She had eight shots of tequila. Eight shots of insanity. She felt she had accomplished a great deal for herself in just one night. She couldn't remember having more fun than she did then. She felt like she wore a mask, lived someone else's life, stole someone else's identity.

"Thanks for the drinks," she told him when he led her to the exit. She walked towards the line of cabs. She didn't wait for him to ask her for her number.

Fat chance!

Guys like Justin Adams engage in flirtations for one moment and forget about the girl the next.

She preferred that he thought she was immune to his charms. She didn't expect more than a sexy dance, or a hot kiss. She wanted to dump him before he got the chance to dump her.

"Hey," he called her. "Need a lift?"

She stared at him and lifted a brow. "In what?"

He pointed at his Ducati motorcycle.

"No thanks! I'm not too drunk. And besides, aren't you drunk?"

"Compared to you, I'm perfectly sober," he teased. She glared at him. Then he added, "I stopped drinking two hours ago. And I only had three light beers tonight. I think I'm way below the DUI limit."

"I might be drunk. But I'm not crazy."

"Come on. It's not like Mommy's going to see you or something." His voice taunted her.

It was the right joke to get her to do anything!

God, could he read minds?

He sounded like he knew exactly which buttons to push.

Does this guy have any flaw at all?

She grabbed the helmet from his hand. He mounted his bike and grabbed her hand to guide her in climbing behind him. She placed her hands on his shoulders and braced herself for the ride. He started the engine and before he drove off, he took her hands and placed them around his abdomen.

"It's safer this way, okay?" he said.

"Where-where are we going?"

She suddenly panicked. She cannot let him take her to her apartment. He will realize that they live in the same building! And she gave him a fake name. Tomorrow, Jamila McBride will cease to exist.

"Um…maybe we can get a cup of coffee in my apartment first," he said.

Coffee? Or sex?

In any case, her heart hammered wildly in her ribcage and no matter how loud her brain screamed at her not to go, she heard herself saying, "Oh…okay."

They drove fast. She felt nervous. It forced her to hold on to him tighter as she rested her head on his back. Being close to him like this made her feel thrilled yet safe. Crashing was the least of her worries.

She thought that this would be a perfect ending to her perfect rebellion. Dressing up wildly. Drinking bravely. Flirting sinfully. And riding freely.

He parked his motorcycle in front of their building. He took her hand and guided her to dismount the bike. She waited for him to get off and they went inside the elevator together. Justin pressed his floor number. She stood on the corner opposite him. She just glared at him, her hands on her side. He had crossed his arms over his chest again as he stared at her with his crystal blue eyes, which, she thought, had strangely turned a shade darker.

Her world still kept spinning because of the tequila and the motorcycle trip. It whirled ten times faster as he stared at her intently, his eyes boring through her soul, making every nerve in her body tingle, and every ounce of her blood sing.

And then it happened.

They met each other halfway. Both of them lunged forward at the same time, where lips met lips in passionate, head-spinning kisses.

This time, he wasn't gentle anymore. This time, he intently demanded her affection. He had become the player he was known to be. He took his time gaining her trust, studying what made her tick. He'd been patient all night, but at that point he began claiming his prize.

They heard a *'ting!'*, which told them they've reached their floor. They didn't stop kissing. He held and kissed her as they walked towards his apartment.

It was three in the morning but neither of them cared. Time stood still. The world stopped spinning. They couldn't get enough of each other's kisses. They couldn't keep their hands off each other.

He pinned her between a door and his hard body. She didn't know which door but she didn't care, either. He kept kissing her, nuzzling her neck, eliciting involuntary moans from her.

All her veins came to life. She felt compelling emotions she hadn't felt before in her entire life. She became bolder, matching his kisses with her own, teasing him with her tongue.

The door behind her opened and she almost fell over but his arms were around her to keep her balanced. His hands went to her thighs and he lifted her off her feet. She wrapped her arms around his neck, and her legs around his waist. He walked inside the apartment. She let out a moan of pleasure when he nuzzled her neck.

She almost shrieked when she felt herself falling backwards as he dropped her on his soft mattress. Then he fell on top of her, pinning her between the soft cushions and his hard body.

She had completely lost her senses. All she could think about were his arms and his kisses.

She felt his skin against hers. It was smooth. Hard. Male.

"I want you," he whispered hoarsely against her lips.

She felt completely lost. She stopped thinking. He occupied her thoughts, as his body dominated hers.

She didn't know when she lost her sandals or her pants, or her blouse. When Justin fell on top of her again, she felt the electric shock radiating from his skin to hers. She felt intoxicated, drugged out of her senses. All these feelings were new to her, she never knew she could feel this way at all.

She didn't know that a man's touch would feel like this... could send her sanity flying out the window...could make her feel a sense of urgency that she could hardly control.

For twenty-five years, she had virtually caged herself, trapped in a box that never allowed her to feel anything beyond normal. With the release of her spirit, she thirsted, she hungered.

Justin kissed her lips again, drugged her even more, making her want to jump off the cliff of insanity.

"I want more..." he whispered against her ear.

"Justin..." Her mind went blank, only one name registered.

"I want you..." he repeated in a hoarse voice.

She moaned once again.

"If you want this to stop, now is the time," he said. He stopped kissing her. He looked at her intensely, in eyes drunk with passion and desire.

He stopped moving, trapping her between the soft mattresses and his hard body. He was giving her a chance to turn back. To return to reason. Or go further towards oblivion and forever be lost.

She reached up and touched his lips with her fingertips. He turned sideways and kissed her palm. And then he looked back at her, waiting for her to make that decision.

She stared at his handsome face. His crystal blue eyes appeared dark with passion. He seemed so devastatingly handsome. She knew just by looking back at him that she couldn't utter the word no. Because right then, she felt that if going to bed with this devil is a prize to claim, then she would blissfully live thereafter as a sinner.

She wanted to feel more. And she desired this dangerous man…with those devilish eyes… nothing less!

She reached her head to nuzzle his neck, and then she whispered, "I want you…" before she could stop the words from coming out of her lips.

The world had turned upside down. As soon as the words left her mouth, he gave it another passionate kiss.

He was out of his pants in less than one minute. He fished a condom somewhere and she felt cold when her own body lost contact of his. She yearned for more.

"Justin, please…" she begged.

Then he was back on top of her. He kissed her, as his knees nudged her thighs. She took a deep breath. She was ready. She was waiting. She was yearning.

"Open your eyes, Beautiful," he stated softly. She did as she was told. "I want you to look at me when I make love to you," he whispered.

She nodded, excitement shooting from every part of her body. And slowly, she felt him at her entrance. She took a deep breath. There is no turning back for her. No one had ever made her feel like this. And she's dying to know what else she was capable of feeling. She wanted to see where else he could take her.

Her family and Troy, even her friends, felt eons away from her mind. She anticipated what would happen next.

And then it did.

She closed her eyes and a squirm escaped her lips as she felt a tearing pain. Her arms flew to his neck and she hugged him to her, as if she thought the pain that he caused her would go away with the comfort that he could provide at that moment.

"Oh shit!" He cursed softly, as he realized what just happened.

They were caught up in a web of passion and he tore into her maidenhead without knowing that it was still intact. She didn't know how they could go on without the pain that seemed unbearable.

He looked down at her. There were tears rolling down her cheeks. He wiped them with his thumb and then he hugged her to him, comforting her. Then he kissed her lips gently.

"I'm sorry. I can't promise that this won't hurt any more than it already does. But I'll try."

Then she felt him withdraw very gently. He reached down and she felt him touch his own manhood. She didn't know why. Then he kissed her again very passionately and yet with so much more gentleness than before.

She felt him again at her entrance and slowly he re-entered her. She felt another tearing pain, but it seemed very gentle compared to the first one. Looking at her deeply, he thrust slowly, and she found it surprising that the pain slowly ebbed away. Then she became more excited.

Soon she felt the urgency and the yearning she possessed a while ago…but this time stronger. Like a tide that swept her away from the shore. She felt madness taking over him…and she realized it had taken over her as well.

He tried to control it, so as to not hurt her. Soon, the pain was gone and she felt unfamiliar sparks shooting from everywhere. She let out a scream of pleasure that she hadn't ever experienced before…bliss she never even knew existed.

She shivered. He caught her mouth and swallowed her screams in his kisses. His thrusts became more urgent until she felt him pull himself out of her. He buried his face in the mass of her hair and she felt his body rock.

When it ended he looked down at her deeply. His lips curved into crooked smile before his mouth descended towards hers.

After the kiss, neither of them said a word. He stood up and turned on his bedside lamp. For the first time, she saw him fully naked. She swallowed hard. She realized as well that for the first time, she appeared naked in front of another human being.

He went to his closet. When he returned he was holding a blanket in his hand. He took her hand in his, pulled her up and caught her by the waist. He kissed her passionately, drugging her again, until she wrapped her arms around him and kissed him back.

He pulled off the blanket they made love in, which she noticed to her horror was filled with blood and something else—she knew what that was.

He threw the new set of blankets over the bed and then he laid down on it and pulled her to him.

They laid there for a while. Not saying anything. Her head rested comfortably on his shoulders. He had one hand rested on her waist. The other under his head.

When she looked up, he found him staring at her with his crystal blue eyes that seem to drown her every time she peered at them.

"What?" she asked.

"I'm sorry," he began gently. "I didn't know…"

She placed a finger on his lips. "Sshh!" she said. "It's okay."

"Do you still hurt?" he asked.

"A little sore, but I'm all right."

They stayed there quietly for a while, lost in their own thoughts. She expected the gravity of her indiscretion to come crashing down on her with a big bang. She expected the feelings of remorse and embarrassment to overwhelm her now that the deed was done.

But to her surprise, she only remembered the intensity of the passion they just had shared and how wonderful he made her feel. For the first time in her life, she felt wanted…and surprisingly cared for at the same time.

He kissed the top of her head. "It was an amazing night," he whispered. "I'm sorry I caused you pain, though."

She smiled. "One man is bound to do so one day."

He chuckled softly. "Then I feel so damn lucky it had to be me. But trust me, honey, that's the only pain I will be causing you."

You're right! Because I don't want anything to do with you after tonight! You couldn't hurt me when I walk out that door and never look back.

Jamila McBride will disappear after tonight.

"Good night…Beautiful," he said, and then he leaned down and kissed her lips gently. He turned off the lights and wrapped his arms around her.

She closed her eyes, thinking, she must be dreaming… a dream she would call to her memory every time she will feel very low in self-esteem. She would treasure this night.

Every time her mother crushed down her confidence or Troy made her feel undeserving, she would think about Justin and how he made her feel that only she meant anything for one night.

As she fell asleep in his arms, she wondered how she stayed in a relationship with Troy for three years and he never made her feel a sense of security and intense desire, but Justin Adams managed to give her all of that and more in just six hours.

A minute later, she fell sound asleep. He kissed her on the forehead and he closed his eyes.

When he woke up, she was gone. He looked around his room looking for any sign of her. She hadn't left a trace.

He sat on his bed, naked. She didn't leave anything. Except for her memory, and her scent that he still could smell when he laid back on his bed, right in the spot where she slept. The same spot where she lost herself for the first time with a man…and that man was him…He looked at the blanket on the floor. It was tainted with her blood. Lost innocence.

He smiled.

She was a virgin. Yet she just did a one-night stand. He couldn't understand why he spent the whole night with her. Why he didn't send her home afterwards. He had never spent a night with a woman in his entire life. It was one of the things that he thought usually led to expectations and commitments. He didn't need that in his life. He didn't even know why he waited for her to sleep first and then allowed himself to sleep with her in his arms, breathing in the scent of her skin, and her hair, which smelled like wild strawberries.

He didn't understand, but he felt drawn to her.

3.
Backslide
To lapse morally; To drop to a lower level, as in one's morals or standards; To revert to a worse condition.

She woke up before dawn, quickly got dressed and took off from Justin's apartment across her own. Good thing, she just lived across from him. Otherwise, this escape would have become so difficult. She intended never to see him again. She would soon look like her old self, with her boring, old-fashioned style and thick glasses.

He's a snob who didn't look down on her kind. She looked quite different last night, even she couldn't recognize herself. She was so sure he would never remember her. She just made it easier for him to ditch her, which she believed he quite certainly would.

She washed her face and soaked in a hot bath to clear her head. She stared at her own body. Almost every inch of it, had been touched by the City's most wanted bachelor—Justin Adams. She couldn't believe that she went so far overboard. She looked for fun. For oblivion. Losing her virginity on a one-night stand to a hotshot playboy seemed way over what she had in mind when she started out last night.

She still felt a bit sore. But she didn't feel guilty at all. She didn't feel like she didn't have any values. She didn't even feel like she cheated on Troy.

It was the first time in her life that she felt alive. That she felt appreciated and adored. And when she felt the pain of the impact of their lovemaking, she felt his concern. It was genuine. She felt cared for. Like she finally mattered.

She remembered that, when the pain became visible on her face, concern and guilt appeared in his eyes as he wiped her tears away. He took off the condom when he realized she was a virgin. Probably, he thought, using it might hurt her more. Her body was not yet accustomed to sex. It would be gentler if he didn't wear the condom.

He probably believed she was safe. He need not wear protection. He was her first.

A thought crossed her mind. She was a virgin. He was a player. She probably seemed safe for him. But what about him for her? Adrienne shrugged the thought off her mind. Justin Adams is most probably too smart and too egotistical to catch something. He must be using protection all the time, not just to be safe, but to make sure that no woman could blackmail him into marriage.

She felt fine when she went to bed after a bath. And this caused her to worry. She spent the night in sin, but all that's left were memories that she knew she would not mind dwelling on for some time in the future.

She was awakened by the ring of her phone. "Hello," she said sleepily.

"Wake up!" It was Jill.

"It's too early!" she told her grumpily.

"What time did you go to sleep last night?" Jill asked.

"Why?"

"Because you're still sleeping and it's past twelve. You never sleep past noon."

"Well, I decided to break the habit," she responded.

"You slept late last night, that's what it is." Jill's tone seemed to accuse her of something.

"I don't know what time I went to sleep," Adrienne said. She stood up to go to her bathroom. "Hold on. I'm just going to splash some water on my face to wake myself up."

Jill waited for five minutes while Adrienne washed her face and brushed her teeth.

"All right. What's up?" Adrienne asked when she finished.

"How was Gypsys?"

That was enough to wake her up. "Ah…great. Nothing different. The same as the others."

Shit! I'm lying!

"Did you leave early? Tell me you didn't leave early!"

"Why?" she asked.

"Well…one of the girls I know from my neighborhood said that Justin Adams attended the opening. And he became attached to some redhead. They didn't arrive together. He approached her and then they danced, kissed and left together."

Now, her heart was pounding.

Damn! How popular can Justin Adams be?

She must remember not to go to Jill's apartment for a minimum of two months at the risk of being recognized.

"So what?"

"Well, Justin isn't known for picking up girls at bars. He does have a reputation of a playboy, but you would never see him holding hands with a girl in public, least of all kissing."

"And the point is?"

"Well…she could be special. Justin likes to keep his reputation of being single. He doesn't go steady with any girl. He doesn't go public with a girl. And that's what makes him more attractive! Like he is an ice king or something. He doesn't pursue and he walks away easily."

"Wow! How can an ice king be a playboy? I thought playboys are supposed to be hot!"

"Yeah, and that's what makes him different! That's what makes him a god! He doesn't have a reputation for pickup lines! But beautiful girls, worthy enough to be models, would just fall at his feet. And last night, it seemed he broke his rules. He picked someone up!"

"Jillian, why are we talking about Justin Adams? You called me to talk about him? Why does everybody obsess about his love life?"

"He doesn't have one," Jill reminded her.

"All right. Then why is everybody obsessed over his sex life?" she asked, correcting herself. "So what? He sees a girl. He could have known her from the past or something. Could be an old girlfriend." She surprised herself there. She didn't know she could lie with so much conviction.

"Nope. He never had a girlfriend! That's the point."

She heard her doorbell ring. She was happy with a little distraction. She lost count of how many lies she just told her best friend in a span of two minutes. She opened the door.

Surprise of all surprises. The man of the hour himself came to her doorstep, and Adrienne thought she would die that instant.

"Holy mother of fuck!" She cursed like she's never cursed before, it rendered Jill speechless on the other line.

He was about to open his mouth to say something but she cut him off.

"Shut up!" she said and his eyebrows shot up behind his sports sunglasses.

"What is wrong with you?" Jill asked.

"Sorry, Jill. I dropped a shampoo on my foot, it fucking hurts! I'll call you back later." She hung up without waiting for Jill's answer.

She faced Justin, who looked amused. He held out a cup of Starbucks coffee in his hand.

"For the hangover? That's assuming I can speak now." He smiled at her.

"How...how..."

Shit! This is embarrassing!

"How do I know where you live?" Justin asked.

Her tongue was tied somewhere inside her mouth. She could only nod.

"I have always known where you lived, since you moved into this building...*Miss Adrienne Miller*."

"You...you knew who I was? You knew my name wasn't really... Jamila McBride?"

He smiled at her. "Yep. I never realized that being fake named by somebody you already know could be hilarious. I couldn't resist playing along. The name you chose actually suited you... Beautiful."

"Oh my God, this is so embarrassing!" she groaned in disbelief.

"It's not embarrassing. I thought it was funny and cute," Justin countered. "Now, do you want to discuss this here in the hallway, or are you going to invite me in?"

She opened the door wider without saying another word. He followed her inside and closed the door behind him.

He placed the coffee on her table and pushed his shades up on his head, revealing his beautiful blue eyes.

"Thanks."

"No sweat," he said. "You didn't give me a chance to make you one this morning."

She turned red. She was now very sober yet his presence reminded her of everything that happened between them the previous night.

"Yeah…last night…It was…it never should have happened," she stammered.

He didn't say anything. He just stared at her with his crystal blue eyes, quizzing her…and for reasons she couldn't understand, drowning her.

After a while, he said, "But it did happen, honey."

"Yes. And I hope we can just forget about it. Like…like we don't know each other."

"But we do know each other now," he stated. "Intimately, I might add."

"Yes, damn it!" She found herself really irritated. She didn't need this. She didn't want this. Sure, she would feel very insulted if she met him in the hall or in the elevator and he acted like he didn't know her, especially if he had another woman in his arms, which most likely would happen.

Although, she realized that since she moved into her apartment and learned that he was her next-door neighbor, she had never seen him bring a woman into the building.

Nevertheless, she thought it would be much better and much more comfortable pretending that she didn't know him than exchanging "hi's" and "how are you's" with him.

"I was not myself last night. I just needed an outlet. I needed to explore, pretend to be somebody I wasn't. Assume a different identity. You were there! That's why I gave you a different name! And I was drunk more than half the time…and it… it got completely out of hand…"

He smiled. "I sort of knew that."

She waited for him to say something more. But he just stood there, staring at her with an eyebrow shot up.

"Damn it, say something!"

He smiled. "All right. You're cute. And you're cuter when you're mad."

She took a deep breath. "What do you want, Justin?"

He shrugged. "Actually, I'm not sure," he admitted.

Then he walked a step closer. She walked a step back, her heart pounding in her chest. He looked so divine in his black jeans and leather jacket. His hair still looked wet, which meant he went to Starbucks straight from the shower.

He kept walking towards her and she kept backing down, until she hit the wall of her living room and Justin pinned her between it and his body. She stared at him squarely.

He tilted her chin up and she almost panicked when his face descended towards hers. He kissed her. Once. Softly. Then his arms went around her waist and he deepened the kiss. Her knees went soft and she felt her nerves come to life. She didn't need that coffee he brought. His kisses thoroughly woke her up. No, not just his kisses. The idea of sleep evaded her the minute she opened the door and found him in front of her.

She wrapped her arms around him and kissed him back. For a minute, she almost felt lost.

He leaned his forehead against hers, his were eyes closed as he took a deep breath. Then he looked back at her. His face no more than four inches away from hers. His lips were curved into a crooked smile. She bit her lower lip, and then she started smiling. He smiled, too. A real smile, which showed her that he had perfect set of teeth and dimples on each side of his lips. He looked more charming and more handsome this close than he did when she saw him from afar.

He pinched her nose gently "You better take that coffee of yours."

She nodded. She started to move towards the table. But both of his hands were now on the wall beside both her ears, caging her.

"Hey, you said coffee," she protested quietly.

He gave her a quick smack before getting out of the way. He took his own coffee.

She took a sip of hers and took out a pack of cigarettes. She went to her balcony. He followed.

They sat there quietly for several minutes.

When she looked at him, she found him studying her.

"What?" she asked.

He shook his head. "Nothing."

"I can tell you were staring at me behind those shades of yours. Like you were sizing me up or something. What?"

He shrugged. "What's the deal with you?"

"What deal?"

He shrugged again. "You said you were looking for an outlet last night. You wanted to be somebody else. Why?"

"Nothing." She sighed. "I just didn't want to live by the rules for once in my life."

"Rules of?"

"My parents. The whole mundane values they taught me for all of my life. Like everyone expects me to be goody-two-shoes...and yet I still wasn't good enough. So I thought, who cares? Screw up for one night. Well...I wasn't literally thinking screw!"

He laughed. "I'm sorry. I wasn't planning to screw someone when I approached you. I knew you and you looked different. Yeah sort of not how anyone would expect you to look like or behave. I came alone for a drink. I realized you were alone, too. So... I just wanted to introduce myself to my next-door neighbor."

"And you know her now... too well, if you ask me!" she said sarcastically.

He shrugged. "Not at all. I believe girls like you have layers in your personalities. And I don't see that too often nowadays."

"Girls like me have secret identities hidden in our closets. You met my alter-ego last night, by the way."

He laughed. "I have a feeling you want to forget what happened between us last night."

She stared at him seriously. "You're not exactly a nobody, you know. Honestly, you're the last guy I expected to be involved in a one-night stand with."

He raised an eyebrow. "So that's what it is? A one-night stand?"

She looked down on her fingers nervously. "Yeah...I guess so. It was not supposed to happen. But it did. I got caught up in the moment and my curiosity made me go overboard. I'm the last person you would want on your list anyway."

"My list?" he asked, quite surprised.

She stared at him. His face showed no sign of any emotion.

"You know...the long line of girls wanting a piece of you. I didn't want any of that. Cross me out of the list of girls who expect you to return their calls."

"I think I didn't have to return your calls since you probably won't call me at all. But then again, I guess you know my reputation more than you know me," he said.

"I don't know you at all," she said squarely.

"You know me more intimately now."

She turned red. He laughed.

"And you can get to know me on a personal level. For all it's worth, I hope we can be friends."

She shook her head. "No. I don't move in your circles. It would be so hard to keep that friendship going. Plus, you live in a world where everything you do almost makes it into the gossip columns. You're one of Manhattan's most sought-after bachelors. It would be very hard to be friends with you. I don't want my girlfriends to be asking about what's happening in your life. I'm not interested in that."

He stared at for a moment and then he asked, "Boyfriend?"

"What?" she countered.

"I'm thinking you have a boyfriend," he asserted.

She stared back at him. So, he really is a smart ass! Harvard straight A's. It seems that part wasn't a rumor.

"What made you say that?" she asked.

He shrugged. "Nobody trashes an offer of friendship if it wouldn't cause havoc to something monumental in their lives."

She stared out at the line of buildings that make up her wonderful New York City view.

"How long have you been with this guy?" he continued.

She sighed. "Three years."

Justin almost choked on his coffee.

Adrienne looked at him seriously. "I know. How did I manage to lose my virginity just last night? And not to him?"

"I didn't ask the question," he noted. "You did,"

She raised a brow at him. "I asked it so I wouldn't have to say the answer out loud."

"Your call," he stated coolly. But if she could see his crystal blue eyes beneath those pair of shades, she knew they danced with laughter.

"Shit! What's wrong with me? I don't even feel guilty about it!"

He shrugged. "You don't love him. Maybe you're keeping him because it seemed like the right thing to do."

She stared at him, unable to believe that he could analyze her almost to a T. "One more psychoanalyzing me and you're out of here, mister!"

He laughed. "Come on, get dressed. Let's go get lunch."

"What? Why?"

He shrugged. "I'm asking you to go to lunch with me. And why not? That answers both your questions, doesn't it?"

"Where?" she asked.

He smiled and again she saw how deep his dimples were. "Somewhere no one knows either of us, since you don't want people to know that we know each other."

"Great idea! It's easy for me. I can eat at Burger King and no one would notice. But it's kinda hard for you."

He raised a brow. "Who do you think I am? Brad Pitt?"

She stood up and went to her room. She realized that she just accepted his offer for lunch without any protest. With questions, yes. But not protests.

She slipped into her white Capri cargo pants, and a white mini T-shirt. She tied her hair in a ponytail. No need to put anything on her face. She didn't need to impress Justin Adams. She already slept with him! And she wasn't planning to sleep with him again. In fact, she didn't have any idea why she's having lunch with him when she should have seen the last of him when she left his apartment this morning.

When she got out of the bedroom, she knew he was staring at her behind his glasses.

"What?" she asked.

He just shrugged, and then he leaned forward and gave her a gentle smack on the lips.

On the elevator, he took her hand in his. Her heart pounded at the touch of his skin.

What is it with this guy that makes her feel like she's being electrocuted? This could not be from the tequila anymore. She never felt this way with Troy. Not even when he kissed her goodnight.

When they reached the ground floor, she pulled her hand away from his grip. He stared at her, raising a brow.

"Bad idea. You: Celebrity. Me: Supposedly spoken for."

He smiled. "Okay, Miss Miller." He held out his hand and motioned for her to go out of the lift first when the door opened. "After you, Miss Miller," he stated, his voice full of sarcasm. Obviously, he mocked her.

She raised a brow at him crossly, and to her surprise he mouthed, "You're a fox!" Which made her blush even more.

He led her to his Red Ferrari. She noticed the dark tint on the windows.

"Great! Maniac tint!"

"Good for your plan, right?" He opened the door for her and she hopped inside quickly.

He took her for a drive. They chatted more about themselves on the way. Adrienne expected to become uncomfortable. What could she possibly talk about with NYC's most wanted?

First, they were so different in many ways! As an heir to a multi-billion-dollar family business, he was born with a silver, even a platinum, spoon! She, on the other hand, barely inherited the genes of her middle-class family. He's a creation fit for the gods. Her own mother didn't even think she looked better than a bit okay. He earned two degrees easily, and people considered him smart beyond belief. According to her mother, she only graduated with honors because her major was a piece of cake. People put him high up on a pedestal whereas her own family and her own boyfriend never professed any pride in her even for a moment.

But as she sat in Justin Adams's sleek Ferrari, she found that she could relax, and not care about how she looked, what she would say next, or where he would take her.

"How long have you been with *Blush*?" he asked.

"Almost like forever. It's my first job," she replied.

"I heard you were good."

She shrugged. "I get a bit bored sometimes, you know. I need more action."

"Judging by the way your colleagues talk about you, it seems you'll be destined for more soon."

"I can't believe Justin Adams engages in gossip." She rolled her eyes.

He chuckled. "No. I have ears. Guys in your office talk about you a lot, you know."

She looked out the window. "Well, I doubted they'd say much about me. Probably because I am the most boring girl at *Blush*. Smart but boring."

"No. Try smart, snobby and undeniably gorgeous."

She laughed sarcastically. "Don't think so, mister. The smart part seems partly flattering. The snobby part probably rings true. The undeniably gorgeous part is undeniably a lie."

He chuckled. "No. Clearly, you are mistaken. You should think more of yourself. The undeniably gorgeous part is undeniably true. Take it from the guy who approached you at a bar, ended up spending a wonderful night with you, and made amazing love to you."

She glared at him. She knew she turned so red, she could be turning violet already.

"Must you always bring that up?"

He looked at her for a moment and then he shrugged. "I'm sorry. I forgot. You wanted to forget last night. But hmmm…the woman I made love to last night was confident…and foxy. I wonder if she's just sleeping there somewhere inside of you."

"I tied her up so she could never come out in the open again."

"It's a pity," he said. "She's a fox."

She didn't say anything. She didn't know what to feel. Flattered? Because Justin Adams told her that she's gorgeous. Embarrassed? Because he knows that he helped unleash a spirit within her that she didn't even know existed. Scared? Because she knew his reputation and suspected that she had gotten tangled in his web as his latest prey.

After lunch, he took her hand in his and led her to a small shopping center. She stared at him in alarm.

"Outside Manhattan," he began. "We don't need to pretend we don't know each other here."

She rolled her eyes but did not pull her hand away. They went around, holding hands, asking each other questions about themselves, like where they grew up and what courses they took in college.

"Wanna watch a movie?" he asked.

She shrugged. "All right. I'm not too busy. Plus, you have the car. I don't even know how to get home."

He chuckled and led her to the movie theater. He bought popcorn and soda before they entered the screening room.

In the middle of the film, Justin reached out for her hand and held it in his.

Later, he brought her hand to his lips and kissed it. She stared at him. His features were illuminated by the lights from the screen. He looked just as her friends described him. Divine. He didn't have his shades on. She could see his long eyelashes and his perfectly straight nose.

He looked at her and their eyes met. He smiled boyishly. Then he leaned forward and kissed her gently. He released her hand, raised his arm and put it around her shoulders. She rested her head on his shoulder.

After the movie, she felt a wave of brand-new emotions. She didn't exactly understand what had unfolded. She didn't ask for it. Least of all, she didn't ask for Justin Adams to barge into her life and take her to the movies and hold her in the middle of the film. Troy would never do such things. He firmly believed that patrons should not cuddle in movie houses.

After the movie, Justin led her to another restaurant where they had dinner.

She must have fallen asleep on the way home. But she remembered that before she drifted off, Justin reached out and held her hand in his.

They were still holding hands when he woke her up with butterfly kisses on her cheek. When she opened her eyes, she was staring at his blue eyes.

"We're home, beautiful," he said softly. And he leaned forward and kissed her passionately. A kiss that left her breathless. He went out of the car and opened the opposite side door for her.

He put an arm around her as he led her to the elevator. She found herself too giddy to protest. In the elevator, he put his arms around her waist and again took her in for an intoxicating kiss. The elevator stopped on the third floor and they immediately moved to opposite corners, as if they didn't know each other. An old couple got in.

She counted up to almost an eternity before the old couple got out on the fifth floor. As soon as the doors closed, they met each other at the center, pulling each other, finding each other's lips, locking each other in a passionate embrace. She felt desire starting to take over her senses once again.

They half-ran to her apartment. As soon as the door closed behind them, they began undressing each other. Their clothes piled up on the floor leaving a trail to the bedroom. When the back of her knees hit the edge of her bed, all that was left on her was her white thongs.

She realized that everything she said about what happened between them being a mistake that shouldn't happen again…was a lie. A product of the supposedly real Adrienne Miller who wouldn't do anything to disappoint her mother and her boyfriend.

He drugged her with his kisses. He made her woozy with every touch. Until her mind went blank except for one word that she kept saying in her moans of pleasure—Justin.

She didn't know how long it took. She just knew that he left her senseless. When it was over, they cuddled in the dark. They talked more about each other. Justin really seemed interested to know more about her.

"I just realized that I am…having a pillow talk for the first time in my life."

He chuckled. "Oh. How was it so far?"

She shrugged. "Not bad at all. I feel comfortable, to be honest."

"Your boyfriend must be blind or mad…or…impotent."

She stared at him curiously. "Why do you say that?"

He shrugged. "You're a beautiful woman. I just couldn't understand why he didn't work on getting to know you… intimately. Is he gay?"

She shook her head. "We just don't see each other often, I guess. And he's…probably as conservative as my mother. We don't even kiss at the cinemas."

"Really? I wouldn't be able to resist kissing you in the dark."

"Well, he's like that. Plus, he doesn't live in New York. It's a long-distance relationship."

And he didn't make me feel the things you made me feel. She wanted to add that but she decided against it. Justin Adams probably knows that he's a cut above the rest of the male species.

"Well, unfortunately for him, he just lost the chance to steal your innocence from you," he said teasingly.

"You didn't steal it," she argued. "I gave it to you."

"And I thank you, honey. I will never forget that." Then he kissed her thoroughly again.

She prepared a bath and he joined her. She had never shared a bath with a man before. And even up to that moment, she couldn't believe that she shared it with Justin Adams.

Afterwards, he led her back to bed where he finished what he started in the bathroom.

By midnight, she felt exhausted. She slept with her head on his shoulders and his arms wrapped around her. She was having the sweetest of dreams indeed.

JERILEE KAYE

4.
Dipendenza
Italian. Translation in English: Addiction.

Adrienne wore a smile on her face when she woke up the next morning. Justin left her apartment early. When she woke up, he was gone. She lay naked in her bed. On her bedside table, a cup of Starbucks coffee sat, with a note:

"You're a fox!"

She smiled again. And because she knew she was completely alone, she couldn't resist putting a pillow on her face and then finally... she fangirl screamed.

She didn't know what had started happening to her. She was shagging the City's most notorious rake. Well... she shagged the City's most notorious rake, that is. For two consecutive nights. She didn't know when she would see him again... if he would even remember her name. Still, she didn't care. That morning when she woke up, she felt beautiful. She felt adored from head to toe.

How many times did he tell her that she was foxy? How many times did he tell her that she was smart and gorgeous? How many times did he kiss her and touch her in places that made her feel all-woman...even a divine woman?

She stretched out in her bed, still drunk with the passion of his lovemaking. Then she got up and took the cup of Starbucks coffee he left for her. It was still hot, which meant that he left a few minutes before she woke up.

She had a smile on her face all day. When she met with Jill and Yuan that night, she was dressed in a silver halter top, a black skirt and a high-heeled sandal.

"Way to go, Adrienne!" Jill cheered when she saw her.

"*Va-va-voom!*" Yuan agreed.

"I see, someone got drunk before going to the party, huh!" Jill teased.

"I'm perfectly sober!" Adrienne protested. "I just felt like dressing up."

"Is this the way you dressed up when you went to Gypsys?"

Adrienne shrugged and looked away from her friends. She knew she had begun blushing. She remembered the night that Justin Adams introduced himself to her and took her virginity away with him before the night was over.

"Well, shall we go in?" Adrienne asked them, changing the subject. "Come on."

The minute she stepped into Gypsys, the memories of that shocking night flashed back to her mind. The hot, sultry dance she had with Justin that led to two nights of passion and mind-numbing lovemaking.

If he was the devil...I wouldn't mind burning in hell for the rest of my damned life.

She knew if she had to do it all over again, she wouldn't change a thing. She couldn't resist sleeping with him over and over again.

To hell with Troy. To hell with her mother. To hell with proprieties!

For the first time in the years that they have been the best of friends, Yuan and Jill saw Adrienne order beer. Normally, she would order iced tea.

"I am loving you tonight, dear!" Yuan said. "If I was a man...I mean, if I were straight, I would go out of my way to hit on you."

Adrienne laughed. "Then you have to be thankful that you are gay. Because I'm not gonna be someone's prey tonight."

The minute that went out of her mouth, she caught a glimpse of jet-black hair falling over a pair of lightly-tinted shades.

She had to blink twice to make sure that she wasn't seeing things. But when she saw the curve on his lips, she knew in that instant that he had been watching her before he went to the bar with his friends.

"Oh my God!" Jill breathed. "Justin Adams is here!"

Yuan looked in the same direction that Jill was looking at. "Right! Manhattan's rakes are here!"

"And what a handsome crowd they make! Look at them. Three guys, all drop-dead gorgeous," Jill began. "But add the two guys multiply them by ten, they still would not equal one Justin Adams."

"You guys talk as if they are a bunch of God's gift to women!" Adrienne rolled her eyes.

"They could well be," Yuan countered. "Look! Half of the girls in this bar are practically ogling them."

"Can't he take his shades off for a second?" Jill complained about Justin's eyewear. "It's dark in here for Christ's sake!" Adrienne raised a brow at her. "Does he have to wear those shades all the time?"

Adrienne noticed that Justin wasn't wearing his usual heavily tinted shades. The ones he has on now are light-tinted, showing a shadow of his eyes, but still refused to give away his true eye color. They looked more like tinted prescription glasses than shades. She actually thought he looked cool.

"Well, you gotta admit, he could pull it off, sweetheart," Yuan said. "It's a part of his style, his outfit. And he looks sexy with it."

"I hope he's not cross-eyed!" Jill stated. Adrienne had to laugh at that.

"Nah! I think Yuan's right. It could be just his fashion statement. He wears it, simply because he can!"

"Yeah," Jill agreed. "He can't be cross-eyed! I think he's physically perfect."

Adrienne nodded at her. But she wasn't just thinking that Justin Adams was physically perfect. She knew that he was. Even without clothes.

Justin looked solely at the bartender in front of him and then his friends. He didn't seem like he was checking out the girls around him. Even though many girls tried to catch his attention, he remained oblivious of the stares directed towards him.

A couple of girls even dared to approach their table with probably a very lame excuse to talk to them, or a very daring line out of desperation. Justin just shrugged when a girl said something to him, and then he stood up and patted his friend on the back and left the bar.

Adrienne smiled. All the more did she feel proud of herself. *He* pursued her. He approached her at the bar and introduced himself to her. She did play hard-to-get, albeit, her efforts proved to be futile, but she liked the idea that she didn't even have to look his way for him to notice her, and more importantly, flirt with her.

In the sinful game of flirting, she felt she had accomplished a lot more than these girls, in spite of her lack of experience.

"Sweetie, I think your phone is ringing," Jill shouted at her over the music.

"You heard that?" she shouted back, fishing her phone from her purse.

An unregistered number appeared.

She sighed. This could be Jada's doing again. She had the habit of giving her number to people who tried to get a feature with *Blush*.

"Hello!" she shouted over the phone, while covering her other ear.

"Come outside!" a male's voice told her.

"What? Who..." And somehow her instincts told her something which excited her every nerve.

She stood up.

"Guys, I have to take this call outside." She said to her friends.

When she got to the reception area where the music wasn't too loud, she put the phone back to her ear.

"Hello."

"Come out," the guy said again.

"Who is this?" she asked.

"I'm hurt. You forgot? Or perhaps I've just kissed you senseless last night?" he suggested smugly.

Her heart skipped two beats instead of one, if that was possible at all.

"How did you get this number?" she asked.

"I was a boy scout," he answered. "Now, get your cute butt outside because I'm waiting for you in my car."

"Why would I do that?"

"I don't know. But when you do maybe you'll find out why."

Smug!

But she knew what he was trying to say. She would die for a taste of him again. She wanted to look at him straight in the eyes once more and convince herself that she didn't dream him.

She hung up and sighed. She started to count one to ten to see if the feeling would still be there after ten seconds.

"... seven, eight..."

"Damn!" She found herself walking out of the bar.

Justin's Ferrari was parked at the front. He opened the door from the inside without getting out, much to her relief. Although, she accepted that she had begun fooling around with him, she still didn't want to be associated publicly with him.

She quickly got inside his car.

"What do you want?" she demanded.

He smiled mischievously and drove off.

"What? Where are you taking me?" she asked. "I can't leave...my friends are inside! They will look for me!"

He smiled at her. "Relax, okay?"

He went to the parking lot and parked in a secluded area. Then he stopped the engine and turned to her.

"I just want to kiss you," he said.

Her breath caught in her throat as she watched him lean over to her and kiss her. Her own arms came to life and wrapped them around his neck. It was a deep and passionate kiss. When he pulled away, her world began spinning once more.

"You look wonderful, by the way," he told her. "I wanted to say hi, but then I remembered, you don't want anything to do with me, so I figured your friends don't know either. I didn't take the risk."

"Good. Because I don't know what lies I would have to spin if they were to ask how I met you."

He raised a brow. "You could tell them we met at *Blush*."

She shook her head. "Jill works at *Blush*, too. She will ask exactly how, and I wouldn't know what to say."

"So you're telling me you're not a liar?" he asked seriously, but it seemed she could see laughter in his eyes.

She shook her head. "I'm saying I'm not a good liar."

His eyes twinkled and then he leaned forward again. "Well, let's make it more challenging then," he teased. He kissed her deeply.

She leaned her forehead against his after the kiss. She took in a deep breath, and tried to compose herself. "Justin...the longer I stay here with you, the more difficult it is going to be for me when I get back."

He chuckled. "You've only been gone a few minutes. You could always say Jada asked some people to call you up and arrange for some interviews, and you couldn't agree on the date and place and they really have to finalize it now."

"And they would be calling me at midnight?" she asked.

"It's a bar. It's only open at nights," he replied.

"And what bar would that be?" she asked.

He laughed. Then he pulled her close to him and kissed her forehead.

"You know what, Miss Prim and Proper, you think too much." He smiled as he spoke. "As much as I want to make out more, I don't want to spoil your night out with your friends and make you invent the story of the year to convince them why you have been gone for approximately...twenty minutes."

He gave her one final kiss on the lips and then he drove back to the front of the bar to drop her off.

Before she got out of his car, he said, "You're a fox."

She stared at him and then she quickly got out of his car and headed straight to the ladies' room. She locked herself inside a cubicle, where she combed her hair and retouched her make-up.

She composed her lines and herself before she went out and headed for her friends.

"My God!" Yuan complained. "You took forever with that phone call!"

"We thought you'd gone home!" Jill said. "Who was it anyway?"

Adrienne shrugged and looked away. If she will lie, she will not look at her friends straight in the eye.

"It's...Troy," she said. "He...I don't know. Nothing that will interest you anyway."

"Sweetie, if you want to talk about it..."

She shook her head. "Negative. Let's talk about... men... other men."

Jill's and Yuan's eyes immediately went to the table where Justin and his friends sat.

Justin had just returned to his seat.

"I actually heard he came here for the opening and he picked up a girl."

"I wonder where she is now."

"Well, you know Justin Adams," Yuan began. "He never stays with one girl exclusively. He beds them and then moves on."

"Well, one night with him is worth a lifetime shag." Jill chimed in breathlessly. "I haven't heard of anyone complaining. Except for, maybe those who believed they could become the first lady of Adams Industries. But he's not the marrying type. That table over there, is full of guys who will take girlfriends for life. I doubt they would want to share their wealth with a woman, anyway...I doubt they would risk splitting their worth."

"Oh well, haven't you heard of pre-nuptial agreement?" Adrienne pointed out.

Yuan shrugged. "Oh yeah. You'll be worth a million dollars after the divorce... nothing more. That's all you're going to get, and a thousand heartbreaks for learning that they only married you to get a legal heir."

"I wonder if Justin Adams grew up away from his parents...if his father had mistresses in every country, and his mother apparently cared for nothing but salon appointments, limitless shopping, and tea room chit-chats with her other rich friends," Adrienne thought out loud.

"Probably," Jill assented. "It's a good explanation as to why he does not commit."

After getting tired of Justin Adams talk, they all went to the dance floor. Adrienne decided she would have the time of her life. She danced and laughed with her friends. She didn't spare a single look towards Justin. She didn't want to see if he spent any time flirting with another woman. She didn't want the memory of kissing him secretly in his car tainted with the memory of seeing him flirt with another girl the same way that he flirted with her when they first met.

They decided to call it a night by two in the morning. Adrienne felt tipsy and exhausted. But she felt wonderful... beautiful.

Justin and his friends were still at the bar when they left.

"I can't believe I didn't see some action." Yuan said.

"What action?"

"You know...I was hoping to see him flirt with some girl so I could know what his type is," Yuan said. "Does he like brunettes, or redheads or blondes?"

"With Justin's history...all of the above." Jill laughed.

When they hailed a cab, Adrienne's phone beeped.

She recognized the number as Justin's. She read the message nervously.

Are you going straight home?

She replied: *Yes.*

After a minute, she received another response: *Don't lock your door.* ;-)

Her heart thumped nervously in her chest.

When she got home, she hopped into the shower quickly.

What is wrong with me?

She barely said goodbye to Yuan and Jill when they dropped her off in front of her building. She ran to the elevator and almost slipped on her front door.

Her heart was beating faster than ever. After she showered, she put on a spaghetti-strapped silk top, and matching silk shorts. She towel-dried her hair, and finally went out to the front door to make sure that she hadn't locked it.

She knew it was a dangerous thing to do. But then again, she considered the tough security as one of the advantages of having an expensive A-list apartment.

She lay on her bed, hugged her body pillow and closed her eyes. But she knew she wouldn't be able to sleep. She essentially waited for him—and the fulfillment of his promise.

Her heart skipped another beat when she heard her front door open and close. She turned to her bedroom door and found Justin standing there, wearing a white shirt and a pair of jeans. He still had his shades up on his head. He must have gone straight to her flat when he got to their floor.

He smiled at her wickedly. And then he walked towards the bed and got into it next to her. Without a word, he leaned over, kissed her passionately and started a wild ride of passion that Adrienne wished would never end.

She woke up the next day by the sound of her answering machine. She still liked some old technology, so she still kept a landline and an old answering machine.

"Wake up! Wake up! Hangover or not we are coming up!" She heard Yuan's voice on the phone.

She panicked. She stood up immediately from the bed and got hold of her bathrobe. She saw that Justin had gotten up already and began to dress quickly.

"Oh my God! It's Jill and Yuan! My best friends!"

"Honey..." Justin called gently.

She ran across her bedroom to gather her clothes in panic.

"Honey..." Justin grabbed her arms gently and gave her a kiss on the lips. "Good morning." He smiled.

She realized she'd been panicking. She took deep breaths to calm herself.

"I'm sorry. Good morning." She reached up to kiss him. "It's just that my best friends are on their way up. And they will see you and they can't..."

"I know." He kissed her forehead. "I'm going. I'll see you later."

He crossed the hall only dressed in his pants, carrying the rest of his clothes and his shoes with him. Adrienne quickly dressed before she threw herself back into bed, waiting for her friends to ring the doorbell.

After barely three minutes, Jill and Yuan arrived. She put them on her visitor's list. Security would just send them straight up. She opened the door, pretending that she just got out of bed.

"Wake up, wake up!" Jill sang chirpily.

"What have you been up to lately, girl? Yuan asked. "You always seem tired. Before, you're up long before the sun was. You always pester us in the morning. Now, it's the other way around."

"Comes with the job description. She's Jada's go-to girl," Jill explained.

"So I heard. And look at this gorgeous apartment of yours!" Yuan grimaced. "Nice taste! It is so you!"

"Coffee?" Jill handed her a cup of Starbucks coffee.

She took a sip, trying to relax herself. Her heart still pounded, and she knew that she still looked flushed.

What am I thinking?

She had firmly decided that it would just be a one-night stand. And then what? Three-nights stand now? And in the second and third nights, it happened more than once?

Jill and Yuan headed for the balcony. She followed, bringing her coffee with her.

"Gorgeous view!" Yuan said.

"You had a visitor, honey?" Jill asked.

"No, why?" she asked. Immediately, alarm signals began shooting from everywhere.

Jill pointed at the two Starbucks coffee cups from the other day. She forgot to clean up her balcony. She stared at the two coffee cups on the table, and it made her remember that Justin Adams had sat there with her. It offered proof that she didn't just dream about him.

"Oh... yeah. Troy brought some coffee for me," she lied.

"Is he here?"

Adrienne shook her head. "The other day, he was. I just haven't cleaned up yet."

"So you managed to fix your problem?" Jill asked.

She shrugged. "It started out...ah...okay...and ended up right where we...started...." She sipped her coffee in between her sentences so her struggles to lie had not become too obvious. "That's why he called last night. But it was useless."

"Oh, sweetie! What is new? Come on!" Yuan said.

"Yeah. Perhaps we should tell Mrs. Miller that Troy is not the right guy for her second child. But what's the point? She considered Troy the only achievement Adrienne ever had." Jill shook her head.

"But still...honey. You already said you were tainted in their eyes. What else is there to lose? Drop that zero! There are plenty of other guys to date!" Yuan said.

"True!" Jill agreed. "Lots of guys in the office have a crush on you. They just see you as this snobby girl who thinks none of them are good enough. And they knew they were up against the likes of a future top surgeon. But honestly though, Troy is cute and all... but other than the great eyes, he's...geeky!"

Adrienne raised her brow. Jill basically confirmed that some guys in the office thought her cute. But then she said, "Come on. I'm not the most fashionable girl at *Blush*, so I doubt anyone notices me like you say they do. And don't be so hard on Troy. I've been with him for three years."

"And you have gone out once a month? That makes it thirty-six times? How many times did you kiss? My God, did you ever make out at all?" Yuan asked bluntly.

"That's it! That's the reason why you haven't gotten laid yet. That's the reason why you are going to die a virgin!" Jill threw her hands up in the air.

Adrienne almost choked on her coffee. If they only knew what she's been doing these last three nights! But she didn't know how to tell them. Would they look at her differently? Would they judge her harshly? And would they forgive her for not telling them the very first time it happened?

She decided she couldn't risk it. Not yet—even if they disliked Troy. And besides, who knows when she would see Justin Adams again? She never imagined she would sleep with him again after she went out of his apartment that night she lost her virginity to him. She never imagined she would spend the previous night with him either.

"Come on, Yen," Jill pled. "Look at you! You look great. I wish I could have those long legs, that straight hair, which makes it hard to determine whether you're a brunette or a redhead. Those dimples. You are gorgeous. But the way you dress...come on. You work for *Blush*. You have to be as stylish as your magazine. And those glasses you keep wearing at work... didn't you know that they have invented contact lenses already?"

Yuan nodded. "Come on. Dress up! Let's go to the salon. My treat! This girl needs a permanent makeover. If she can show up looking like a hot chic last night, it means she's not hopeless. She just needs a little push."

Adrienne moaned. "Come on, guys. I haven't written the Gypsys thing yet. It has to be perfect and on Jada's table by ten o'clock sharp tomorrow."

"Yes. And you're a gifted writer, you know that. It's a piece of cake for you!" Jill said as she hauled Adrienne out of her seat and tucked her inside the bathroom.

Adrienne took a quick shower. Each minute she spent there, reminded her of Justin's presence. It was as if he was still there with her. Touching her. Kissing her.

She decided to shake the memory out of her system.

She went to her closet and dressed in a pair of blue jeans and for once, she wore a Sabrina blouse that hugged her body to perfection.

When she exited her bedroom, Yuan and Jill started staring at her.

"Now, that's what I'm talking about!" Jill said.

"I'm dressing up for your little game, 'girls.'"

"Adrienne, did Troy stay here the other night?" Yuan asked.

She shook her head nervously. "No why?"

Yuan lifted a pair of shades that he found seated on her bedside table.

"Cartier?" Jill asked, reading the brand. "Wow! That sure looks like an attempt to have style."

Adrienne carefully took the shades from them. "Give me those."

"Justin Adams wears shades similar to these. But on him they look hot!" Jill said.

Adrienne swallowed hard. If they only knew that they actually referred to the same pair of shades.

"On Troy…hmmm…they should have marked the box, 'For humans only.'" Yuan laughed.

"If Troy would fancy a pair of shades, he should get an Oakley. They have a model called Monster Dog!" And Jill and Yuan launched into a laughing trip about Troy.

Adrienne felt relieved that the topic shifted to Troy versus Justin. She really hated lying to her best friends.

"Come on, guys, you've had enough fun already," she said.

"My God, Adrienne! Do you know how connected you are with the apartment across the corridor?" Yuan said staring at her window.

"Look! Your bedroom windows face each other. And there's a platform that allows you to cross and enter that flat through the window!"

"Really?" Adrienne asked nonchalantly. "I didn't notice before. Why would I want to do that?"

"You may not want to, but what if your neighbor is a killer or a rapist? It's the worst way to lose your virginity, my dear. Some guy could just go right through your window and rape you or even murder you."

Adrienne laughed. "My God, Jill! You should have been a novelist! That plot would make a good movie adaptation!"

But she felt guilt gnawing at her. Her neighbor had taken her virginity, all right! But he didn't have to break in and enter. She went into his apartment, and handed her precious virtue over to him on a silver platter!

"Who lives there anyway?" Yuan asked.

Adrienne turned her back on them and swallowed hard again. "I don't know. I don't spy on my neighbors."

Yuan and Jill kept looking through the window and then they shrieked! "Oh my God!"

"What?" Adrienne asked nervously. She had been jumpy since Justin left that morning.

Guilt, guilt, guilt!

"Torso! Perfect abs! Perfect body!" Yuan was drooling, looking over the window.

Adrienne squeezed in between her friends to see what Yuan and Jill had seen.

She saw a body she knew well from the past three nights. A body that not three hours ago, had been touching hers. Justin had his blinds half-open so that only his chest and abs were showing. His face remained completely hidden from them, much to Adrienne's relief.

"Who is that?" Jill asked.

Adrienne shook her head and turned away from the window.

"I have no idea. I don't stalk my neighbors," she lied.

"This guy is worth stalking! God! You gotta love that body! Not the wrestle-mania type, and yet, perfect abs, tough… hard…" Yuan said dreamily.

"Guys! Just get out of there! Don't drool in front of my window. You don't live here! I do! I don't want my neighbors to think I'm a complete freak!"

"Balcony, balcony!" They screamed and hurried off to the balcony.

Oh God! She should call him and tell him to stay away indoors!

Yuan and Jill lighted their cigarettes and waited for the torso guy to come out.

"What are you doing?" Adrienne hissed.

"Nothing! We just want to see his face!" Jill whispered.

Adrienne groaned. She was about to haul her friends away from the balcony when her phone rang. She ran to answer it before the machine could get it.

"Hello."

"Hey…" a guy said on the other line.

"Who's this?" she asked hastily.

"Me. Remember? We just spent three amazing nights together?" Justin said with a chuckle.

"How did you get my landline number?" She asked.

"I told you I was a boy scout," he replied. "And I have photographic memory."

Adrienne stared at her landline phone. She saw that her number was written on the bottom part of it. Justin must have seen it.

"Okay, whatever you do, stay away from your balcony!" she hissed.

"Why?"

Because my friends saw what a gorgeous body you have and now, they hope to see your face."

He laughed. "So what if they see my face?"

"They can't! They can't know you live across from me."

"I see. You're too embarrassed of our connection, huh? You won't let people know you know me. Or that I live next door from you." Adrienne could swear there was pain in his voice.

"God, Justin, this isn't a time for an argument! I'm inside my closet and I'm whispering! And I'm mad right now!"

He chuckled. "Okay. Stay away from the balcony it is."

She sighed. "You left your shades here."

"That's fine. I can get them later. I have a spare."

Later? Was he planning to see her again?

"Why did you call by the way?"

He paused for a while and then he said, "Forget it."

"Justin. What is it?"

"Dinner tomorrow night?" he asked quickly.

She sighed.

"Justin… I thought this was just a one night thing," she said softly.

He sighed. "Three nights thing. And now, I'm asking you out for dinner."

"I have a boyfriend. I shouldn't be seeing anyone..."

"You aren't. We're secret friends remember?" And there was a trace of laughter in his voice.

She took a deep breath. "Friends don't do what we did the last three nights."

"So I'm a friend who allows you to fool around once in a while behind your other friends' and your boyfriend's back."

Adrienne heard Jill calling her. "God, I have to go. Just send me a text. The time and place." She hung up quickly as soon as she heard footsteps coming her way.

"What are you doing?" Jill asked behind her.

She shook her head. "Nothing. Just trying to find a phone number for my sister. I thought I placed my dentist's calling card in one of my bags here. So, how was the torso hunting?"

Jill shook her head.

"He didn't come out. He just disappeared."

"Come on, let's go!" Yuan said. "Let's just hope that his face justifies the body he has!"

Adrienne bit her lip. *You have no idea!*

They took a trip to the salon, and Adrienne got a haircut. The stylist layered her hair, which turned out perfect since it highlighted the red strands of her hair. Afterwards, all three went shopping.

Adrienne beamed as she tried on some clothes. Instead of the conventional pants she wore to work, she decided to try on some more clothes that would accent her curves and highlight the colors of her hair.

In the back of her mind, there was Justin Adams. And every time she thought about him, she would smile. Even if only to herself. She didn't know why he haunted her so much. If all the girls he'd been with felt like this, then half of Manhattan must be heartbroken by now!

The thought scared her. She wanted him out of her mind. Otherwise, she believed he would disappoint and hurt her. He was far too charming and far too dangerous.

Her phone rang.

"Hello," she answered.

"I'll pick you up at your apartment tomorrow. Say sevenish?" Justin asked from his end of the connection.

"I normally work late," she replied.

"Okay. Then I'll pick you up at your office."

"No! Wait!" She almost wailed. Jill turned towards her and raised a brow. She walked away slowly so Jill wouldn't hear her.

"You can't do that," she began. "Seven-thirty, my place."

"All right. I'll see you then."

"Justin…"

"Yes?"

"Why are you doing this?"

"Doing what?"

"Can't you just drop me? Like what you normally would do?" she asked.

He didn't answer.

"Justin… Are you still there?"

"Yeah. I'm here."

"You are making my life complicated." She began giggling desperately.

"Well, maybe we've been following the same paths for all our lives. And it's time for a change."

"I thought you've been living this life all along."

"My reputation precedes me," he said quietly.

She sighed. "What do you want?"

"Nothing," he responded. Then he took a deep breath. "Well, maybe…just you."

Her heart skipped a bit. She knew that she was being handled by a professional in the game of flirting and heart-breaking. And she's scared that she's close to falling deeper and deeper into his realm.

"All right. Seven-thirty tomorrow then."

"Okay. Take care. If you need a ride or anything at all… you know my number," he added.

She smiled. She thought that was actually sweet. "I'll remember that. Bye."

She remained smiling when she hung up.

"Who was that? Troy I suppose?" Yuan asked.

She didn't answer because she thought she might scream if she opened her mouth.

"Boy! This is new! Troy? Making you smile like that? Is he on the brink of proposing—that you go to bed?" Jill asked with a sarcastic tone.

Adrienne raised an eyebrow. "What's that supposed to mean?"

"Your relationship with Troy is completely extraordinary… extraordinarily boring!" Yuan said.

"And it has never made me smile like this before?"

They nodded. "So the tides could be changing. Probably, someone in med school gave him a Viagra!" Yuan started laughing.

She shook her head. Yet she still smiled like a teenager.

I never smiled like this with Troy ever?

Truly Justin Adams had turned her world upside down.

The three headed to Starbucks for coffee.

"I still cannot believe that you didn't see Justin Adams at Gypsys. I mean the place is not really a labyrinth. You can stand by the bar and you will see everybody in there. And you can't miss Justin Adams!" Yuan said.

"Well, maybe I did see him, but I just didn't care," Adrienne said.

"Why wouldn't you care?" Jill asked.

"There are other cute guys in New York too. Why must you obsess over just one?" Adrienne countered. She didn't really want to talk about Justin much. Because now, she had something to hide and feel guilty about.

"Justin is not your classic playboy. He seems... the smuggest of them all! He acts like he got more class than any other playboy!" Jill said.

"What?" Adrienne asked. "Playboys have class now?"

"Look at his profile!" Yuan looked like he's starting to drool. "He's only twenty-seven. He's the heir of Adams Industries. He's got Harvard degrees. He graduated with distinction. Although, he has a rebellious personality, he's got no drugs and no gambling in his profile. He refused to work for his father. Instead he made millions of his own on the stock market. His hobby—Photography. Never had any girl attached to his name. He's straight. He just didn't have any steady relationship. He's clean. He's highly sought-after. He doesn't pursue. He's a mystery. And would you look at that gorgeous thing? He is absolutely divine!"

"Divine?" Adrienne practically scoffed. "Have you even seen how he really looks? Doesn't he have like a pair of shades on or something all the time?"

"Yeah...so smug!" Yuan giggled. "But still, the whole package. Him with the shades. He is absolutely gorgeous! That black hair that keeps falling over his forehead. I would take that, even if he was cross-eyed!"

"I wonder what his eye color is," Jill pondered.

"Crystal blue," Adrienne thought out loud. The moment she realized what she just said, she turned red. She took a gulp of her coffee, hoping to hide the redness of her face.

"What?" Jill stared at her curiously.

"Well...I...ah...think it would be nice if his eyes were blue," she said.

"Yeah, like a black-haired Ken doll!" Yuan agreed.

Just then, a group of guys sat at the table next to them.

"Don't look now, but it's the man of the hour!" Yuan whispered and took a sip of his coffee.

Adrienne and Jill looked at the same time, and, indeed, they saw Justin with two of his friends.

"I just said 'don't look!'" Yuan hissed at them crossly.

Justin wore jeans, a black leather jacket and another pair of pitch dark shades over his eyes. She looked away, pretending she didn't see him.

What is he doing here? How can my life be entangled with his like this?!

"Oh my God!" Jill hissed.

"Come on, guys. Time to change the topic. I'm fed up with this," Adrienne said.

"Honey...we always talk about hot bachelors, and this guy is our favorite," Jill whispered. "You didn't seem to hate the topic before."

"Well, it's getting old!" Adrienne hissed back. "There are other cute guys around."

Her phone rang. She answered it, relieved to be distracted.

"Hi," Justin said.

She looked at his direction. He didn't seem like he was looking at her behind those shades of his.

"Um...excuse me?" she asked nonchalantly.

"I just wanna say hi. I didn't want you to think I was a snob or something." His lips curved into a crooked smile.

"O-kay. Bye now."

"Bye." This time, he smiled widely.

She swore she couldn't control her blush. Jill and Yuan eyed her curiously.

"Cousin of mine. Reminded me to pick up a book that was nice. Well...where were we?" She asked.

"Still there, still with hotshot, himself," Jill replied.

"I wonder who he picked up at the bar the other day." Yuan mused.

Adrienne sat quietly while Yuan and Jill discussed other boys, more often, focused on Justin. She became lost in her own thoughts. But she couldn't help feeling self-conscious. She didn't know if Justin was watching her. With those pitch black shades, it was impossible to tell what he was looking at.

After a while, Justin and his friends stood up and left.

She received a text message after a minute.

Justin: *See you. I'll be with these guys. It's poker night tonight.*

She replied: *Okay. You didn't have to tell me that.*

Justin: *But I did... and by the way, you look stunning in your new hairstyle. I couldn't take my eyes off you.*

She knew she was blushing when she replied: *Liar.*

Justin: *Nope. I'm bad at lying. Do you know you chew on your straw when you pretend to be interested in a conversation with your friends?*

Her: *What?*

Justin: *And you bite your lower lip when you're nervous. You look so cute.*

Her: *You were watching me!*

Justin: *Of course. What else would I be looking at?*

Damn! This is guy is a pro at making hearts flutter.

She didn't reply. She wondered how she could take it all back. She met him, been with him, and now, she couldn't seem to escape him.

She didn't even know if she really wanted to get away from him. He had a reputation, certainly. But she couldn't help noticing that he was rather sweet. Maybe he's right. It's time to take a different path. For all it's worth, she can pursue her alter-ego. Explore that different side of herself with him. Have fun behind the back of the old boring Adrienne.

She smiled to herself. As long as she kept her heart intact, he couldn't damage her, right? It might even do her more good than bad to play this game.

It wouldn't matter what Troy thought of her. She need not die of insecurity because her parents and boyfriend all thought she could never measure up to Kimberly.

She could have fun on her own. This time, she would find her real self. She would unleash her spirit and discover if Jill and Yuan were right. Maybe she could become a much more beautiful creature by being who she really was.

5.
Amizade
Portuguese, meaning: Friendship

She donned a white skirt that went all the way down to her knees, pairing it with a white turtleneck sleeveless blouse that hugged her body to perfection. The dress partly revealed her perfectly flat tummy. She tied her hair in a bun and put on very light make-up. She finished the look with a pair of white gold hoop earrings and white, high-heeled strappy sandals.

She felt quite satisfied with herself when Justin rang her doorbell. He stared at her for about ten seconds. He didn't say anything.

"Too much? Too little?" she asked uncertainly.

He chuckled. "For a woman perfectly confident of her IQ, you aren't quite as confident that you can make heads turn even if you were in your pajamas.

She blushed. "Then I trust that I look okay."

He nodded and then pulled her close to him. "More than okay. You're a fox!" He leaned down to kiss her on the lips.

"That's against the rules, chief." Adrienne said after the kiss. "The kiss has to be towards the end of the date."

He laughed. "It's not every day you get to date a goddess."

That was overly flattering. But Adrienne managed a shy smile. "It's not every day you get to date a god, either."

He took her to a French restaurant. They were taken to a VIP area. It was perfect. No one except for the waiters would see them there.

"Do you find the place suitable?" he asked her.

She nodded. "Yes. I don't know what I will do if Jill's date decided to take her here as well."

"So you still haven't told your best friends that you know me."

She shook her head. "No. I don't even know what I'm doing."

"You're having a dinner date with me," he said coolly.

"Yes. And I don't know why."

He took her hand in his. "If I were not me…would you tell them about this?"

It was a difficult question and she didn't know how to answer without hurting his feelings.

"I don't know," she admitted. "I cheated on my boyfriend. Five times for three consecutive nights, to be exact. I'm not sure I should tell anyone about that. And I didn't tell my friends the first time it happened. That's enough to piss them off. Especially because it's with you."

"I'm just a guy, Adrienne," he told her softly. "I hope you can see me as me, and not as Justin Adams."

"Why? Justin Adams has a secret identity as well?"

He sighed. "Justin Adams is a name. A name I sometimes don't like carrying at all. The person behind the name doesn't necessarily resemble what you hear about him…at least I hope he doesn't."

"We'll see about that, won't we?" Adrienne managed to wink.

He nodded. "Yeah…we'll see."

They enjoyed a perfectly fun and relaxing date. When he walked her to her door afterwards, he kissed her softly. Then he looked deeply into her eyes. And then he kissed her again… passionately, this time.

He sighed. "You better go in before I lose my control."

She smiled. "Good night. Thank you for dinner."

He nodded. She closed the door behind her and leaned against it. She was smiling from ear to ear. It was a perfect date and he was a perfect gentleman. They may have started out on a one-night stand, but he seemed to want to prove that he's not just after sex. Maybe he tried to prove himself to her… that he's not all what his reputation says. That Justin Adams is just a name. And the man inside wanted to call himself just human.

And yes…he wasn't notorious like what his reputation claimed. He was actually gentle and sensitive. And he's surprisingly sweet.

She didn't think that he was screwing someone else other than her at the moment. He hadn't asked her to go on a threesome with him and another girl, or another guy. She might expect those sorts from notorious rakes. But Justin didn't seem capable of doing those things. If she didn't know his reputation, she might even believe that he was wooing her. At least that's what it felt like he was doing…for now.

She took a shower and got dressed in a pair of lavender pajamas and a white spaghetti strap blouse.

Her phone rang. It was Troy.

"Hey. Surprised you still remember me," she told him sarcastically.

"I'm sorry, sweetheart—I was stupid," he said. "I know it's hard to cope with the pressure you receive from your mother. I shouldn't do the same thing to you." Troy took a deep breath. "I'll make it up to you when I visit, okay?"

"Okay." She couldn't manage more than that. She tried so hard to feel excited at the thought of Troy visiting her. She waited for that nerve to tick, for the thrill to flow…but there was just…nothing.

"So, what were you up to this week?" he asked.

The first and only thing that came to her mind was Justin Adams. She waited for the guilt to start gnawing her. But it almost shocked her that it didn't.

"Well, I went to Gypsys. It's a bar. There was an opening. I had to write about it."

"Who did you go with?" he asked.

"Just myself."

"Did you drink?"

"Of course I drank! Soda!" she lied.

He was silent for a while. "Adrienne, isn't that... dangerous? I thought you only reviewed restaurants and small shops. And now? A club? Next thing I know you'd be telling me you went a strip club."

Adrienne bit her lip to keep from shouting at him.

"Adrienne, aren't you thinking of making a career change? I'm sure you're good at what you do. But... going to bars and fashion shows, honey...that's not a career! I mean...you could try at least try a newspaper. Are you even sure you're safe in your job?"

She took a deep breath. Didn't he just say sorry for pressuring her like her mother?

"I hate to agree, but sometimes, your mother is right. Look at your sister. She's in med school. I know you're smart. But why accept a lower level of career? You could at least be a manager of some company. But writing about bars?"

"I told you before. Kim is into medicine. I'm just... not. She got that from our parents. I have a knack for writing. No one in my family knows how to write. But this is what I'm good at."

"I know. I just hope we can have a more intellectual conversation sometimes. I talked to Kim last week. She gave me a lot of pointers for my internship. She's so good. It's not that I'm comparing you to her like your parents were. I just want you...to harness your potential. Kim will become head surgeon of some hospital someday, and you will be at home writing a novel you may never publish. You're still young. It's never too late, sweetheart."

Adrienne realized that Troy sounds like a lovesick twelve-year old when he talks about Kim. This infuriated her, actually. Of course. There was a time in her life that she convinced herself that she was in love with him.

"I have a deadline to meet, Troy. Let's talk about this some other time." She hung up.

Now she was really mad. She wanted to hit something and break it. Even her boyfriend compared her negatively to Kim! Can't anybody see that she did extremely well on her own? And even if she hadn't gotten there yet, must Kim always have to be the measuring stick of all her achievements?

She wiped the tears away from her eyes. She took her keys and went out of her apartment. She wasn't sure what she was doing. But soon, she was ringing the doorbell of the apartment across her.

Justin answered after two rings. He wore just a pair of pajama bottoms. One look at her softened his expression.

"Hey, what's wrong?" he asked.

She shook her head. He pulled her to him and gave her a hug. She cried silently on his shoulders.

He caressed her head, showering light kisses on her temple. She pulled away and stared up at him. He wiped the tears on her cheeks.

"Wanna talk about it?" he asked.

She shook her head.

He stared at her for a moment and then he nodded. He pulled her inside and closed the door behind them.

"Did I disturb you?" she asked.

"No, not at all," he replied. "I was…just about to…well, call you."

This surprised her.

"Why?"

He shrugged. "I have nothing to do. I wanted to see if you're up for a chat. But your line was busy, so I figured I'd try again after a few minutes. And here you are."

He took her hand in his and led her to his bedroom. He pulled the covers away and lay on it. He pulled her by the hand to motion her to lie beside him. Then he put his arms around her and she nestled her head on his shoulder.

"Parents?" he asked quietly.

She shook her head.

"Boyfriend?" he asked again.

She shrugged. "All of them. It's like my life is made up of one significant thing—my sister's shadow. I'm happy for her. But can anyone just be happy for me or at least accept me?"

He caressed her head. "No one likes what they don't understand," he stated. "They don't know you that well. Just stop living your life the way other people want you to live it. Live it for yourself."

"Like you?" she asked.

"Yeah. Maybe. My parents wanted me to be someone else as well. And I know I can't escape that path. So I'm trying to learn as much from life now. So that I'll be more ready when I finally face my destiny."

"You were doing well by yourself," she said.

"Yes. But I can't live in photos and stocks all my life. And who's going to take over the family business? My cousins from the mother side? It wouldn't be right. My father's father started the empire. It has to be his blood to continue growing it."

"So, when do you intend to start learning the ropes that you should have learned years ago?"

He shrugged. "After this year. I've done well for myself. At least people can't say I became rich because I had a rich dad. That's just the stereotype I wanted to escape."

"At least your future is brighter than mine," she grunted.

"What do you really want to do with your life?" he asked.

"I love what I do now," she answered. "I love writing. It's my passion. It's not just a hobby. But I also want to invest in something. I want to earn money somewhere else."

"Like what?"

She shrugged. "I don't know. Stocks maybe. But I have no idea what to do. So I couldn't possibly play."

"You're serious?" he asked.

She shrugged again.

"I can show you. I can teach you how to play. You don't have to invest that much. You can start with a thousand bucks. See where it gets you. If you feel that it's for you…we'll increase the investment. I'll guide you all the way."

"Really? A grand?" She stared up at him.

He nodded.

The idea actually excited her. She felt like this could work. She can write and invest at the same time.

"Okay. What do I have to do first?"

"Look up Wall Street numbers and find a company you like." Justin replied. "Read about how they're doing in the past year and in the previous months. That's how you decide first which company to play for."

She smiled. "I could do that."

He nodded. "Yes. Don't worry. I'll teach you how to call the shots. If I screw up on my advice and you lose money, I'll cover your losses."

"Why would you do that?"

"Because it will teach me how to be a better teacher."

She laughed. "It's a deal then."

They were silent for a while. Then she said, "Thank you, Justin. And I'm sorry. I shouldn't have bothered you. But…" She sighed. "You live closer to me than Jill and Yuan."

He chuckled. "See? You can even joke under distress. That's the Adrienne that should always be out in the open. I think it's the real Adrienne all along. Don't try to be somebody that other people wanted you to be. The real Adrienne is wonderful and beautiful just as she is."

"That's the Adrienne you met at Gypsys," she admitted.

"That Adrienne has a long, happy and colorful life to live," he responded.

They lay silently for a while. Then he tilted her chin up and kissed her. After the kiss, he pulled up the covers to her chin and turned off the lights.

"Good night, Adrienne," he calmly spoke.

"Good night, Justin," she whispered.

He's really going to sleep now?

Part of her felt happy that he didn't suggest they make love then. That he seemed content to just sleep with her in his arms. But a part of her was disappointed, because deep inside she knew she craved him with every fiber of her feminine being.

She looked up at his face in the dark, illuminated by the light coming from the window.

God, he really is handsome!

And she's there in his arms! Without the need to say that she'll spend the night, knowing that she just had a bad moment, and she needed company, he held her, comforted her.

She reached up and traced his chin with her fingers. She traced his jawline gently. She was surprised when suddenly he shifted and pinned her between the bed and his body.

She shrieked and laughed.

She found him looking at her with his devilish eyes. He was half-smiling.

"Didn't it ever occur to you that I could just be holding on to the last string of whatever control and chivalry I have in my body?" he asked her wickedly.

She shook her head. "Come on. Let's go to sleep."

He shook his head. "You had that chance a minute ago, miss. You didn't take it."

She laughed. "Please, Justin…"

She watched helplessly as his face descended towards hers and he took her lips in one head-spinning kiss.

Then he nuzzled her neck. She moaned in pleasure. She wrapped his arms around him and caressed his hair. He kissed her lips again. She kissed him back.

They made love slowly. He caressed her. He kissed every inch of her skin. He made her feel adored… like she's the most beautiful woman in the world.

She realized that Justin made her feel appreciated whereas Troy compelled her to feel like she wasn't good enough. Her parents kept telling her that she will never be good as her sister. But Justin…he wanted her to believe that she's perfect just as she is.

Afterwards, they cuddled, locked in each other's embrace.

"You okay?" he asked gently.

She nodded. "Hmm…tired. Aren't you hungry?"

He looked down at her. "Are you?"

"Suddenly…I feel a bit hungry." She smiled.

"Dinner wasn't good enough?" he asked her, smiling.

She giggled. "It was. But the…" She trailed off. She was going to say sex but not quite sure how to say it.

"Lovemaking was better?" He suggested smugly.

She jabbed him gently on the ribs.

"How smug!" She laughed.

She stood up and quickly got dressed.

Justin followed her to the kitchen where she raided his fridge and he sat at the counter.

"Hmm…you have microwaveable pasta?"

He smiled sheepishly. "What did you expect? Living life in the fast lane. Everything has to be on the go."

She raised a brow, sort of like scolding him silently.

He held his hands up. "All right. Maybe sometime you can cook for me. Can you cook?"

She raised a brow at him. "All right, mister! What do you want? Thai? Chinese? Japanese? Mexican?"

He laughed. "Whoa! Never challenge Miss Miller on her cooking skills."

She decided to fry some patties.

"Beer? Soda?" she asked.

"Let's have beer," he answered.

"You have beer," she said. "I'll have a soda."

"Not a beer person, huh?"

She shrugged. "Not a drinking person."

"Come on. Time for change, remember?" He dared her, his eyes filled with challenge.

"All right. I'm with Justin Adams."

"We both learn something from each other." He grinned.

They went to the balcony to eat and drink.

"How old is this sister of yours?" he asked.

"Twenty-eight. Three years my senior."

"So, what is she? Miss thing?"

She shrugged. "At least that's what my mom and my boyfriend thought. They kept telling me that my writing was just a lame excuse to make a living."

He looked over at her apartment. "I'd say it's a hell lot more than that for you to afford that apartment of yours. Have they been there?"

She shook her head. "They don't even know my address."

"Well, I'd say don't think too much about that. We're not so different, you know. My father thinks I will live on the streets and won't be able to sustain the lifestyle I grew up in unless I work for him. But I think I'm doing fairly well. I have money and time in my hands. I can sustain my vices."

"Vices?" She echoed, suddenly alarmed.

He shrugged. "Cars. Gadgets."

She felt relieved. He must have noticed because he took her hand in his and laughed.

"No, ma'am. Don't do drugs, no gambling, no white slavery or dealing with terrorist acts, not even prostitution or encouragement of such."

Then he kissed her hand gently.

After they were done eating, Adrienne insisted she wash the dishes, while Justin cleared the bottles in the balcony.

"So, are you serious about the stocks thing?" he inquired.

She nodded. "I will give it a try."

He smiled. "That's great. You're learning to risk more now."

Her eyebrows shot up. "Yes. And it started the day Gypsys opened. That damned place should be shut down! I should have written a nasty review."

He laughed. "Don't blame the place. It was in you. You have a free spirit dying to get out. You sound like you've never had fun in your life."

"Well, you didn't have the parents I have."

"Yours can't be stricter than mine. But still, it didn't stop me from doing what I wanted in life."

"At least they spoiled you a little."

He shrugged. "Maybe. But that didn't stop me from having sense, either."

"Yeah…among other things. You were known to be a snob. And you…" She stopped.

"What?" He essentially urged her to continue.

"And you were known to play around…with women…" She hesitated, putting the last plate in his dish dryer.

He was quiet for a while.

She thought she must have hurt his feelings. She felt guilty.

Finally, he took a deep breath. "If you thought that was true about me…how come you're here?" He asked quietly.

That ticked something inside her. That was the same question she had been asking herself. If she knew who Justin Adams was, then why did she stay here? Why had she come to him in the first place?

Suddenly, she felt mad. At herself more than anybody. "You know what?" she snapped. "You're right! Why am I here?"

She turned on her heel and hastily headed for the door.

He ran after her and grabbed her by the arm. She struggled to get away from his grip but he didn't let her go.

"Damn it, Justin! Let me go!"

He wrapped his arms around her waist.

He didn't say a word. He just hugged her. Tightly. She took deep breaths and bit her lip to prevent herself from saying anything that would further ruin the night for both of them.

"Honey, help me out here," he whispered in her ear, very gently, it made her want to cry.

She didn't answer.

"I'm sorry," he said. He tilted her face so he could look into her eyes. "I just…think it's unfair. You have been looking at me based on my reputation from day one. For a moment, I believed that you could see me another way. You could see the man beneath the Justin Adams coat."

She stared at him. She could see that he was struggling with his words.

"Why does it matter what I think about you?" she asked him squarely.

His expression softened and he smiled sheepishly. "It just does."

She took a deep breath and managed to calm her emotions down. "I have to go."

He shook his head. "Let's please not leave it like this." He seemed to be pleading.

Then she realized that he was right. And anyway, it shouldn't matter if Justin acted like the asshole his reputation said he was. She promised to keep her heart intact.

And she realized it was unfair to think of him that way, because he gave her a chance to see underneath the Justin Adams nametag.

He was actually a great guy. He did have a soul. What she said was unfair. She didn't look to this thing to actually end in happily ever after. It never would. This was simply the breather she needed.

Justin Adams gave her a chance to live her life the way she should live it. He inspired in her the courage to try things she had never tried before. This thing they shared—the temporary insanity...the mutual but short-term passion...provided her with more good than bad, anyway. And she was being unfair thinking that he was an ass, when she was the one playing games here.

She felt sorry now. She felt guilty. She reached up and touched his cheek gently.

"I'm sorry," she whispered. "I was out of line. I don't care what your reputation says. I mean...it doesn't matter to me. I'm the one who's cheating on my friends and my boyfriend here. I'm sorry."

He smiled. "It's not about the cheating, Adrienne. I know you feel guilty about it. But look at it this way. For once, you're thinking about what you want. You're teaching yourself how to live...and at the same time, you're actually teaching me to do the same."

She smiled at him. "Yeah...I know. I guess we should leave it for what it is."

He nodded. He kissed her passionately. She responded with the same passion.

He bent down and carried her in his arms.

"Hey...I said I had to go."

He grinned. "Oh no. You were set out to spend the night here two hours ago, miss. You're going to do just that."

She raised an eyebrow.

"You're impossible!"

He laughed as he set her down on his bed.

"I'm gonna need to brush my teeth," she said.

He laughed and pulled her up on her feet and led her to the

bathroom, where he took out a brand new electric toothbrush and handed it to her.

"You're not giving me any other choice, are you?"

He shook his head. "Nope."

She laughed and put toothpaste on her new toothbrush.

After brushing their teeth, they both went to bed and slept in each other's arms.

6.

Ferveur

The intensity of feeling or expression; intense heat. Passion.

*W*hen she woke up, she was lying flat on her back and Justin still slept soundly beside her with his arm around her. She looked at the clock on the bedside table. Eleven o'clock.

"Shit!" She quickly stood up.

Justin woke up and sat up on the bed.

"What's the matter?"

"It's eleven o'clock! I needed to be at work at nine!"

He smiled. "So what? When was the last time you took a day off?"

She stared at him. "I don't know. A year ago."

He shrugged. "You're too much of a workaholic. One day of rest wouldn't hurt."

"Justin...I can't..."

He grinned. He pulled her hand and made her sit back on the bed beside him.

"Miss Workaholic!" he teased. "I think you're in dire need of a vacation. Learn to lighten up a bit. You're doing well with everything you do. You're smarter than that sister of yours. You can't prove yourself to be book-wise all the time. You know what I believe in? The person who lived more out of life is the more successful one. Chill okay?"

Hearing Justin say those words made Adrienne realize that she never gave herself much of a break because she was always chasing after her sister's accomplishments. And every single day counted.

Maybe Justin made a good point. She has to learn to let things go. Some things at least. She doesn't have to be uptight all the time.

She sighed. "Okay." She smiled at him and then she leaned forward to give him a kiss on the lips.

He smiled at her.

"What about you? Don't you have to go work today?" she asked. She didn't even know if he really worked at all.

"Done," he replied. "I woke up about nine in the morning and I did some trading."

"Really? That easy? Did you make money?"

He nodded. "I got lucky today. A hundred thousand bucks."

Her eyes widened. "Hundred thousand? How is that possible?"

He shrugged. "I worked hard for it to happen. It took a great deal of investment and patience. It was risky and I needed to wait a whole year for the right time. And today, things turned my way. You must be my lucky charm."

"My God! My one thousand dollars sound like a...tip or

something."

He laughed. "I've been trading since I was twenty, honey. And besides, I'm not asking you to start on one thousand to make money. It's just for trying to learn how it works without having to invest a lot."

"You were awake at nine and you didn't wake me up? You know it's Monday!"

He smiled. "I knew you didn't sleep until late last night. So I decided not to wake you up."

"All right. Then you better treat me for lunch or something."

"Done. Anywhere you want, honey. We can go to Paris for lunch if you want!"

She laughed. "No. I wouldn't want to go that far. And besides one lunch in Paris wouldn't be enough for me. I gotta stay there for at least a week!"

He smiled. "Okay. Where do you want to go then?"

She shrugged. "Can we just have it here? Or in my apartment? Delivery perhaps?"

He stared at her for a moment, as if he was trying to read her thoughts. Then he nodded. "All right. Can't be seen with Justin Adams on the streets," he muttered quietly.

She felt guilty. She hugged him. "Can't be seen anywhere on the streets if I will call in sick, anyway."

"Indeed, Miss Miller. You got me there. What do you want then?"

"Chinese?"

He nodded. "Okay. Let's eat in the terrace. Myla, my housekeeper will be here in thirty minutes."

"Who, what?" she asked.

"My maid," he replied.

"You have a maid?"

He nodded. "Comes here Monday, Wednesday and Saturday."

Somehow, she panicked at the thought of someone else seeing her with him. Even though she trusted Justin, she didn't want to take the risk. She could be Justin's flavor for a week (or two), but when he walked away, she wanted to be as unscathed as possible.

"Tell you what, let's just go to my apartment. I need to check my mobile and my answering machine anyway. Jill would be screaming in it already since I didn't tell her where I was."

He raised a brow. "See? You don't even want to my housekeeper to see you with me."

She groaned. "Justin! Are we really going to argue about this? You made me miss Jada for a day so we can have a fight?"

He shook his head. "All right, all right. You win. You go back to your place. I'll order from here and be there in fifteen minutes."

Back in her apartment, she headed straight for the answering machine. Twenty messages.

"Hi Yen, it's Troy. I'm sorry, baby. It's just that you know my brother just got married last year. And Lisa is a top-notch lawyer."

"She's ten years older than your brother," Adrienne muttered.

"I know you have a game plan. Let's talk things over. When I have time, I will come to New York so I can see you. I love you."

Each day that passed, she realized more that her relationship with Troy seemed hopeless. She had come to a comfortable place where she knew she couldn't care less if Troy dropped her... if she didn't do it first.

Sure, her mother would berate her for breaking up with him. But she's been disappointing that woman forever. No matter what she did, her mother would never see her in a different light.

For the first time in her life, Adrienne wanted to do what she thought would make herself live a complete life in spite of being a failure in her mother's eyes. At least she didn't have to be a failure in her own eyes.

There was another message on the answering machine.

"Hey Yen...it's Jill...lunch tomorrow with Yuan? He'll pick us up."

Adrienne panicked.

The next messages came from Yuan and Jill all asking her where the hell she was.

She dialed Jill's number.

"Damn it, where are you?" Jill demanded.

"I'm home. I overslept and I'm not feeling quite well," Adrienne replied.

"My God, sweetie? Are you all right?" She asked, switching moods from anger to concern.

Adrienne nodded.

"Hello?"

"Sorry, I'm actually nodding," she said. She felt guilty for lying to her friends. Jill sounded so concerned. They knew that she didn't usually feel sick... or she was never too sick to not go to work.

"Want us to come down there?" Jill asked. At the same time, Justin entered her apartment, without so much as a knock.

"No! Don't. I'll be fine. I just need to rest," she lied.

"Honey... are you sure you're okay?" Jill asked.

"Yep. I'll be fine."

"All right. I'll tell HR now. I'll call you after work, okay?"

"Sure. Bye."

Justin was looking at her, with a raised eyebrow.

"My friends. They wanted to come down here and check on me. I said no."

He smiled. "Good idea. I think I'm going to head out the window if they knock on your door."

She giggled. "You can actually do that, I think."

He nodded. "I checked that the morning they called saying they had gone to the elevator already. That would be the last resort if you want to keep this little secret of ours."

She went to him. She wasn't quite sure if he meant it's okay to keep this a secret.

She gave him a hug. He hugged her back.

"I'm starving," she whispered.

He chuckled. "Food will be delivered in fifteen minutes, don't worry."

And true to his word, it was. Justin ordered spicy beef, noodles and dim sum.

After lunch, she cleared the table and joined Justin in the balcony.

"You know, you are a bit ironic," he stated.

"Why is that?"

He shrugged. "You seem to be so prim and proper most of the time. And yet, you smoke."

"Like you said…most of the time." She smiled. "I didn't start smoking until last year. I had a worse relationship with my mother. And that time, Troy acted like a jerk because he wasn't doing too well in one of his subjects. And I also had too many deadlines. I needed a breather to think clearly and get something done."

"And the habit just proved to be useful that time," he suggested.

She nodded. "And then it proved to be addicting as well."

"And I figure, Mommy doesn't know," he guessed.

She nodded. "Yep. It'll be another stain in our relationship."

"Why is it like that?" he asked.

She shrugged. "I remember she started comparing me to Kimberly when we were both in high school. She was three years my senior. She always stayed at home, always seemed bookish. I was always out with some friends. I started dating ahead of her. But I kept getting straight A's. My mother was not happy with my partying or being out with friends. She always complained that I should be like my older sister, whose life revolved around school and home.

"Kimberly never liked me very much. She always bullied me, as far as I can remember. When I tried to learn how to play the guitar, she already held piano recitals.

"I used to be rebellious. I never did the right thing. Whenever Mom scolded me, it would be like…look at Kimberly… Kimberly never gave me these problems…When Kimberly made it to UCLA, my mother was ecstatic. She seemed so proud of her and she implied that I would never make it as big as Kim. Kimberly will get anything she wanted in life, and I would end up being a secretary of some company…if I didn't get pregnant as a teenager.

"I remember being so angry that night. I went on a date with this jerk, who's a senior. I thought it was cool because I was dating a hotshot older guy. But I almost got date raped. I used pepper spray on him and had to phone my father to pick me up in the middle of nowhere. I felt so scared. And Mom was so mad.

"That's when I started going the other way. I wanted to earn her trust instead of rebelling against it. I stopped dating in high school. I almost didn't go to prom. I used to dye my hair dark brown, to hide the red highlights. I loved my red strands 'coz I thought it looked cool. But my Mom always made me feel like a harlot because of them. So I had a whole stock of dark brown hair dyes.

"I still earned straight A's as a student. I did much better in junior and senior year. I got accepted in all the universities I applied to. I took communication arts at Stanford. I have always wanted to write. My mother still thought it wasn't good enough. Kim had gotten into med school and she did well.

"It seems like all my life, I attempted to live up to my mother's expectations. But I still can't make her love me as much as she loves Kim..." She didn't realize that tears already began rolling down her cheeks.

Justin took her hand and pulled her close to him.

"But you are doing well," he said softly.

"I thought so too. I'm one of *Blush's* top editors. I thought it was big. *Blush* is big. And I made it to that position in three years. My mother never saw that. She said, *Blush* is a magazine read by models and women obsessed with their looks, who never cared much about their brains."

"I don't think that's true. Women read a lot of these magazines for empowerment—because it's a magazine that holds the secrets of your gender. You'll be surprised some guys read it, too. You know...just to know how to charm a woman." He chuckled.

She smiled. "I don't know, Justin. I went there because I have passion for it. I love to write. And *Blush* is prestigious. But I also wanted to do other things. I want to invest. I want to make a whole lot more money than what I'm earning now."

"You're still young. What are you? Forty?" He gave her a mocking look.

She pinched him on his side.

"Ouch!" He laughed. "All right. Twenty-five. You're doing great at *Blush*. You could do more. On the side, you can invest in some things. You could even start up your own business if you want to. When the business turns great, you can choose whether you want to go on with full-time writing or contribute to *Blush* or another magazine or write your own novel or book."

She pulled back and stared at him. "You know what? I have always wanted to do that. And I swear I will when I have more time or if things become more stable."

He reached up and pushed a lock of hair away from her face.

"Do it. I know you'll do well. And surgery... it can be learned in school. I think you could be a better surgeon than your sister if you chose to be. But writing...not everyone can be a writer. It's a gift. And you have it."

She smiled and then reached up to kiss him.

"Thank you for saying that. I wish my mother thought of it that way."

"What about your father?" he asked.

"I always thought I was Dad's favorite. But my father was more the *'Yes Dear'* kind of husband, if you know what I mean. He's quite smart, and he loves all of us too much. I never felt my father treated me unfairly. I know many times he stood up for me. But nothing he did ever changed my mother's opinion of me. Maybe that's just the way it is."

"Well, at least it's not both of them. And hey...you turned out okay. Sometimes, it's the challenges that stand in the way that force us to be better persons. If you ask me, you're perfect, just as you are, honey."

"No one is perfect." She laughed.

He shook his head and looked at her deeply. "You're smart. You've got a good heart. You know how to handle your finances. You're independent. You've got a classy apartment; a stable job. You've got friends who love you... a guy who's crazy about you."

She laughed sarcastically. "I don't really think Troy was crazy about me at all."

Justin stared at her for a moment. He fell silent. His eyes were narrowed and an eyebrow was shot up.

She stared back at him.

Shit!

"You mean... what do you mean?" she stammered.

Justin Adams couldn't possibly be crazy about me!

He looked away from her. "I'm sure this Troy character is crazy about you. Otherwise, he wouldn't be sticking around like what he's doing now, considering you don't see each other much."

Shit! I just ruined that perfect moment, didn't I?

It suddenly felt awkward.

This is Justin Adams! Hello! Hotshot playboy who could have any woman he wants! Women who are on the A-list, even royalty!

"Justin..." she started.

He just stared at her for a while.

"You meant...Troy, right?" She asked in a broken voice.

He shrugged. "He is the current and official boyfriend, isn't he?"

What kind of an answer is that?!

She gazed at him. She knew she didn't have any right to get mad.

It's only been a few days!

Could he really say that he was crazy about her?

He pulled away from her and lit a cigarette. "What's his story, anyway?"

She watched him intently. She tried to figure out the expression on his face. He had none. He just looked out onto the view from the balcony.

She decided to let it go or else she might say something to ruin the moment even more. She has no right to demand anything from Justin. She has a boyfriend! She merely fooled around with him.

"Well... I met him when I first started working for *Blush*. It was my parents' anniversary party and they were friends with his parents. To tell you the truth, I didn't think he was actually my type at first. But he sounded so mature, and my mother adored him. When he picked me up for our date, it was the only time my mother seemed ecstatic for me. As if it was the only time, I brought good news to her.

"Troy and I got along just fine. The relationship became stable. He went to med school, yet we managed to keep things going. We had our problems...we don't always see each other eye to eye. But the relationship was safe. I thought that was all that mattered. I felt it was going somewhere. We've been dating for three years. I think he was the only trophy I ever brought home to my mother."

Justin listened quietly to her story. Adrienne wished she was a mind reader. She wanted to know what he was thinking. She didn't want to answer his question about Troy...but he asked!

She thought it weird and way too complicated talking about Troy with Justin. Especially after he just pointed out that some guy was crazy about her and she automatically thought about Troy. She realized that her words told him that she had no regard for the last nights they spent together. For that, she felt remorseful.

But she didn't even know what they were! And it's hard to hope for something stable with a guy like Justin Adams... and harder to believe that a guy like him could be crazy about her!

Her phone rang. She went inside the apartment to answer it.

"Yen... how are you?" Yuan asked.

"I'm okay. I'll return to the office tomorrow."

"You're falling sick, sweetie. You need a vacation. You work too much!"

"I'm okay. Really. I just didn't feel too well to go to work this morning. Maybe it's stress. And one day of rest took care of it. I feel better already."

"Maybe it's your virginity eating away your insides and working its way to destroy the rest of your body," he teased.

"Ha-ha! You're very funny!" she said sarcastically.

She felt guilty. How could she bring herself to come clean to her friends now? How could she say to them that she lost her virginity a few days ago and the recipient of her precious virtue currently sat on her balcony? A.k.a God's gift to women? A.k.a the most sought after playboy in the City?

"Why don't we drop by tonight?" Yuan asked.

"No need for it, guys. I want to sleep early to make sure I go to work tomorrow."

"Okay. It's just that...I'm not used to this falling sick thing of yours. You never do that!"

She laughed. "First time in many years."

"Yes... oh well...call me if you need anything, sweetie."

"Will do. Bye."

When she turned around, Justin sat on her sofa. He hadn't made a sound. Now she really felt guilty about talking about Troy.

No! He can't be jealous! He's Justin Adams!

But how come she had a feeling that she hit him hard when she said that it was Troy who's crazy about her...and hit him again when she said that Troy can keep a stable relationship, which suggested that he can't?

She sat beside him and rested her head on his shoulder. He didn't budge. She wanted to ease him in her own way. But she didn't want to say anything because that might be assuming that she meant something to him.

He didn't say anything for a whole minute. But then she felt him wrap an arm around her shoulders and plant a kiss on her head.

She smiled to herself. All this unspoken affection that he shows her drove her mad! She felt that he somehow had grown fond of her over the last couple of days they spent together. Still, for a guy like Justin Adams, she couldn't believe it was possible at all.

The signals he sent her chased her out of her skull. She knew she couldn't nail down a guy like him. And she didn't know when this will be over. She promised herself she would keep her heart intact. But she knew it was just too darned easy to fall in love with him! When Justin would leave her, she didn't think she would be able to handle it if he took her heart with him.

She wondered what would happen in two weeks. Justin's reputation says he drops a woman after two weeks, right? If he is like this with every woman, then he leaves a trail of heartbreaks at least twenty-four times a year. And she didn't intend to be a part of that trail.

"Do you want to watch a DVD?" he asked mildly.

She looked up at him and smiled.

"Yes."

He smiled back this time. Then he stood up and pulled her up on her feet.

"Let's go to my place," he said.

They watched *How to Lose a Guy in 10 Days* in Justin's bedroom.

"My God! Even I would drop this girl like a hot potato if I were her boyfriend!" Adrienne pronounced while watching the film.

He laughed. "Hey… some girls are like that. They demand too much."

"But not all, mister," she countered.

"Yeah. I said some."

"But you guys…I don't understand why you guys run off when a girl leaves something at your place. I mean, you're too afraid of commitment. We don't mind if you leave something at our place. You guys…immediately think we're marking you as our property if we leave as much as a lipstick on your table!"

"No. It's just that, we like to have our own place. And our time. And sometimes girls can't get that."

"Leaving something of ours in your place doesn't necessarily mean we are marking it as our territory. As if we want to move in with you or something."

"You can leave some of your stuff. But you don't have to write your name all over the place."

"What? Write our names? Leaving our stuff in your place is like writing our names on it? What are we? Cats?" She started to raise her voice.

He laughed. "Honey…chill, okay? I'm not generalizing women. And I'm not saying it's all true for men, either. I don't mind if you leave some of your stuff here. You have a toothbrush here, remember? And I gave it to you. You didn't leave it here."

She realized that she sounded so furious and so she laughed as well.

"It's just that some things…for guys…take some time to get used to. And bachelors, who get accustomed to doing their own thing at their own time, take more time to get used to the fact that they can't do it the same way anymore. Like toilet seats, for example. Girls don't like it up, because you use it. Hey…you're the one using it. So why don't you put it down yourself? We don't complain if you leave it down. And we grew up being taught by our mothers… this is a toilet seat. Put it up when you are using the toilet. Flush. And then put it back down. You grow up and realize that you did it for the girls."

"That's like etiquette or something!"

He laughed. "Come to think of it, honey, I'll bet that rule was made by a woman! Were you ever taught…this is a toilet seat. Put it down when you are using it. Flush and put it back up?"

"No. Because that is not the way it was supposed to be."

"Come on. What's the rationale? Because there might be a girl who will use it one time and it's only proper that it's all ready for her to sit on."

"Chauvinist pig!" she snapped.

He laughed and then pulled her to him into a hug. She pulled back, refusing.

He laughed harder. "Honey…I was just making a point. Look in the bathroom. The toilet seat will always be left down for you. I'm not arguing."

"Okay. From now on, always leave it up. If I use it, I will put it down myself!"

He pulled her again and hugged her, laughing. "No. I will not break the rules of my mother and of the society that dictated this principle."

She jabbed him lightly on the ribs. "You're impossible. You do one thing and yet you make fun of it."

"I'm not. There are some things that you just can't change."

She pinched him.

"Ow! What was that for?"

"For being a chauvinistic jerk!"

He laughed. Then he tilted her chin up and kissed her.

The kiss deepened, became more passionate, and then suddenly, raging. Before she knew it, Justin began taking her on a passionate ride again.

When it was over, they were both catching their breaths.

Justin lay on his back and pulled her to him. She rested her head on his shoulder. After a minute, they were both asleep.

When she opened her eyes, she found herself still in Justin's arms, naked, with a blanket tucked to her chin. She looked up. Justin had awoken already. He was watching a movie. He put the volume on low with the subtitles on, sort of like he was careful not to wake her up.

She just stared at his profile. His perfect nose. The cleft on his chin that was barely there at all. He was very handsome indeed.

He looked down at her. "Hey beautiful," he whispered.

"How long have I slept?" she asked.

"Two, three hours? It's already seven."

She closed her eyes for a moment, then she stretched her arms and sat up, tucking the blanket under her arms.

He caressed the side of her waist. "Do you want to go out?" he asked.

"Where?"

He shrugged. "Just dinner. Anywhere your friends don't normally hang out in so you won't have to worry about anyone you know seeing you with Justin Adams."

She peered at him, trying to see if he was angry about it. But he actually smiled this time.

"Okay. Just let me shower first."

He nodded.

She got dressed. Then she kissed him on the cheek. "Pick me up at eight?" she asked, smiling.

"You bet." He smiled back.

She took time getting ready. She wore a pair of white capri pants and a red sleeveless blouse that accented her curves, which she never paid much attention to before. She put on very light make up and tied her hair in a half-pony. Finally, she slipped into her while high-heeled sandals. She smiled at the sight of her reflection.

How come I never wore these clothes before?

The doorbell rang at exactly eight. Justin studied her for a whole minute when she opened the door.

"Should I change?" she asked.

He shook his head. "I'm thinking, let's not go out at all. Let's just stay here."

She laughed. "Justin!"

He smiled. Then he pulled her close to him and whispered in her ear, "You're a fox!" And he kissed her on the side of her neck.

She giggled. "Come on. Let's go before you think of going farther."

"Oh trust me, honey. I'm already thinking about it."

She pinched him on the arm and laughed. "We just did what you were thinking about."

He shook his head. "That was almost five hours ago."

She pulled him towards the elevator. "Let's go. I don't sleep with a guy before a date."

He laughed. "You've never slept with a guy before me, honey."

She turned red. He laughed again and wrapped an arm around her waist.

"And that makes me so damn lucky!" he whispered and kissed her temple.

He took her hand in his. He led her to his Ferrari, and they drove to a Mexican restaurant in the City. Arrangements were already made so that they were seated in a secluded VIP area again.

After dinner, they took a joyride. Most of the time, he would take her hand in his and kiss it.

When they got home, he walked her to her door. They kissed passionately. She felt drugged. Excited. Like her world had flipped upside down again. And yet there was a sense of knowing. She knows this man... Justin... she feels comfortable at the same time. She felt the same excitement as ever, but the fear was gone.

When he pulled away, he looked as lost as she was. He smiled and kissed her on the forehead.

"Goodnight," he said.

"Goodnight," she whispered. She felt disappointed. She knew that she would miss sleeping in his arms that night. And she didn't want to break the magic just yet.

Then she dared ask him, "Do you want to come inside?"

Triumph glinted in his eyes. He replied, "Honey...you know if I come in, I would stay the night."

She smiled and wrapped her arms around his neck. "Then stay the night," she murmured.

He smiled at her. He looked genuinely happy she asked him to stay.

She turned around and opened the door. He followed.

She went into the bathroom to take a shower and change into her pajamas. When she got out, she found Justin on her bed, watching the news.

"Hey…" she called.

He smiled at her and then took off his shirt, which exposed the torso and abs that melted her knees when she first looked at them… and they still did.

"Toothbrush?" he asked.

She went into the bathroom and took a brand new toothbrush head and placed it on her electric toothbrush.

"Sorry. I don't have the whole brush. But I have spare heads."

He laughed. "That's fine."

After brushing, he took a quick shower. Adrienne placed a clean towel on the towel bar and closed the bathroom door behind her.

When Justin got out of the bathroom, his hair was wet and he had a towel wrapped around his waist.

"What are you watching?" he asked.

"Nothing interesting."

He sat beside her and kissed her. "I can think of something interesting to do," he whispered mischievously.

She laughed. "You! You sound like you're not tired of me yet."

He shook his head. "Why should I be? You're a fox!" His face descended towards hers and he gave her a soft kiss that turned passionate and deep. He nuzzled her neck and she moaned in pleasure.

After they made love, she felt senseless but happy.

She felt comfortable in his arms. She felt adored…and at the same time, safe.

She smiled even in her sleep. She thought, from the day she walked into Gypsys, she would never be the same.

7.
Junpu manpan
Japanese. Translation: Smooth Sailing.

It was true. Adrienne was never the same.

Her spirits soared so much higher when she went to work. She didn't dress in boring square pants and skirts anymore. She still exuded an executive look and yet became…foxy!

She didn't wear glasses anymore. She just kept them with her whenever she read or wrote. She frequently styled her hair down, either straight or in perfect waves behind her shoulders. She actually loved its red highlights. It made her look smart and naughty at the same time.

She became a little worried, though. On the fourteenth day since they began seeing each other, she still expected Justin to walk away.

Two weeks. This was his reputation. After two weeks, he would just disappear like a bubble.

She sighed on her desk and promised herself that she wouldn't get hurt. That she would accept things as they were. When he walked away, she would still be the same Adrienne that she had become. She wouldn't go back to her old wardrobe or her eyeglasses. This whirlwind thing had done a great deal to her confidence and self-respect. Regardless of how sinfully she acted, she got her self-love back. She wouldn't regret a single moment of her time with Justin.

"Are you okay?" Jill asked her.

No! He hasn't called me or texted yet! And it's after lunch!

It took all her effort not to scream that. Instead, she said, "I'm fine. Whatever made you think that I'm not okay?"

Jill shrugged. "You looked tense."

You think?

Adrienne sighed. "Too much work, I guess."

From the seventh day since that night at Gypsys, Justin had always sent her messages throughout the day.

You're a fox.

It never failed to bring a smile to her face. Yet when she got to Day Fourteen, she was starting to feel like she didn't exist at all. She didn't want to swallow her pride and call him. Not at the end of the two weeks, when rumors said that he'd lose interest in a woman.

She composed herself and went back to work.

"Miss Adrienne Miller?"

She looked up and saw a guy dressed in a Khaki uniform in front of her.

"Yes?"

He put a large bouquet of red roses on her desk.

She looked up at him. "From whom?" she asked.

"There's a card, ma'am. Please sign here." The delivery guy took her signature, and left.

When he was gone, she scanned the card nervously. Jill went to her side, curious and excited at the same time. "My God? Who sent those?" she asked. "Troy?"

"I don't know."

She read the card. Hoping against all hopes that it's from Justin, but also hoping that it wouldn't say so in the card because Jill stood right in front of her and definitely would snatch the card from her fingers after she read it.

The card read, *You're a fox...* She recognized Justin's neat handwriting.

She sighed in relief. She smiled to her ears.

Justin.

She only waited for a text message. He gave her more than that. He gave her roses! First time she ever received a bouquet of roses from a guy. And he was discreet enough not to put his name on it, but he left no doubt that he sent them.

Jill seized the card from her.

"Oh my God! You have a secret admirer! Do you know who it is?"

Adrienne shook her head. She didn't say anything. She feared she would scream if she opened her mouth at that moment.

"So sweet! And mysterious! I can say some guy is gaga over you! I told you! You're hot! You know why Kim had to be prude and had to pretend she is smart? Because it's so evident that you have the looks!"

"Jill!"

"And now that you're coming out in the open, see what happens?"

With all of Jill's excited wailing, other girls soon crowded in her cubicle, talking about who could possibly be the sender. They had some suspects and names to suggest, which surprised Adrienne.

"Jake from Marketing, he was asking about you," Cynthia asserted.

"And oh...Matt from Accounting, also asked if you had a boyfriend, the other day," another colleague said.

Adrienne just half-listened to the conversation. She wasn't interested in any of it. She found herself quite thrilled with her own thoughts. This is the first time she received flowers in her life.

Yes! My relationship with Troy was that pathetic!

Then somebody went, "Ssshh!!!" And then they all fell silent.

When she looked up, she saw Justin walking past her cubicle. He had an eyebrow raised and a corner of his lips curled into a half-smile.

She knew he gazed at her. And she felt good. When all of these women drooled over him, she knew his eyes were on her.

She bit her lip and just stared at him. And then he was out of sight.

The girls sighed in unison.

"All right. Back to work ladies. Jada will have my neck if she finds out I'm causing this commotion."

She brought home the bouquet of roses and placed them in a vase. She thought herself on cloud nine.

After five minutes, the doorbell rang.

When she opened it, Justin wrapped his arms around her waist, lifted her off her feet and carried her inside her apartment. She wrapped her arms around his neck.

"Did you send them?" she asked.

"Did you like them?" he countered, his crystal blue eyes sparkling.

"I love them!" She leaned down to kiss him.

They had Thai food delivery and afterwards, they watched DVDs in Justin's apartment. She fell asleep in his arms.

* * *

One month and a half elapsed since that night she went to Gypsys and met Justin Adams, who had become monumental in her life. They spent almost every night together. When he and his friends would have poker nights, he would borrow her key, so he could slip into her apartment and into her bed after midnight. When she woke up, she would find herself comfortably nestled in his arms.

She started trading stocks as well. She found it quite exciting. Her one thousand bucks paid twenty percent. Well, it was Justin who called the shots. She put her money on some blue chip company he was trading on. And it wound up being a good choice.

She invested more money. An amount she thought she could do without. She wanted to prove that she had learned how to risk some things. Every move she made, Justin would tell her if he thought it good or not. She saw him as a genius in this game. No wonder he made his own millions here.

Troy would call her at least once a week. She would indulge him in his med talks, and when it would normally freak her out to hear him say Kim's name more than once in every phone call, it didn't matter to her anymore.

Whenever he'd say I love you, she would reply goodnight, or remain silent. She actually found herself looking at the door when Troy embarked on a monologue, hoping Justin would walk in. And he always would.

And that's the time her face would brighten up.

"Kimberly gave me another pointer today...blah...blah... blah..." Then he went on and on.

She raised a brow, then let out a yawn while she let him talk to himself.

She knew it was only a matter of time before she broke up with Troy. She just needed time to be ready for what her mother would say to her. And she's definitely not going to end their relationship over the phone.

She reveled in high spirits that day. Before she went home, Jada called her and gave her another column. And she promoted her to Assistant Editor-in-Chief. The title raised her salary by a whopping twenty percent. But she figured Troy wouldn't be interested in hearing that. Even if she became a major stockholder for *Blush*, she didn't think he would be proud of her.

Justin opened her door and went into her apartment. She smiled at the sight of him. He did so in return.

He held a bottle of wine and a bouquet of roses.

"What?" she mouthed.

He shrugged. He didn't say anything. He knew she was speaking to someone on the phone. If he knew it was Troy, he never asked. In fact, he never asked about Troy anymore or where she stood with him. It was like when they're together, there's only the two of them.

"Hey...I gotta go...My boss just texted me. I need to go back to the office. Something came up," she lied.

"Sweetie, what kind of a profession does that? Pays so little and demands so much of your time. You gotta have time for yourself, you know."

"And what? Being doctor is an eight-hour job?" she snapped back at him.

"But at least it pays a lot more..." he started.

"Look Troy, you do your thing, I do mine. I don't fancy being a doctor, and you can't be a writer! Now, I have to go. Goodbye." Then she hung up.

She closed her eyes and took deep breaths to calm herself down.

Justin went to her but didn't say anything for a while. She looked up at him.

"I should remember not to argue with you, honey." He smiled. "You have a hell of a temper."

She sighed. "I'm sorry. Let's drop that."

"You want to talk about it?" he asked.

"Why would you want to talk about Troy?" she asked him, raising an eyebrow.

"I don't," he began softly. "But if you want to talk about it, I will endure it."

She smiled and shook her head. Then she threw herself in his arms and gave him a hug.

"I don't want to talk about it. I just want to be with you," she whispered.

"Hmmm...what are you doing with a guy who gives you a lot of problems anyway?" he asked quietly.

She shook her head. "It's complicated, Justin. My mother...she might never forgive me for breaking it off. I can't imagine what she will say to me. Besides, I can't break up with him over the phone. I have to plan this appropriately. And I can't think about this now."

He took a deep breath. "I just wish you would think about it someday." He hugged her tighter.

She didn't answer. She looked up at him. She couldn't make out any expression on his face.

"You could be a shrink, you know that?" she teased.

He raised a brow. "I don't think my Dad would name me his heir if I choose to be a shrink, though."

She laughed and then reached up and kissed him on the lips.

"Now, what's with the wine and the flowers?" she asked as she pulled away from him.

He handed her the roses. "For you."

"Hmmm. Justin Adams is a romantic soul." She giggled.

"Not every first impression proves to be true," he responded. "And we've been together for more than a month now, you should know that by now."

She nodded. "I know." She gave him a reassuring smile, sort of saying to him that she doesn't see him based on his reputation anymore. He's become a totally different person to her. "And what's with the wine?"

He placed the bottle of Chardonnay on her table. "Somebody received a promotion. I thought there's a reason to celebrate." He was beaming.

She was touched. She didn't tell him about the promotion yet. How did he find out?

"Oh, thank you! But how did you know?"

He shrugged. "I work part-time at *Blush*, remember? I have ears. Your friend, Jill, was talking about it with the layout artist when I came into the guy's office."

She smiled. "Thank you!"

"I'm really proud of you, hon," he said.

She hugged him. Now, more than ever, she felt what it was really like to have a boyfriend. How is it that Justin actually acted more like her boyfriend than Troy ever did? Come to think of it, Justin treated her the way she hoped Troy would treat her in the three years they were together.

She served dinner. Earlier, she cooked beef and pasta, thinking Justin might want to have dinner at her apartment. And now her plan worked out even better. Justin even brought wine.

The continued drinking the wine on her balcony.

"I have something for you," he stated.

"Really? Now how could you possibly top the wine and bouquet of roses?" She smiled.

He didn't answer. He took out a box from the pocket of his jacket and gave it to her.

"What is this?"

"My congratulations gift to you." He smiled. "Go ahead, open it."

The box was Tiffany's. Her heart pounded. She took off the ribbon, and slowly opened the box.

She lost breath when she stared at what lay inside.

A pair of dangling diamond earrings. The diamonds looked like raindrops, and it looked like to it could be at least two carats. She only could admire their absolute beauty.

"Justin…" She could barely breathe.

"Come on, I want to see them on you." He cut her off.

"Justin…this is expensive. You didn't have to…" She started.

He reached forward and silenced her with a kiss.

"But I want to, okay?" he whispered. "Do you like them?"

She nodded. "Yes…but you didn't have to get me something expensive…and not this expensive! Don't spoil me this way."

He chuckled. "It doesn't matter, honey. I walked by the shop, saw them in the window and I thought they would look stunning on you. I'm spoiling myself."

She leaned forward and gave him a kiss.

"Thank you," she whispered. Her eyes became wet with tears as emotions overwhelmed her. No other human being had ever made her feel this appreciated before. Not even her parents. She was the hand-me-down girl of Kimberly. She never had anything as beautiful or as expensive as Justin's present for her.

He smiled. "You're welcome. Now, let's see them."

She put the earrings on and pulled back her hair so he can see them on her.

He stared at her for a full minute. Not saying anything. Just giving her an intense look that suddenly made her nervous.

"What? They don't look good? The store can take them back, right?" she asked, almost in a panic.

He smiled at her. "They're gorgeous. Fifty times more beautiful than when they were sparkling in the window."

She smiled at him, released her hair and leaned forward to kiss him.

Troy never gave her anything extravagant or romantic. Two out of three birthdays of hers that they were together, he didn't even remember. And he never gave her flowers at all… not a single one…

8.
Réaliser
French. Etymology of the word: Realize

*A*drienne woke up that morning with the sound of the doorbell.

"Shit!" She panicked. She realized that she was naked and lying in Justin's arms.

"Who is that?" Justin asked, lazily sitting up from the bed.

"I don't know. It must be Jill or Yuan or both of them," she said, hurriedly getting her clothes and getting dressed.

"How will you hide?" she asked him.

"What if I just don't?" he asked squarely, getting dressed himself.

"Justin…this isn't the time okay? I need a good timing to tell them about us. I've kept it hidden for so long and they would hate me if they found out I didn't share something this huge with them," she explained.

"Do you realize that every day you don't tell them is keeping it from them longer? I'm still gonna be with you tomorrow, Adrienne. And the days after. If you don't tell them today, you will only increase the number of days that you have lied to them. They are your best friends. And besides, I wanted to meet them. I know Jill, but I've had to pretend I didn't because you didn't want her to know about us."

She sighed and went to his side. "I need more time. I need the perfect timing. And the perfect spiel." She felt desperate.

He stared at her. "Why didn't you tell them in first place?"

"I don't know. I just didn't…and I wanted to…but…" She stammered. To be honest, she didn't have an answer to that question. She knew she couldn't break up with Troy until he visited her. But she didn't know why she kept lying to her friends who never really cared for Troy, anyway.

Justin's eyes narrowed at her. "You didn't think it would last this long, did you?" he asked her seriously, his tone a little grave.

Bull's eye! Justin Adams, the smart ass!

Shame and guilt crossed her face. The doorbell rang again, this time the person on the other side of the door was getting impatient. "Justin, please?"

He threw his hands in the air. "All right, all right! I'm going!"

"How? You can't go out the door without being seen?"

"Who said I was going out the damn door?" he muttered, and then he opened the window of her bedroom. She watched nervously as he crossed the platform, that is about one and a half meters wide and six meters long, to the window of his own bedroom.

When he was safely in, she hurried towards the door.

"What took you so long?" Jill asked, entering her apartment immediately.

"I was asleep?" she replied sarcastically.

Yuan gave her a kiss on the cheek.

"Good morning, Sunshine!" he said, mimicking an early morning talk show host.

"What the…" Jill started.

Adrienne realized that the bouquet of roses that Justin gave her still sat on her dining table and wine glasses remained on the table in the balcony.

"Oh my God, is Troy here? Did he finally stay the night?" Yuan asked.

Adrienne shook her head. She felt so guilty. She felt bad about having an argument with Justin, too, after the previous night, which was perfect. He treated her wonderfully well. He had made her feel more special than anybody ever had in her entire life.

He sounded so dead serious about not keeping this thing a secret anymore, at least to her best friends. She knew she should tell them. But she couldn't quite find the right time. Because it would mean she lied to them from day one.

But it seemed flattering to know that Justin had given her a little promise…at least of some sort. He just said that he'll still be with her tomorrow and the days after…for how long, she didn't know. But at least she knows he wasn't walking away soon.

"Where is he?" Jill whispered.

Adrienne shook her head. "He's not here." She took a deep breath, nervously facing her friends and decided to face the truth and reality like ripping off the bandage. "I was actually with another guy. Justin."

Jill raised a brow. "Justin who?"

Adrienne took another deep breath. "Justin…Adams," she croaked.

Her friends blinked back at her. Then they stared at each other and then back at her again. Adrienne nervously waited for the screams and the curses. She balled her fists and bit her lip as she waited for almost like an eternity for them to react.

Then suddenly, they laughed…very hard! They even held on to their stomachs and sat on the couch and continued rolling in laughter.

"That's…that's a good one!" Yuan managed to speak in between his fits of laughter.

"Oh my God!" Jill uttered, struggling to compose a sentence. "He's a god in bed, right? He was with me the other day, too! And what can I say…best orgasm of my life!" And she laughed again.

Adrienne bit her lip to keep herself from crying. Her friends found it so hilarious that she could actually be with Justin. Well, how can she blame them? Sometimes she found it unbelievable herself.

When they finally calmed down they smiled at her. "That was the best joke you've said ever since we met you!" Yuan admitted. "Really! You cracked me up!"

Adrienne forced a smile. "Is it so unbelievable?"

"Justin Adams only beds supermodels," Yuan began. "And you're too smart to have sex with him! You did not hold on to your virginity for so long, only to waste it on a guy who wouldn't give a damn that he was your first. You're too smart to get yourself involved with a playboy. That's why you can't break up with Troy! You're too…safe, too careful."

"Plus! You would never keep that from us! I will never, and I mean…never forgive you if you even spoke to him and you didn't share that with us! That's a friendship ender!" Jill went over to her fridge and getting a soda for herself and Yuan.

Shit!

Adrienne gulped. Although she knew Jill didn't mean it, but there was a hint of truth in it. They would never forgive her if they found out what's she's been doing the past six weeks and who she was doing it with.

"What is happening south of your earlobes?" Jill exclaimed.

They both came closer to her. Yuan checked out her ears. Too late. She forgot to take off the earrings that Justin gave her from the past night.

"How gallant!" Yuan exclaimed. "My God, Troy must have been struck by lightning! He had suddenly gone romantic!"

"Are those Tiffany's?" Jill asked.

Adrienne nodded.

"Those cost a fortune, you know!" Yuan continued. "That's two carats! Probably more! He must love you so much to spend all of his medical school allowance on a trinket!"

"Who said they came from him?" Adrienne asked almost in a snap, stepping away from them.

Her friends fell silent. They realized that Adrienne wasn't in a good mood. She went to the balcony and lit a cigarette. She was biting her lips to stop herself from crying. She started melting with shame and guilt.

She realized now more than ever what a mistake it was to hide Justin from her friends. Even Justin didn't seem happy to be kept inside the closet anymore. But what could she do? How can she bring herself to confess to them when Jill just gave her a fair warning that it would be an instant deal-breaker?

"I have something to tell you, sweetie!" Jill started, finally dropping the subject of her earrings. "I was talking to Garry, the layout artist, yesterday, and guess who walked in?"

Adrienne knew exactly who walked in. And the thought made her feel even more guilty.

"Justin Adams!" Jill exclaimed. "He looked absolutely handsome. But as always, he had those shades on. But that makes him hotter though.

Like he just stepped out from the covers of a magazine or something. And this is the story. When he walked in, he said, '*Hi Garry.*' And then he looked at me and said, '*Hi Jill.*' He knows me! He knows my name! My God! Unbelievable! We're on first-name basis now!"

Adrienne stared at Jill. She was practically drooling. She felt more and more ashamed of herself. But what should she say?

Of course, he knows you! He's been hiding from you guys for almost two months now because I didn't want you to know that he was sleeping with me! And yes, I've been sleeping with him almost every night!

She closed her eyes for a moment.

"Sweetie, you're still sleepy?" Yuan asked.

"I read a book last night. Slept late," she lied yet again.

"My God, when I see him again, what will I say to him? I'll say, '*Hi Justin.*' Do you think it'll be weird? Do I sound bold? Or too assuming?" Obviously, Jill wasn't ready to give up talking about Justin Adams just yet.

"You can try—and then tell us about it," Yuan suggested. "My God, that guy is known for being a classic snob! But he's got every right to be. And speaking of hot guys, I wonder when Torso god on the other side would show himself."

"Yes, have you seen what he looks like, Yen?" Jill asked.

She shook her head slightly. She couldn't concentrate. She still couldn't get Justin out of her mind. She kept repeating their conversation over and over in her head. That was their first fight. And who knows if they will make up and last long enough to have another one, the same way normal couples do?

Then her phone beeped. She read the message.

Justin: *I'm going to Chicago for a week. Duty calls. I mean, my father. I'll catch the twelve-noon flight. Obviously, I can't come over to kiss you goodbye. So, I'll just see you when I get back.*

She was too confused to answer. And worse, she felt miserable with shame and guilt.

"What's bothering you, Yen? You don't seem like yourself lately. Well, you did change a lot for the better. But now, it seems like you didn't want to talk at all. Are you okay?" Yuan asked.

She shrugged. Because she couldn't lie any more, she decided to answer with something that has truth in it. "Troy. This thing with him isn't going anywhere. We argue a lot. And I don't seem to care anymore. I don't care if we have a fight. I don't care if he's been having too many study dates with Kim."

Yuan and Jill stared at her. None of them could say a word.

"I mean, we're so incompatible. And that's not good. And… every time we talk these days, it's not complete without an argument. I did change a lot. And I feel good about myself. It's like for the first time in years, I felt like I'm great. Like I'm amazing. And I didn't have to live in someone's shadow. I want to experience magic with someone. Someone who doesn't have to love me. But just make me feel adored. Admired. Like I'm good enough just being myself."

Like Justin! I want to be fair to him! But only God knows until when our thing is going to last.

Yuan reached for her hand. "We've been trying to tell you that for years, sweetie. But you love the guy…"

She shook her head. "I don't anymore. I liked him, yes. But I realized that maybe I am with him because he fits this whole trying-to-please-Mommy charade I've been keeping up for years. And I give up. Mom will never love me as much as she loves Kim. And it's okay. As long as she loves me. I don't care."

"Think about this, honey," Yuan began. "Because your mother might not be able to forgive you for this. She seemed hell-bent on making Troy her son-in-law."

"Are you guys trying to change my mind on this?" she asked.

Jill shook her head. "No. But we just want you to be emotionally ready. Because it's like waging war with your mother. And we know how much you hate fighting with her."

She tried to weigh her situation, the pros and the cons for two straight days. That's what Justin told her the last night she was with him. Think about her relationship with Troy. It did last for three years but that didn't mean it would last forever. Come to think of it, she didn't have a lot of good memories with him, if she had memories of him at all.

Adrienne couldn't do anything right. More often, she stared into space. She jumped every time her mobile phone rang or beeped. She waited for Justin to call or send a message. He didn't. She didn't hear from him for three straight days, quite contrary to what he said to her before he left…that he would stick around some more days.

She didn't feel like this with Troy at all. Never. She seemed okay with him not calling her or texting her for days. She would still be herself. But why was it different with Justin? Why did she miss him every single minute of every hour of every day? And why did she worry that this could be very well the end of them.

He might have come to his senses! Why did he stay with her in the first place? He could have better looking, richer and more confident women. Women who would be proud to be seen with him! Why did he stick with a girl with a very low self-esteem, who decided she didn't want to be seen with him at all? Who was ashamed of his acquaintance? He is Justin Adams! He didn't need that crap!

On the fourth night without Justin, she just lay in her tub thinking. She didn't realize that tears had begun rolling down her cheeks. She hated to admit it but she missed him like hell.

She knew she didn't love Troy anymore. She even questioned herself if she ever loved him at all. It wasn't going anywhere. And she didn't feel for Troy anything like what she felt for Justin. Maybe the thought of her mother's approval blinded her, her constant need to seek it made her think she was in love with Troy, when she didn't even know what and how love should feel like.

And suddenly she realized that she can't be in love with Troy, especially not…when she's already fallen in love with someone else.

Oh, damn it!

She changed into her pajamas and went to bed. Before she turned off the lights, she took her cellphone and sent Justin a text message, before she could stop herself.

Her: *Hey… I hope you're okay. Take care… I miss you.*

And she pressed SEND before she could either erase the whole message or add '*I love you*' to it.

She waited a whole hour. He didn't reply.

She blew it for sure. First, she made him feel like she wasn't proud to be associated with him in any way. And with her text message, she realized she had just given him the first sign of what she really felt for him.

She might have blown it there as well. Maybe the whole thing worked for him because she wasn't demanding anything. What if he was just having fun? And it's cool because he thought she was, too.

Yes, he definitely became fond of her. The flowers he sent her said so, as did the Tiffany earrings. But he's filthy rich. The price of those earrings wouldn't cover even one tenth of what he earned every day. It said they were good. But it didn't say he loved her, too. It said he's fond of her…for the moment, but not forever.

She cried herself to sleep that night. She hugged her pillow tight, remembering the moments when it was Justin's body she held and he embraced her, comforted her, made her feel safe.

Finally, she allowed sleep to take her. In her dream, he had her in his arms. They were together, and they didn't fight anymore.

Her alarm went off at seven-thirty in the morning. She had a bad headache from all the crying. She still clutched her pillows, but something wasn't right. A pair of strong arms also draped around her.

She spun around and found Justin sleeping beside her. She blinked to make sure that she had actually woken up and didn't imagine this. She bit her lip and took a deep breath. She prayed: *If this is a dream, don't wake me up! 'Coz this is just too darned romantic right now!*

She watched him sleep. He wore only a pair of pajama bottoms.

How could he be here? He said he would be in Chicago for a week. It had only been four days.

She took her mobile phone on the bedside table. She didn't have any messages. She sent a message to Jill, saying she cannot go to work that day.

"*Headache. Bad one. But don't worry about me. I'll call you later.*"

She gazed at Justin again. And then she leaned forward and kissed him on the lips.

He tightened his arms around her. "Adrienne," he whispered.

She smiled to herself, closed her eyes and went back to sleep.

She woke up again an hour later. When she opened her eyes, she found Justin watching her lazily.

"Good morning," he said.

She touched his cheek with her fingertips.

"Morning." She smiled. "What are you doing here? I thought you'd be gone for a whole week."

He smiled. "I finished business early. And besides…"

"Besides what?" she asked.

"You said you missed me." He smiled boyishly.

She blushed and looked away.

He tilted her chin up so she could look him in the eye. "Well? Did you?" he asked.

She smiled shyly and then nodded. "And did you miss me?" she countered.

He leaned forward. When his lips were just an inch away from hers, he said, "Like hell." Then he kissed her deeply.

After the kiss, he leaned his forehead to hers. "You have to go or you're going to be late for work," he said.

She shook her head. "Not today."

"Really? Why?" he asked.

"I missed you like hell, too." She smiled boldly.

He grinned. "Really? Show me."

She pushed him flat on his back and then she leaned forward to kiss him passionately. She started it, and he finished it. When it was over, her world had started spinning again. They lay there naked for a while, their legs tangled, their arms wrapped around each other.

"Hon…" he started. "I'm sorry I raised my voice the last time we spoke before I left."

"I'm sorry we argued in the first place," she confessed.

He smiled. "I know you're not yet ready to tell your friends about us. And I'm sorry if I put pressure on you. But sometimes, I just don't understand why you can't tell at least your friends. I mean…they are your best friends. Do you really think I'm such an asshole that you don't want them to know that we're seeing each other? Are you…ashamed of me or something?"

She shook her head. "No. I'm just worried they won't forgive me for hiding this from them. And you're not an asshole. I thought you were, though."

He looked down at her with a raised brow. "You thought I was?"

She smiled. "Don't get mad. I just thought you were conceited. You were giving women false hopes, that's bad."

He was silent for a while. Then he said, quite carefully, "I typically don't look for a girlfriend. I don't stick around longer than two dates. If I knew it wasn't going somewhere, I just…get out. And I never promised a girl it would last forever. I never swore my heart to a woman before. So no one should say that I gave them false hopes."

"Didn't you even try?" she asked, smiling.

Justin seemed lost in his own thoughts as he caressed her arm. Then he said, "You don't have to try in love, Adrienne. When it comes, you're hopeless to even try to stop it from happening to you. Even if sometimes…you couldn't and shouldn't fall in love. It still happens." He sighed. "Contrary to my reputation, I actually feel with my heart. Not with my dick."

"Can I ask you something?"

"Shoot."

"Do you marry for love? Or for power, wealth and money? I mean are you allowed to choose whoever you want?"

Justin gave her a squeeze. Then he kissed the top of her head. "Power and wealth aren't the only things to consider in marriage," he admitted. "I don't speak for everybody who was born with the same privilege as me. But…if it were up to me, I would marry for love, anytime, any day."

"Did your parents marry for love?"

He thought for a while, then he replied, "My parents are as in love with each other as two lovers could ever be."

Adrienne stared up at him. Justin looked serious. But she couldn't read the expression on his face. He reached forward and pushed a lock of stray hair away from her face.

"You're beautiful," he whispered.

She smiled and leaned forward to kiss him.

Suddenly, he chuckled. "You thought that I was an asshole and yet you still went home with me when we met at Gypsys?"

She smiled wickedly. "Well, the tequila made you look like a god! It was whispering in my ear, *'Go on! Lose your virginity to this asshole! At least he looked hot as hell!'*"

He laughed. "Tell me you didn't mean that."

"Which one? The tequila made you look like a god thing? I think I mean that. But the kisses you gave me made me lose myself all the way."

He laughed harder. "I picked up the wrong girl that night then. I thought you would think highly of me."

"So conceited! Just because the whole of New York thinks you're a god, doesn't mean I do, too."

"And you were the one that mattered." He shook his head. "Damn! I think I made a move on the wrong girl that night."

She raised a brow. "Okay, so you're sorry now? All right. I won't put up a fight!" she snapped and started to stand up from the bed.

He pulled her back and pinned her between his body and the mattresses.

"You... have a hell of a temper, honey. You get mad easily. I was kidding. I would never, ever, *ever* trade you for any girl that night."

"Yeah... since we're having this conversation, why did you pick me up anyway? Of all the girls there, why me? Did I look like I would sleep with you?"

He smiled and shook his head. "You were the only one who looked like you wouldn't. And it made me want you even more."

"You're a bundle of conceit, you know that?" she snapped. "I was a challenge? And now you know I would sleep with you. Does that mean you don't want me as much as you wanted me then?"

He chuckled and pressed closer to her. She felt him pressed on her abdomen. He was rock hard.

"Does it feel like I want you less than that night?" he asked in a sober voice.

"Justin...we just..."

He grinned at her wickedly. "That's how much I want you." His face descended to take her in a kiss that led to another wild ride of passion.

9.

Salaisuus
Finnish for Secret

The following Friday night, she made plans to go to Gypsys with her friends. She texted Justin to tell him this.
    Justin: *I'll see you there.*
    Her: *What?!*
    Justin: *Relax! I'll be with my friends. But look my way sometimes, okay?*
    Her: :-)
    Justin: *When you're there, remember that there's one SMOKING HOT guy in the bar who couldn't take his eyes off you!*
    Her: *Smoking hot? Who? Oh, did you mean you?*
    She smiled when she sent him that message.
    Justin: *The one and only!* ;-)
    Her: *Let me get a needle. Your head needs deflating!*
    Justin: *You're unbelievable! LOL! See you later!*
    When she stared at her reflection in the mirror, she couldn't help feeling proud. She curled her hair with an iron. It looked more reddish brown. She applied light pink blush and silver and gray eye makeup to emphasize her startling long-lashed green eyes. She wore a glittery white dress that ended a few inches above her knees and showed her perfect curves. The high-heeled sandals gave her extra height and extra allure.
    Yuan gave her a missed call, which meant that they're already in front of her building.
    When they arrived at Gypsys, they immediately found themselves a spot in the center of the bar.
    "It had to be in the middle of the floor, huh?" Adrienne rolled her eyes at Jill and Yuan.
    "Of course. This is where the action is!" Jill replied, laughing.
    A group of guys entered and walked to the bar in front of the bartender as if that spot was reserved for them.
    "Manhattan rakes!" Jill swooned.
    "It's good to see Justin Adams back!" Yuan said.
    Adrienne raised a brow. "What do you mean it's good to see him back?"
    Yuan shrugged. "Lately, he's been out of circulation. No one saw him partying at all. His love… excuse me! Sex life seems pretty quiet."
    "Yeah. I have friends who blogs gossip here and there. And apparently, they don't see him much these days. Before, he went to bars almost every night. Then it's like he disappeared! How lucky could we be

that he's here tonight?"

Adrienne didn't say anything. But she couldn't help smiling, because she knows exactly where and how Justin had spent his nights lately. In his apartment or hers, watching movies, drinking on either of their balconies and only twice, poker nights with his friends.

Adrienne stared at the bar where Justin stood. He sported those light-tinted Cartier glasses again to shield his eyes. He leaned on the bar, holding a bottle of beer in his hand. He looked in their direction. Adrienne knew that Justin was watching her. And because she knew her friends weren't looking, she smiled and winked at him. She noted the upward curl of his lips before she turned back to her friends.

After a couple of seconds, her phone beeped.

Justin: *Stop flirting with me!*

She bit back her lip to prevent herself from grinning widely in front of her friends. If they got too curious, they just might snatch the phone from her to look at what she was smiling about.

She sent him a response: *Then stop staring at me!*

Justin: *Impossible. I couldn't stop looking at you since the day I laid eyes on you. ;-) You're a fox!*

She grinned at her phone, then she straightened her face when she remembered she was with Jill and Yuan.

She sent another message to Justin: *Now it's your turn to stop flirting with me!*

She looked over to his location. She found him staring at his phone and then he grinned widely at it. He looked at her for a while, the smile still pasted on his face, and then he typed something on his phone. Then she saw him bring it to his lips and kissed the screen. Then he looked at her again, smiling crookedly.

Her phone beeped again.

Justin: *Justin Adams just gave Adrienne Miller a thorough kiss on the lips!*

She couldn't help giggling this time and she knew she began blushing all over. When she looked up, she found two pairs of curious eyes staring at her.

She cleared her throat. "Nothing. Kimberly sent a broadcast on chat. Medical joke. Wanna hear?"

Please say no! She silently prayed.

Jill wrinkled her nose and Yuan rolled his eyes. "No, thanks!" they said in unison, much to Adrienne's relief.

After a bottle of Breezer, Adrienne excused herself to go to the ladies' room. She went through the first door and found two other doors in front of her. The door on the left led to the men's room and the other to the ladies'. She took the door to her right.

As she retouched her lip gloss, she noticed the women around her.

Some of their outfits seemed too skimpy for her taste. She thought one or two girls had started hurling in one of the cubicles. Most of them still spoke about how many cute and available guys came that night and how each hoped to score one of them.

She couldn't help wondering where she'd been all her life and what made her oblivious at how liberated the world had become. Was she really too prudish and too sheltered?

She went out the first door. As she reached for the handle of the second one that will lead her to the bar, it opened and two girls rushed inside. One had her hand to her mouth, obviously trying to make it to the ladies' room to throw up but it didn't look like she was going to make it. Unfortunately, this girl had come directly in front of Adrienne. She feared she was too shocked to react or stay out of the way. She watched in horror as the girl lunged forward and made a puking sound.

Suddenly, she felt somebody pull her waist and yank her out of the way. The girl vomited a meter away from her, much to her relief.

It took her a moment to realize that whoever pulled her still held her. She looked up and saw a pair of gorgeous aquamarine eyes. His hair was brown with a little tint of red. He was looking back at her in surprise as well. A sense of familiarity shot toward her, which made her aware that he was still holding her.

She took a step back from him. His eyes were narrowed, as if he was trying to place her. His face looked familiar too, which she found quite odd.

"Have…we met before?" he asked.

Standing half a meter away from him, she got the chance to look at him further. He was taller than her, probably as tall as Justin. He appeared lean, and the white long-sleeved shirt he wore outlined a bit of his well-toned physique.

She would have remembered meeting him. He was very—and she meant *very*—good-looking. Like he stepped out of the covers of a magazine. But she was positive she hasn't seen him around yet. But something about him seemed oddly familiar.

She shook her head. "No, I don't think so."

"Sorry. I thought I've seen you before." He smiled, flashing her his perfect set of teeth and deep, adorable dimples on either side of his cheeks, just beside his lips. Then he reached forward and extended his hand to her. "I'm Jin. Jin Starck."

She stared at his hand for a moment and decided to shake it. "Adrienne. Adrienne Miller."

Adrienne heard a cough behind her. She turned around and found Justin, a grave look was plastered on his face. Immediately, she pulled her hand away from the guy.

The guy looked from her to Justin, and Adrienne saw the realization crossing his face. He took in the look on Justin's face and immediately concluded that Adrienne was with him.

"Well, you're welcome," he said to Justin, his eyes glittering.

Justin shot an eyebrow up. "For what?"

"I just saved your girlfriend's dress from going in the trash bin," he said cheerfully. Then he stared at Adrienne and smiled. "See you around, Adrienne Miller." He winked at her before he exited the room.

Adrienne turned to Justin who didn't look too happy. "Yeah, a girl almost puked on me," she said, pointing at the nasty vomit on the floor that was now being cleaned up by a female maintenance worker.

He glared at her for a long moment and then he shook his head.

"What?" she asked.

"You have ten seconds to get back to your table. Or I'm taking you there and you will have a lot of explaining to do to your friends," he said in an arctic-clad voice.

"Justin…" she started.

"Ten… nine…" He started counting which made her panic. She quickly turned on her heels and she took a run for the exit.

Adrienne was panting when she got back to her table.

"What happened to you?" Jill asked.

It took a moment for Adrienne to compose herself. "Some girl almost puked on me."

"And it's only eleven, ladies and gentlemen! Welcome to the twenty-first century!" Yuan chuckled.

When she peered at the bar, she found that Justin had already gotten back to his seat. He had his back to her.

An ugly, guilty feeling gnawed her and she couldn't understand it. Was she wrong to shake that guy's hand? He introduced himself to her politely, and he saved her from a disastrous wardrobe emergency. It seemed only right to shake his hand, no?

Then why did she feel like she was cheating? Why did she feel like Justin had every right to be pissed off?

She took out her phone and started typing: *Are you okay?*

She didn't receive a response. She kept looking at her phone and at the bar where Justin sat. He still had his back to her and it looked like he was drinking quietly.

She tried again. *Hey, handsome! Smile, okay?*

She saw Justin looking down, probably reading her message.

Finally, her phone beeped. Her heart skipped a beat as she read his message.

Justin: *Can't smile. Some guy ogled my girl.*

She smiled at those last two words. *My girl.*

She replied: *He was not ogling! And besides did you see her ogle back?*

Justin: *No. But I still feel bad. So, she has to make up for it!*
Her: *How?*

She waited for like forever for his response. Then finally, her phone beeped again.

Justin: *She has to go on a date with me. This time, I name the place and the terms.*

She bit her lip. She had to keep herself from screaming her heart out.

Her: *She says okay. But you have to remember the rules. Nothing public.*

Justin: *Nope. I said I will be the one to name the terms.*

Adrienne sighed. She knew in her heart that she loved this guy. And he'd done so much for her. He knew what he's doing. He promised not to pressure her. So she typed her answer and hit send: *All right Mr. Adams! You got yourself a date!*

After a minute he responded: *Now, Miss Miller… I'm smiling all the way!* :-)

She looked at him. True enough, he started looking in her direction, his lips curved in a smile that she knew was meant only for her.

10.
Kidnappad.
Swedish for Kidnapped

*W*hen Adrienne woke up the next day, her head rested comfortably against Justin's shoulder. She got home at around two and he came to her apartment thirty minutes after, dressed in a white shirt and a pair of Calvin Klein pajamas.

He pretended to look pissed, but once she pulled him to bed and kissed him, he caved in. Then, they fell asleep.

"Wake up, sleepyhead," Justin said. "You have a date in two hours."

Her eyes widened. "Two hours? Justin…it's ten in the morning! We're going out in broad daylight?"

He raised a brow. "Yeah, why not?"

"You know we can't! No one knows we're seeing each other. The minute we get photographed together, somebody could post about it on social media and it will definitely reach Jill! And she already warned me…this is a friendship ender."

Justin sighed. "So what's your plan, Miss Miller? You will never introduce me to them at all?"

"I haven't even broken up with Troy yet!" She threw her head back against her pillow.

Justin propped up on an elbow so he could look at her. "Adrienne…no one has ever been ashamed of me before."

She shook her head. "I'm not ashamed of you. God! If circumstances were different… if I didn't have a boyfriend… I would be proud to be seen with you."

"Can I ask you something?" He looked gravely serious.

She nervously nodded.

"Do you even have plans of breaking up with Troy?"

She gazed at him and smiled slowly. "Of course."

Justin stared at her for a moment, searching her eyes. Then finally, he gave her a crooked smile. "Then that's good enough for now." Then he leaned forward and kissed her on the lips thoroughly.

"Justin… now, can I ask you something?" Her heart pounded in her chest.

"Anything."

"Why do you put up with this? I know you hated being kept a secret. You can have a pick of any woman…"

She wasn't able to finish that sentence because Justin's lips were on hers, cutting her off.

When he pulled away from her, he gazed into her eyes gently. Then he said, "Because the only woman I want, Adrienne, is in this bed with me."

She smiled at him. She thought she would die right then and there. He didn't say he was in love with her too, but that was close enough.

"Now, dress up. I'll pick you up after an hour and half," Justin said, standing up from the bed.

She raised a brow at him. "Justin…"

He silenced her with a kiss again. "Don't you trust me, honey?"

She nodded. "Okay."

"Great. I'll see you later." He stood up from the bed, grabbed his shirt on the floor and wore it. Before he exited her room, he turned back to her and grinned, "You're a fox!"

After showering, she wore a pair of skinny jeans and a sleeveless top. Her mobile phone rang. It was Justin.

"Hey."

"You don't look warm enough," he said.

She turned around and saw him standing in his room, looking at her through the glass window.

"I have a coat."

"Still not good enough. Wear a sweater under your coat."

"It's not even snowing outside and it's almost noon!"

He grinned at her. "Didn't you promise me last night that I will be the one to name the terms?"

She laughed. "All right."

"And wear a pair of boots, too, okay?"

"Okay, fine." When she hung up, she scanned through her closet and found a blue knitted sweater. Then she took a black shawl and placed it around her neck. She wore her black knee-length boots.

She couldn't help wondering about Justin's plans. She wanted to wear one of her hooded jackets so that if they walk the streets, she could lessen the risk of recognition.

She figured he must be getting tired of hiding all the time. The previous night, he didn't hide the fact that he was not happy to see another guy introducing himself to her. It made her feel happy to know that he felt jealous and unafraid to show it. But it also broke her to realize that she couldn't give him what he wanted. Until she faced Troy and officially broke up with him. Until she comes up with a plan on how to confess her situation to her friends, who she couldn't lose no matter what.

She took out her phone and decided to send Troy a message: *We need to talk. In person. When you have a day off, let me know. I could come to see you.*

She hoped that Troy was smart enough to sense that something was wrong.

Come on! Who are we kidding?

Justin acted more like a boyfriend than Troy ever had. Troy must be dense if the thought this relationship was going somewhere.

Her doorbell rang. She grabbed her purse and opened the door. Justin looked at her for a moment.

"I look okay?" she asked, uncertainty all over her voice.

His eyes glittered and he pulled her to him. "You look more than okay. You're a fox!"

She laughed and closed the door behind her.

"So what's your plan, Mr. Adams? Just make sure I'm in for a big surprise!" she teased.

Justin laughed as they entered the elevator. "You have no idea, honey!"

In Justin's heavily tinted Ferrari, no one could see her even in broad daylight. She still wondered where he would take her. She still worried that somebody could recognize him. Why did he have to be quite famous in this state? Why did he have to be the City's most wanted?

Adrienne realized that they reached the airport and Justin used a private entrance.

"Where are we going?"

He just grinned at her.

Finally, he stopped the engine in what seemed to be a private parking lot.

He got out of the car and rounded it to open the door for her. He took her hand in his. She noticed there were people around, and a guy followed them, carrying a small traveling bag with him.

Adrienne stared at Justin nervously.

"Justin…I'm getting really freaked out," she whispered.

He laughed. "Your problem has always been that you didn't want to be seen with me. You're always scared that somebody you know would run into us when we're together in New York. I, on the other hand, wanted to be free to go around town with you in my arms. I want to drink coffee with you in the local coffee shop, or watch movies with you, go around shopping with you, and be free to hold you, hug you, kiss you, without you worrying that your friends would kill you if they found out. I want to go on a whole day date with you…without you worrying about anything at all."

Adrienne bit her lip. She felt happy, and guilty and sorry all at the same time. She squeezed Justin's hand.

The door in front of them opened. Adrienne was surprised to see the runway. She saw a private plane from a distance. She almost gasped when she saw the markings on the body of the plane, *"Adams Industries."*

She stared up at him. "Justin…"

He grinned at her. "I'm taking you somewhere no one knows either of us. And both of our problems are solved."

Her heart melted. If she wasn't in love with him already, then she would have fallen…right then and there.

The flight stewards greeted them warmly.

"Good afternoon, Mr. Adams." To her, they said, "Welcome aboard, Miss Miller."

She was stunned that they knew their name. But then again, they would have the flight manifesto beforehand. Justin must have arranged this after she said yes to him.

The interior of the plane looked luxurious and classy. It had long leather couches, an eight-seater dining set, all in rich combinations of gold and cream colors. She sat on the sofa and Justin sat down beside her.

"Your plane?"

Justin shrugged. "My family's."

"So when you go back to Chicago, this is what you use?"

"Yes. Are you hungry?"

She nodded.

"We'll have lunch after take-off."

"Where are we going, Justin?"

His eyes glittered. "Somewhere we're sure no one knows either of us."

She rolled her eyes. "Where is that?"

"Alaska."

Her jaw dropped. It took a while for her to recover. She heard somebody asking them to fasten their seatbelts.

"Justin… it's a couple of hours flight."

"Seven."

"When do you plan to get back?"

"Monday."

"I work on Monday!"

"I'm sure you can take a day off."

"What… what will I tell my friends?"

He leaned back on his seat. "Aren't you a creative writer for *Blush*?"

She nodded.

"So do what you do best. Be creative!" He grinned.

She groaned. She leaned back on her seat. She kept silent all throughout take off. Finally, the plane climbed high in the air, and the pilot informed them that they can unfasten their seatbelts.

Justin quickly got off his seat and went to her. He unbuckled her belt, and to her surprise, lifted her off her seat and brought her to the sofa, so she could sit on his lap.

"Are you mad?"

She pouted at him and then she pinched his side. He laughed and hugged her to him.

"Justin, I didn't bring any clothes."

"I know. I couldn't tell you what to pack. Otherwise, knowing you, we'd still be at your place right now arguing about this trip. So I figured I'd just kidnap you."

"So what am I going to do?"

"We'll stop by a mall as soon as we land there. You can go shopping for your weekend needs."

"And wear those clothes without washing them? No way!" She sounded so abhorred that Justin couldn't help laughing hard.

"No, silly. We're checking into a hotel. You can send your new clothes for rush laundry. I'll pay for the premium. I'm sure they'll get them to you in an hour or two."

A flight attendant informed them that their lunch awaited them. Adrienne pulled away and stood up. She reached her hand out and pulled him up on his feet.

After lunch, Justin led her to another section of the plane. Adrienne was surprised to see that it was actually a small room. It had a double-sized bed a small coffee table and two one-seater chairs.

Justin opened the small door to his left. "Bathroom's here if you wanna freshen up."

The bathroom was small, but oddly big enough, considering they were travelling inside a plane. It had a shower, a toilet and a sink. She found a new set of toothbrushes by the sink. She brushed her teeth and splashed water on her face.

As she stared at her reflection, she realized that she had glitter in her eyes. Her blush seemed permanent and she couldn't stop grinning.

Justin Adams sure knew how to make a girl swoon! Her official boyfriend may be a troll and sure lacked a romantic bone, but her unofficial boyfriend sure made up for everything that was missing in her love (and sex) life.

Justin just lay lazily in bed when she came out of the bathroom. She removed her boots and used one of the new slippers she found under the bed.

Justin stood up and kissed her lips. Then he went to the bathroom. Adrienne looked around the room. It was small but the luxurious furniture was cleverly arranged to make it look big enough. It was cozy and almost felt like home. She noticed some pictures hanging on one of the walls.

She looked at a family portrait of Justin and his parents. His father had the same jet-black hair as him. His mother appeared dark blonde. His mother seemed young, and every bit sophisticated and beautiful. Justin's father on the other hand…looked exactly like him. Only about twenty years older.

Suddenly, she felt Justin's arms around her waist as he nuzzled her neck.

"You look like your Dad," she said.

He rested his chin on her shoulder. "Everybody says that."

Adrienne laughed. "Everybody's right. Your mother is beautiful. Your parents look very young in this picture."

"They are. They got married when my Dad was twenty-five and my mother was twenty-three."

"Whoa! That's young. They must have been really in love when they got married."

Justin fell quiet for a little while. Then she heard him take a deep breath as he pulled her closer to him.

She turned around to face him. "Are you okay?" she asked, noticing his quiet reaction.

He nodded. "Aren't you tired?" he asked. "We've got five and a half hours left. You might want to sleep first."

"I could use a nap." She pulled him towards the bed. "Come, lie down with me."

They quietly lay in bed. Adrienne wondered why Justin's mood changed when she mentioned his family and how in love his parents were when they got married. She wondered why that seemed to bother him.

She looked up and found him staring at the ceiling, lost in his thoughts.

"Justin," she called. "Did I say something wrong?"

He looked down at her and shook his head. "I'm sorry. I just remembered something my parents…asked me to do." He looked at her deeply.

"What? Some sort of errand?" she asked brightly, hoping to change his mood.

"More like some sort of obligation," he sighed.

"And you haven't done it yet?" she asked, propping up on her elbow so she could stare at him.

He pushed back a lock of hair away from her face. "I…forgot about it."

"So? Can't you go back and do it then?"

He shook his head. "No. I can't go back now."

Adrienne drew her brows together. Justin didn't seem like he wanted to elaborate on the subject. And she knew better than to pressure him to tell her about his family affairs.

"I'm sure it's not yet too late. You can still tell them you'd get to it as soon as you can."

He shook his head. "It's too late," he whispered.

"Why?"

Justin drew a heavy breath. "Because I don't wanna do it anymore."

She was about to ask more but he pulled her neck and closed the distance between them. His lips found hers and he kissed her passionately, as if he was pouring out his soul in that kiss.

11.
Liberté.
The French Translation of Freedom.

*W*hen Adrienne woke up, she found that Justin had gone from the room. She went to the bathroom to freshen up. Justin walked in just as she was putting on her boots.

"Hey, where have you been?"

"Having a chat with the pilot," he replied.

"Can you fly a plane?" she asked.

He grinned. "I have a license. I don't think they give it out to just anybody."

She smiled. "Justin Adams, the pilot. What else don't I know about you?"

She stood up and wrapped her arms around his neck. He leaned forward and kissed her lips. "A lot. But that's why you're going on a weekend date with me, right? So I can show you what I'm like when I'm...unrestrained."

Adrienne laughed. "Nice choice of word."

As soon as they landed, a limousine took them to a local mall. Adrienne turned on her phone and immediately, it kept ringing, indicating text messages and voicemails.

Jill: *Trying your phone. It's off. Where are you?*

Yuan: *Hey, where are you? Coffee this afternoon?*

She sent them a text message telling them that she had to fly to Boston to see her parents. Hopefully, they wouldn't ask her to elaborate. She did that once in a while anyway.

While at the mall, in broad daylight, Justin pulled her to him and put an arm around her shoulder. She felt a kiss at the top of her head.

She got herself some sweaters, pants, underwear, gloves and a thick coat. Just enough for the next three days. When she brought her stuff to the counter, Justin was quick to hand over his Infinite credit card.

She glared at him in protest. "No, Justin. It's my stuff!"

He grinned at her. "And it's my treat. I don't let a woman want for anything on our date."

"But this is not a date! This is...shopping!"

"The whole weekend is a date, honey," he argued. "And besides, I didn't give you a chance to pack some clothes. I owe you on this."

The cashier swiped Justin's card.

She stared up at him. "Thank you," she said in defeat.

Justin smiled and leaned forward to kiss her. "You're welcome, hon."

They decided to explore the local shops, all the while holding hands and frequently kissing. Adrienne felt free. She didn't care about the people around them, or what they would say or think. All she cared about was the man beside her, whose arms wrapped around her, whose lips kissed her.

And for the first time in her life, she felt what it was really like to have a boyfriend…to be in a real relationship.

They checked in to a hotel, which seemed quite remote. And Adrienne couldn't help teasing Justin.

"What?"

"You said you didn't want to hide. And yet this hotel is really more than a little bit remote," she said, giggling.

He laughed. "Trust me. I have my reasons."

She raised a brow at him.

"Patience, Miss Miller. It just might turn out to be a pleasant surprise if…nature agrees with me."

She smiled brightly. "Now, I'm curious!"

After checking in, Adrienne immediately sent her clothes for laundry. Express service returned them all back to her within an hour.

They enjoyed a candlelight dinner in one of the fine dining restaurants in the hotel.

"Where's your plane?"

"On its way back to Chicago," he answered. "One of my cousins might need it. Or maybe my Father. He flies to our different branches once in a while."

"Are you working for him now?"

He shook his head. "No." He fell silent for a while.

Does he have a rift with his parents? Is this why he becomes quiet every time I mention them?

"So, what else don't I know about you?" she asked, trying to make his mood lighter. "Any brothers or sisters?"

He gave her one hard look and then he replied. "I have a twin. I mean, I had a twin."

This almost shocked Adrienne.

"Identical?"

He nodded.

She thought that the world could barely handle one Justin Adams, just imagine two.

"What happened?"

He shrugged. "I was eight minutes older than him. I lived. He didn't."

Adrienne reached for his hand and gave it a squeeze. "It would have been a blast," she said quietly. "I'm sure you would have had a better relationship than Kim and me. We…never really jived. She hated me. I knew it even if she didn't want to admit it."

"I wondered what it would be like if Jeffrey lived. I always wanted a brother."

Adrienne smiled. "I did, too. But all I got was a sister who I share nothing with…except for a DNA."

"Do you look like your Dad?" he asked.

She shrugged. "Kim is a spitting image of our Mom. Blonde hair, blue eyes. Dad has dark hair and brown eyes. Yeah, I did look like him in a way."

"What about cousins? Sometimes a cousin is good enough to take the place of a sibling."

Adrienne shook her head. "I never met any of them. It was always just Kim and me."

"I have a lot of cousins," Justin replied. "Three guys, and one girl. We all sort of lived in the same house, except for one who lives in Italy. My parents have a huge house in Chicago. Like ten bedrooms. Each of my cousins has a room there. It's always a full, loud house. Sure, they have their own homes. But they seem to love living there more."

Adrienne smiled. "You're really lucky. When it came to family, you hit the jackpot!"

Justin seemed thoughtful for a moment. Then he said, "Well, someday, your mother will change her mind about you. She will see what a beautiful, wonderful and smart daughter she has. And she will learn to love you as much as she loves your sister."

Adrienne bit her lip to keep from crying. "I sure hope you're right."

They retired to their room at around ten at night. When Adrienne got ready for bed, she found Justin in the balcony. He stretched out in one of the loungers with layers of blankets on top of him.

"What's going on?" she asked.

He smiled at her. "My surprise. Come." He pulled her to lie down with him. She leaned on his body and then he wrapped the layers of blankets around them.

She was still tired from the trip. She rested her head on Justin's shoulder and closed her eyes for a moment.

After a few minutes, she heard him say, "Open your eyes, beautiful."

When she did, she didn't expect the sight before her. The sky was suddenly covered in a curtain of multi-colored lights over the mountains.

"Oh my God!" she gasped.

The sight before her was more than spectacular. Tears welled up in her eyes. She had always dreamed about seeing the Northern Lights. And the sight had just become more surreal because she was wrapped in the arms of a man as equally magnificent as the dancing of blue, green, yellow and red lights before her.

"Do you like it?" Justin asked.

She stared up at him and smiled. "I love it," she whispered. "Thank you, Justin." She leaned forward and kissed his lips.

They lay there quietly, warm beneath the sheets. Adrienne felt warmer, wrapped in Justin's body heat. But moreover, the warmth came from deep inside her as she realized she had just fallen more in love with New York City's most wanted bachelor.

***

When Adrienne woke up the next morning, she found herself snuggled against Justin. She stared up at Justin's handsome face and smiled. She didn't know how long this thing they had would last, but she knew she would have no regrets. She had never felt more alive or free until the day she met him.

He never failed to make her feel adored…cared about. He made her feel, for the first time in her life, that her thoughts and feelings actually mattered. And that she didn't have to be afraid, or to care about what others think about her. For that, she would always feel grateful towards him.

He opened his eyes and stared at her lazily. "Morning."

She smiled wildly. "Morning." She leaned forward and kissed him.

In a minute, he got on top of her, kissing her urgently, passionately. Adrienne realized that they hadn't made love in two days. And somehow, it never seemed to bother her. Their relationship had turned to a different page. They still had this fire, this passion that tended to consume her every time, and yet, they shared a bond built on friendship, trust, and comfort. And that's wonderful, too.

After breakfast, she asked him what his plans were.

"Do you know how to ski?"

When she was in high school, back when she was still rebellious, she used to sneak behind her parents back to go on ski trips. She told them she was going to the beach house of one of her friends for the weekend. But when they thought she bathed in the sun, she was actually rolling on the snow. They didn't really care much about her to ask her why she didn't have a tan when she got back home.

"I'm not a pro, but I can balance myself on a pair of skis."

The thought of skiing again excited her. They took a trip down to a nearby ski mountain. Justin brought his own gear and he bought Adrienne new ones for herself.

"It's temporary. Can we just rent for me?" she asked.

He shook his head. "Nope. Who knows? You might want to keep doing this. Consider this another treat. And besides, if you change your mind and decide not to breakup with that asshole boyfriend of yours at all, I want something in your apartment to remind you…that you deserve better than him."

She stared up at him. "Justin…"

He silenced her with a kiss. "I know. No pressure. Do it when you're most ready. I can wait."

Justin helped her put on her new ski boots, helmet and goggles. They headed to a beginner's slope to get her accustomed to skiing again, as it had been a long time since she did this. Pretty soon, she was getting the hang of it again. As they ventured into more challenging terrain, Adrienne felt her blood pumping into her system, and she screamed to her heart's delight.

Justin always stayed close, making sure she was safe and he would reach her soon enough in case she tumbled or struggled.

When they came close to the station, Adrienne felt tired but extremely happy. She fell to her knees, causing Justin to ski faster to get to her. He reached her side the very first second.

He bent down. "Are you okay?"

She let go of her ski poles and then grabbed a handful of ice on her hands and threw it at Justin. He was caught unaware. She got out of her skis in a minute, standing up on her feet, and tried getting away from him, scooping another handful of snow.

"You're dead!" he said, unfastening his skis.

Adrienne balled the snow on her hands and then directed a perfect aim at Justin. It hit him on the shoulder. She shrieked when she saw him coming for her. She turned around and tried to run away but he was agile, fast even though he was wrapped in layers of clothing and wearing a heavy pair of ski boots.

He caught her by the waist and lifted her off the ground. She struggled to free herself. She couldn't help shrieking and laughing. Justin put her down and spun her around. He lifted her googles off her face and also took his off. He smiled at the rosy color on her face. Slowly, he leaned forward and gave her a kiss on the lips.

They deepened the kiss. Then suddenly they heard a camera clicking behind them.

They pulled away from each other and looked at the person who just interrupted their moment.

Adrienne saw a very good-looking guy with sparkling blue eyes, a shade almost similar to Justin's. His blond hair was peeking out from under his helmet.

"This is a sight you don't see every day," the guy teased, seeming to be taunting them…particularly Justin. "Actually, it's a sight you don't see *ever*!"

"What are you doing here?" Justin asked in an annoyed tone.

The guy lifted the snowboard he held with his right arm.

"This is why the plane was unavailable yesterday? We were going to the same place, and you didn't want to share, Just?" His eyes danced and he obviously succeeded in needling Justin. Then his eyes went to Adrienne. He studied her quickly and then he smiled. "Of course, now, I understand why."

"Go away, Gian!" Justin said to the guy.

"You're not even going to introduce us?" The guy feigned a shocked look on his face, enjoying Justin's irritation.

Justin sighed. "Adrienne, Gian. Gian, Adrienne." Then he turned to Gian. "Now, can you…evaporate?"

The guy didn't back down at all. He took a step towards them. He looked at Adrienne. "Sorry. My cousin has better manners than that. Don't get turned off."

"Cousin?" Adrienne echoed, peering up at Justin.

"Now I'm thinking…how unfortunate, right?" Justin said, rolling his eyes.

Adrienne finally smiled. She extended her gloved hand to Gian and he shook it, although barely because his gloves were much thicker than hers.

Gian smiled at her. "I can see why he doesn't go home frequently anymore. I can't see what you see in him, though."

"Nah! He's a great guy…if he chooses to be," Adrienne teased.

Justin pulled her closer to his side, and then he turned to Gian, "Now, can you leave us in peace?"

Gian took a step back. "Aww! I was hoping to show Adrienne my impressive moves on the board."

"Not gonna happen." Justin raised a brow at him.

"What's the matter, Justin? Afraid of some competition?"

Justin narrowed his eyes. "Remind me again who taught you how not to fall on your ass in a halfpipe?"

"That's what I'm talking about!" the guy jeered. "Come on, big cuz. Show your girl what you got."

Adrienne actually smirked. She wanted to see Justin on a snowboard. She was curious and she felt sure Justin would be pretty good at everything he did.

"That would be interesting!" she announced.

Justin turned to her. "Really? You're listening to this guy?"

She laughed. "It's not like I present any sort of challenge to you on the slopes. Have fun. I'll watch."

Justin shook his head. He turned to Gian. "Just so you know, it's rude to interrupt somebody's date."

"Just so you know, it's not good to antagonize family when one of them runs into you while you're on a date," Gian responded evenly.

"One more word and I'm kicking you out of my house!"

Gian backed down, his eyes dancing as he pressed his lips together.

"See you on the pipe in fifteen minutes," Justin said, then he pulled Adrienne with him.

Adrienne turned to Gian. "Good luck!"

"Oh, he's the one who's going to need it, sugar!" Gian then walked away.

"Unbelievably annoying!" Justin groaned.

Adrienne smiled up at him. "So…you seem close."

"Sometimes, I think… too close! You know like one of those annoying little brothers?" Although he was groaning, Adrienne didn't miss the affection that was disguised in his voice.

Then she remembered that he took a picture of them while they were kissing.

"He…took a snapshot." She sounded a little worried.

"Don't worry about it. The most he'll do with it, is blackmail me into borrowing one of my cars for a week to impress one of the girls he's dating."

Half an hour later, Adrienne stood in one of the viewing decks overlooking the snowboarding halfpipes. Justin had arrived there with Gian.

She watched proudly as Justin took off from one side and went to the other side hanging mid-air for a few seconds. Then came Gian's turn. He looked like he knew what he was doing, too.

Then both of them showed off their freestyle moves, somersaulting, spinning three hundred sixty degrees in the air. Adrienne took out her phone to take a video of Justin. He was amazing. He could totally go into one of those X-Games competitions. Gian seemed extremely good, too. But in the end, Adrienne understood exactly what Justin said. He had taught Gian those moves. He remained the better one on a snowboard.

When they finished, Adrienne met them at the station, smiling widely.

"So, did I totally kick his ass out there?" Gian asked her.

She laughed. "You were magnificent!" she said. Justin raised a brow at her. She smiled at him. "But he still owned you!"

Justin laughed proudly and pulled her into a hug. "You're saying that because you're dating him," Gian complained.

"Yeah. And he owns the transportation that got me here. So you can see that my hands are tied." She winked at him.

Gian laughed. "Yeah. He owns the plane that got both of us here, so let's give it to the guy."

"You two are unbelievable," Justin groaned. Then he added, "Come on. Coffee's on me."

Gian turned out to be actually funny and sweet. Adrienne learned that he was only twenty-two and still in college. He had a twin. Adrienne guessed that twins ran in Justin's family.

That night, when they got back to the hotel, Adrienne showed Justin her video. He watched it happily.

"You're really, really good," she told him. "Do you do that a lot?"

"Whenever I have the time. I usually go snowboarding with my cousins at least once a month."

"It looked dangerous."

"It is. If you don't know what you're doing." He grinned.

"Smug!" She rolled her eyes.

They made love again that night. Slowly, passionately. Here in this place, she felt like she belonged to Justin. He belonged to her. Here, in their own little world, where no one can stop them and nothing holds them back.

Justin never told her how he really felt about her but what right did she have to demand that? She couldn't ask him to commit to her, when she can't commit to him in the first place. He was single…and she was the one who was supposedly spoken for.

As Adrienne rested her head against Justin's shoulder, she looked through the glass windows and watched the Northern Lights. She realized there that she didn't know if he felt the same way about her, but she never would until she risked everything she had. Troy. Her mother's respect. Her friends. She might end up losing them all. But all this freedom to love and be loved by Justin…had become something absolutely worth risking everything for.

12.

Curiosus

Latin etymology of the word Curious meaning "inquiring eagerly" meddlesome or diligent.

Adrienne returned to the office on Tuesday. She felt confident and proud of herself. True, she still hadn't figured out how the heck she would tell her friends about Justin, but other than that, everything was perfect.

Justin is perfect.

He deserved to be sought after, drooled upon, dreamt of, but not for the reasons they all believed. Not for his face, his body, his money, his cars, or his privilege. He was a total dream guy because he's romantic and sweet… he's wonderful inside and out.

Now, to tell my friends…

She figured she needed to break up with Troy first. And then tell her friends. And then her mother. In that order.

Whatever happened after that, she would have to take it. She'd gone too far. She owed it to Justin. She owed it to herself.

Jada called her to her office.

"Adrienne, since you took a long weekend, I trust you are more well-rested than I am," Jada started. Adrienne rolled her eyes. "So, you have to make up for my lack of sleep yesterday by attending this meeting with a potential advertiser. This is going to be a huge account."

"Don't we have a department that handles that?" Adrienne asked.

"Yes. But I don't want them to mess it up. I want to send my best weapon to make sure that we bag this account. Plus, the decision makers are within your age group. I'm sure you can better reach out to them."

Adrienne sighed. "All right. What time are they coming?"

"Unfortunately, they would only be available at seven tonight. You have a dinner meeting with the representatives of AB Wellness at The Sixth in Lever Du Soleil Hotel."

She blinked back. "ABW? That's good. What rates do you want me to give to them?"

"Standard less thirty."

"Thirty?" she asked in surprise. Their magazine enjoyed a great reputation, and, as a well-known venue for advertising, companies almost fought for an ad space. *Blush* typically only gave their best customers a maximum ten percent discount.

"I want this account, Adrienne. Their health clubs are booming and that's the direction we want to go to. They will make us look good."

Adrienne stood up from her seat and turned to leave. "I'll keep you posted."

She received a message from Justin as soon as she got back to her office.

Justin: *Dinner tonight, honey?*

She sighed glumly. She wants nothing more than spend the evening with him.

She replied: *Can't. Working again. Meeting some advertisers at Lever Du Soleil. Jada's job—assigned to me. Her punishment for me taking the day off yesterday.*

Justin: *Sorry, hon. My fault she did that. I'll see you after your meeting. I promise to make up for your evening. ;-)*

She smiled. She felt sorrier that she couldn't have dinner with him instead.

At seven o'clock she arrived at The Sixth, a restaurant in the five-star hotel, Lever Du Soleil. "I have a meeting with somebody from AB Wellness," she told a reception attendant.

A restaurant hostess led Adrienne to her table, which surprisingly was only set for two.

"Aren't there going to be more people coming?"

"We were only told to arrange for two," the waiter said. "Can I offer you something to drink?"

"Okay. White wine please."

"Right away, ma'am."

She reviewed her notes as she waited.

After five minutes, she heard somebody in front of her say, "I'm sorry, I'm late."

She looked up and found herself staring at a pair of aquamarine eyes. Eyes she'd seen before. She stood up from her seat and stared at the man dressed in a dark gray suit that screamed luxury with every thread. He was smiling at her, showing the deep dimples on either side of his lips. His reddish brown hair was not disheveled this time. It was combed perfectly in place, which made him look professional and formidable, far from the seemingly fun and carefree guy she bumped into a few days ago.

He extended his hand to her. "We meet again, Miss Miller."

It took her a moment to speak. What was his name? She was embarrassed to admit that she forgot.

He grinned. "You forgot my name, didn't you?" he said in a teasing tone, catching her off-guard. She was about to say something but immediately he added, "Jin Starck."

She shook his hand. "I'm sorry."

"That's fine. It's a first for me, though." That should have made him sound cocky, but the tone he used made it easy for Adrienne to pass it up as a joke. "Please, have a seat."

"I was… expecting to meet with some people from ABW."

Jin nodded. "Yes. Me."

"But…" Jin hardly looked like a guy who worked for a wellness spa.

"Were you expecting a bouncer-type muscle man? Or perhaps a healthy looking female?"

Yes!

But Adrienne simply said, "Sorry. Jada didn't mention the names of who I was meeting today. And I also thought that I would meet more than one."

"Well, my team is still in Paris," he said. "I'm already here on business, so I decided why don't I just meet with you instead."

She nodded. She didn't miss the words, "my team". Jin Starck must be the head of their marketing department or something. And Adrienne couldn't help thinking that he looked so young.

She remembered that Jada was dead-set about getting this account. She would have her head if she messed this up just because she was caught unprepared by the guy she was meeting.

"So, I was told you were looking to put an ad campaign with us."

Jin nodded. "Yes. Our two lines of Health and Wellness services, Rain and Soleil are looking more into cosmopolitan men and women. We'd like to get it in line with this market with our set of elite services."

They were interrupted by the waiter who took their orders.

Afterwards, Jin proceeded with the specifics. In fairness to him, he looked like he knew what he was talking about. He looked young, but obviously, he was smart and he came prepared.

Adrienne discussed his options and what *Blush* could offer to them. She even threw in a first-hand feature and review of their services in one of her columns, to which Jin Starck seemed pleased to obtain.

When Adrienne gave him the standard rate, he didn't seem to flinch at all. Instead, he replied, "Draw up the contract, send it to my office and my secretary will return it to you with my signature."

That's it? He is signing up without negotiating the amount?

"Um, all right. I would include the payment terms along with our offer."

"I can pay via telegraphic transfer or check," he said. "No need for terms. I can pay upfront if that's what you require."

Now, he didn't sound like he just heads Marketing, unless his other job is also Head of Finance.

"So, it's settled? Do I get your verbal confirmation then?" Adrienne asked carefully.

Jin grinned. "You can email me and you'll get an email confirmation if your boss requires it from you."

Adrienne smiled. "No. It's just that, it will be a privilege for us to secure this account," she said honestly. "She would want to ensure that the deal is a go, and we will make a space for you in next month's release. There are other ads in line. Needless to say, she would kill me if I reserved a spot and then the client backed out."

Jin nodded. "It's a done deal, Miss Miller. I can assure you that."

What if he has no right to decide?

"And of course, your word is good enough because you're..." she trailed off, subtly asking him to supply her the information she needed. She realized that even his business card didn't state his position.

Jin smiled at her mischievously, obviously, realizing what she was getting at. "Because I'm Jin Starck," he said, much to Adrienne's frustration.

He watched her expression for a while. Then as if he decided to end her agony, he said, "Miss Miller, ABW is a subsidiary of Starck Hoteliers. So I think, you can tell your boss that my word is good to go."

Adrienne scanned her brain for a moment, while trying to keep her face steady. Then she remembered. Starck Hoteliers owns more than fifty five-star hotels, spanning three different continents. No wonder, Jin Starck looked so young and yet he seemed to know what he was doing, and had full decision-making powers.

Shit! I looked like a fool!

"I'm sorry, Mr. Starck..."

"Jin," he said calmly. "You can call me Jin, Adrienne."

She nodded. "Jin," she said. "I'm sorry. I should have had that information beforehand." Instead of making up excuses, she decided to own up to her mistake.

He grinned. "It's okay. I get that reaction a lot," he said. "I guess I look like I still belong in school rather than in the boardroom, making decisions on my parents' behalf."

Adrienne smiled. "I must admit I did wonder how old you were."

"Twenty-three. And I'm managing one fourth of our hotels. I also look after ABW..." He stared at her for a moment. "On my mother's behalf."

Adrienne was impressed. Most twenty-three year olds barely have finished college. And Jin Starck managed a chain of hotels all over the globe.

"Your mother?" she echoed.

Jin nodded. "Yes. AB stands for Ariana Blanc. It was her concept. But sometimes she couldn't attend to it. So I help out. She's a very busy woman."

"I think you have a busy family." She smiled.

He nodded. "Yes. My mother doesn't work much on the business though. She works more on her passion. You might know her."

She looked up at him curiously.

"She goes by the name Amanda Seville."

Again, Adrienne scanned her brain. Then she blinked back. "Amanda Seville as in...the writer?"

Jin's smile spread across his face. "Yes."

Adrienne was surprised. She read many of Amanda Seville's novels and she was one of her favorite historical romance writers. She couldn't believe she actually had dinner with her son.

"Wow," she whispered.

"I know. She makes me proud. Not only because she's a talented writer. But also because she's the best mother anyone could ever ask for."

Hearing him say that pinched Adrienne's heart. How she wished she could say the same about her own mother.

"So now, you know more about me personally, and since we're done with our negotiations and not even halfway through dinner, perhaps you can tell me more about yourself, Adrienne. Where are you from?"

"Boston," she replied.

"What do your parents do, if you don't mind me asking?"

"My parents are both doctors. My father is a neuro-surgeon. My mother is an OB-GYN. My sister studies medicine, too."

Jin looked at her for a while and then he smiled, "So I guess, you're the odd one out." Again, the light, teasing tone he used made it difficult for Adrienne to feel insulted by what he said. She actually smiled at his attempt to tease her.

"You can say that. But I have a passion for writing. I love working for *Blush* and I love what I do now."

"Didn't they pressure you to go into medicine too?"

"Story of my life," she murmured.

"Well, at least you aren't working at all." She raised a brow at him. He added, "Because if you love what you do, it's not work at all. It's all fun and games every day."

"Do you like what you do?"

He nodded. "Oui, mademoiselle. I was born and raised to manage our family business."

Adrienne was surprised by how easy Jin was to talk to. She didn't feel like she was having a business meeting at all. More than half the time, they weren't talking about business. They spoke about their families. Of course, she didn't tell him how broken her relationship was with her mother. That part used to be Jill's and Yuan's territory, and now it belonged to Justin. She only answered his questions where she grew up in, which college she went to and then stuff she did at *Blush*.

Contrary to Justin's belief, Jin didn't ogle at her at all. He seemed actually funny and easygoing. Nothing in his actions or lines made her feel like he flirted with her. But of course, she didn't consider herself an expert in that department.

By the end of dinner, although she insisted on paying for the bill, Jin didn't allow her to do it.

"It's my hotel, Adrienne," he said, chuckling. "You can consider this as part of my advance payment for advertising with you."

He walked her to the front of the hotel. "Do you have a ride?"

She almost told him that she didn't when she saw a familiar figure stepping out of a familiar Ferrari. Her heart leapt out of her chest. She involuntarily smiled.

Jin noticed her face as she watched Justin approach them.

"Well, I guess I don't have to worry about you getting home safely," Jin said. She turned to him. "I'll send you an email confirmation first thing in the morning. Please send me your final proposal and contract."

He extended his hand to her and she shook it. "Nice to meet you, Jin."

"Likewise, Adrienne."

He gave her a final nod and went off before Justin could reach them.

Justin's eyes narrowed as he watched Jin Starck disappear into the elevators.

Adrienne turned to him. "So… the world seems really small," he said a little tartly.

Adrienne laughed. "I know, right? He's advertising in our magazine."

"Hmmm…" Justin said. "For what? Playstation?"

Adrienne laughed again. "I know. He didn't look like the type. But he's actually advertising for a spa."

"Shouldn't he still be in school?" he asked.

"He said he's only twenty-three. But I guess if you operate a family-owned chain of hotels, you start young."

Justin took her hand in his, and Adrienne almost panicked. But Justin only gripped her hand in his tightly. He pulled her gently towards his car.

"It's a few meters walk, Adrienne," he said. "And right now, I'm beyond caring."

She sighed and quickly followed him to his car. When they got in, he pulled her to him and crushed his lips to hers. He took her breath away, like he wanted to remind her who she belonged to. And God, how could she ever forget that?

When he pulled away, she smiled at him. "Are you mad?"

He shook his head gently. "No. But sometimes it kills me that I can't punch the life out of any guy who shows interest in you."

Adrienne smiled at him apologetically. "Jin Starck is not interested in me. He didn't even flirt with me. And I'm not usually interested in boys younger than I am." She stared at him, trying to give him some reassurance. Then she took a deep breath and asked, "How long can you wait?"

He took a deep breath and kissed her lips again. Then he breathed, "As long as it takes."

He pulled away from her and then he started the engine. Before he drove off, he asked, "What did you say his name was again?"

"Jin Starck. Apparently, they own Starck Hoteliers. And oh my God, his mother is Amanda Seville! She's like... my favorite writer of all time!"

Justin stared at her for a long moment. And then he turned towards the road. His face turned sober and he gripped the steering wheel tightly, before driving off.

"Justin, are you okay?"

He didn't look at her. Instead, he continued staring ahead. With a hard look on his face, he murmured, "Peachy."

JERILEE KAYE

13.
Broken
Etymology: Middle English breken, from Old English brecan; akin to Old High German brehhan, which means to break

Over the week, Adrienne finalized the contract with ABW. True to his word, Jin sent the signed contract to her within one hour of her sending it to him.

Jada sounded pleased. She was even surprised that Adrienne managed to get the contract without a discount.

"I just offered a page feature, that's all."

"Wow! You must be charming!" Jada said. Adrienne didn't know whether she meant it or she was just being sarcastic.

She told the news to Jill as well.

"What did he look like?" Jill asked. "I read in a blog that the heir of Starck Hoteliers is an absolute stunner!"

Adrienne narrowed her eyes at her best friend. "What blog is this?"

Jill bit her lip and shyly admitted, "The one that…blogs about steaming hot bachelors with…bright futures ahead of them."

Adrienne raised a brow. "You mean with huge bank accounts and unlimited credit card limits?"

Jill giggled. "It isn't bad to dream about one of those kinds once in a while, you know."

She raised a brow at Jill. "Is Justin Adams on that list?"

Jill grinned. "Topnotcher!" She went over to her desk and typed something on her keyboard. Then Jill gasped. After a while, a naughty grin spread across her face. "Well, hello, competition!"

Jill turned her monitor towards Adrienne and she saw a picture of Jin Starck staring back at her. He had a boyish smile on his face and his eyes were a bluer shade of green.

"You have his number?" Jill asked.

She frowned at her friend. "Confidentiality agreements in my contract preclude me from giving you any of our clients' contact numbers, Jill. No matter how much you beg me, you won't get it."

Jill pouted. "You're such a bore!"

Just then, her eyes drifted to something behind Adrienne and she fell quiet. Adrienne turned and saw Justin walking in the halls. He looked in their direction, and his mouth slightly curved.

Jill gasped. "Did he just smile at me?"

Adrienne turned to her friend guiltily. She shrugged.

"One of these days, I am totally going to start a conversation with him! I may not get to have him, but it's good enough just to talk to him.

Even just a little chit-chat. Do you think that will work?"

Adrienne shrugged and turned away from her. Guilt ate her insides and slowly bore a hole through her.

She walked back to her office. She thought she'd give Troy a call. He didn't answer her last text message. She really needed to talk to him. And fast! The sooner she breaks up with him, the sooner she can get her mind straight about admitting to her friends what she's been up to these last few months!

She hated lying to Jill and Yuan, especially with something big about her life. And this is not just big. She: Losing her virginity to the City's so-called rakehell on a one-night stand and then later falling in love with him! This is bigger than big!

She didn't know if they could forgive her if they found out. *Hell!* They wouldn't even forgive her if they found out that he lived across her apartment and she didn't tell them.

When she tried Troy's number, she only got a voicemail. He must be out of coverage or his phone may be off.

She went to see Garry for the layout of the article she wrote. She was surprised to see Justin there.

She didn't greet him. She pretended that she didn't notice he was there at all. She told Garry everything she needed for him to do. She tried to muster all her confidence. She felt so nervous and excited at Justin's presence. He sat on a couch, wearing those pitch black shades of his, but she had no doubt that he was staring at her.

Her knees shook a little when she turned on her heel and left the room. She saw Jill and some of the girls chatting in the corridor. She stopped by to join them. After a few minutes, Justin passed by them. They all fell silent. When she looked up, he had an eyebrow up and he gazed in their direction.

When he was gone, the girls sighed.

"My God! He looked at us!" Meena, the girl from Circulation, said.

"He is just bloody hot!" another girl said.

"He doesn't even have to be the heir of Adams Industries. I'd take him any day even if he was poor!"

Adrienne smiled when she went back to her office. The other girls were drooling over him when she knew his eyes were on her. Sometimes, she still thought she'd just been dreaming. And she just hasn't woken up yet.

After fifteen minutes, she received a text message from him.

Justin: *You're a fox! Let's go out tonight? Let's break this rule of yours a little and go somewhere. I promise, minimum risk of being named.*

Adrienne heaved a frustrated sigh. Justin said that he can wait, but she knows that his patience just may run out one of these days. And she also became aware that no matter how hard they tried to hide, one of these days, Jill and Yuan just might run into them in the streets, or in her apartment and she would be in deep shit, big time!

That evening, she got ready for her date with Justin. She wore a pair of white skin-tight pants, and cropped black sleeveless top. She tied her hair in a pony, and she put on light makeup.

She smiled at her reflection. Each day that passed by, she saw more in herself what Justin has been saying to her at least once a day. She's a fox. She felt more confident.

She grew up always being overshadowed by a prettier and smarter older sister. But she didn't care about that anymore. She had started to appreciate herself and how amazing she could be, once she let go of her inhibitions.

The doorbell rang.

He came early. Fifteen minutes. Normally, he's exactly on time, which she loved, because he doesn't pressure her to hurry up and he's not making her wait either.

She got her tiny purse and headed for the door.

When she opened it, she was shocked to see Troy and Kimberly standing in front of her.

"Shit!" she muttered.

"What's that, sweetie?" Troy asked.

She stared at him. She remembered that he didn't curse at all. "I said '*Shit! Holy shit!*'"

An eyebrow shot up. He was about to say something, when Kimberly cut in. "Expecting somebody else?"

God! Was she right!

"No. I just didn't expect to see you," she said. "Come in. I was just on my way out. I was supposed to dine in this place I will feature in our next issue."

They went inside her apartment. Immediately, they looked around, as if examining it for safety violations.

"Nice place," Kimberly said and Adrienne almost clapped at the fact that she threw a compliment her way.

Kimberly lost weight. She was wearing a skirt that goes all the way to her knees and a long-sleeved blouse. Her blond hair looked blonder. Adrienne had to admit that she looked prettier than the last time they saw each other. But still, so prim, so proper. So angelic.

"What are you wearing?" Troy asked staring at her from head to feet.

"Yes, I'm fine too, Troy. It's so nice to see you!" She smiled sarcastically. "Yes, you can sit down for a moment and I will go get something to drink." She motioned for them to sit on the sofa.

She took deep breaths as she took out two cans of Pepsi from her fridge.

"Bad news, Kimmy. I don't have diet," she said.

"You never needed to diet," Troy said.

Good! He can say something nice to me for once.

"It's okay. I never needed diet, either," Kimberly said. "Sorry, to drop in without warning. You were heading out to do that…" she trailed off. "That work you do."

Adrienne nodded. "I will write a feature for this place on Sixth Avenue."

"Exciting job!" Kimberly beamed too enthusiastically. But she knew her better. Kimberly never had much affection for her. She always tried to put her down to lift herself up. And Adrienne got so accustomed to it. There was no use in trying. No use in fighting.

"What about you guys, what are you doing here? This is so unexpected."

"Well, we have a medical conference here for a week. We decided to surprise you," Troy said.

And I was shocked!

"So thoughtful of you!" she said instead, smiling. She caught a glimpse of the time on her wall clock. Exactly eight. Justin has synchronized his watch with hers, which she thought was quite sweet, but that's not the point here. She knew that he would knock at her door any second.

"Shit!" she murmured.

Troy stared at her, raising a brow again.

She smiled. "Let me just go to the lobby to check whether my boss left me the passes I was supposed to get tonight. Be back in a sec."

She dashed for the door, not giving them a chance to argue, praying that Troy would not follow her.

When she opened the door, Justin was just about to ring her doorbell. She pushed him gently and closed the door behind her.

"Quick! Inside your apartment," she hissed.

He quickly fished his keys without asking and then they went inside.

"What's wrong?" he asked.

She screamed in frustration. "Kimberly! And Troy! In my apartment!"

Justin didn't say anything.

"My God! What did I do today to deserve this ordeal?" she asked desperately.

"Troy… the current and official boyfriend?" Justin asked quietly.

"Troy, the ghost of a boyfriend, and Kimberly, the ghost of a sister, yes!"

Justin took a deep breath. Then he said, "All right. Go out there. I'll just call some of my friends tonight then."

She stared at him. She couldn't make out any expression on his face.

"I don't want to go out there, Justin. I really don't."

"She's your sister. You can't do anything about that. The boyfriend... you could ditch anytime...actually, should have ditched a long time ago...but still, for now, you have to go through with this." He oddly tried to encourage her.

"Are you sure it's okay with you?" she asked.

He smiled. "Positive. If you can't endure it, give me a call. I'll think of something."

She smiled and reached up to kiss him on the lips. "I'd probably do that, just to see what you could come up with."

He laughed.

She headed for the door. "You look great, by the way," he told her.

She looked down at herself. "It's a waste now, isn't it? I didn't dress up for them."

He went closer to her and pulled her waist. "Just make sure you mean that."

"Mean what?" she asked.

"You dressed up for me. Not for him," He smiled sheepishly.

She giggled. "I mean it. I was supposed to go out with you, remember? If I were meeting him, I would have worn a pair of trousers, long-sleeved, ruffled blouse, and a pair of eyeglasses."

He kissed her again before she went out of his apartment. She took some time, took deep breaths and then opened her front door.

Troy and Kim still sat on the sofa.

My God! They were like the king and queen of good conduct and behavior!

She found them right where she left them.

She remembered that many times in her life she actually felt intimidated by Kim because of Troy. Because she thought that the only way that she could keep Troy is to be like Kim.

But now she couldn't say for sure why she wasted three years of her life, trying to be something and someone she wasn't. When she could have been herself all along. Free-spirited. Fun. And according to Justin, foxy!

"Want to go have dinner instead, guys?" she asked them.

"What happened to the work you need to do?" Troy asked.

"My boss couldn't get me the passes. I called her up and told her that I could do that tomorrow."

Kim just smiled.

"But you have to change your outfit, sweetheart," Troy said. "You can't go out in that!"

She looked down at herself and raised a brow at him.

"Oh jeez, Troy! Grow up!" Kim said. "It doesn't show much flesh! Come on, I'm starving."

Troy didn't argue. Like he regarded Kimberly as his teacher.

Ma'am, yes, ma'am.

They all went to Casa Mexicana.

Troy and Kimberly talked about their convention and their escapades at med school. It seemed that they have been members of the same clubs and they belonged to the same crowd. Adrienne sat there wondering how many hours a day Kim and Troy spent with each other.

That thought should have eaten her alive, left her reeling with jealousy. But since Justin came into her life, she felt happy about herself. And she no longer felt that tinge of insecurity. That awful feeling inside her that she couldn't keep Troy because she wasn't good enough had totally disappeared.

When their orders came and when their drinks got refilled, Adrienne noticed that the waiter kept looking at her. She felt self-conscious. Like she felt there was something wrong with her face.

"Excuse me. What's your problem?" Troy asked the waiter. He also noticed the number of times he stared at Adrienne.

"Troy, please," Adrienne pleaded. She didn't want to cause a scene.

"I'm sorry," the waiter said.

"No. Tell me. Why were you staring at my girl?" Troy asked...a little too aggressively this time.

The waiter looked apologetic. "Sorry, sir. I just thought you're a lucky guy. Your girlfriend is very beautiful."

Trying to avoid a scene, Adrienne smiled at the waiter. "Thanks, sweetie. Now, could you get me my margarita?"

He nodded. "I'm sorry. Right away, madam."

Adrienne turned to Kim and Troy. "So, back to the pep squads you do at med school."

Luckily, Troy decided to let it go. Kimberly engaged them again in a topic about a vulvar cancer and Adrienne just plainly lost her appetite. She fiddled with her fork and wondered when she would get Troy alone to finally break up with him.

It has to be tonight! So tomorrow...

She smiled. Tomorrow, she can tell Justin that they no longer needed to hide. He might need him to come with her when she tells Jill and Yuan about them. She couldn't forget the last time when they laughed in her face when she attempted to come clean about Justin.

Her phone beeped and she was thankful.

Justin: *How are you holding up?*

Her: *I'm still surviving. But God! I miss you!*

Justin: *I'm at the Oxygen, with Mike and James. We're waiting for my cousin, Gian's twin, Ian. Vacation from college.*

Her: *At least your night sounds more fun.*

Justin: *I'm not with you, where is the fun in that?*

She smiled and she was certain she started blushing.

"Everything okay, sweetheart?" Troy asked her.

She nodded. "It's just Jill. Another one of her escapades."

Troy raised a brow. She thought he didn't believe her. She just smiled at him nonchalantly.

She figured, tonight when they drop her off at her building, she would talk to Troy alone. It will be quick and easy.

But when they got out of the restaurant, Troy said he would get a cab for them and he would go back to their hotel alone. Adrienne looked at them in confusion.

"I'm staying with you tonight, Adrienne." Kimberly stated suddenly.

"What?"

Kimberly shrugged. "Dad suggested I spend the night with you. I figured, why not?"

Shit!

"Yes, Adrienne. It would make your parents really happy to see both of you together. You haven't seen each other in a while, right? And Kimberly could use some girl talk for a change." Troy grinned and Kimberly giggled. Adrienne, on the other hand, found none of it to be amusing.

But her parents…yes, her parents would be happy to know that she and Kim had some sister bonding time. They never do that. It would warm her parents to know that she's trying to spend time with her sister.

"Okay," she said to them.

"Yay!" Kim reached out and hugged Adrienne. Adrienne actually smiled and hugged her back. "You're the best sister!" Kim said sweetly. Adrienne wanted to cry because it was probably the first time she felt Kim show some affection for her. Maybe not seeing each other often made her realize she wasn't a bad sister after all.

Then Adrienne turned to Troy. "Can we talk?" she asked.

"I'm tired, Yen."

"I won't take much time," she insisted.

"I'm picking up Kim early tomorrow. We start at eight and you know I hate to be late for anything. I'll see you when we get back. Kim and I have two days off. We can talk for forty-eight hours if you want, sweetheart."

"But Troy, there's something I really need to tell you."

"It can wait, Yen."

He hailed a cab, not giving her a chance to argue.

"No, Troy, it can't. We really need to talk."

Kim got into the cab.

"Come on, Adrienne. The cabby's waiting. Hurry up!" Kim said impatiently.

"Go. We'll talk later," Troy said. Then without warning, he bent down and kissed her lips.

Her first thought was: *Bad kisser!*

Her second thought was: *Shit! I'm never cheating on Justin! God, what is wrong with me?*

She doesn't feel guilty about sleeping with Justin behind Troy's back, but she feels terrible about being kissed by Troy behind Justin's back. Troy is the official boyfriend. Justin was...well, he is Justin... and she's in love with him.

She didn't kiss Troy back. She gently pushed him away and willed herself not to vomit in front of him and Kim.

"Good night, Troy," she said and went inside the cab.

They rode the cab in silence. Kim was looking out the window, enjoying the scenery before her. And Adrienne really didn't know what to say to her.

As soon as they entered her apartment, Kim turned to her, "So which room do I stay in?"

Adrienne showed her the guestroom.

"All right...good night," Kim said.

"Wait! Didn't you say, we should... bond?"

Kim actually laughed. "Come on, Yenny! We don't have to pretend we actually get along when we're alone," she said. "Let's just tell Mom and Dad that we spent almost the whole night catching up, then I had an early start the next day. Get the program?"

Then she closed the door behind her.

Adrienne stared at the door for a long while. Then she thought to herself, *Nah! We weren't really close anyway!*

She took a shower and brushed her teeth about three times to make sure there was no more trace of Troy in her. The thought of kissing somebody else besides Justin made her want to puke.

When she left her room to get a glass of water, she found Kimberly on her living room watching Medical Detectives.

"I thought you were sleeping."

"And I thought I didn't have to talk to you for the rest of the night," Kim said flatly.

Adrienne gripped her glass tightly. She prevented herself from throwing it at Kim's beautiful face.

"You're actually in my apartment, Kimmy," she said coldly.

Instead of feeling ashamed, Kim just smiled sweetly at her. "And I'm helping you score points with Mom. You're welcome!" Kim turned back to the TV.

Adrienne closed her eyes. In her head, she took a firm hold of Kim's hair, pulled it so hard and then slammed her face on the coffee table.

When she opened her eyes, Kim was still there. Still in one piece.

Adrienne walked to her bedroom without another word.

"You should change your television set!" Kim called to her. "It's not good for your eyes to watch on such a small screen."

Adrienne smiled at her acidly and then slammed the door behind her.

She looked through her window and found that Justin wasn't home yet.

She sent him a message: *Kim is at my place! Really trying my best not to murder her!*

Justin: *If you can wait up, I would do it for you. :) Seriously, what did she do this time?*

She replied: *Just being herself. Apparently, her staying over was gaining me points with our mother. So she thought she's actually doing me a favor!*

Justin: *I'm coming home with my cousin. Want to come to my place? I could introduce you to each other.*

Her: *I would love to! But the thing is, Kim seems to be camping in my living room, watching TV, which she said by the way was too small for her taste! Anyway, I can't go out. Kim can smell things from within a mile away! It's safer if I stay here. You know…until…*

She trailed off purposefully, hoping Justin would get what she meant.

Justin: *Okay. Sweet dreams. I'll miss you tonight. It's been a while since I slept alone. ;-) And by the way, I have a surprise for you. See you tomorrow, hon.*

When she woke up the next day, Troy was already in her apartment. He and Kimberly drank coffee in the living room.

"We have an early start," Troy said, smiling at her. "We were about to leave. Guess you two stayed up late with your girl chit-chats, huh."

Kimberly winked and smiled at her sweetly. "I wish we could have stayed up longer. But we have this early morning thing."

Liar!!!

Why was she lying? Am I the only one privileged to see what a real bitch she was?

"After the conference, my parents have invited both of you to join us to a weekend at a resort here. Your parents may come too," Troy said.

"Oh my God! That's so lovely!" Kim shrieked but Adrienne knew she was being overenthusiastic.

Troy went to Adrienne. "We need to talk, sweetheart." He gave her a bright smile. And then he leaned down and kissed her. At least he attempted to. Adrienne averted her face so that Troy's lips just landed on her cheekbone.

"I guess I'll see you," she murmured. "Text me when and where we're going."

When they left, she hoped that Troy got her subtle messages. He didn't give her a chance to break up with him. For all it's worth, she wanted to make this as clean as possible. If they can end up being friends, it would be better. That could help her mother forgive her.

She took a shower. Then she put on a pair of jeans and mini tee. She dried her hair, took her keys and rang Justin's doorbell. She needed to clear her head. She needed to plan how to breakup with Troy and she needed to execute that plan well.

She rang the bell twice.

No answer. She tried again.

Finally, the door opened. She had prepared herself to fly into in his arms. She missed him so much. Last night was the first night she spent without him in many weeks. And she was happy when he said he would miss her too.

But what she saw made her stop. Wet blonde hair. Perfect skin. Blue eyes. Barbie doll in the flesh. And she's wearing one of Justin's robes.

"Excuse me, can I help you?" she asked.

God, even her voice was a perfect pitch!

Adrienne bit her lip. She didn't know what to say. She couldn't find her voice. She looked like she wore nothing but Justin's robe and she still managed to stun Adrienne with her beauty. And she's not even a man!

"Who is that?" She heard Justin say from inside the room. When the girl didn't answer, he went towards the door. He was topless, with only a towel wrapped around his waist. He looked like he just gotten out of a shower.

No! It looked like 'they' had just gotten out of the shower.

Adrienne took a deep breath and summoned all the strength she had left in her body just so she could raise her chin and say something.

"I'm sorry. I didn't realize you were busy," she snapped. Then she quickly spun around.

"Honey, wait!" Justin shouted and ran after her. But Adrienne was quick enough to slam the door in his face, refusing to give him a chance to either spin lies for her to believe, or break it to her gently that they never had a commitment in the first place, they weren't exclusive, so he's free to screw somebody else.

She had a boyfriend. He had waited for her to break it up with him. Maybe his patience finally ran out and he went after what he deserved: A girl as perfect as the one standing in his living room.

14.
Remorsus
Medieval Latin. Gave birth to the word Remorse.

"Adrienne, this isn't what you think. Could you open the door and talk to me?" Justin said on the other side of the door.

She didn't answer. She turned on her stereo so loud so she couldn't hear his voice. She knew that she should find the strength. It was the first night she spent without him in more than a month. The first night that she was not with him. And he did what he normally does.

She felt like she cheated on him when Troy kissed her! That same night, Justin had shagged somebody else in his room. In the bed where she had slept in on many nights.

She went to her room, locked her windows and closed the blinds. She threw herself in her bed and cried. She felt pain in her chest…hard, pinching pain. Her stomach began to tie itself in knots. She let the tears fall freely as she hugged her pillow.

What did she expect? Guys like Justin Adams did not want to commit…were never known to commit. Did she really expect playboys like him to be loyal and faithful to only one girl? Of course not! She got her hopes too high without realizing it.

She loved him…so much! And it did hurt. Yes, she had made him the guy on the sidelines, but he was also the guy she loved. And he knew she had a boyfriend from the start.

How could he bring a girl home the way he brought her home? And God, she was perfect! She was a hundred times prettier than Kimberly! How could she compete with that? And maybe, Justin couldn't resist, either.

He kept calling her. He left messages on her answering machine. He sent her text messages. She didn't listen or read a single message. She didn't need his excuses. The evidence had stood in his apartment. Nothing could be as clear as that.

Sure, a stranger couldn't just come to his place and use his bathroom, right? And use his robe? And he certainly wouldn't walk around in a towel around the house if there was a complete stranger with you…unless you two have just spent the night banging each other's brains out.

That thought twisted a knot inside her chest and she thought that her heart broke some more.

The thing that they had…it was good for both of them… for a while. From the start, it never spelled ever after. There were some things that you just take for the moment until they end. After that…it was over. You just have to thank your stars that it ever happened. Remember the good things that it taught you. Because some things don't give you bad memories at all until they are over.

She fell asleep. When she woke up, it was already six in the evening. Her house remained quiet. She erased the fifty voice messages in her answering machine without listening to them. She erased all the text messages that she received from Justin without reading them.

Then she packed a bagful of clothes and snuck out of her apartment, hoping she wouldn't run into Justin in the hallway, elevator or in the lobby.

She hailed a cab and went to Yuan's house.

When he opened the door, he was shocked to see her expression. "What the fuck is wrong with you, girl?"

She shook her head. "Can I crash over here for a week or so? I don't want to be alone in my apartment."

"What happened?"

She shook her head.

"Nothing. I just need time to clear my head and think. I'm seeing Kim and Troy this weekend. I have been planning to break up with Troy for a long time."

Well, that wasn't exactly a lie.

Yuan didn't ask any more. He just nodded.

She was trying her best not to cry. If she looked so overdramatic he would grill her for the details.

Jill came over and slept over that night, as well. Her phone kept ringing. Justin was tireless in his pursuit but she wanted to think straight. And she couldn't get the image of that girl out of her head.

"Are you gonna get that?" Yuan asked her. "Must be Troy."

She shrugged and then turned her phone off.

"By the way, I have a scoop," Jill said suddenly, trying to get Adrienne's mind off her problem.

Adrienne looked at her, thankful for the distraction.

"Justin has a new car," Jill said. "We saw him driving it from the office today. He was heading out of the building and he rode a sleek brand-new yellow Porsche."

"He's rich," Yuan remarked. "That's not much of a news. He can change cars every single day if he wants."

"I know that," Jill agreed. "But I'm not really sure if it's his. If it is, then something is going on."

"Why?"

"Because the plate says I-E-N-N-E."

Adrienne's head shot up and she stared at Jill. "What?"

"It could stand for anything," Yuan theorized. "Probably a different language. He's multi-lingual anyway."

"Or!" Jill raised her voice. "It could also be a nickname for a girl."

Yuan raised a brow. "What kind of a name is that?"

Jill pointed at Adrienne. "Adrienne's nickname is Yen, but it could also be spelled as I-E-N-N-E."

"That must be pronounced as ee-yen," Yuan said.

"It would be sweet if he's suddenly named one of his cars with a girl's nick, right?"

Adrienne turned away from her friends. Tears rolled down her cheeks once more. She hoped that her friends wouldn't notice.

It could all be lies! It could mean anything! That car could even belong to the girl I found in his apartment this morning.

But didn't he tell her that he has a surprise for her?

What if that was the surprise he was talking about?

What if his new car's plate meant... my name?

But still...

Why the hell did he have another girl in his apartment?

* * *

She tried to concentrate on her work the next day. She sure knew she looked like hell. She had worn her eyeglasses again to hide her red swollen eyes that said she stayed up all night, crying.

Even Jada knew she felt horrible. She didn't say anything. But to her surprise, she wasn't the bitch from hell that she used to be.

Oh! She does have a heart after all!

She was staring at the blank page on her screen when she realized that Justin was standing in front of her.

She looked up at him nervously.

For a handsome guy, who looked so playful and carefree, Justin looked like shit, as well. He hadn't shaved and it looked like he didn't sleep at all.

"What are you doing here?" she asked him crossly, but trying to keep her voice down so no one could hear.

He shook his head. "Honey, don't do this. Please...listen to me first." He sounded almost like he begged her.

She shook her head. Right now, everything was just plain confusing for her. She and Justin started out wrong. Their four-month relationship seemed to be built on passion, but never entirely on trust. It was a good thing. But that didn't mean it was right. Because if it was right, then they shouldn't have to keep it a secret.

She wasn't being fair to him either. She couldn't keep stringing him along and making him wait on the sidelines while she couldn't bring herself to break up with Troy. As much as she felt hurt with the fact that Justin brought another woman home, she also hated the fact she had no right to demand for his faithfulness. She didn't even exactly give him hers. She's still with Troy, wasn't she?

"I need to clear my head. I need to think about what I need to do. The thing we have...let's just be thankful it lasted that long. It was just supposed to be a one-night stand anyway. I can't tie you down. And I have too much excess baggage." She took a deep breath and tried so hard not to cry. "I can't keep on lying to my friends and cheating on my boyfriend. I'm not some loose woman who plays around. I made my mistake. I have to make things right this time. I'm not being fair to anyone. And it's time I become fair to you."

She didn't know where she got the courage to say those words, without even blinking.

She stared at him. His eyes were narrowed a little and for a moment, she thought she couldn't contain the cold fury she saw there. She felt almost scared.

"So, just like that?" he asked coldly. "You couldn't break up with Troy for the longest time! And you're giving me up just like that? Without even giving me a chance to explain?"

No! I don't want to give you up!

She wanted to scream that to him.

"You didn't have to explain. You don't owe me an explanation."

Justin balled his fists and gave her table a frustrated punch. "Okay!" he said. "I slept with her! I banged another woman. What can I say? I was in...heat! I would fuck anything that wears a skirt! And she happened to be there! Willing! And easy! So I took her back to our bedroom and screwed her brains out!" He gave her a stone-cold stare. "Is that what you wanted to hear?!"

Adrienne stood up from her seat and without warning slapped Justin on the face. Tears were rolling down her cheeks. Every word he said felt like knives stabbing through her, shredding her, tearing her apart.

When Justin looked at her again, his eyes were shining with tears.

"I thought you trusted me, Adrienne... thought better of me," he said in a cold and frustrated voice. He shook his head. "I guess you still believed my reputation more than you believed me." He took one last deep breath and said, "See you around, Miss Miller." And then he left.

Adrienne sat back on her seat and this time, she really cried. She didn't hold back.

The other day, she was contemplating on breaking up with Troy. How did things go the wrong way and she broke up with Justin instead? The guy she actually loved.

She took a tissue and wiped the tears from her cheeks and her eyes. Then she gathered her bag and went out of her office. She was thankful that most of her officemates had gone to lunch. No one saw Justin come to her office and no one heard them fight. Jill sat in a meeting in Jada's office, so she couldn't ask Adrienne why Justin Adams just went to her office. Knowing her, she would ask for every single detail.

She got out of the building with no particular destination in mind. She didn't want to go home. She didn't want to risk running into Justin. He must be so pissed at her. She was still angry at him, too, for the words he said to her. He said his piece, and he could have just provided her with a clear explanation. Instead, he said words that made it difficult for her to know what happened for real.

She was a big mess and she couldn't even turn to her friends for advice. She could never consult her sister on anything. And Troy was definitely not on the options list.

Twenty minutes later, she was sitting in a bar in a hotel, drinking daiquiri. Yes, maybe in this case, liquor helps!

The lady bartender was looking at her wearily.

"You okay, sweetheart?" she asked.

Adrienne looked up at her. "I've been better."

"Boy trouble?"

Adrienne let out a sarcastic laugh. "Boys troubles."

The bartender smiled. "Then consider yourself luckier than the rest of us." Then she turned to serve another customer a drink.

"Now this is the last place I expect to see you at this time of the day." somebody said beside her.

She turned to her left and saw a familiar guy sitting beside her. He motioned for the bartender to give him a beer. The bartender smiled at him widely, obviously flirting.

Adrienne groaned. That was the last thing she needed.

"So what's up, Miss Miller?" Jin Starck asked taking a gulp of his beer.

Adrienne shook her head. "Nothing."

"You could have fooled me!" he said lightly, trying to make her smile.

"I don't discuss my personal problems with my clients, Mr. Starck," she said.

He smiled. "Do you see me wearing my suit?"

Adrienne took a second to look at what he was wearing. He wore a dark green long-sleeved shirt over his jeans. His hair was again disheveled. He didn't look like the tycoon she met at the hotel a week ago.

"Guess you're not. But why would I tell you all my troubles?"

"Because I happen to be an unbiased stranger." He grinned. "Don't worry. Nothing you say to me gets out of this bar. And I totally won't judge you after this."

Well, she was desperate to talk to somebody. And right now, nobody she knew would forgive her if she told them the truth.

Adrienne took her drink straight up. Then she motioned for the bartender to give her another drink. "Okay. I must be crazy for telling you this."

Jin smiled. "You look more desperate to me than crazy, to be honest."

"You're right." She took a deep breath. And then finally, she talked…about the first time how she met Justin, how she ended up in his apartment, and how they were keeping a secret from everybody for the last four months.

She told Jin that she had a boyfriend and why she was with him in the first place. She told him why she couldn't tell her friends. She told him almost everything…except for the details of her sex life of course, and the names of everybody involved, in case Jin Starck happened to know any of them.

"So this guy that you were with at the bar the night I met you…the one who picked you up at the hotel… that's the official boyfriend? Or the mistress?"

Adrienne raised a brow at him. She laughed at his choice of word. *Mistress!*

"He's the unofficial boyfriend," she replied.

"But he sounded like he's also the one you want to be with."

Adrienne nodded. "I love him." Tears rolled down her cheeks. She wiped them off with her fingers and then asked the lady to give her another drink.

"Now, I understand," Jin said.

"Understand what?"

"That night I met you, I watched you afterwards, trying to figure out where I've seen you before. I was curious why your boyfriend sat in the bar and you were at one of the tables with your friends. Now, I know. He's your secret, other boyfriend."

"Pretty much."

"How'd you break up?"

So she told him about the girl she found in his apartment.

"She is so beautiful!" she said. "How could he say that he didn't screw her after I found her in his apartment wearing his robe?"

"He's a pretty boy, Adrienne. I'm sure he's got girls falling over his feet. His concept of beautiful just might be different from yours."

"He's a player! A rakehell!" she said. "At least that's what his reputation said."

"And you believe that?" Jin asked. Adrienne looked up at him. Jin sighed. "Let me guess. This guy…rich, smart, heir to some throne someday. Girls just follow him everywhere and he can take a pick wherever whenever? Never had a steady relationship. Never committed to anybody?"

Adrienne nodded. "Sadly so."

"Welcome to my world!" Jin said and Adrienne looked up at him thoughtfully.

Yeah, he was right. He's exactly another version of Justin Adams.

"But not all of us are heartless, Adrienne. Not all guys who are like that think with their... excuse my French... dicks! Just because he doesn't commit to a girl doesn't mean he's just after the sex. Maybe he's waiting for the right one to come. Maybe that was you. You got a chance to see what he was really like, and you still believed what others thought about him."

Adrienne stared back at Jin and tears welled up in her eyes.

He's right!

Oh God! Justin didn't screw that girl! But what was she doing in his apartment?

"So...I should...call him?"

Jin raised a brow at her. "Are you single? Have you broken up with your official boyfriend? Have you come clean to all your friends?"

She bit her lip. "No. No. And no."

"Then no," Jin said. "If you're going after a guy you hurt and insulted, make sure you have something to offer in return. And right now, after all that you said to me, I can tell, he only wants one thing from you." He took a gulp of his beer. "I think you know what that is, *cherie*."

Adrienne covered her face with her hands. "God! I just want to call my boyfriend now and break up with him! Maybe I should. Just rip off the bandage."

"Doesn't always work. Not in your case," he said. "You were with him for all the wrong reasons. You were trying to please your mother. Now, be brave enough to do the right thing this time. If you can end up as friends, then that just might cushion the blow for your Mom."

Adrienne drank another daiquiri. Her world seemed to be spinning now. She turned back to Jin. "You're too wise for a twenty-three year old."

He smiled. "I was raised by a wonderful woman. Too bad for you...the woman who raised you sounds like a horrible person who didn't care about your feelings." Adrienne wanted to cry at that, because she actually believed that Jin felt sorry for her.

"She was horrible!" she murmured. "She loved my sister but she never loved me. My sister hated me too. My father... was helpless to defend me most times." Then she laughed. "I lost the one person who made me feel like I mattered at all. I screwed it up, big time!"

She felt Jin put his arm around her shoulders and hug her. Adrienne cried on his shoulder, unable to stop now. She was thankful that she spoke to Jin. He was so comfortable to talk to. She felt like she's known him all her life. She felt like right now, with him, there was somebody on her side.

"How on earth are you so mature and wise?" she asked in spite of her tears.

Jin heaved a sigh. "Of course, if the world wasn't mad...if we were in the ideal world...it would be you giving me advice, Adrienne. Not the other way around." Adrienne knew her world was already spinning. And before she passed out, she thought she heard a little sadness in Jin's voice.

15.

Entrevue.

French. Etymology of the word Interview.

*W*hen Adrienne opened her eyes, she was rested on a soft mattress. She immediately stood up and her hand went to her head.

"Headache?" She heard a familiar voice ask her. She opened her eyes and turned to see Yuan almost glaring at her. "Serves you right!"

He looked like he was so angry at her, but still he stood up and handed her aspirin and water. What happened?

She was dressed in her pants and long-sleeved white shirt. The same ones she was wearing in the office yesterday.

She looked around the room and discovered that she was in Yuan's bedroom.

"Why am I here?" she asked. She didn't even remember seeing Yuan yesterday.

"Your hot-looking friend called me. You're so lucky he's such a gentleman. In your state yesterday, you could have been gang raped and you wouldn't even have a clue when you woke up the next morning."

Adrienne squeezed her temples. "What time is it? God, I have to get to work."

"Forget it." Yuan said. "Jill already told Jada you weren't feeling well. She said she needed to interview somebody for her article and then she'll come back here."

Adrienne lay back on the bed and closed her eyes.

"Come on! You could use caffeine in your system."

Adrienne took a quick shower as Yuan made them coffee. When she emerged from the bathroom, she was wearing a fresh pair of pajamas. She felt better but she still had a headache.

Damn those daiquiris!

"Who called you?"

"Jin Starck." Yuan replied.

Adrienne finally remembered how she poured her heart out to Jin yesterday.

Oh God, this is embarrassing!

"How did you meet him anyway? He's not even from New York. He lives in Paris."

"He's here on business. He's a client of *Blush*."

"Well, you don't get wasted in front of your clients! Or are you mixing business with pleasure?"

"Hello—no!"

"Well, he said he insisted that you go for a drink after your meeting.

He didn't know that you have low alcohol tolerance. I told him you had zero."

Wait? What? Jin told Yuan we had a meeting yesterday? He didn't tell him that he found me drinking my problems away? Thank God!

"Wondered how he knew to call you," she thought out loud.

"He called using your phone. Maybe he checked who you had on your speed dial."

After having coffee, she went to the bedroom and slept some more. Honestly, with the pain she felt in her heart after losing Justin, there were only two things she wanted to do. Drink and sleep.

She checked her phone, hoping for the impossible. That somehow, Justin must have called her or sent her a message.

But she only had one message from an unregistered number: *Hey, hope you'll feel better when you wake up. Don't forget to laugh once in a while, okay? – Jin*

She smiled at his thoughtfulness.

She replied: *Up now and still alive. Will learn how to laugh again soon, I hope. Thanks! I owe you one.*

Jill got to Yuan's place in the afternoon.

"I had a wonderful day!" she squealed. "You'll never believe what happened today!"

"Do tell!" Yuan said curiously.

Adrienne's heart pounded inside her chest. With Jill's excitement, she figured this has got something to do with Justin again.

"Jada gave me a new column, right? I'm featuring anybody from town. Real people with their interests and some personal stuff. So to launch this column, we asked some interesting people to be the firsts to be featured. And guess who we interviewed first."

Please don't say Justin!

"Justin Adams!" Jill squealed and jumped for joy.

"What did he say, what did he say?" Yuan asked excitedly.

"I know you will not be content with my narration, so I got him on camera!"

"Oh my God, oh my God!" Yuan said excitedly. "Let's play it!"

"Come on, Adrienne! Let's watch!"

Adrienne shook her head. "No, guys. I'm really not in the mood."

"When were you not in the mood to hear about Justin Adams? Come on! I'm giving you uncut, unedited scoop on the City's most wanted!"

"Really not interested," Adrienne insisted.

Jill grinned at Yuan. "I know why she's not interested!"

"Yeah! I can't say I blame her." Yuan said grinning back at Jill.

"What?" Adrienne raised a brow at them.

"Maybe she doesn't fancy black-haired rebels. She wanted brown-haired, green-eyed tycoons."

Adrienne blinked back at both her friends. "What? No way! It was just a situation that got out of hand."

"Come on, Yen!" Jill insisted. "That guy is hot! He can give Justin a run for his money. Ditch Troy and see if you can make something out with your sudden closeness to Jin Starck!"

"You look cute together, by the way." Yuan smiled.

"Yes. Maybe the universe is pointing you to the right direction. Break up with Troy and go for Jin Starck."

Adrienne shook her head. "You are unbelievable," she groaned. "Jin is a kid!"

"He's two years younger than you, silly! Two years don't even count anymore when you're past puberty!" Yuan argued.

"Anyway, suit yourself. We're just saying that we think Jin Starck is interested in you. Otherwise, he wouldn't ask you to come to the bar with him, right? It was like a lame excuse to get you on a date! He didn't even care that you were still dressed in your office attire."

Adrienne squeezed her temples. "You guys are giving me a headache!"

Her friends laughed. "No. Jin Starck is giving you a headache! You know he's attractive. He's *smoookingg* hot! You may be attracted to him, too, but you just refuse to admit it."

"Just stop it, guys! I don't picture Jin that way. He's a client. And he's way too young for me. Could we please drop this now?"

Jill shrugged and then she turned to Yuan. "Before we watch this clip, I'll tell you a rumor I just heard. Tara Lambert, that hot lingerie model, in an interview was asked who she would like to go with her to her lingerie line's grand launching. And you know what she said? Justin Adams."

Adrienne stared at Jill. Pieces of her already shattered heart were somewhere on the floor and Jill was stepping all over them. Now, she wished they just stayed on the subject of Jin Starck!

"Even the supermodels have their eyes on him. What chance do we mortals have now?" Jill sighed.

"How could she even hear about Justin Adams?" Adrienne asked, trying to disguise the pain in her voice.

Jill shrugged. "Well, Tara used to be a lady bartender. She was discovered there. Probably met Justin Adams at a bar since he hangs out in these elite places."

What Jill said only made Adrienne feel worse. Long legs, big boobs, perfect body, all bared and paraded on Fifth Avenue. Then that perfect Barbie in the flesh. Beautiful goddess who looked like an angel sent from heaven. What does the assistant editor-in-chief of Blush have to say to that?

"I hoped you asked him about this," Yuan asked.

Jill beamed. "Right ahead of you, friend."

Yuan got even more excited. "Let's watch already!"

Jill hooked up her camera to Yuan's flat screen. Adrienne didn't want to watch but her friends forced her to. And if she refused even more, they might know that something was up. And she was not yet ready to confess to them. She needed to break up with Troy first. And that would only happen this weekend.

Justin's handsome face appeared on the screen. Adrienne's heart broke just a little bit more, if that was possible.

"I'll tape this, if you don't mind," Jill said. "I'm bad at writing notes."

Justin just shrugged. He didn't look like he was in a good mood at all.

"How are you doing, Justin?" Jill began.

"Not bad," he replied. "You might need to excuse me for not taking off my sunglasses though."

"You got a shiner there?" Jill teased nervously.

"No not really. But I haven't had much sleep lately."

Jill asked about his credentials first. His age, education. Nothing Adrienne didn't know about. Then Jill asked him about his hobbies and where he hung out more often.

"I go out with my friends, play poker with them," he replied. "I also ski and snowboard with my cousins."

"What's your idea of perfect date or night out? With a girl, I mean." Jill asked.

"Hmmm…tough one. But normally, I just like hanging out with her at home, cuddling…being with each other. Nothing grand, really. But that's the point. If you like being with a person, it doesn't matter where you are. You can have the best time of your life."

His voice was so sincere that Adrienne felt like crying.

"Best date you ever had?" Jill asked again.

He laughed humorlessly. "Watching the Northern Lights in Alaska."

"You actually took a girl in Alaska just to see the Northern Lights?" Jill asked.

"Yep, pretty much."

"That's a lot of effort for one date," Jill said in a dreamy tone.

"Well… she was worth it," Justin said in serious tone.

Jill and Yuan sighed in unison.

"You know the rumor that Tara Lambert is interested in you, what do you have to say to that?" Jill asked boldly.

Justin chuckled uneasily. Then he said, "I'm sorry. Who is Tara Lambert?"

"You know her. She's the girl bold enough to show her twin C's on the Fifth," Jill said in a low voice.

Justin laughed. "You're not going to print that, are you?"

Jill giggled. "Of course not." She winked at him. "Okay, back to Tara Lambert, now that you know who she is. What do you have to say?"

Adrienne rolled her eyes.

Justin shrugged. "Well, rumors are rumors. I'm not sure if it's true, though. But I'm not really looking for anything right now."

Gees! That's embarrassing!

"Really?" Jill asked. "Does that mean you have a relationship with someone now? Is she the one behind your car plate number? Ienne?" Jill was relentless.

Justin sighed. He bit his lip and thought for a while. Then he said, "I was deeply involved with someone. It's a little... messed up now, but I still feel deeply involved."

Jill was silent for a while. "What happened?"

He paused thoughtfully and then said, "On paper, you can write, 'miscommunication,'" Justin said.

"Okay...but off the record?"

Justin stared at her for a moment. "Okay, promise not to print this, okay?"

Jill smiled wildly. "Sure, you can trust me on this. No one will ever see this video too."

Liar! Adrienne thought about Jill.

"Okay, between you and me... my reputation preceded me... yet again. She thought I was cheating on her when she found a girl in my apartment."

Jill giggled. "But Justin...if you have a girl in your apartment, then that would constitute cheating, right?"

"Depends on who the girl is," Justin replied.

"Okay, so who was the girl?"

"Her name's Ian. Short for Julianne. She's my cousin, who visited me from a short college break," Justin said soberly.

Ian? Gian's twin. His cousin?!

Now, she remembered Gian and the girl she found in Justin's apartment. Somehow, she realized how much they look alike.

Adrienne stared at Justin's handsome face on the screen. She didn't listen to any of his voicemails nor did she read any of his text messages.

Justin was smart and private enough not to confide to a stranger. And yet, here on camera, he freely told Jill what happened. Because he knew... she would see this. If she didn't, then Jill would tell her. Just as if it wasn't enough that her heart remained broken, she could feel her world crashing all over her.

"Lucky girl, that one," Jill said.

"Tell me about it. He really seemed into her. I mean, that's a first. Justin Adams admitting to the world that he's not really the cold and unattached playboy the world believed him to be. He can fall in love. That is just romantic," Yuan said.

"I was too shy to ask him her name. Figured that would be too private. But if I knew, I'd hunt her down and tell her, thanks for making him single again, *stooooppidd*!!!"

"I kinda feel bad for him," Yuan said. "A good guy with a bad reputation."

Adrienne found herself lost in her own thoughts. She didn't listen to him. She just immediately assumed that he slept with somebody else. Defense mechanism. She wanted to protect herself from getting hurt by him by immediately assuming that he would.

She felt like throwing up. She felt like crying. And she knew she would. Right then and there. In front of her friends.

"Honey, are you okay?" Jill asked.

She nodded. "Excuse me," she said to them and locked herself in Yuan's bathroom. Luckily, her friends blamed her actions on her hangover.

She silently poured all the tears she's been bottling up inside once she was alone in Yuan's bathroom.

Now, she remembered everything Justin did for her. He was wonderful. He treated her far better than Troy ever did. But she didn't give him a chance. She gave him a deaf ear and a blind eye. She had so convinced herself that he was the cheating type. That nothing good could ever come out of what they had anyway. That it was bound to end someday. And when they encountered a bump, she immediately gave up, and didn't even fight for him, or gave him a fighting chance.

Oh, God! What have I done?

***

Next day, Adrienne saw Justin in *Blush*. He didn't even look her way. She tried so hard not to cry. All she wanted to do is run to him and throw herself in his arms, but maybe it was too late for that now. She made her bed, she has to go lie in it!

She hurt him deeply. And she knew no matter what she did, she couldn't get him back. At least, not yet. She had to fix herself first and remove all her excess baggage. Someday, when she's free, when things no longer seemed complicated with her life, she just might give it a try again…she can try to win him back. Because she knew that Justin deserved to be more than just the guy on the sidelines.

However, it seemed that Justin's recovery was coming at blinding speed. Every night, he was seen in bars, partying with his friends.

"You know what? A friend of mine saw Justin Adams in Oxygen last night. Clubbing with guess who? Tara Lambert," Yuan said to her Friday night when Adrienne went out with them for dinner.

And he said he didn't know her? Bet he does now!

"Well, girls like Tara Lambert have a certain advantage," Jill said.

"Yes. They're called C-cups!" Adrienne muttered under her breath.

"I wondered what happened to the girl he said he was 'deeply' involved in," Yuan said, thoughtfully.

Jill shrugged. "She probably decided to stand by her stupidity. What do you say? One girl's loss is another girl's gain. In this case, it looks like Tara Lambert is on the winning end. It looks like he will be replacing his Porsche's plate to spell T-A-R-A."

"Yes. Until now, it still says the same name. He must have been really into her, huh," Yuan said.

That made things even worse. Adrienne tried to endure thirty minutes of another Justin Adams conversation. Most of it, much to her pain, included how compatible he was with Tara Lambert.

"They would look good together, don't you think?" Yuan asked.

Jill sighed. "Yeah, with her legs that go forever. Perfect curves. I don't think she's really pretty though. Her facial features are too strong, if you ask me. Justin's face is aristocratic. If you ask me, features-wise, he would look great with someone who looks like a cold and yet angelic princess."

"Sometimes, I think Tara Lambert's face looked too boyish," Yuan began. "But she's got that appeal. Maybe that's why she's hot these days."

Adrienne hated the feeling of not being able to tell her friends to shut the fuck up! Because it affected her. Because she's in pain for ending things with Justin Adams for stupid reasons... for all the wrong reasons!

She received a call from Troy. Even though she knew she faced another problem, she was thankful with the distraction. She didn't know where she was getting all the courage to endure the Justin-Tara loveteam talk.

"Hi Yen," he greeted. "The convention is done. My parents are booking a weekend getaway for all of us."

"Troy... can we talk first?" she asked. "I don't think I should go to this thing with your parents."

She heard a sound and then she was talking to Kim now. "Yenny! Mom and Dad will be onboard a flight tomorrow. They'll meet us at the Seasons Holiday Resorts at noon. It's in New York so you really don't have an alibi."

Adrienne closed her eyes for a moment. *Damn!* How could she not be given any peace with Troy so she can finally break things up with him?

Troy got the phone back from Kim. "We'll pick you up at your apartment early in the morning."

"Troy, we really have to talk," she insisted.

"Then we'll talk there. I have something to tell you too. We'll pick you up at seven."

Adrienne closed her eyes again and then she sighed. "Okay. I'll see you."

When she hung up the phone, she told her friends what she was going to do over the weekend.

"Let's go!" Yuan said. "We're coming with you!"

Adrienne figured this could be a good way to end things with Troy. She could talk to him during the weekend. At least, he won't have too much pressure and he's got his *Sensei* Kim to tell him what to do. Knowing Kim, she would support her in this decision. She was never happy with her relationship with Troy. Kim was Troy's mother's first pick anyway.

God! Kim was our own mother's first choice for my boyfriend!

"They're picking me up at seven."

"Great!" Yuan responded. "I will call my agent. I'm sure they can book us. But we might go there later. Probably noontime. Which hotel are you staying at?"

"Seasons Holiday." Adrienne sighed. "This will not be good."

Yuan shrugged. "Come on. Now, that you are sure that you have to spread your wings and explore greener pastures, you have to find the courage to stand by your decisions, sweetie. No one said it is easy. But eventually, this should make you happier."

"Yes. And we will go with you! Don't worry. You have all the support you will need."

"Look at you!" Yuan stated. "Since you got that apartment of yours, you have changed so much."

"You've stopped wearing glasses. You've started re-evaluating your wardrobe. You let your hair down often. You've become Assistant Editor-in-Chief."

"Made some money on stocks as well," Adrienne added.

"You invested in stocks?" Yuan asked.

Adrienne realized that even her playing the odds on Wall Street was unknown to her friends.

"I gave it a try. And I had beginner's luck. But it was fun and liberating, thinking I can earn so much more in some other way. I thought I was going downhill when I signed the mortgage papers. But I was luckier than I thought. Except for my mother, Kim and Troy, I can't say that I have any right to complain about my life."

If Justin was still with me, then things would have been perfect!

"And you've got an opportunity of meeting someone perfect for you."

"You need not die a virgin!" Jill asserted with a mischievous smile. "And you can have your first time with someone who will wake up every single nerve in your body."

I already have and I just lost him!

"All right. Jill and I are going to meet you there by noontime. I need to go to the office to sort out some things."

"Yeah, me, too. I need to submit something to Jada first thing tomorrow."

Adrienne's hands felt cold and her heart was pounding in her chest. She knew that she had to go through with it. She might not have enough courage, but she believed she'd know when the time came. And she would be braver than she needed to be.

16.

Verraten

German. Meaning Betrayed in English

"Come on, come on. Get ready, we're leaving in thirty minutes," Kim announced when she and Troy appeared at her doorstep.

"I'm ready," Adrienne said but she still felt a bit sleepy.

She wasn't able to get enough sleep the night before. She thought of ways of telling Troy that it's the end of the line for their 'pretend' relationship. If he's in the same boat with her, he wouldn't mind. But if he really still loved her like he said, then it's going to be a nightmare. That's not even mentioning that her heart still suffered every time she thought about Justin.

She wondered, will she by chance see Tara Lambert on the elevator? Is she the one warming his bed now? Would he take care of Tara the way he took care of her? Would he make her fall hopelessly in love with him?

She just hoped Tara or any other girl that Justin would be with would see him better than she did. Would believe in him more, and would trust him better. Justin deserved that.

They rode a taxi to the resort. Troy checked them in. His parents still hadn't arrived.

"They're coming with your parents late afternoon," Troy said. Then he turned to Kim. "Kim, you'll be in Room 204," he said when he returned. "Adrienne, we'll be in room 313."

What?!?

Adrienne felt the first pangs of panic.

This cannot be happening.

"No, Troy," she managed to say. "I will stay with Kim."

"Why?" he asked sharply.

"Why not?" she asked back.

He raised a brow. He whispered to her angrily, "I'm your boyfriend, Adrienne. Your job is to stay by my side whenever you can."

She raised her chin. "No, Troy. I'm not your bodyguard!"

He threw his hands up in the air.

"All right. Do whatever you like! You are so good at that anyway!"

She rolled her eyes and looked over at Kim.

Kim's room was a bit small. It had a double bed though and a big couch.

"I can sleep on the couch, don't bother," she told Kim. "I guess Troy didn't anticipate that I won't be rooming with him."

"What's the fuss anyway, Yenny? It's not like you're still a virgin.

We actually sleep with our boyfriends, you know. While you're still single, you should have all the fun you like! You used to sleep around when you were young. Then you changed and became boring!"

She couldn't believe she was hearing this from Kim. The prim, the proper, Kim. And yes, she knew that. A girl can sleep with her boyfriend. God! She can even sleep with someone else. And fall in love and get heartbroken. Kimberly didn't need to lecture her on the world's favorite secrets!

Adrienne could only stare at Kim. Though, if she was holding something in her hands, she would have flung it to her face.

"For the record Kim, I never slept with anyone in high school…or college. It's a pity we never talk much. You could have shown me some pointers since you sound like you normally do this sleeping around thing," she said with a tang, trying to sting Kimberly for once.

To her surprise, Kimberly laughed. "Come on, Yenny. Lighten up. Just because you receive too much pressure from Mom, doesn't mean you have to do what she says all the time. You just have to show her what she needs to see. And then when you are out of her sight, you can be free! You never learned the rules of the game! You're so dim."

"And you're such a hypocrite!" Adrienne snapped. "And not rooming with Troy isn't about pleasing Mom. It's about me, what I want and don't want."

"Then I don't think you will keep Troy for long, dear. Surprised you managed to hold on to him for three years."

"Maybe it's him who didn't want to let go," she said.

Kim rolled her eyes before turning away from her.

Adrienne's phone rang.

"We're here," Yuan said. "We're just going up to our room."

"All right. See you, guys," she said. She turned to Kim. "I'll go change. Then I'll see my friends."

She took out a pair of one-piece suit and a sarong. She tied her hair in a pony.

Kimberly was watching TV when she went out of the bathroom.

"I'll catch you later," she said to her and went out.

She was still confused about Kimberly's words as she waited for the elevator. Was that what she was doing? Was she just trying to please their mother and did what her mother wanted in front of her eyes and then went wild behind her back?

But she knew Kim was doing well in med school anyway, so it didn't really matter. And what has been done is done. She could have used this sort of information when she was younger. No matter what, she'd remain the black sheep in the family. She couldn't change that. What she could do is to just make sure that she didn't fail herself in life from this point forward.

When the elevator opened, she was shocked to see Justin in it.
What the hell is he doing here?
He was wearing his heavily tinted shades and she didn't know if he was looking at her. She looked away from him as she entered the lift. She wanted to touch him. She wanted to throw herself in his arms. She wanted to feel him. To know that one time in her life, he existed. He was real. She didn't just dream him.

Just one word, God. Please! Just one word, I will throw myself in his arms, no questions asked.

The elevator door opened. He went out without a single word or glance at her. As if she didn't exist to him at all.

Tears rolled down her face. She wiped them before she knocked on her friends' room.

"Have you spoken to Troy?" Yuan asked.

"Honey, my piece of advice?" Jill began. "The sooner the better. Before you start having doubts. Before your parents come tonight and you chicken out just by looking at your Mom."

"Justin Adams is here," Yuan said all of a sudden.

Why is it that he just appears out of nowhere?

When she doesn't expect him to be in this place, he shows up. When she doesn't expect him to be brought up in any conversation, his name just keeps popping up.

"Yes! I saw him in the lobby as well. He must have arrived the same time we did. I just ran into him at *Blush* this morning. I told him that we were going here and I had to rush out. He's nice really. He smiles at me when I run into him. He doesn't act snobby to me anymore since that interview."

"Well, lucky you!" Yuan teased. "But sorry dear, you are up against a lady with big breasts who is not afraid to show herself in lingerie all over Fifth."

"I am not after Justin Adams! I know he is way out of my league. But it is nice that he knows I exist."

Adrienne didn't say anything the whole time. The whole problem with secretly sleeping with the guy your friends dream about is that you get to hear about him all the time even after you part ways! She found it especially hard since she just fell in love with him and drove away a once in a million chance because she decided to be stupid.

"Was he with someone? Was he with Tara?" Yuan asked.

"I don't know," Jill admitted. "Didn't see any girl with him. I saw him chatting with some guys in the lobby. But no sign of Tara. But knowing the likes of her, she will be here by evening. God! I think she would follow him to the ends of the Earth!. That billboard comes in very handy for her!"

"Yeah. But I don't think you can get Justin Adams to commit to a girl who used to work as a bartender, and now parades around in lingerie on a catwalk. She could be good for a month's shag, but knowing Justin's dating history, or lack of one, she would be picking up the pieces of her heart this same time next month."

Adrienne swallowed hard. She wanted to tell them that Justin deserved a better impression than that. That Justin is human! And he can be considerate and sweet.

She had lunch with Jill and Yuan. She felt guilty about not bothering to go to lunch with Kim and Troy, but she needed to clear her head first and find enough strength, so that the next time she sees Troy, it would be to break up with him.

Jill was right. The earlier the better.

After lunch, she decided that the time has come. She went out to find Troy. She didn't need a script. She will just tell him straight what she needed to say. If he tries to evade her again, she will be firm.

She knocked on his door. No answer. She must have knocked for a whole five minutes, but it looked like he wasn't in. He must have taken a late lunch with Kimberly.

Oh God! Why are you making this so difficult for me?

She decided to go back to her room. When she opened the door, she was shocked by the sight in front of her.

First, she saw Kimberly. She had her back to her, her head pulled back, she was naked, her legs were spread apart. She was on top of…Troy. Troy had his hands on her waist. They were moaning…

She swallowed hard. Anger and embarrassment ate her up. She wanted to puke at the sight in front of her.

She knew this moment will happen only once and she didn't want to go back in her history and remember that at the moment when she should have held her head up high, she lost it and ran away. No. She would be strong. She would stomach this! So she stood there, and waited for them to realize that they were no longer alone.

Suddenly, Troy realized that she was standing there.

"Oh shit!" Troy muttered, then he immediately pushed Kimberly off him. He stood up, not minding that he was naked. His sex in full display.

Well, at least she had a peek before they broke up.

God! Troy would never make me as happy as Justin did.

She smiled sarcastically.

"Oh, I just came to find you to say something important. I was quite worried how you would take it, but it seems that you've been quite busy yourself." Adrienne said, trying to keep her voice calm. "You made it so much easier for me to break the news to you, Troy. We're over! Goodbye!" Then she looked at Kimberly, who is hugging the blankets to herself. "Mommy's going to be happy about this. Her favorite daughter is screwing her son-in-law candidate. I'll bet she wouldn't even care that he was her other daughter's boyfriend!"

Then she stormed out of the room.

She was shaking as she waited for the elevator. When the door opened, she found herself eye to eye with Justin.

Shit! Could things get any worse?

She tried hard not to cry. She pressed Yuan's and Jill's floor. Seeing Justin at this time, when she needed refuge, made her want to break down and lose herself in his arms. His phone rang before she could endure the awkward silence inside the lift.

"Who's this?" he asked the person on the other line. "Tara? Tara? Lambert?"

Shit! Apparently, things could get worse!

"Oh hi. Yeah. I'm cool. I was…" She didn't wait to hear the rest of what he will say. She's had enough for the day! The elevator doors opened and she immediately stormed out and headed to Jill's and Yuan's room.

Tears were rolling down her cheeks when Yuan opened the door. She knew it was because of the mixed anger, embarrassment and pain that she was feeling.

She wasn't heartbroken but she felt betrayed. She didn't expect much from Troy, but Kimberly's betrayal ate her up.

Some things are just way below the belt! There are some things that you just don't do to your sister!

It was just like when they were young. Every little thing she had, no matter how cheap, no matter how small, if she seemed happy with it, Kimberly would try to take it from her. And worse, their mother would always take Kimberly's side.

"Holy shit!" Yuan said she told them what she came to discover. "You were so worried about how you were going to break up with him. He just gave you the perfect reason. But my God! Kimberly is a classic. God only knows what a bitch that sister of yours is! Like, who does that?"

Adrienne was lost in her thoughts. She didn't want to go back to her room. Her mind was messed up…with thoughts of Justin, with the image of Kim riding Troy madly.

"I don't know whether I should be mad or happy. Mad because they must have thought so little of me to do what they did. Happy because the blame of this breakup didn't have to be a burden on my part."

"You could use this, you know," Jill said wickedly. "You could use this to blackmail Kimberly."

Adrienne laughed in spite of her pain. "No matter what I do, Kim has my mother's love and trust. And I don't think I would need something from Kimberly bad enough to blackmail her!"

"So, did they say anything?"

"I think they were dumbfounded," Adrienne replied. "I don't think they were able to recover fast. I was standing there for more than a minute, watching them… ride each other! My God! It was disgusting!"

Jill laughed. "No, sweetie! You're a virgin. You would think it's disgusting. But with the right guy, intimacy is actually great."

Adrienne knew that. With Justin, it was bliss! But seeing Troy do it with Kim felt like she had eaten her own vomit.

"What does Troy want?" Yuan protested. "I mean, look at you, Adrienne. You are pretty, sexy and smart! You have done so much for yourself. You're independent and decent! What was he looking for? Kimberly is not even half as attractive as you are! What was he thinking?"

"Guys, let's not forget I was going to break up with him," Adrienne said.

"Yes. But he didn't know that. He doesn't have any reason yet to look somewhere else," Jill said.

"Do you want to go to the beach and get some air?" Yuan asked.

Adrienne shook her head. "I think I'm just going to sleep for a while. Maybe when I wake up, I will forget the sight I just saw in my room. It still makes me want to hurl." She sighed. "I wish I found him earlier. So we could have broken up and parted in a more civil manner."

"Yes. And he could hump your sister after that!" Yuan said sarcastically.

Adrienne rested on Jill's bed. She received a text message.

Jin: *Just checking up on you. Everything well?*

She replied: *If by well, you mean I finally found the guts to break up with my boyfriend and found him beneath my sister, then yes! Everything is right in the world again!*

It took a moment for Jin to reply: *I have assassins on my beck and call. You want me to order a hit?*

She actually smiled at that. Then she replied: *No. Totally not worth it.*

Jin: *And your secret fling?*

She sighed sadly when she typed the message: *Unfortunately... still... flung.*

Jin: *Hey Adrienne! One step at a time, okay? And smile once in a while. Just a little while more, and you'd have a better life to look forward to. I promise you that.*

She: *I hope you're right. Thanks.*

She smiled at Jin's words. She didn't know how Jin Starck became her confidante. He was easy to talk to. And he seemed sincere in giving her advice, like he feels for her and he wanted to make her feel better in whatever way he could.

She must have slept for three hours. When she woke up, she saw Jill and Yuan enjoying a cigarette on the balcony. She felt guilty. She must have ruined their weekend getaway already. They haven't been under the sun yet.

"I'm really sorry, guys. I dragged you into this."

Jill hugged her. "Sweetie, that's what we are for. We're your best friends. We are here when you need us the most."

"So now, we can go out in the sun and catch the sunset?" Yuan asked.

Adrienne smiled and nodded. She wondered if her parents have arrived already. Although she wasn't ready to face them just yet.

As she watched the sunset while they swam on the beach, Adrienne knew that she would be okay. She believed she lost Justin for good. But if there's one thing she learned from him, it was that she needed to love and appreciate herself. She's more than what she gives herself credit for. She's beautiful. She's strong. She's a fox. She would get through this.

17.
Vapas Karo
Hindi. Translation: To take back

Adrienne took out a pair of two-piece suit from the bag she brought with her when she first went to her friends' room. Now that she'd relieved herself of Troy's chains, and Kimberly had just shown her that she is not entirely prudent like she appeared to be, Adrienne thought that there's no harm in wearing a perfectly decent two-piece suit. If her parents arrived in the evening and if her mother lectured her on the virtues of being prudent, she must remember to point out that her favorite daughter did more than wear a piece of revealing clothing.

When she finished dressing, she was happy to see that her suit highlighted her flat tummy, her curves and her long legs. Jill lent her a pair of very sheer white capri pants. The outfit looked decent, but showed a hint of her bikini underneath. She felt sexy and stylish. She thought that if she was still with Justin, she knew exactly what he would say to her.

Her phone rang. It was her father.

"Sweetheart," he started. "We can't make it. Your mother and I both have emergency surgeries. We just can't get out of this. Troy's parents decided not to go too. We figured you kids can have some fun without us."

"All right, Dad," she answered.

Kim is already having more fun than I am.

"Take care, okay?"

She looked at Jill and Yuan. "One problem out of the way. My parents aren't coming anymore."

"Good. At least you didn't have to pretend to be civil to Troy and Kim in front of them."

They went down to the restaurant to have dinner. She chose a table in a secluded corner outside. She sat with her back on the crowd. If Kimberly, Troy or Justin walked in, she didn't want to see any of them.

Fortunately, none of them showed up and she was able to eat a full meal in peace. All Jill and Yuan talked about were their latest dates and escapades. They also planned a night out the following week, where they would go bar hopping.

"The best way to meet guys!" Jill said.

"Both straight or not," Yuan agreed.

After dinner, they hung out by the beach front. Yuan got them some beers.

"All right, Adrienne, whatever pain you feel, let's talk about it. Now. With spirits! Don't go Miss Prude on me, darling." Yuan handed her a bottle of beer.

She took a gulp. It was very cold, thus, she didn't mind the strong taste.

"Will you ever forgive Kim?" Jill asked.

She shrugged. "I don't know. I'm aware that she hated me, but I never expected her to sleep with my boyfriend, either. I mean, sure, Troy is barely a boyfriend, but still, if she had the decency, she wouldn't do it with him. Or at least wait until we break up before she did something like that. It's disgusting!"

"Have you ever thought about seeing somebody else aside from Troy?" Jill asked.

She stared at them. Has the time to be honest finally come? She did promise herself she would come clean to her friends once she broke up with Troy. Well, she and Troy are history now!

She nodded. "Yes, of course. My relationship with Troy was absolutely less than perfect and I did... feel the need to be with someone who lights up my fire."

"During those dry spells, didn't it even cross your mind to explore... you know... other horizons? Or were you just... so resigned to the fact that you're gonna marry a vegetable?" Yuan tried to put it mildly. But Adrienne knew that what he really meant was, *'Didn't you even think about sleeping with somebody else while you were with Troy?'*

She sighed and took a gulp of her bear, for liquid courage. Then she replied, "Yes. Yes...I did."

I slept with somebody else. I cheated on Troy. She wanted to add those sentences but the words never came out.

"Why did you wait this long to break up with that loser?" Jill asked.

"Troy was the only guy she went out with," Yuan told Jill. "Could you blame her for not having anybody else to compare him to? She wouldn't know that Troy was the sorriest excuse for a boyfriend because she didn't know any better."

Adrienne took a deep breath again and mustered all the courage she could. "Actually...I know that. I was able to compare my relationship with Troy with someone who was..." She took a deep breath. "Pure perfection. The relationship was an absolute bliss." Again, she felt her heart break a hundred more times.

Her friends blinked back at her. "What?"

"Sometimes, I couldn't believe what I was doing. Like one time, I went to Gypsys. I dressed up in this very sexy outfit that Jacob picked for me. I went to that bar like a vixen in search for my latest prey. And...sometimes, I still think I just imagined it. Like it was a dream."

"Adrienne, what the fuck are you talking about?" Yuan asked.

She smiled at them bitterly. "I'm sorry, I didn't tell you earlier, guys. I hope you can forgive me."

"What?"

"There was somebody else. Troy was the official boyfriend. But he wasn't the guy I was in love with. There was someone else. I know what you're saying about sharing passion and intimacy with a guy. And you're right. It was perfect. It was pure bliss."

Yuan and Jill went silent for a moment. Adrienne looked at them and realized that they weren't even looking at her. They were staring at somebody behind her.

She turned around and found Troy staring down at her. She stood up and faced him. "What do you want?" she asked.

"What did you just say?" he asked angrily. "There was somebody else?"

"That's beside the point, Troy. We were done a long time ago, you know that!"

"Adrienne...we can still fix this!"

"We were nothing before, Troy! You were... a ghost of a boyfriend! You were not even a friend most of the time! Where did you think our relationship was going? And then you screwed my sister? That just made it so impossible for me to even think good thoughts about you!"

Troy's face turned red. He took deep breaths. Then without warning, he took hold of her wrist and pulled her to him.

"Let me go!" Adrienne said, yanking her arm away.

"We lacked intimacy! That's why it went downhill for us!" he said. "But it didn't have to be like that, Adrienne. I planned this weekend so we could finally cross that line!"

"And you decided to be intimate with my sister as well? That's beyond thinkable!"

"It's you I love, Adrienne! Kim was a mistake! She was... she was always there! And I always missed you. It killed me to have to be so far away from you. It's you I really want! What Kim and I had was just sex. And it won't happen again!"

Adrienne shook her head. "But I don't love you, Troy. There had been nothing between us for a long time. It didn't matter whether you were screwing my sister behind my back. I was going to break up with you anyway."

"Because there was someone else?" he asked in a grave tone. "Who was he?"

"It doesn't matter, Troy. It's not about him. It's about you. I don't love you."

Adrienne saw the anger in Troy's face turn to fury. Then without warning, he took her by the forearm and pulled her away, this time with so much more force.

"Damn it, Troy! Let me go!" she cried, struggling to pull away from him.

He started dragging her, not listening to her pleas.

"Troy, please, let her go!" Jill said.

"Let her go or we're calling security!" Yuan said.

"You two stay out of this!" Troy fired back at them.

He turned to Adrienne and grabbed her other forearm. He was bruising her arms now.

"I waited for so long and got nothing! And somebody else got to enjoy your body, you slut!"

His face had gotten within only a few inches away from hers and he smelled of beer. Adrienne realized that Troy was drunk! She panicked when she realized that he was leaning forward to kiss her on the lips. She struggled but he was too strong for her.

She could hear Yuan and Jill screaming. With all her might, she launched a slap on Troy's face that made him fall back.

"You bitch!" he roared. And before she could see what was coming, she felt a sharp pain on her cheek, so strong that it made her fall to the ground.

Yuan launched a punch at Troy, but he jabbed him in the ribs and he, too, fell to the ground.

Jill screamed again. "Help! Help us!"

Adrienne started to get up. She saw what could be the scariest thing she had seen in her entire life: Troy's face, filled with fury, as he started for her again.

Just when he was about a meter away from her, somehow he got pulled back. The next thing she saw was Troy, on the ground being beaten up.

There were two other guys. They had pulled on Troy's assailant to stop him.

"Shit man, stop it!" one blonde guy said. "You could kill the guy! He's down already."

It took her a moment to realize that it was Justin. He had mounted Troy and punched him to the core. His face was red and Adrienne realized that she had never seen him raging like this before. When he finally stopped attacking Troy, his friends had to hold him back to make sure that he didn't go for him again. Troy sat up from the ground, holding his jaw in pain, and looked like he didn't know what had hit him or why.

Justin bent to pick up his shades that fell to the sand.

"What the fuck?" Troy shouted at him, when he found the voice to speak. "What's your freaking problem? Mind your own damn business!"

Justin didn't answer. He turned to Adrienne. The minute their eyes met, she knew he saw the terror on her face. She had turned pale. He went to her.

"Justin," she whispered.

He didn't say anything. Instead, he put an arm around her waist and tilted her chin up to see the damage that Troy's slap did to her. Troy had hit

ALL THE WRONG REASONS

her harder on her lower lip, and it had started bleeding lightly.

"Oh, honey…" he said very softly. Amidst all the terror that she had just gone through, Adrienne wanted to break down and cry. Not because of the fear she just felt, but because of the gentleness in Justin's voice. And because she heard him call her honey again.

Justin bent down to touch her lips with his, on the part that it was bleeding. She realized that he sucked the blood that was coming out of it.

"What the fuck…" Troy cursed when he saw what Justin did.

Justin turned to him again. Fury and rage returned to his face.

"Didn't your mother tell you not to raise your hand to a girl, Troy?" Justin asked coldly. Justin still obviously fumed. He released Adrienne and started for Troy again. "And guess what? You picked the wrong girl to mess with, asshole!" Then he punched him on the jaw one more time. Troy fell to the ground again.

"Justin, please?" Adrienne pleaded softly. He looked at her and nodded slightly.

He went to her again and seeing how terrified she was, he enclosed her in his embrace, as if telling her that everything was going to be okay. She could feel safe with him now.

"I'm sorry, honey. I'm sorry, I didn't come soon enough," he said to her as he caressed her head. "I wouldn't have let him hurt you."

She shook her head, as tears rolled down her cheeks. She didn't know whether it came out of relief, or because of the fear she felt, or because she was so happy being in his arms again.

She felt him kiss her temple. She closed her eyes and prayed that it wasn't a dream. That he was here for real. That she was back in his arms again.

"Justin, man…" one of his friends called him. "Can we have a word?"

Justin nodded and pulled away slightly from Adrienne. He stared at her for a moment and then kissed her forehead. "Wait a second, hon."

She nodded and Justin went to talk to his friends.

Yuan and Jill went to her in obvious awe. She realized that the moment of revelation had come. Fifteen minutes ago, she considered being honest with them. She planned to take it slow, and offer explanations…to break it to them gently. But now, they were staring at her as if they had just been bitch-slapped with the truth.

Troy had gone to sit on the sand. Kim had magically appeared at his side. Adrienne turned to Yuan and Jill again.

She felt lost for words now. She knew that there's nothing she could say that would make them not hate her at all.

Finally, Jill was able to find her voice. "'Honey?' Justin Adams just called you 'honey?'"

She opened her mouth to say something in her defense but no words came out.

"What is going on, Yen?" Yuan asked. "I mean, clearly, Justin Adams came here to rescue you from your lunatic ex. That part we get. But…him hugging you, kissing you, and calling you honey, with so much familiarity…it makes no sense!"

"And you were right. His eyes are blue. That wasn't a guess, was it? You knew that before. I remembered you saying crystal blue. The exact color of his eyes. We barely see him without the shades. But it looks like you've looked into his eyes more often than anyone else." Jill shook her head.

"Adrienne…were you the girl that Justin was referring to in the interview?" Yuan asked. "The one that he said he was involved with?"

Adrienne whimpered. Tears rolled down her cheeks. Then she nodded slightly.

"Oh my God!" Jill breathed.

Yuan threw his hands in the air. "I can't believe this!"

"I tried to tell you before," Adrienne said. "But you laughed at me. You thought I was joking."

"Then you should have slapped both of us and told us you were serious!" Yuan said in a frustrated voice.

"I was about to tell you before Troy came to us," Adrienne said in a quiet voice. "And I will tell you everything. I'll explain everything from the beginning. But I can't do that now, not after what just happened. I hope you can understand me and give me some time to sort things out."

They didn't say anything. They stared at the figure standing behind her. Justin reappeared at her side and wrapped an arm around her waist.

"Hey, Jill, Yuan," he greeted them casually. Finally, he met them. And this was not the way Adrienne imagined introducing Justin to her friends.

Jill and Yuan nodded at him, but they still gave Adrienne a cold, murderous look.

Justin turned to Adrienne. "We better get you inside, honey," he told her. "You're cold, and we need to attend to that wound."

Adrienne nodded. She turned to her friends. "I'll talk to you guys, later. I'm really sorry."

Justin put an arm around her shoulders and walked her back towards the hotel silently.

She felt too shaken and too confused. But she was also happy. In her mind, she kept asking if he was real. If this was real. Did he really walk with her? Are his arms really around her once again?

When they entered the elevator she said, "Justin, I can't go back to my room. I'm sharing it with Kim, and I can't stand to be in the same room as her now. I just can't."

Justin stared at her for a moment. "I never said we're going to your room," he said. His voice was serious and a little cold. The look that he gave her was distant. "You and I need to talk, too. And I'm not taking no for an answer this time."

Her heart pounded in her chest. Justin stood next to her, but didn't touch her. It seemed like forever before the elevator stopped on his floor.

Justin led her to his room. He rented the suite, with a king-sized bed and a big balcony. The room she shared with Kim was even smaller than Justin's living room.

He closed the door behind him. She stared at him nervously. He looked back at her.

"Thank you," she said quietly.

"For what?" he asked.

She shrugged. "Rescuing me from Troy. I realized Yuan couldn't do much to him."

"I would have done more to him had you not pleaded with me to stop," he stated coldly.

"Justin, you could get into trouble for that. What if Troy sues you for damages? You gave him the beating of his life."

Justin shook his head. "I don't care. He shouldn't have touched you! He deserved what he got."

Tears were shining on Adrienne's eyes as she looked up at him. "Thank you," she whispered. "I'm so glad you're here!"

He didn't move. He just kept looking at her, studying her, waiting for her to say something. In his eyes, she could still see how deeply she hurt him. How small she made him feel.

"Oh God, Justin, I'm so sorry," she whispered. Tears rolled down her cheeks.

"For what?" he asked.

"For...not listening to you. For not giving you a chance to explain." She continued weeping.

He raised a brow at her. "And?"

"For...lying about you to my friends. For making you feel like I'm ashamed of you...of what we had."

When he still kept silent, she stared back at him, wondering what was going on in his mind. "Go on," he urged.

She smiled bitterly. "For not fighting for you. For giving you up. For not believing in you in spite of all the things you showed me. For not trusting you...even though I should know better. For thinking... that you were cheating on me."

"Do you still think I slept with her?" he asked in a steady voice.

Adrienne looked down on her feet, feeling ashamed of herself. She shook her head. "No."

She felt Justin tilt her chin up so she could look at him. "Do you still think I would cheat on you?"

She bit her lip. "Would you?"

Justin groaned. Suddenly, he snatched her by her waist and crushed her into his arms. "You are unbelievable! You drive me crazy sometimes." His voice was gentle, his arms tight and warm around her. Then he pulled away and looked into her eyes. "I know you lived your life around inconsiderate people who did nothing but crush your spirit and made you feel that everything that you are, and everything that you do… is mediocre.

They're wrong, Adrienne! I am here in front of you, and I'm telling you now… that you're the most beautiful woman in my eyes. You're amazing. You're beautiful, inside and out. And I am absolutely, undoubtedly crazy about you. And no! I would *never ever* cheat on you."

Adrienne smiled in spite of her tears. She couldn't believe that she heard these words from Justin. That finally he spelled it loud and clear that he's crazy about her.

Justin looked into her eyes and wiped the tears from her cheeks. "So now… Troy is history?"

She nodded.

"Sure? You told him it's over? *Finito?*"

"I did," she replied. "I wished I said it to him before I found him in between Kimberly's legs though. But nevertheless, I told him."

Justin raised a brow at her. "He was sleeping with your sister?" he asked, obviously finding that hard to believe.

"Yup. I wish they just told me, you know. I didn't need to see the evidence." She let out a little shiver.

Justin grinned. "So, the position of current and official boyfriend is finally open?" he asked, his eyes dancing.

She smiled at him, her heart pounding inside her chest.

"Yes," she replied.

"If you don't mind, Miss Miller, I would like to apply."

She grinned at him. "Well, I'll have to see if you pass the audition first," she teased.

Justin's eyes gleamed and he smiled at her mischievously. Adrienne realized then how naughty and kinky she sounded.

Justin pulled her to him just a little roughly. She shrieked. "Justin, wait! I didn't mean…" she started protesting.

He lifted her off her feet, his hands cupping her thighs, making her wrap her legs around his waist and he started carrying her to the couch.

"Don't worry, Miss Miller. I know exactly what you mean!" Her laughter died in her throat as he crushed his lips to hers as soon as she landed on the soft cushions. A few minutes later, she was screaming his name as he took her to the edge of oblivion, and soon after he met her at the gates of Nirvana.

18.

Opinbera

Icelandic. Meaning Official.

Adrienne lay on the couch, resting her head on Justin's shoulder. She smiled contentedly. True, her life was still less than perfect. Her friends fumed at her, her mother would soon do the same when she found out that she broke up with Troy. Her relationship with Kim was worse than before. But somehow, she still felt this surge of happiness within her. She felt that everything would turn out just fine. And she knew why. She was back in Justin's arms. He said he was crazy about her. And she felt the same way. Tonight, he just became her official boyfriend.

Justin gave her a squeeze and she felt him kiss her forehead. They savored being in each other's embrace again.

"How did you know I needed help?" she asked.

"I sat in the bar and watched you. I saw him come up to you. I didn't know you were fighting, until I saw you slap him. That's when I made a run for it. But I didn't get there fast enough. He hit you first."

"Thank you!" she said again. "Thank God you were there! And by some good coincidence you came to this resort."

"I knew you'd be here," he admitted sheepishly.

"What?"

He took a deep breath. "I ran into Jill this morning. I asked her why she was rushing. She said you guys were coming here. Lucky for me, she was so excited about it, she even mentioned the hotel you were staying in and who came with you." He paused for a while. "I don't know…I just…" He sighed. "I wanted to see you with your friends and your boyfriend. I wanted to see if you're happy… so I could convince myself that you don't need me in your life anymore… so I could finally work on getting you out of my mind, out of my system."

Adrienne shook her head. "I wasn't happy, Justin. I was… miserable! You acted like you didn't know me at all, like I was nothing to you. And you don't want anything to do with me." A tear slid down her cheek. "And I know I deserved it. Because in spite of everything you said to me, everything that you did for me…I still didn't trust you. I didn't believe that you would never hurt me."

"I tried explaining to you who she was, Adrienne. Her name is Julianne. She's Gian's twin. I told you I had a cousin who visited. Her nickname is Ian. That must have confused you. You must have assumed Gian had an identical twin."

Adrienne nodded sheepishly.

"I did explain it to you. In your voicemails, in my text messages.

You must have deleted them without reading them or listening to them…" He took a deep breath. "At that time, I thought maybe you just wanted to end what we had."

Adrienne stared up at him guiltily. She knew she couldn't say anything that would make it enough for him to know how sorry she was. She reached up and kissed his lips. He kissed her back. She felt Justin smile against her lips.

"God, I missed kissing you."

"God! Justin, I was so stupid!"

He leaned forward to kiss her on the forehead. "I'm sorry, too, honey. I should have told you the night before. I should have told you…"

"You didn't have to, Justin. You didn't owe me that. You didn't have to tell me everything that you do."

"But I wanted to," he said. "I was quite excited to show you my new car, actually. I had a plate especially made…"

"Ienne," she whispered.

He nodded. "I wanted to see how you would react when you saw it. I know you would be furious at me, as I'm defying your request to keep us a secret. But it was my little way of showing that we…belong together."

"And when Jill told me about it, I thought it belonged to the girl I found in your apartment."

He shook his head. "It meant you."

She pulled his face to hers and kissed him again. When he deepened the kiss, she felt a sting on her lip.

"Ouch!" She giggled. She had forgotten about the wound that Troy gave her. In her excitement to make love to Justin again, she didn't even feel any pain when he crushed his lips to hers.

"I'm sorry, honey. I forgot."

She nodded. "It's okay. I forgot it, too."

"Come on, let's go freshen up."

"Justin, I have to go back to Yuan's and Jill's room. I was sharing a room with Kimberly. And I just can't bear to see her right now."

He raised a brow at her. "Who said you were going to stay with Yuan and Jill? You're staying the night here with me, honey."

"But Jill and Yuan are mad at me."

"If you go back to your room will it make a difference? They already know about us. I'm sure they would have guessed that you're spending the night with me."

"They won't. They still believe I'm a virgin." Adrienne rolled her eyes.

Justin grinned. "Then when you stay the night with me, they won't think that about you tomorrow morning. I'm the most wanted rakehell in town, remember?"

She pinched his side. "You are so conceited!"

He laughed.

"Did you have dinner already?"

"Barely—I didn't have the appetite," she replied.

Justin called room service. Then he gathered her in his arms and carried her to the bathroom.

"I can walk, you know," she said, staring up at him.

"Pretend you can't, so your new boyfriend will feel he's such a hero." He winked at her.

"New boyfriend? Did I say you passed the audition?"

He grinned. "Considering you screamed my name thrice, I think I just earned the right to claim that position."

Adrienne's face turned red and she pinched Justin's arm again.

"Ouch! Adrienne! Do you want me to drop you?" he asked, laughing.

"Don't you dare!"

He settled her down on the shower. He helped her remove the remaining pieces of her clothing and did the same to his. Then he gave her a mischievous smile and before Adrienne could ask what he was up to, he turned on the shower and Adrienne shrieked as the cold water hit her skin. He laughed and hugged her to him.

When she looked up at him, he looked like a playful little boy. His crystal blue eyes were dancing. She realized he was exactly like this in Alaska. This was Justin…unrestrained.

"I missed you so much." She leaned forward and kissed him on the lips.

"Really? What did you miss most about me?" he asked.

She smiled. "Your eyes."

"My eyes?" he echoed.

She nodded. "You always keep them hidden behind those shades of yours. Your face looks expressionless, sometimes, even cold. But your eyes are frequently dancing with laughter. I love the way you can be so serious and yet your eyes are very warm."

"Really? You were the first one who's noticed that."

"Maybe I was the first one who looked at them very closely." She smiled.

"Indeed, you are."

"You know… I was especially curious about the color of your eyes. I have…" She remembered the novel that she started writing after she moved into her apartment. She realized that she hadn't thought it since she met Justin.

"What?" he asked.

She blushed and turned away. But Justin knew her better.

He tilted her chin up. "What is it?"

She felt embarrassed to admit this. But she realized that she promised to trust him. And she should...no matter how small or embarrassing it could be.

"Well, you were a popular guy. My friends talk about you all the time. I thought you were cute and all, but I never fantasized about you. I just didn't understand why some girls would lose their breaths at the sight of you. And then...I discovered that you were my next-door neighbor. I grew fascinated by you. I decided to see what the fuss was about. I was... watching you sometimes...trying to see what you were like."

She stared back at him. She was watching if his expression would show signs of panic. She was scared that he would be screaming '*Stalker Alert! Stalker Alert!*' inside his head. But when she looked into his eyes, they were dancing again.

She smiled shyly. "I started writing a novel. And...I drew out the character after you."

He raised a brow. "Really? What type of novel?"

She shrugged. "Historical romance. You were a rogue knight. For sure you were a rakehell." She giggled.

He asked. "Was there a red-haired damsel in distress?"

She stared back at him. His eyes were sparkling. She nodded shyly.

"And how did that turn out?" he asked.

She shrugged. "I didn't finish it yet."

"Why?" he asked.

"I met you. And I haven't written a single word on it again."

"How do you think that will end?" he asked. She smiled because she felt that he actually seemed interested.

"I haven't thought about it yet," she said. "But I sure hope it would end in happily ever after."

He stared at her for a while and he sighed. Something crossed his face. A thought, an expression. But he pulled her to him too fast, she wasn't able to decipher it.

"I'm sure he would do everything he can to make sure it ends that way." He hugged her to him tightly, keeping her warm against the cold water pouring over their skin.

After the bath, Justin kissed her softly on the lips and then went out to answer the door.

She put on a fresh bathrobe and then towel-dried her hair.

When she went out, Justin had just finished setting the food he ordered from room service.

She realized that she didn't have clothes to wear.

"Oh my God. I'm gonna have to go to Kim's room after all."

"Why?"

"I don't have clothes to wear, Justin."

He went to her and wrapped his arms around her waist. Then he smiled mischievously. "You don't need any tonight."

She giggled. "Jus-tinn!"

He laughed. "Here." He handed her a bag. "I had room service deliver a fresh pair of underwear from their souvenir shop. They're dry cleaned already."

"Really? They do it that fast?"

"Considering I tripled the price, I'm sure they would do magic."

He handed her a white long-sleeve shirt from his closet. "I hope you don't mind wearing something of mine tonight." He smiled. "I'll call the shop again to have a bathing suit delivered up. Then tomorrow, I will go to your room to get the rest of your stuff."

"Thank you." She headed to the bathroom to dress up.

Justin studied her from head to toe when she emerged from the bathroom wearing his shirt.

"I look okay?"

He pulled her into his arms and kissed her. "You're a fox."

She smiled and kissed him back. She realized she missed hearing that line.

She laughed and kissed him back. Then he said, "I'm happy that you made a character out of me. To be honest with you, I was watching you whenever I can, as well. I knew you from *Blush*. You were snobbish. I was intrigued. And whenever you sat out on your balcony, it fascinated me to see you lost in your thoughts. I saw you talking on the phone and I couldn't make out the expression on your face. But now that I know you, I realized that during those times, you were talking to your ex-boyfriend or your mother."

"You can see my frustration from afar?"

He shrugged. "I didn't see your happiness. That's why I was so surprised to see you at Gypsys. Looking the way you did. And God! You looked so hot!"

"And I thought you wouldn't even recognize me, or remember me afterwards."

He laughed. "I was… short of stalking you whenever you're at home, to be honest. That's why it was so hilarious when you introduced yourself as Jamila McBride. I already knew a lot about you when I approached you that night."

"That night changed my life. It changed the way I looked at things. I got to appreciate myself more now." She looked at him. "Thank you, Justin Adams. For stepping into my life…when I wasn't even asking you to."

He smiled. "And thank you, Adrienne Miller. For looking at me in a different light." He leaned forward and kissed her lips gently. Then he said, "Come. Dinner's getting cold."

After dinner, they sat on the balcony and drank some beer.

"Tell me again what happened with your sister?"

"I came here to clear my mind. And to break up with Troy. When I couldn't find him in his room, I went back to mine and Kim's room. I found him there all right. Between Kim's legs."

Justin stared at her for a while. "Can your sister do any worse?" He shook his head. "Are you sure you have the same genes?"

She shrugged. "I don't know what I ever did to her."

"And this Troy character? What a loser! I don't understand what else he was looking for. He's got you. And you...are perfect just as you are."

"No, I'm not. For him, I would be a disgrace to his family. His brother married a hotshot lawyer, and he somehow couldn't accept the fact that he, on the other hand, will be marrying a vanity writer."

Justin shook his head. "Why? Did he expect his wife to make a living for him?"

"It was all ego for him."

Justin took a deep breath. "If a person...had the right to choose who he marries, he should marry for love. It's a privilege to be able to choose your own happiness. Doesn't he realize that? Not everything is about money and prestige. I would rather be penniless and married to the girl of my dreams."

Adrienne smiled. "Your parents must have been so in love with each other for you to think that way, in spite of who you are."

Justin looked away from her. It was a while before he spoke. "My father has always been Jac Adams. He inherited my grandfather's empire. But he was married to a woman that he was excited to go home to. A woman he felt content to be with...who stirred his blood, affected his senses, and challenged his intelligence."

"I'm sure they're happy."

Justin smiled and nodded. "Very. Every day I see them, they still look like they were newlyweds. My father adores my mother from head to foot."

"Your mother...what does she do?"

"She came from a good family, too. She didn't work a day in her life."

"By good, you mean...wealthy, powerful, decent."

Justin took a deep breath. He nodded. "Heiress to one of four companies her family owned. But she didn't have any interest in managing it. How could she be interested in mining?"

"So what happened to her family's business then?"

Justin gave her a serious look and then in a quiet voice he said, "It became part of Adams Industries."

"Your father acquired it?"

Justin nodded. "During that time, my father's family business was the biggest in the industry. Acquiring my mother's company made it even bigger."

"Your parents must be really lucky to find each other."

Justin sighed. "I don't believe in luck. You want it, you go for it." His voice became firm and sober.

Adrienne smiled. "No wonder you're branded as the rebellious heir of Adams Industries."

He grinned at her. He reached out for her hand. "I have a feeling I will always be."

"If your parents are so in love with each other, how come you were an only child?" she asked.

"When Jeffrey died, my mother didn't take it well. After a few years, they tried having another baby, they just…couldn't."

Adrienne squeezed his hand. "You would have been a wonderful brother. You're a wonderful cousin."

"I always wondered what Jeffrey would be like. Would he be as stubborn as I am? Would he defy Mom and Dad? Would he like the same things that I do? Would he rather be a businessman like I am now destined to be, or would he like to be a lawyer or a doctor, instead?"

She reached out and squeezed his hand again.

"You have a blessed life, Justin. You don't know how lucky you are. Maybe Jeffrey became your guardian angel. He would always look after you. Since you were the one who lived, he made sure your life would be a blessed one."

Justin stared at her eyes deeply, and she thought she saw a hint of tears in his eyes. He smiled and squeezed her hand back.

"I think you would have been better brothers than Kimberly and I were sisters," she added. "Our relationship is a pity, really. And worse, my parents didn't do anything about it. Somehow, I even think that the root of all this was my mother. When we were young, Kim would always want what was mine. No matter how cheap or shabby my little toys were, if she saw that I am happy with it, she would always try to get it from me. And my mother would always take her side." She looked at him. "I think Jeffrey would love you more than his life. I think that he would always be there for you. He would want what is best for you."

Tears rolled down her face. Justin rose from his seat and pulled her up gently and enclosed her in his arms. Then she lost it. She let him comfort her. She cried hard and hugged him tightly. He didn't say anything. He just allowed her to cry. He caressed her head while leaning a cheek against her forehead. He let her pour it all out, but through his embrace, he told her that he was there for her. That he would catch her when she fell. That with him, she would always be adored and appreciated.

19.

Nar

Arabic, meaning Fire

They got ready to sleep. By the foot of the bed, Adrienne watched Justin come closer to her. He took her face in both of his hands.

"My sweet, beautiful Adrienne..." he whispered.

Then he kissed her gently. He wrapped his arms around her waist. She kissed him back and wrapped her arms around his neck.

He unbuttoned the shirt she was wearing. And soon, they were kissing each other passionately. She took his shirt off. He nuzzled her neck. She moaned. She felt the familiar desire creeping in her every vein, slowly consuming her, blocking her senses.

Adrienne thought she wouldn't feel like this anymore. For days, she thought that all she could do was call Justin's memory to her mind, just so she could feel alive again. Because she thought it was over. That she had lost him forever.

She could hardly believe that she was back in his arms. And he ignited all of her passions again, arousing her until her mind went completely blank with need and longing.

"Justin," she whispered hoarsely. "Oh God! Justin, please..."

"I missed you so much, honey," he whispered hoarsely. They kissed each other, feeling the effects of the time they spent apart. They held on to each other, devouring each other with their kisses. "I wanted you so badly!" he said to her.

"Then take me, Justin!" she whispered hoarsely.

They fell to the bed and barely a second after, they were one. When he looked at her, his eyes were a shade darker. They were drugged with desire and consumed by passion. She felt familiar sparks creeping in her every vein, until it took her to the brink of insanity.

"Justin!" she screamed. His lips descended on hers and he swallowed her cries. Then he moved with more urgency until she heard him scream her name, "Adrienne, honey!" Then he hugged her tightly to his body and she felt his body rock.

When it was over, he looked up and stared at her deeply. He leaned down and kissed her lips gently.

"My Adrienne. Finally... my Adrienne..." he whispered.

She smiled at him weakly. He lay on his back and gathered her gently into his arms. He tilted her chin up and she gazed into his eyes.

"I'm sorry. I wasn't quite gentle. I've missed you so much, I almost feared that you weren't real."

She smiled. "Me, too. It's okay. I wanted you as much as you wanted me."

"We've got plenty of time to catch up on the time we've lost," he suggested.

She sighed. "I was stupid, Justin. I judged you. I guess, I was scared of your reputation in spite of knowing you better."

"I know," he responded. "But it's okay, honey. We're both here now."

She took a deep breath. "And since we're on the subject of your reputation, I need to ask you something, just to make it clear and to hear it from you directly."

"Okay. What is it?"

"Someone said you were clubbing with Tara Lambert."

He laughed. "I was not! I was out with my friends and she happened to know one of them. She was there at Oxygen. But no, I didn't dance with her. I didn't flirt with her. I didn't even exchange three sentences with her. All right?"

"You were talking to her this morning on the phone," she said.

He rolled his eyes. "Somehow, she got my number. I must remember to cripple whoever gave it to her." He looked at her for a moment. "If you heard me well enough, I even asked her first who she was. It means, I didn't have her number. And because I think you will ask anyway, I'm going to tell you now, that she was asking me how I was, blah, blah, blah. She asked me where I was, and I told her straight out that I was in the elevator with my girlfriend. But you hopped out of the lift too fast. I don't think you heard that." He smiled at her gently. "At that moment, I wanted to know what it felt like to call you my girlfriend."

"And?"

He kissed her lips gently. "It felt so damn good, I realized how badly I wanted it to be true."

"Oh, Justin. I'm sorry it took so long for us to get here."

"It doesn't matter. It's true now." He smiled at her. "And trust me, hon, I haven't been with any other woman since I met you. Before you, the last woman I've been with was named Jamila McBride. And I've been faithful ever since."

Adrienne laughed.

Then Justin added, "How could I talk to her, when all the time, I was cursing the day Ian slept over at my apartment?"

She laughed. "Why?"

"Because I almost lost you." He kissed her again. Then he chuckled. "I can't believe it! You were jealous."

"I was not!" she denied, pulling away from him.

He laughed and pulled her to him for a tight hug. "Too bad," he whispered. "I would have liked it if you were. Because I sure as hell wanted to punch the walls every time I think about Troy."

She laughed. "Okay, maybe I was jealous. A little," she admitted. "I mean when I saw Ian I was…stunned. I'm a woman… and I'm straight. But I thought, wow, she's so gorgeous!"

Justin laughed. "She better be! She's my flesh and blood."

Adrienne's eyes widened and she pretended to choke. "Help! I can't breathe! Your inflated head is taking up all the space in the room!"

Justin laughed harder and squeezed her to him again. "Come on! Don't I at least look a little bit cute to you?"

She rolled on top of him. "Cute is a huge understatement, actually." She smiled at him. "You're sinfully handsome." Then she leaned forward and kissed him until they were lost in the heat of love once again.

They made love again when they woke up in the morning. Adrienne sighed contentedly. She was happy. It was bliss.

Then she realized that her time was up. It was time to face Jill and Yuan, and then Kim and Troy.

She felt her heartbeat double its speed.

Justin rolled on top of her and looked down at her, studying her face.

"Honey, are you okay?" he asked.

She reached up to caress his hair. "I was thinking that…it's time to face the music."

Justin smiled at her apologetically. "You know I'm with you on this, right?"

She nodded. He leaned forward and kissed her. "Let's go have breakfast," she suggested.

"All right. But promise me we will come up here around noontime just so I could make love to my sweet and lovely Adrienne again."

She giggled. "I'm surprised you are saying that fifteen minutes after we just did."

He grinned. "I haven't been with you for more than a week, what do you expect? Do you think it was easy for me to run into you at *Blush*? To see you sulking in your office?"

"I wasn't sulking!" she protested, laughing.

He laughed. "Really? So the puffy eyes and the bad moods weren't because of me?"

She pinched him. "Lucky bastard!"

She wore a two-piece suit and a sarong was wrapped around her waist. They went down to the beach hand in hand.

They found Yuan and Jill already having breakfast in the restaurant. She nervously approached them.

"Hey guys," she greeted them.

"Yuan. Jill." Justin nodded at her friends.

Yuan and Jill smiled but didn't say anything.

Justin looked down at her, his eyes asking her if she wanted him to stay with her while she talked to her friends.

She took a deep breath and whispered, "I'll be fine."

"Okay. I'll go find Mike and James. I will be back in a while."

She nodded. Justin leaned down to give her a smack on the lips.

"I'll see you later guys," he said to Yuan and Jill before he left.

She sat down on the table. Yuan and Jill were just staring at her. They didn't speak…but if looks could kill, she'd be dead within a minute.

She took a cigarette from Jill's pack. At that moment, she could really use nicotine to calm her nerves.

Then she said, "All right. First of all, I wanted to say, I'm sorry. There is absolutely no valid excuse for what I did. I can't offer any specific explanations. But if you ask me your questions, I will answer them. Truthfully."

Yuan and Jill looked at each other for a while. Then Yuan leaned back on his seat and said. "First off. Are you still a virgin like we thought you were? Yes or no?"

Adrienne bit her lip. Then she shook her head.

"Thought so," Yuan murmured.

"Who was it?" Jill followed up.

Adrienne took a deep breath. "Justin."

"Did you ever sleep with Troy?"

Adrienne shook her head. "You know I didn't."

"Oh, I'm sorry!" Yuan began sarcastically. "We wouldn't know! Because all the while, we thought Troy was the boyfriend."

"You weren't the two-timing type, Adrienne. Who would have guessed, right?"

Adrienne didn't have anything to say to that. She didn't want to aggravate them further. She figured she would accept their anger because they deserved to lash out at her for lying to them for so long.

"You wanted to break up with Troy because of Justin, didn't you?" Jill inquired in an accusing tone.

She shook her head. "No. I broke up with Troy because I'm not in love with him. I haven't been for a very long time. And I don't even know if I really was in love with him in the first place or if I was just in love with the idea of being with a man that my mother approves of."

"How the hell did you hook up with Justin Adams?" Jill asked. "I work with you at *Blush*. We were always together when we go out. When we saw him in the bars, you didn't even stand less than five meters away from him. How could this happen?"

"He couldn't have met you just yesterday. He calls you honey," Yuan pointed out. "And you know what? He knows me. He hasn't even met me. And moreover, how the hell does Justin Adams know Troy?"

"Did you see his face when he was punching the life out of Troy? He was furious! He freaked out when he saw you were hurt! If he was just rescuing us, he wouldn't have felt so…involved with your fight with Troy! You can't just…have met him."

Adrienne took a deep breath. "Jill, remember you told me about some girl that Justin picked up at Gypsys?"

Jill nodded.

"That was me," she admitted. "I went alone for Gypsys' opening. I was drinking. I felt frustrated with Troy, my Mom. Justin approached me. Introduced himself, bought me a drink… things got out of hand…I ended up going home with him."

"Gypsys opened more than four months ago!" Jill exclaimed.

Adrienne nodded guiltily.

"You've been seeing each other for more than four months now!?" Jill asked. Her voice was full of shock.

"The shades in your apartment," Yuan interjected. "The same one he was wearing now. That was him who spent the night with you, wasn't it? It wasn't Troy."

She nodded. "I went to Gypsys. I was mad at my mother and at Troy. I felt like a total failure. I felt that no matter how hard I tried, they would never look at me in a different light. I will always be the inferior one. The less pretty, less smart second daughter. The black sheep of the family. So why bother? I dressed up in this sexy outfit that Jacob had picked for me. I drank a bit and didn't care that I was alone. He approached me. I pretended not to know him. I even gave him a fake name. Things happened fast, and I spent the night with him."

"You lost your virginity that night? After just hours of meeting him?"

Adrienne nodded shyly. At times, that part didn't really make her proud but she really was hopeless to resist Justin's charms.

"I thought that's all I'd ever have with him. One night. Make myself feel good in spite of Troy's and my mother's efforts to constantly shoot me down. I deserved Justin Adams. Even for just one night.

"Anyway, I was sure that he would forget about me the next day. He wouldn't even remember the fake name I gave him. But I was wrong. He showed up on my doorstep the following morning. Turned out, he knew who I was from the beginning. He even knew where I lived."

Jill raised a brow. "And how would he know where you live?"

She took a deep breath. "You know the guy next door to my apartment… torso god you called him. Well, that's Justin."

"Oh my God!" Jill sighed in frustration.

"So you went with him, and you gave him the virtue you've been saving up for Troy."

Adrienne took a deep breath. "I wasn't saving it for Troy. I was saving it for the right moment… the right guy."

Jill raised a brow. "And Justin Adams… the City's most wanted playboy seemed like the right guy? Well, I can't really say I blame you!"

"It's not just that, Jill." Adrienne said, trying to be calm. "Justin made me feel things I never felt before."

"I'm sure he did!" Yuan said. "He wouldn't be a rakehell for nothing, you know."

"Would you please just listen to me!" Adrienne finally raised her voice, which silenced her friends.

Adrienne took a deep breath. "You see... I got tired of my life. I realized I've been living each day for all the wrong reasons. One night. I decided to just finally live it for my own! And my paths crossed with Justin. I felt this... this sense of need that I couldn't control...that I haven't felt with Troy before. I actually forgot that I was a virgin, until he...until he was in me."

She stared back at them. They listened to her quietly. Their silence encouraged her to go on.

"I wanted to feel guilty. I knew it was wrong. I had spent one night...in sin...with the City's most notorious playboy," she said. "But I didn't feel guilty at all. I felt like... for once in my life, I did something right. I did something that made me happy... regardless of what others would think about me. But I never intended for it to happen again."

"It was supposed to be just a one-night stand?" Jill asked.

She nodded. "It started out to be a one night thing. And yet, he showed up in my apartment the next day. And then again the following day. Until...we just saw more and more of each other. I couldn't believe that I lost my virginity to Justin Adams. And I had planned to stop. I knew that after a day, he would forget about me but he didn't. He was persistent. He...pursued me. Until I got more and more attached to him."

She looked at her friends. "Guys...the real Justin Adams is far... from the playboy we all thought he was. He is sweet. And caring. He brought out the best in me. He made me feel cared for. He appreciated me for who I was... the way Troy never did. Not even once. He taught me how to trade stocks. He spent almost every night in my apartment. I couldn't seem to get rid of him."

"Why didn't you tell us?" Yuan asked.

She shrugged. "There could be absolutely no excuse for what I did and didn't do."

"He didn't want it to go public," Yuan said. "He was the one who didn't want people to know. That would make sense. Justin Adams wanted to keep his reputation of being a bachelor."

Adrienne shook her head. "No. It was me. And it annoyed him so much. Once when you went to my place, we had an argument. Because he didn't want to hide anymore. He was getting tired of being kept a secret. He felt insulted every time I wondered if he would stick around for a long time.

"I tried telling you, too. But you laughed at me. You thought it was the biggest joke on earth. And then you told me, Jill, that if you were to find out, it would ruin our friendship. I got so scared of losing you guys.

"I just didn't know what to do. I never expected Justin Adams to be...a relationship type of guy. But that's what we had for months. Troy may have been the official boyfriend. But Justin was...the real one. He was the one I spent my nights with and told my dreams and frustrations to. I never expected him to be so much different from what we know about him."

"Justin mentioned about the best date he ever had. Northern Lights in Alaska?" Yuan asked.

Adrienne slowly nodded. "Yes. That weekend I told you I was going to Boston, Justin actually took me to Alaska. He wanted to be with me without my fear of being named or being seen with him."

"Oh God!" Yuan breathed. "How many lies did you tell us, Adrienne? We were your best friends!"

"I know. And I'm really sorry."

"That day you crashed over my apartment, you weren't fighting with Troy either, were you?"

Adrienne shook her head. "When Kim spent the night at my place, the next morning, I went to Justin's apartment and some blonde opened the door and I thought, he was with another girl..."

"But it was his cousin," Jill finished for her.

Adrienne nodded. "Yeah. He called me, sent me messages, even talked to me at *Blush*. He wanted to explain. I didn't want to listen. I realized that I still believed his notorious reputation in spite of knowing him better. I was so stupid."

"That's why he told me the reason why he broke up with the girl he was seeing. But he told me not to print it. He knew I might talk about it with you or you might see the video. That was his way of letting you know what really happened that night," Jill realized, thoughtfully.

"Now, that makes sense! How else would he be confiding in you like you were BFFs?" Yuan said to Jill and Jill actually glared at him.

"His car plate. I-E-N-N-E. It was short for Adrienne, after all," Jill mused.

Adrienne nodded. "Before we fought, he said he had a surprise for me. But we never got to that part. I even thought that the car belonged to the girl I found in his apartment that morning. But then, I think I've always known what he meant when he got that plate. I just stubbornly refused to believe it. I didn't think that he would do that for me. That I was worth it."

Adrienne stared at her friends ruefully. "Guys, I'm sorry. I didn't know how to deal with it. It was something that I didn't expect to last. I thought it was nothing serious. Because Justin Adams wasn't known to be serious. But now...I know this is real. For the last four months we've been together, I can say that I couldn't ask for anything more from a man. He is everything I want, everything I was asking for in my prayers. If you thought the Justin Adams you knew was drool and swoon-worthy...well the real Justin Adams happens to be much more than that. He's worth falling head over heels in love with... over and over again."

"And have you fallen in love with him?" Jill asked.

Adrienne took a deep breath and nodded. "Hopelessly."

"Does he love you back?" Yuan asked.

She shrugged. "I know that we want to be with each other. I never asked him to be with me, to stay with me, but somehow at the end of each day, I wind up in his arms. I know that I'm important to him. When I got mad, I saw the efforts he made to get me back. Last night, when Troy hit me, I saw the rage on his face. I know he cares about me. He said he's crazy about me. He didn't say the 'L' word. But for now, that's good enough."

Yuan and Jill stared at her for a moment and then Jill said, "You let us talk about him and Tara Lambert! How could you have endured that?"

Adrienne giggled humorlessly. "That wasn't fun. I wanted to cry, but I had to keep a straight face. That was tough."

"But just so you know, my friends, who write gossip columns, did confirm that Justin Adams was ignoring Tara Lambert. She chased him. But he seemed to her a slippery fish to catch."

"And now, we know why," Yuan said. "At first, we thought that Justin just wasn't interested in a relationship because he's just a big-time player who couldn't be tied down. But now...we know why he was single. He was waiting for the one. And it's you."

"He wants me, I know. I don't know for how long, though. But I don't care. For once in my life, a guy wants me with every fiber of his soul. And he happens to be a god! And I feel good about myself. All my life, I believed I wasn't worthy... that I wouldn't attract a man who's more than good enough for me."

"That was your mother talking," Yuan began. "But you are pretty and smart. You've got this appeal that draws men to your feet. But you were raised believing that Kimberly defined beauty. Yet, she won't even hold a candle to you, Adrienne. You overlooked the fact that you have your own charm."

"And you wasted years trying to make the Troy thing work," Jill added. "We never believed it would. You needed a guy who could challenge your spirit to come out. Not clip your wings and make you stiffer than you already were."

"So now...you and Justin?" Yuan finally asked. His voice lacked the trace of anger now.

Adrienne smiled. "Yes. He said he didn't want to be the sideline guy anymore. And he doesn't deserve to be." She took a deep breath. "I love him, guys. There's just no...turning back for me anymore. I don't care about what my Mom will think. I don't care if she curses me all my life. For once...I just feel like I'm fighting for what I want... what I believe in."

Adrienne looked at her friends again. "I'm really sorry. I hope you will be able to forgive me."

Jill and Yuan looked at each other. Then they looked at Adrienne soberly.

"Well, I guess it's not entirely your fault," Yuan said. "If we didn't gossip about Justin a lot or if we didn't laugh at you the first time you attempted to tell us, then you would have the guts to come clean."

Jill had tears in her eyes. "You know that I was only kidding when I said that hooking up with Justin and not telling us would be a friendship ender, right?"

Tears welled up in Adrienne's eyes. "Oh, guys! I'm really sorry!"

Jill and Yuan stood up from their seats and gave Adrienne a hug.

"Oh, honey, if you're happy, we're happy," Jill said. "Just don't get hurt, okay? And we're here for you. I mean, Justin is known to be a playboy, yes. But he never seemed committed to anyone. Never been seen with one woman exclusively. And look at what he was doing here with you, Yen? It's like telling the world that what we know about him were all lies. That he's human after all. And to tell you the truth, we knew it was serious when we saw his face last night, when he saw that you were hurt."

"And if he ever hurt you, I will be the first one to kick his ass! Or at least...I would try," Yuan said. He was tearful, too.

"So, I'm guessing, murder plans are off the table now?" They heard Justin ask behind them.

Jill and Yuan both stared at him for a second and then they smiled.

"Well, if you hurt her, it will come back faster than you can blink," Yuan said.

Justin sat on the chair beside Adrienne and put an arm around her. "I will remember that," he said to Yuan in a serious tone and then he kissed Adrienne's forehead. "I'm starving. Why don't we order? Do you mind if I join you guys?"

"Go ahead," Yuan said.

Justin ordered breakfast for all of them.

"Thank you for coming to our rescue last night, Justin," Yuan stated. "I realized then that I couldn't stand up to that lunatic."

Justin shrugged. "Thank you for trying to protect Adrienne, in every possible way you could."

Yuan laughed. "You are welcome. She's our best friend. I will rise up to the occasion, when needed. But still, that guy was a psycho, and the fact that he was drunk made him bolder and stronger than me."

"I thought the fact that he was drunk made it easier for me to put him down," Justin said.

"No, I don't think that is true—you have martial arts training in your profile," Jill pointed out.

"But I wasn't supposed to use that to assault raging, drunk lunatics."

"He deserved it."

"Although, I've been wanting to do that to him for a while now," Justin admitted, looking at Adrienne.

"Oooh, Justin Adams is a jealous guy," Jill said, with a teasing grin.

"Speaking of which, who was that moron you had a meeting with at Lever du Soleil?" Justin asked Adrienne.

"Who? Jin Starck?"

Justin nodded. His face tightened a bit.

"He's a client, Justin."

Yuan and Jill looked at Adrienne for a moment and she knew exactly what they were thinking. Adrienne felt guilty. In truth, Jin Starck is a really nice guy but she never felt that he had become interested in her romantically. But still…she started this relationship with Justin with lies. She wanted none of that in the future.

"After we fought in my office, I got drunk at a bar. He ran into me there."

Justin stared at her for a moment. He didn't say anything. He waited for her to continue.

"Justin… he's not interested in me. In fact, he gave me good advice. He made me realize that that I was wrong about you. That I should have trusted you."

Justin raised a brow. "Hmmm… interesting," he murmured. "I'll send him my compliments in the future then."

"You have martial arts training?" Yuan asked, changing the topic.

He nodded. "Since I was young. Either I mastered some arts and appear capable enough to defend myself or my grandfather will stuff me with bodyguards. And I didn't want to look like a wimp."

"It was quite handy that you happened to be here," Jill noted. "You didn't tell me that you were coming here when I ran into you yesterday."

Justin smiled sheepishly. "Actually, I didn't plan to come until then."

Adrienne blushed and hid her face partly in Justin's shoulder. Justin gave her a squeeze.

"I have been wanting to meet you guys, for months now. Did Adrienne tell you that?" he asked Yuan and Jill.

They nodded.

"We were shocked, actually. We never had a clue."

"And you forgave her too easily?" he questioned, teasingly.

He received a playful pinch on his side.

"Ouch!" He laughed.

"She's still going to pay for it," Yuan said brightly. "This will not go without punishment."

"I'm sure," Justin responded. "I'm just glad that the secret is out in the open now. Honestly, I don't want to cross that platform between our bedrooms anymore when I could conveniently use the door."

Adrienne couldn't help laughing at that. He smiled at her and leaned down to give her a quick kiss on the lips.

"Where are your friends?" Jill asked.

"On the beach. Busy scouting some chicks, I think."

"Has Adrienne met them?" Yuan asked.

He shook his head. "No. They've been dying to, though. But Adrienne was ashamed of her association with me."

Adrienne pinched his side. "I'm not! How long before that gets old?"

Justin laughed. "Probably a long time, honey."

Yuan and Jill smiled at Adrienne happily. And Adrienne couldn't help smiling back at them. She knew that they're truly happy for her. And at that same time, she felt that Jin Starck just might be right. From now on, she had a better life to look forward to. With these three people on her side, fighting with her, she doesn't have to feel scared and defeated.

She stared up at Justin. His eyes were dancing. Then he leaned forward and whispered in her ear, "You're a fox!"

JERILEE KAYE

20.
Incandescere
Latin. Etymology of Incandescent

After breakfast, Adrienne remembered that no matter how hard she tried to avoid Troy and Kim, she has nothing to wear for the rest of the weekend. And she couldn't go buying stuff from the hotel shop. Yes, Justin could afford it, but she wouldn't allow him to keep buying her clothes.

"I'll pay up for your room till noon," Justin offered. "I don't want Troy to think you owe him anything when you leave. You will be staying with me now."

"I'll pay you back."

"Useless. Come on, it's a small price to pay for spending the rest of the weekend with you." He kissed her.

Justin went to the reception and she went up to her room to get her stuff and say a few things to Kim, if necessary.

When she got to the room, Kim wasn't there. She started gathering her things. But after a minute, Kim entered, with Troy.

She swallowed.

Awkward!

"You're leaving?" Kim asked in a bored tone.

She shook her head. "No. Justin checked out this room already. It's paid up until twelve. You guys can just rebook it if you want." She tried her best to be casual.

"Who is he, Adrienne?" Troy asked quietly.

"None of your business now, Troy," she said angrily. "Sue him if you want, I could always go on the witness stand and say that he just came before you beat the life out of me."

"I'm not stupid, Adrienne," Troy responded. "I know what I did. And even if you don't believe me, I am sorry. I didn't mean for things to get out of hand. I didn't mean to get too drunk."

"So you mean to tell me, you can beat a helpless girl and the fact that you are drunk gives you the right to do so?"

She stared at him. His nose looked broken, and he had a shiner on both eyes. He did look pretty beaten up. And she didn't feel the least bit sorry for him. In fact, she suppressed the urge to laugh.

"So all along there was another guy lurking in the shadows?" Kim asked.

Oh, really? She's going to pin this on me?

She couldn't even begin to decipher what a sorry piece of trash her sister really was. *How did I end up with this family?* She felt fury coming back to her.

She took a deep breath and stopped herself before she could cross the room and haul Kimberly by her pretty blond hair.

"Just like there was another girl lurking in the shadows all along, right, Troy?"

Troy closed his eyes. He fell quiet.

Guilt! Guilt! Guilt!

"Never mind. We didn't need to cheat on each other to realize that this was going nowhere. We were nothing for a very long time. But you know what? Yesterday, before I broke up with you, I still hoped we could at least be friends. But I guess that's out the window now!"

"Fine!" Troy threw his hands in the air. "Who is he anyway? What kind of guy did you replace me with? Can he even give you the life your mother wants for you?"

She wanted to laugh. Clearly, Troy thought his profession and wealth was a trump card. "This is not about money, or profession, Troy. This is about dignity and fidelity. Don't you get that? But I guess you wouldn't. For you it's all about prestige and fame and success. Regardless if there's misery underneath! You two really deserve each other."

Troy stared at her. She couldn't make out the expression on his pretty banged up face. And she didn't care.

"It was over even before I found you humping my big sister. I had decided to end us. It was over a long time ago. And not just because of him."

Adrienne turned to Kim. "You know I only made Mom proud just once. And that was when I dated Troy. And you weren't happy about it. You always made sure you made better choices than me. Now, go ahead. You can have Troy. You didn't have to steal him so deceitfully, you know! You could have just asked! I would have given him to you on a silver platter!"

"And what will you tell Mommy? I took the surgeon away from you, that's why you ended up with that guy... who looked like a brainless model? Come on, Adrienne. I will not let you make me look bad. If you were ending things with Troy, I won't let you tell our parents that it was because I slept with him!"

She laughed sarcastically. "No. Don't worry. I won't do that. Nothing I say can taint your spotless reputation in Mom's eyes, anyway. But you're filthy, Kimberly. And someday, all of this hypocrisy is going to bite you in the ass!"

Adrienne finished packing her bags.

"You know what? I can forgive Troy for cheating on me. Hell! I was cheating on him, too! At least I was brave enough to admit that. We never slept together, anyway. We pretended to be in a relationship. And it wasn't going anywhere. But you? I could accept it if he slept with any other girl. But my own sister? While we haven't broken up yet? That's too damn low, Kim. Even for you!"

She grabbed her stuff. "And since I have always been the villain in mother's eyes, I would just tell her that I didn't really want the surgeon. She wanted him for one of her daughters. She wanted him for you, I remember. But I ended up with the trophy, didn't I? And I bet that was killing you, huh, Kim!"

For once, Kim didn't have anything to say to her. Adrienne saw guilt cross her face, confirming what she already knew. Kim had always been out to get Troy…because she couldn't admit that she lost him to her.

"Don't worry. I will tell Mom I am so sick of everybody around me being a doctor! And I found a man who is a hundred times better than what she could have imagined for me." She turned to Troy. "I hope you manage to hold on to Kim after I'm gone. I think... and this is just a hunch…that she was only interested in you because you were mine! But how will you manage to keep it together this time?" The concern on her face was fake, and she was taunting him with something that he might have already known.

Both Kim and Troy looked away from her. They also refused to look at each other and Adrienne knew she hit them spot on!

She took her bags and started for the door. But before she went out, she turned back to them.

"And oh, by the way…his name is Justin Adams. He does look like a model. But he's not brainless. He's a straight A Harvard graduate, a Wall Street genius, and soon he's going to be the CEO of Adams Industries." She couldn't disguise the pride in her voice. "And Kim…if you ever, ever seduce my boyfriend like you did with Troy, I swear to God, I will make sure you won't be able to attract another male in your entire life again! And too bad for you neither of our parents are plastic surgeons!" And then she closed the door behind her with a bang.

She took deep breaths. She was reeling with anger. She didn't know where she got the courage to say all the things she said. But she was glad she said them. For once in her life, she stood up for herself in front of Kim and Troy.

When she looked up, she found herself staring at Justin. Suddenly, she felt nervous. She told them who he was. It sounded like she was bragging about who he was. She didn't know he was listening outside the door, which was left ajar by Kim and Troy when they entered.

He stared at her seriously, and Adrienne feared he would get mad at her for involving him in the conversation. Then he said in a sober voice, "Number one, I don't find your sister half as attractive as you are. Number two, I'm not as dumb as Troy. Number Three, I may have the reputation of a player, but I never cheat."

She stared back at him. "Justin, I'm sorry…"

He smiled at her. Then he pulled her into his arms. "Sorry for what?"

"For involving you in the conversation…for telling them who you were…"

He shook his head. "It sounded to me like they were pinning the cheating thing on you, and overlooking the fact that you caught them in bed together."

She nodded. "Oh God Justin, how could I feel this much hatred for two people who I thought were very important to me?"

"Sshh...sometimes, you have to see that you matter more than anyone else," he began softly. "Especially, when you weren't treated with the love and respect you deserve. And I'm proud of you, honey. For standing up for yourself. For fighting back. And it's good to hear you stake your claim on me for a change. And God, your feisty self is so damn sexy!"

They went to their room holding hands.

Justin kissed her thoroughly as soon as he closed the door behind him. And true to his word, he made love to her again.

When they went down, Adrienne met Mike and James at the lobby.

"Guys, this is Adrienne," Justin said softly.

"Finally! I have been wanting to meet the woman who achieved something we thought was impossible." Mike smirked, teasing his friend

"Which is?" Adrienne asked curiously.

"Giving in to the pull of attraction. Defying the rules of gravity." James had joined in on the teasing.

"Ha-ha! You're very funny," Justin said sarcastically. He gave James a murderous look and before Adrienne could react or ask further, her friends made an appearance.

She introduced Yuan and Jill to Justin's friends.

They spent the whole day with Mike, James, Yuan and Jill. They swam on the beach, played volleyball and pool. That night, they partied in the bar.

She had the time of her life. She felt freer than before. She loved being able to hug Justin anytime she wanted. And it looked like he felt the same. He seemed keen on showing the world what they have. That they belong together. When she went to the ladies' room, he walked with her and waited for her at the door. Then they walked back hand in hand towards their table.

"Do you always do that?" she asked him.

"Do what?"

"Wait for a girl outside the ladies' room."

He shrugged. "Probably. But you never gave me plenty of chances before."

She smiled and pinched him on his side jokingly.

"Owww!" He laughed.

That night, they made love slowly, passionately. Like they were savoring each second that they had together.

She went through the whole week with a smile on her face. She asked Jill and Yuan not to say anything about Justin to their other friends. She wanted to keep it low-profile. He was still somewhat a celebrity. And the last thing she wanted was for rumors to ruin what they had.

She'd been sleeping over Justin's apartment since the night they returned from the resort. They were spending each and every night together.

He took her to the office and picked her up every day. He would take her out to dinners, sometimes fancy, sometimes fast food. He took her to the movies one time, and that Friday, they returned to Gypsys.

"Now, we arrive together. I hope you don't mind if I buy you a drink, flirt with you on the dancefloor, kiss you and take you home with me again." His eyes twinkled mischievously, reminiscing the first night they met.

She laughed. "I would love that."

She had seven shots of tequila. He took her home on his Ducati motorcycle, just like the first night they met.

"This is very familiar," she teased.

He laughed. In the elevator, he took her in a passionate kiss. They half-ran to his apartment, and as soon as he shut the door behind him, he grabbed her by the waist and kissed her again.

After a few minutes, they were in bed, naked.

She smiled at him. "This time, you can't hurt me."

He nodded. "You're not a virgin anymore, honey. And I intend to give you only pleasure."

And he kept his promise. When they were done, she felt completely satisfied. She felt beautiful. She felt like a woman.

It felt like reliving the memories of that night. But this time, she knew the man. She trusted him. She was completely in love with him.

She also felt glad that she wore Jacob's outfit that very first night she went to Gypsys. That she had decided not to be prim and proper for once.

She may have done all the things she did that night for all the wrong reasons, but at that moment…she knew that she's in Justin's arms for all the right ones.

JERILEE KAYE

21.
Obligación
Spanish for Obligation

"You seemed glowing, Adrienne. Something you're not telling us?" Cynthia, one of her officemates asked her when she and the girls were chatting at the corridor.

Adrienne shook her head. "No. Not really. I just feel better than any other day in my life, that's all."

At the same moment, Justin appeared on the corridor.

She looked at him. He stopped by her side. She didn't say anything, quite uncertain how she should behave with him in front of her other female colleagues. The same ones who drooled over him.

She was surprised when he put his arms around her waist.

"Pick you up after work?" he asked.

She smiled shyly and nodded. Then he bent down and gave her a quick kiss on the lips. Then he looked at the other girls and said, "Have a nice day, ladies."

When he was gone, all the girls in front of her were open-mouthed and wide-eyed, except for Jill.

"What the hell..." Cynthia started.

"Okay, so you're the mystery girl?" Anna, the receptionist asked.

"Mystery girl?" Adrienne echoed.

"Well, when Ivan, Garry's new assistant, asked Justin to go clubbing with him where he'd introduce him to some girls, he told him he can't because he has a girlfriend."

Girlfriend.

That word made her heart skip a beat. She's Justin Adams's girlfriend when he was known to dodge commitments any chance he got. And now...he's hers. Somehow, she still couldn't believe that all this was happening to her.

"That's why you are in full bloom! You're shagging a god!"

"Cynthia!" Adrienne knew she was red as an apple.

"This is very interesting," Anna said. "I never thought that guy could settle down."

"We're seeing each other. We're not getting married," Adrienne stated.

"So, the IENNE on his car plate is actually short for Adrienne?" Cynthia asked with a shocked expression on her face.

"Yes!" Jill replied. "Trust me girls. They only have eyes for each other. You should see them together. It's like you are a painting on the wall. They just look at you, but you are inanimate and you don't really exist." Jill smiled.

"And you didn't tell us about this, Jill. I can't believe you!"

"I didn't know until last week, to be honest," Jill responded. "Apparently, they've been seeing each other for more than four months now." Adrienne glared at her.

"What kind of gossip columnist are you?" Anna asked Jill.

"It made me feel bad about my abilities. Both as a gossip columnist and as her best friend."

"Come on, Jill. You already forgave me for it. You already know about it now." Adrienne giggled.

"Yes. Along with the rest of the world. You never let me savor the moment for myself."

Adrienne put an arm around Jill. "Don't forget, I am treating you and Yuan big time for this," she whispered.

"Oh right. I have a right to shut up after all." Jill smiled.

They talked about going to Boston. Adrienne wanted a break and try to see her father on a weekend. Yuan and Jill would go with her—on Adrienne's treat.

"This is big!" Cynthia said. "There will be at least two guys in this office who will be heartbroken with this information. How could they compete against Justin Adams? And it's not just a flirting kind of thing, it seems. It looks serious."

"Come on, ladies. We're just taking one day at a time," Adrienne said and then she went back to her office.

She got an email from Jill after a few minutes.

To: amiller@blush.ny
Fr: jdurmont@blusy.ny
Subject: You!

You have to wake up already! You're not dreaming this thing you have with Justin. It's real! And you deserve it.

All of us can see that both of you are head over heels for each other!!!

Even Mike thought so. He actually told me that Justin suddenly stopped being interested in women months ago. They could only conclude two things. Either he's turned gay or he's got it bad for one girl. And that girl turned out to be you! You're so lucky, dear!

And to kiss you in front of a crowd like that?

Wow! Knowing that Justin Adams had been slippery and evasive with women...and now he's suddenly mushy and romantic.

Mike says you are all he talks about! And that plate in his car is like advertising to the whole city that he's not single anymore.

He's in love with you! He hasn't said it straight out. But I bet you,

you should be prepared to be Mrs. Justin Adams in the future!

Jill

Adrienne smiled and replied:

To: jdurmont@blush.ny"
Fr: amiller@blush.ny
Subject: Re: You!

Jill,

Thanks!
I AM head over heels with him and I know he's crazy about me. I don't know if he wants to marry me, but I don't care about that yet.
What's important is that we are with each other and I'm happy. I'm not thinking about how this will end. Because that's how we started anyway. Not thinking how it will end and how long it will last.
I am just happy and thankful for him. And yes, I do feel lucky! I feel blessed every minute I am with him.
Happy?

Yen

Justin's Porsche was parked in front of her building when she went out of the office.

She gave him a kiss on the lips when she went in.

"How's work?" he asked.

"Great. How about you?"

He shrugged. "Met with some of Dad's accountants. Made some money on stocks. I'm thinking of just keeping the blue chips now. I don't want to do risky playing anymore. I won't be able to focus on it when I start with Dad's companies."

She nodded. "I think that's a very sound choice."

He smiled. "My priorities have changed. I'm done goofing around."

"You don't look like you're goofing around, hon. You actually made so much for yourself, just goofing around."

He chuckled. "Actually, thanks to you."

"Me?"

He nodded. "Remember we were talking at the balcony that night we got back together?"

She nodded.

"You told me that Jeffrey was looking over me. That he made sure I had a blessed life. I figured, I wouldn't want to let him down. I thought that if he were me, he wouldn't want to waste our legacy. He would feel duty-bound and honor-bound to help Dad run the business. And since I was the one who lived, I am the one who will carry that out…for both of us."

Tears threatened to pool in Adrienne's eyes.

"That's why, I thank you, hon. For making me realize how lucky I am. And that in return, I shouldn't be avoiding my obligations to my family. I owe it to my father for giving me the life I have now. I owe it to Jeffrey. I'm living both our lives. And I want to make it worth it. I want to make him proud."

She squeezed his hand. "I'm happy for you, Justin."

"I am happy, too. And I'm lucky to have you, honey."

"Really? As far as I know, you were doing just fine before we met"

He shook his head. "I thought I was fine. But when I met you, I realized that some people have to work to be appreciated. I never did. I never felt that my family's trust in me wavered. I couldn't believe that someone like you, who's beautiful, smart and successful would think so little of herself. That you couldn't see all the wonderful things that make you—you. Make you perfect. You made me see the things that I have been taking for granted. And it's time to make things right. While it's not yet too late."

She squeezed his hand again. "Thank you, Justin. For making me love myself the way I do now."

He took her hand and kissed it. "And thank you. For making me love the things I have the way I do now."

"So where are we going?" she asked.

It took him a moment to reply. "I'll just drop you off. I…actually need to go back to Chicago tonight."

"Everything all right?" she asked.

He looked at her for a while. Then he said, "Yeah. Peachy."

She traced a hint of worry in his voice. But she didn't want to pressure him. And besides, he's Justin Adams. She's sure that whatever worried him, he'd find a solution for it.

She thought about Justin's parents. The man who looked so much like his son, and the beautiful heiress he married made this wonderful man she found herself now head over heels in love with.

"You look a lot like your Dad." She wondered out loud.

"And he looks exactly like my grandfather," Justin said. "People say it's because they married women who were head over heels in love with them, and not with their money. Thus, their heirs had inherited exactly their physical features. But it's all just very dominant genes, to be honest."

Adrienne laughed. "Maybe my Mom wasn't very in love with my Dad then."

Justin laughed. "Yeah. Like I said, it's just genes."

"Kimberly and my mother look the same. They both have blond hair. My father's hair is dark brown. So I guess, I look like my dad."

"Where did the red highlights come from?" he asked.

She shrugged. "Genes skipping generations and landing on me, I guess."

"They look great on you. Added a foxier effect." He winked at her.

She laughed. "I wish my mother looked at it that way. She believes it makes me look like a harlot."

Justin shook his head. "It's pretty. And it's you. It's part of what makes you…you."

"Glad you liked it. Otherwise, I would dye it back to plain brown again."

Justin laughed. "No, honey. You're perfect just as you are."

"Your parents are still so in love with each other. I couldn't say that my parents act like they were crazily in love with each other."

"I envy my parents for what they have. My Dad grew up with business instilled in him by my Grandpa. He didn't have much fun in his life. He was always so responsible, strong and focused. But when he met my Mom, he went out of his skull."

"Who wouldn't? Your mother is absolutely stunning."

"And she's smart too. When they met, she was twenty-three years old, and my Dad was twenty-five. They were married within the same year."

"Really? That young?"

Justin nodded. "Makes sense to me. I don't believe in marrying at an older age. Two people in love can get married as early as they want. If they feel they are right for each other, what's the point in waiting? I don't believe that you find your soul mate when you reach a certain age. She comes, she comes. And it's up to you if you will hold on to her or let her go. And as far as I know, you will always regret it if you let her go."

She stared at Justin, quite unable to believe what she's hearing.

"I admire you, Justin. Not all guys think the way you do. Actually, I never thought that would be your point of view. I mean, before I met you, I thought, you were just playing around. But I know now, Justin Adams really is just a name. The guy underneath is ten times the man who wears the name tag."

He smiled. "I've had my share of fun. I told you, I'm done goofing around. You taught me how to look at things in a different light."

Justin dropped her off their building. He gave her a thorough kiss when he walked with her towards the elevators.

"I'll see you in two days," he told her. Then he sighed. "This is gonna be so difficult!"

"Why?"

"I didn't want to leave you this early. I mean… we've just been officially together for about week."

"Officially, huh," she repeated.

"I'm not going back to the sidelines again, honey. I patiently waited there. Somebody should actually build me a monument!" He chuckled.

"Yes," she said. "And thank you, Justin. For waiting for me to come around," She kissed his lips gently.

He leaned his forehead against hers. "Maybe... next time... you could come to Chicago with me."

She stared back at me. "What?"

He shrugged. "Let me... let me prep my family first," he said. "They're not really used to me having a girlfriend. Never introduced a girl to them before. But I'm thinking... it's time I introduce you."

She smiled. She felt really happy. But at the same time, she felt nervous. She really hoped his parents would like her. She knew she wasn't an heiress like his mother was, but she hoped that his parents would accept her. Because she sincerely loved their son.

When she got back to her apartment, her phone was ringing. She ran to get it.

"What did you do to Kimberly, Adrienne?" her mother asked angrily. "And you were cheating on Troy? What a disgrace! I did not raise you to be a slut! How could you embarrass us like this?!"

Before she could say something, she heard a click on the other line and her father spoke. She realized that her father picked up the extension line to join in their conversation.

"Adrienne, I'm sure you would have a good explanation for this," her father said.

"Dad..." Tears rolled down her cheeks. She could strangle Kim for turning this against her.

"If you didn't love Troy anymore, then you should have been honest with him about it. Kimberly told us that your other boyfriend was at the resort, too. And he beat the hell out of Troy."

"His parents are quite mad! They're thinking of filing a lawsuit but they couldn't understand why Troy refused to do it!" She heard her mother say.

"Troy was going to propose to you, sweetheart. That's why the whole family was going there."

Propose? Is Troy crazy? He must be delusional to think that I would say yes.

"But he cancelled everything. Said he changed his mind," her father said. "And then, they came back to Boston and he's got a broken nose and a shiner."

"Dad, this isn't all my fault..."

"Who's the guy, Adrienne?" her mother asked. "You, ungrateful girl! I was trying to look out for you! Troy is your best chance at life. You wouldn't make it on your own! Your only chance is to marry somebody who could give you a good life!"

"Wait a minute, Marina," her father said. "Let's give her a chance to explain."

"Dad, I'm not in love with Troy. It would be wrong to continue being with him. I wasn't happy!" she said in between tears.

"When you get married to a good for nothing bastard like your boyfriend now, then you would really be miserable! He'll just get you pregnant and then leave you because he has no means to support you!"

"Mom!" Adrienne raised her voice. "Justin is not good for nothing! He's ten times the man that Troy was and will ever be!"

"And how can you say that? How well do you know him?!"

"Almost everybody knows him!" Adrienne replied. She was getting frustrated. "You want to know why Troy didn't want to file a lawsuit, Mom? Because he knows he couldn't go against Justin Adams and win! Justin could afford the best lawyers in the country and the fact that I will testify against him will make it a sure loss!"

"Justin Adams?" her father echoed. "That's your boyfriend's name?"

Adrienne sighed. "Yes, Daddy."

"Justin Adams as in Jac Adams's son?"

Pride swelled in Adrienne's heart. "Yes."

"What? You know this guy?" Her mother seemed surprised.

"If you read business news and Forbes' magazines, Marina, you would know who he is. They own Adams Industries. Adrienne, your boyfriend is… a billionaire. A third-generation billionaire."

"It's a common name! Maybe we're not even talking about the same person!" her mother hissed.

"We're talking about the same person, Mom. My boyfriend is the heir of Adams Industries. I'm sure of it. He's quite famous here in Manhattan. And I've been on his private jet, so there's no doubt he is what Dad says he is."

"Oh! So that was your plan all along?! Troy wasn't good enough, then?"

"Mom, why are you doing this to me?" she asked, unable to stop the tears now. "I wasn't happy with Troy. I was miserable! We don't match! Can't you just please be happy for me for once? I'm going for the guy I love, the guy who made me complete! That's what marriages are all about. Even if I didn't have an… affair with Justin, I still wouldn't have said yes to Troy. Because he's not the guy for me! He's the guy you want for me!"

Her mother fell silent for a while. Then her father said, "Adrienne…come to Boston when you have time. Let's talk about this as a family. There are matters that we cannot discuss over the phone."

Adrienne suppressed a whimper. "Okay, Dad. I love you."

Then she hung up. She sat on the floor of her living room, leaning her body against the counter. How could her mother act like this towards her? How could she love one daughter so much and despise the other? What did she ever do to her?

She wiped the tears from her face. And then she grabbed her purse and keys. She couldn't be alone at a time like this. She needed to see her friends. Justin must be onboard the plane by now, and she couldn't burden him with something this petty.

When she got to the elevators, a couple was standing there, waiting for the lift. The man was dressed in an expensive suit and the woman was wrapped in a Burberry coat. They looked rich and classy. They had their backs on her and didn't even notice her presence behind them.

"I cannot believe he would go off like that!" the woman said. "I know he was always rebellious. But I didn't know he would go to extreme lengths like this!" Adrienne only listened half-heartedly.

The man put his arms around the woman and Adrienne thought that was sweet. "Honey... come on. We can fix this. It's not too late. It's not like he's married already."

"But I feel different about this. I know he's been with some girls before. But something tells me it's different this time. I think he's serious about this one. Where is he, by the way? How come he's not in his apartment?"

"He is probably at the airport now."

The elevator stopped on their floor. The couple stepped inside and Adrienne stepped in after them. She got a glimpse of the handsome man and the elegant woman. They both looked like they were in their fifties. Somehow, Adrienne thought they looked familiar.

"This is embarrassing, honey!" the woman spoke in a low voice. But Adrienne still heard her. "Ana has been my longest friend. Our parents were the best of friends. You know this arrangement had been finalized when Justin was just a baby!"

"I know," the man admitted.

Adrienne's heart skipped a beat. She realized now why the couple looked familiar. These were Justin's parents. Her knees shook and for a moment, she forgot how to breathe.

"And he grew up knowing that. He didn't complain about it. We constantly reminded him of this. It's his duty. He even promised my father on his death bed that he will fulfill his wish."

"And we know he will," the man continued. "My son is a man of his word. He made you and your father a promise and he will keep it. I know because he's my son. This family is more important to him than anything else. He'll go through with this wedding."

"It's not like we chose badly. This girl comes from a very good family. Decent. Wealthy."

"And has a set of beautiful genes to give us absolutely stunning babies," the man added jokingly.

"I won't forgive him if he defies us, Jac," the woman breathed. "He can't back out on his word now. I will... disinherit him!"

The man just laughed. "Now, now. Don't be so stressed out, sweetheart."

The woman paused and Adrienne heard her laugh. "Your son has given me more wrinkles than I want!"

The man laughed again. "No, honey. You're very beautiful. You're a fox!"

The elevator opened on the ground floor. Adrienne stood still as the couple walked past her.

Every nerve in her body screamed. Every muscle shook. She was certain that her face had turned white, bloodless. Her heart pounded loudly inside her ribcage. She couldn't breathe.

Realization crept through her, took control of her body and threatened to suffocate her.

She remembered the many times when Justin would fall silent and sad when he talked about his family and his obligations to them. That was it. That was what his parents asked him to do.

Her heart shattered into a million pieces. She walked out of the elevator like a zombie. Her tears threatened to blind her. She didn't hear anything, didn't see anything. Only one thought dominated her mind and she couldn't escape the blinding pain that came with it.

Justin is engaged.

22.

Agwat
Filipino for Space / Distance

*W*hen Adrienne arrived at Yuan's apartment, her friends knew instantly that something was wrong.

"What?" Yuan asked. "Did he break your heart? Was he cheating on you? Where is he? I will kill him!"

Adrienne sat on the couch silently. She stared into space, still unable to recover from her shock. How could this happen to her? A few hours ago, she was happy. She was floating on air.

But that seemed so far away as she sat with her heart broken like shattered glass. She didn't know how she would be able to recover from it. Her world had fallen apart.

"Adrienne, what is wrong?" Jill asked, taking her hands in hers and gently squeezing them.

She stared at them for a long time.

"Please don't tell me you caught him cheating on you?"

Adrienne shook her head. "He wasn't cheating on me."

"Then why are you like this?"

She took a deep breath. "Apparently… Justin was sort of… cheating with me."

"What?"

"I…" She took a deep breath. "I shared the elevator with his parents. They didn't know me. They haven't met me. But his Mom was so upset, she couldn't help talking about her…dilemma with her son." Pain came rushing to her again. "She said…that Justin has this obligation to the family. An arrangement that goes way back when he was still very young."

"What is it?"

"They… arranged for him… to be married to some… rich heiress," she stammered and then tears rolled down her cheeks.

"Oh my God!" Yuan and Jill breathed together.

It took a moment for her friends to recover.

"Maybe…maybe it's not his parents. How could you know? You haven't met them."

"I saw a picture of them," Adrienne replied. "And his father looks exactly like him. There's no mistake about it. They mentioned his name. So I'm pretty sure it's them."

"Have you spoken to him?"

Adrienne shook her head. "Not yet. I just…want to organize my thoughts first."

"He never mentioned this to you?"

"Never. But there were moments in the past when he would look worried or sad when he remembered something. He mentioned a family obligation that he forgot about. He didn't say what it was. He was always changing the topic after that. I'm pretty sure this was it."

"But maybe…maybe he doesn't want to do it."

Adrienne remembered Justin say, *'It's too late. I don't want to do it anymore.'*

"Okay, you said they agreed on this a long time ago. Maybe because you came along…Justin wouldn't want to go through with this anymore. His parents wanted him to do it. But did you hear him say that he would?"

Adrienne shook her head. "But his parents will disinherit him if he defies them. And I know how much Justin's family means to him, guys."

"But you mean something to him too."

Adrienne took a deep breath. "He hasn't told me he loved me. But I know he loves his family more than anything."

"Just because he hasn't told you doesn't mean he doesn't," Jill said. "Because we see him. And we know he is deeply in love with you."

"But why didn't he tell me about this?"

Yuan sighed. "I don't know. Maybe he's trying to fix it. So when he does tell you, there would be nothing for you to worry about anymore."

Adrienne wiped the tears from her face. Her friends were right. Justin probably did want to fix it. That's why he went back to Chicago with his parents. He said he would prepare his family first and then he would ask her to come to Chicago with him. He wouldn't say that if he still planned on pushing his engagement to some other girl, right?

"Oh God! I hope he can convince his parents," she breathed. "Because I don't want to let him choose, you know. I won't let him sacrifice his relationship with his parents for me. I know what it's like to live with a mother that hates you and a father who couldn't stand up for you. I won't let Justin have that life, guys. I love him too much for that."

"Sweetie… we're sure you guys will be okay," Jill said. "Believe in Justin. He won't hurt you. He will fight for you."

"I really hope you're right. I…I don't wanna lose him. It's too soon." Adrienne let out frustrated sigh. "God, can't I have like…a month's peace?" she asked, looking up. "I mean… Justin and I have been together officially for like a week. And now this."

"If he really loves you, he will fight for you. Maybe he went to see his parents this weekend to call off his engagement with this bitch."

"No wonder Justin was non-committal before. Maybe this was the reason why he never did relationships. He couldn't commit because…he was already committed to somebody else. And the other girls were all like flings. To pass the time. To have some fun before he finally serves life imprisonment with some bitch who earned the right to be his fiancée just by being born." Adrienne said, thinking out loud.

"But you weren't just some pastime, Adrienne. He got serious with you."

"Maybe he never meant to, but he couldn't help it," Jill suggested.

Adrienne sighed. "I can't hold him back from his destiny. I can't make him leave his family. He was a twin, you know? His brother died at birth. He's the only one his parents got."

Jill and Yuan smiled at her apologetically.

"Just wait. I'm sure he'll fix this." Yuan said.

"God, I hope he does. And soon! Because I need some strength to face my parents."

"Why? What happened?"

"My parents called me. Apparently, news of Troy's black eye reached them already. My Mom is pissed with me. Kim failed to mention to them that I found her on top of Troy, moaning her lungs out!"

"Of course. Whoever makes it to your parents first gets to throw the first stone." Jill rolled her eyes. "Ooohh! I want to poke her eyes out!"

"It doesn't matter whether they cheated on me. I cheated on Troy, too. And I was going to break up with Troy even before I found out. This was doomed to happen. My best bet is for my parents to understand that for once, I'm doing something I want. Being with the person I love. And not just to please them."

"Any parent should understand that!" Yuan groaned.

"Not my Mom. Apparently, she was doing me a favor for pushing me to date Troy. She said, I'd never do good in life. My best chance was to marry somebody successful. How pathetic did she think I was?"

"I wanna bitch-slap your Mom sometimes!" Yuan said. "I'm sorry. But I really don't get how mean she is to you! Like you didn't come from her! How could she demean you like this?"

"And there's nothing to demean! She's got a smart, beautiful daughter whose only wish is to please her! What more could she ask for?" Jill said.

"Well, now at least you can tell her that her choice wasn't good enough for you," Yuan added. "You managed to snag one of the richest bachelors in the country. Eat that Kimberly!"

"It doesn't matter. Justin didn't have to be rich. I'd still fall in love with him. Remember, when I did fall for him, we were just having dates in our apartments. We barely went out. I never got first-hand experience of knowing how rich he really was. We kept things low-key... quiet and simple. And I still fell in love with him."

"But still, it must have been quite a shock for Kimberly!" Yuan asserted. "I wonder how she reacted when she first realized who you're dating now. And how Troy felt when he found out who he lost you to."

"Yeah! Justin freaking Adams!" Jill said cheerily.

"Must have been quite a shock for them," Yuan continued. "Unfortunately, they weren't shocked enough to have a heart attack. That would have been lovely!"

"Seriously, guys! I should be the one wishing them dead, not you. Whatever happens between Kim and me, she's still my sister. She's still family."

"Tell that to her. She doesn't seem to know!" Yuan rolled his eyes.

"So you still need to go to Boston?"

Adrienne nodded. "Yes. And I was hoping Justin would come with me."

"He would," Yuan said confidently. "He's a decent guy. He won't leave you in the air."

"And not for some bitch who's only connection with him is a business tie-up," Jill added.

Adrienne buried her face in her hands and prevented herself from crying. "Oh, God, I hope you guys are right."

That night, Adrienne decided to spend the night in Justin's apartment, instead of hers. Justin had given her keys to his apartment they moment they got back from the resort. It was the first time she used her key without him actually being in the place.

She wanted to feel close to him. She laid down on his bed, the bed they usually spend their nights in. She hugged his pillows. They still smelled faintly of his aftershave.

She flipped her phone and dialed his number.

"Honey," he greeted her after one ring.

His voice sounded so sweet to her and she immediately felt like crying. She realized just how much she loved him and wanted to keep him forever.

She took a deep breath. "I miss you," she whispered. She tried to keep her voice steady. She didn't want to let him know that something was up. She didn't want to tell him yet that she knew about his engagement. Especially not over the phone.

It took him a moment to respond. "I hate being away from you," he responded. "If I didn't have… some things to fix here, I wouldn't have gone at all."

"Yes. I wish you were here, too."

"Where are you?"

She sighed. "In your bed."

He paused for a long while. Then he said, "If that's your way of making me suffer even more, you're succeeding."

She giggled. "I've missed you. I thought if I spend the night in your bed, I'd still somehow feel like you're just here next to me."

"I'd come back right now, if I could."

"It's okay. We'll see each other on Monday."

"Until then, it will be torturous."

They both fell quiet for a couple of seconds... just feeling each other's presence, no matter how far they were from each other.

Then finally, Adrienne said, "Good night, Justin."

"Good night, honey," Justin said soberly. "I'll be making love to you... in my dreams."

When Adrienne hung up the phone, she hugged his pillow and let all the tears fall.

23.

Al Haqiqah.
Arabic meaning The Truth or Reality.

It seemed like an eternity before Adrienne faced Justin again. During the two days that they spent apart, she tried to act normally. He'd call her at least three times a day. She didn't want him to think that something was up. Because knowing him, he just might fly back to New York earlier than scheduled and he only got two days to spend with his family.

Monday evening, he appeared on her doorstep.

"Hi," she greeted him, pasting a smile on her face.

He stared at her for a while. And without a word, he pulled her to him and crushed his lips to hers.

"Justin," she whispered against his lips.

"I missed you," he said, lifting her off her feet and carrying her to the bedroom.

When he put her down on her feet, she stared up at him. She could see fatigue in his eyes. "I missed you, too."

He smiled at her, but she knew him better now. His eyes didn't sparkle and it looked like he was forcing the smile on his face. Adrienne already knew that something was up.

"Are you okay?" she asked.

He nodded. "I am now."

"Justin..." she started.

He silenced her with a kiss. She kissed him back. Their kiss became passionate. It was evident that he didn't want to talk. He just wanted to lose himself in her. And she allowed him.

Within minutes, they were in bed, panting. They rode the tide of passion that threatened to consume both of them.

"Adrienne..." Justin whispered. He was more urgent than usual. She matched his kisses, his passion with equal fervor. She loved this man and she didn't want to lose him. She wanted to claim him, as much as he was claiming her.

When she reached her peak, she screamed his name in ecstasy. In the midst of their passion, she managed to remember that they got lost too soon, Justin wasn't even wearing protection.

"Honey...we don't have protection," she panted.

He stared back at her in eyes drunk with passion, consumed by desire. His expression was so intense, she almost didn't recognize him.

He took her mouth in his in a rough, passionate kiss. She kissed him back, holding him close to her.

Then he leaned his forehead against hers and he whispered in a hoarse voice, "Tell me you love me, Adrienne."

She blinked back at him, finally gaining back some of her senses. "What?"

She stared back at him, unable to understand what he was asking of her.

"Tell me… that you're in love with me," he said, his voice pleading. He drew in a deep breath. Then he added, "The same way that I am so, so… in love with you."

Her heart pounded inside her chest and she struggled to find her voice. Emotions enveloped her all at once and she fought for air. She smiled at him, tears glistening in her eyes. "Justin…you know I am."

A slow, triumphant smile spread across his face. "I wanna hear you say it, honey."

She pulled him to her and kissed him passionately. When she came up for air, she said, "I love you, Justin Adams. With all my heart."

He kissed her back. "I love you, Adrienne Miller. With all my heart. With all my soul. With all that I am," he said. And with that, she felt him move within her, more passionately and more urgently that it brought her once again to her peak.

"Justin!" she screamed.

"Adrienne, I love you so much!" he screamed her name and within seconds she felt his body rock within her.

He tightened his arms around her as he buried his face into the mass of her hair, taking in her scent, feeling her every heartbeat, listening to her every breath. They remained joined, still one with each other. And all Adrienne could think of was how he told her he loved her.

Justin continued kissing her, nuzzling her neck. Her eyes were half-closed. She was consumed by the power of their lovemaking. It was intense. And she knew that she had just given herself completely to him. Her heart and her soul now both belonged to Justin.

"You're beautiful," he whispered to her.

She smiled. "So are you." Then, she again remembered that they weren't wearing protection. "Justin… you weren't wearing any rubber."

He stared back at her. She expected him to panic, and realize what just happened. They were both lost in their passion that they actually forgot about the risks. But he said, "I know." He leaned down and kissed her once again.

"Justin, I'm not on the pill." She remembered that she should have thought about this since the day she lost her virginity.

"I know," he said again.

"Justin…"

He silenced her with a kiss.

"Do you think I would worry, Adrienne?" he asked. "I love you, honey."

She bit her lip and kissed him back. "I love you, too."

He smiled back at her. "Then we have nothing to worry about."

Finally, he pulled out of her and rolled on his back. He gathered her in her arms. She rested her head on his shoulder.

They got lost in their thoughts for a while. Justin silently caressed her arms and kissed the top of her head once in a while.

She wondered what happened in Chicago. Did he manage to convince his parents not to go through with their arrangement to marry him off? Did he win? Is he finally free?

She took a deep breath. "Justin... is everything all right with you and your parents?"

It took a moment for him to answer. "Nothing I can't handle."

She stared up at him, searching his face. Again, his eyes weren't dancing. Something was there beneath their depths. Something that worried Adrienne.

She didn't want to tell him that she knew about his engagement. She wanted him to tell her at his own time. When he managed to fix things. When he's ready.

"If something's wrong, you would tell me, right?" she asked.

He smiled at her. "The woman I love just told me she feels the same way about me. Right now, I'm invincible. I'm the king of the world! Everything is perfect."

"Justin!" she pinched him on his side.

He pulled her to him and kissed her forehead. "Nothing's wrong, Adrienne. Everything is just fine."

***

The next day, Adrienne tried to concentrate on her work. But she stayed anxious. She should be happy. Justin loves her. Everything was perfect. But somehow, she still couldn't forget that nagging feeling that this bubble she was in would just blow up in her face. That she would lose Justin. Because even though his heart belonged to her... he was still Justin Adams. And his name... belonged to somebody else.

"So, did you talk to him?" Jill asked, sitting on the chair in front of her desk.

"No. I tried to get something out of him. But he wouldn't talk. He just tells me that I have nothing to worry about."

Jill stared at her apologetically, not really knowing what to say.

"He finally told me he loves me."

Jill's eyes widened. "Wow!" She suppressed a scream. "Then...you have nothing to worry about, Adrienne!"

"I know. But I can see it in his eyes. Something's bothering him and he doesn't want to talk about it."

"Maybe it's not yet all peachy. Maybe he's still trying to sort it out.

But he loves you. And that's your assurance. He's fighting for you."

Adrienne took a deep breath. "I know. I just hope he wins, though."

She decided to cook that night. Something special for both Justin and her. She knew that even though he's happy with her, things still seemed off when it came to his parents. His mother was determined to change his mind and make him fulfill his promise to go through with their arrangement. He loved her. And she knew it must be tough for him to defy his parents.

"Something smells good," he said when he entered her apartment and found her in the kitchen.

"Hey!" she greeted him. "I hope you're hungry. Dinner will be ready in fifteen minutes."

He stood behind her and wrapped his arms around her waist. He gave her a kiss on the neck and looked at what she was cooking.

"Stroganoff?"

"Yes."

"My favorite," he said. He kissed the top of her head. "I love you."

She smiled and turned to him. She reached up and kissed his lips. "I love you, too," she said. "Now, go wait in the living room, so I can finish this."

Just after they sat down for dinner and Justin had taken a taste of what she had cooked for him, he stared back at her in awe.

"What?" she asked.

"Wow! You really can cook!" He took another bite. "This is awesome!"

She smiled. "I'm glad you like it."

"Love it!" he said and ate as if he hasn't eaten the whole day. And it made Adrienne feel proud and happy.

After she washed the dishes and tidied up the kitchen, she found Justin on the balcony. Lost in his own thoughts, drinking beer and staring into space.

Her heart almost broke. She knew the burden he carried. She promised she wouldn't pressure him about it, but at that moment, she felt like maybe it's time for him to share that burden. She realized that it was bad enough that he's defying his parents' wishes. He carried the burden of not telling her, too, because he feared he would hurt her or he would lose her. She wanted him to know that she knows. That it was okay. That she trusted him.

She took a deep breath and said, "You don't have to be strong all the time, you know."

He turned around to face her. "Hey," he whispered softly.

"Justin…" She took a step closer to him. "I know…I know what's bothering you."

He blinked back at her. "Nothing's bothering me."

She raised a brow at him. "Liar," she said softly and she smiled at him ruefully. "I know you're engaged, Justin."

He stared at her. Blood almost draining from his face. She stepped closer to him. "Justin…you don't have to hide it from me."

"Adrienne…I'm not engaged."

"I know you are. Stop pretending that everything is peachy! Like there's nothing wrong. I know you have a fiancée somewhere and you're scared to tell me about it."

He closed his eyes for a moment. He took a deep breath and said, "As far as I'm concerned, I'm not engaged."

"Justin…please!" She's getting frustrated. "How could you say that? I know what's going on with you!"

He groaned softly. "I am not engaged, Adrienne! Because if I was, then you would be wearing a huge rock on your finger!" He sank on the chair and refused to look at her.

Adrienne took a moment to think about what he said and what that meant. Her heart swelled at the thought that if Justin was free to ask somebody to marry him, he would ask her.

She went to him and knelt in front of him, taking his hands in hers.

"Okay. You're not engaged…by your own free will. Your parents arranged you to be married to some heiress they chose for you. Am I right?"

He gave her a hard look. He squeezed her hands. "How did you know?"

"It doesn't matter how I knew. But I do. And I know it's bothering you."

He shook his head. "It's not bothering me, Adrienne," he began in a broken voice "It's killing me."

She knew that. But what's important is his choice. What did he really plan to do about it?

She took a deep breath. "So what's your plan, Mr. Adams?" she asked. "Because I'm only willing to stand by your side if you say that your choice is…me."

He released her hands, leaned down and gave her a hard kiss on the lips. Then he said, "What are you talking about, Adrienne? The choice will always be you!" He pulled her up so she could sit on his lap. He drew her closer to him.

They stayed quiet for a while. She rested her head on his shoulder. He gave her a tight squeeze. Then he said, "You don't know how relieved I am to hear you say that you will stand by me."

She looked up at him. "Is that what was bothering you?"

He pushed a lock of hair away from her face. "The only thing that's killing me is the fear of losing you if you found out."

"I love you, Justin. And I know it wasn't your choice."

He took a deep breath. "I've already made my choice," he said. "My parents won't be happy about it, but there was never a question of ever giving you up for some rich brat I haven't even met."

"You haven't met her?"

He shook his head. "All my life, my mother told me I would marry the daughter of her best friend. Their family had been very good friends with mine. Even our grandfathers were the best of friends. They got it in their heads to join our families and they believed the only way to do that is through marriage. Unfortunately, my mother never had a brother. And the girl's mother was an only child. So marriage was impossible in their generation. They thought about making me miserable instead."

"How long have you known?"

He sighed. "Ever since I was boy," he replied. "I promised my grandfather I would do it. Back then, I thought my Mom's friend was beautiful. So her daughter couldn't be that bad. And I didn't care about those things yet. Even when I became an adult I never found somebody I could fall in love with. So it never bothered me.

"I was raised with this arrangement like it was a part of my system... a part of who I am. And besides, my mother and my father came from that sort of arrangement and they were so in love with each other. It worked out well for them, so I thought, maybe, I would fall for the girl, too."

Adrienne rested her head on his shoulder as she listened to his story.

"That's why I never committed to anybody. Because I knew not to become emotionally attached. I know every girl I got to be with is just... temporary. In the end I'm still going to marry my mother's friend's daughter. So it didn't matter if I never had a relationship before. What was the point?"

"You were a bachelor for a reason," she murmured.

He took a deep breath. "Then I saw you one day, in your office. You were beautiful and I was entranced. The fact that you ignored me and didn't seem interested in me got me fascinated with you even more."

Adrienne giggled. "That's your ego talking."

Justin chuckled. "I always watched you. You didn't seem interested. I saw you move into this apartment and I got excited because it meant I would get a chance to get your attention."

"Maybe I presented a challenge, that's why you were interested in me."

"Maybe at first. But the more I watched you, the more I got intrigued by you. You were always serious, but I felt like you have a shell that I just had to crack and something even more beautiful would come out. That night at Gypsys, I saw a crack in that shell. So I pursued you. Because I knew that was my only chance."

Adrienne giggled. "Jamila McBride gave you a chance."

"That was hilarious. I already knew so much about you, and when you gave me a fake name, I tried so hard not to laugh."

"I thought you would easily forget me."

"Now, you know, I won't," he said. "I never meant for this to be just a one-night thing. And the more I got to know you... the more drawn I became to you. You have layers in your personality that I find enthralling. You were smart, funny and tough. And I felt privileged that you showed me sides of you that you don't allow anybody else to see. The fact that I was the guy you gave your virginity to, made me feel like somehow, I did something right in my life to deserve such a special prize.

"Our secret made me live in your world... the world you try so much to hide. After two weeks of being with you, I realized that I was way into you for this thing to be called just a fling. When I saw that guy, Jin Starck, looking interested in you, I felt a pang of jealousy that I never felt before. I became possessive of you. I wanted you all to myself and I didn't care anymore if I was previously arranged to somebody else. I don't want her. I want you."

"Did you tell your parents about this?"

"Yes," he replied. "Last weekend, I told them that I'm calling off the whole arrangement. They can't choose my wife for me. I already know who I wanted to spend the rest of my life with."

"How did they take it?"

He sighed. "Badly," he whispered. "My mother was threatening to disinherit me."

She pulled away from him and looked into his eyes. "Justin...she couldn't do that to you, can she?"

He smiled ruefully. "I was hoping she would get it someday. She didn't know what it was like. She accepted her fate willingly. She was never in love with somebody else when she married my Dad. And then they got to know each other and fell madly in love. So after a few months, it wasn't a business arrangement anymore."

"How sure are you that you won't like this girl, too?" Adrienne asked him.

Justin shook his head. "How could I even like her? I'm already too far in love with you."

She leaned forward and kissed his lips. Her heart swelled with joy and broke in pain at the same time. She was happy to hear him say he loved her enough to fight for her. But she also knew that he's sacrificing his family for their love. And a part of her didn't want that for him.

"What are you going to do now, Justin?"

He smiled at her ruefully. "I can't live without you now, honey. I won't. Even if it means I lose everything."

"Are you ready to do that?"

"Will you stay with me even if I'm not Justin Adams anymore? Even if I make a living bussing tables?"

"You know I will," she replied. Then she grinned. "Maybe I just might love you even more."

He stared at her for a while and said, "Then you just made me the happiest man alive, honey." He leaned forward and gave her a passionate kiss on the lips.

24.
Dit is die moeite werd om aan te hou.
Afrikaans: Worth Keeping. Worth fighting for.

The next few days were a total bliss. Justin was almost back to his usual, jolly self. They didn't talk about his marriage arrangement anymore and Adrienne trusted what he said. That his choice was her and he will fight for them.

They stayed together every day. After work, she returned to his apartment. She only came back to her own place to check her voicemail and to get some clothes. Every night they slept with each other, as if they lived together.

One night, they sat together in Justin's chaise lounge on his balcony, staring at the Manhattan view. Adrienne leaned her back against Justin's chest as she sat between his legs. She rested her head against his shoulder.

"Do you love me?" Adrienne whispered softly.

"With all my heart, honey," Justin said and hugged her to him tightly.

"Seriously?" She smiled.

"Seriously," he whispered and she kissed her temple.

"Justin...if...if you didn't have me, do you think you would be married by now?" she asked.

Justin sighed. "I don't know," he replied. "Usually... they don't throw you into a wedding ceremony immediately. What happened with my Mom and my Dad...they were introduced to each other, and then my father was told by my grandfather to... get to know his fiancée. They had to spend some time together.

My father had to court my Mom. Woo her so...she won't feel like she was forced into this fate. And even if they didn't fall in love, they would at least be friends when they got married." Justin fell silent for a while. Then he added, "They usually set the wedding a year after the meeting. So, the couple gets like a year of courtship...a year to fall in love. My parents...they got married in six months."

"Six months? Way ahead of the one-year courting period?"

Justin nodded. "My Dad couldn't wait. He proposed to my Mom after six months, and she said yes. It was just formality because they were already arranged to be married. And so they did. And here I am! Being made to suffer the same fate."

"You get one year to make her fall in love with you?" Adrienne asked, her heart tugging inside her chest. She refused to burden Justin with just how much this bothered her.

"Yes. Or at least become her friend, so the arrangement wouldn't be that bad."

Adrienne sighed sadly. "She *will* fall in love with you."

"Why do you say that?"

She stared up at him, tears shining from her eyes. "Because you're Justin Adams," she said glumly. She felt proud of him. But somehow, she couldn't help worrying even more. "As if the guy who wears the name tag isn't great enough, the guy underneath is so... so much more worth falling in love with."

Justin stared at her wearily. "But Justin Adams will never fall in love with her," he stated. "His heart is already chained to somebody else. He wants no one else in his present or his future." He paused to take a deep breath. Then he added, "I want you to remember that, Adrienne." Then his lips descended to hers and he kissed her thoroughly.

Thursday evening, she went into Justin's apartment from work. He was in the balcony talking on the phone.

"No," he said. "You can't make me, Dad!"

She stopped in the living room and listened to him. He had his back on her and he didn't hear her come in.

"Why are you being so unfair to me?" he asked angrily. "You love Mom! You're married to your soul mate. Every day of your life, you wake up beside the woman who means the world to you! I found the woman who means the world to me. This is not a game, Dad! I love my girl! I'm going to marry her. And you can disown me all you want, but I won't change my mind about this!"

He paused for a while. Obviously, his father was saying something on the other side. She saw Justin gripping the rails in front of him tightly.

Then he heaved a frustrated sigh. "I've done well enough for myself. I don't need your money. My girlfriend is a simple girl. She doesn't need to live in your fancy world. And I'm pretty sure I can still give her a comfortable life with my money alone. I'm wealthy enough on my own."

He paused again. After a few minutes, she heard him say, "Fine! I'll move out this weekend!" Then he hung up. He took deep breaths and then he punched the rail in front of him.

Adrienne closed her eyes for a moment. She felt his pain. Justin chose her, fought for her. But it came with a great price. His family. And Adrienne knew, unlike hers, Justin's family was perfect. And they were everything to him before she came along.

She stepped forward and then she hugged him from behind, resting her cheek against his well-sculpted back. He took a deep breath, grabbed one of her hands and kissed it.

"Well, I'm officially disowned by my parents," he whispered.

He turned around and faced her. Tears welled up in her eyes. She shook her head. "It shouldn't be like that, Justin. You can still fix this." Even as she said this, her heart broke for him.

He pushed a lock of hair away from her face. "The only way to fix this is if I leave you for some brat I don't even know. And that's not an option for me."

"But Justin...it's your family."

"And on the other hand, Adrienne, it's you," he said ruefully. "My life."

Then he bent down and kissed her lips thoroughly.

"Justin, are you sure you're making the right choice?"

He sighed against her lips. "I think I am. Because my father just asked me to move out of the house and all I can think about is making love to you right now."

He cupped his hands on her thighs and lifted her off her feet. She wrapped her legs around his hips and kissed him. He carried her to his bedroom and dropped her on the bed. He took off his shirt and soon they were both screaming each other's names in the gates of Nirvana.

***

"That did not happen!" Yuan said over lunch on Friday when Adrienne told them what happened to Justin.

"Is he okay?"

"He tries to look okay. He doesn't want me to feel bad about it. But I know it's painful for him," she said guiltily.

Still, she felt glad about Justin's choice. She was so happy that he's willing to sacrifice all that he is, all that he has for her. But Justin's situation with his family now was no better than hers. And she knew what it was like to have a broken, almost irreparable relationship with family. She couldn't help asking herself if she did the right thing in not giving him up.

"He really does love you."

"Yes, but it feels like those 'you and me against the world' sagas now. And I know it's more painful for him than it is for me. I can't help thinking that maybe I am being too selfish."

"It's not about being selfish," Jill countered. "It's about being honest about your feelings. You could be saving Justin from a lifetime of misery that this marriage to some rich bitch will cause him."

"I know that. I know I will do everything that I can to make him happy. But what if she was the right one for him all along and I was just in the way of...destiny."

"He doesn't seem like a guy who believes in destiny, Yen," Yuan said. "He's always been like somebody who likes to write his own. It's his choice. The only way you could make the load seem lighter is if you don't make him regret ever choosing you."

"I thought arranged marriages are a thing of the past," Adrienne heaved a frustrated sigh.

"It's a rich people thing," Jill responded. "Gives them the kicks."

"That's why the rich get richer, sweetie," Yuan said. "Justin's parents just want to secure their family's wealth and gain more."

"I wonder how she feels," Adrienne said. "That girl. I wonder if she feels as repulsed about marrying Justin as he is."

Jill looked at her as if she was out of her mind. "Hello! Have you *met* your boyfriend? Didn't you not know, better than the rest of us, that he's a god? That girl must know who he is and must have been pulling all her influential strings to make this marriage happen."

"She's lucky she's rich!"

"Unfortunately, I'm not," Adrienne said. "Apparently, I'm not fit to be Mrs. Justin Adams."

"But you are. Because Justin should be the only judge of that. And he already made it loud and clear that you're going to be someday."

Yes, she did hear him tell his father that he would marry her. He hadn't asked her formally, but if he said it to his Dad and it caused his father to disown him, then he must really mean it.

"Now I understand what Justin's friend said when I met them. I made him give in to the pull of attraction and made him defy gravity," Adrienne said. "He was single for a reason. He was already essentially engaged, so what's the point of having a relationship?"

"But he fell in love with you. So he had to defy his parents' wishes."

Adrienne nodded. "I thought that after I broke it off with Troy, things were going to be easy. I didn't know that a bigger bomb was just about fall on the top of my head."

Her friends smiled at her apologetically. "Well, his parents have already disowned him and you're still going strong. So what could be worse than that?"

At that point, she thought her friends were right. The worst of the storm had come and all they needed to do is just ride it out. As long as they're together, it couldn't be all that bad. What could be worse than that?

Over the next couple of days, Justin was quiet. Adrienne tried to cheer him up. He would smile and laugh with her, but she could see from his eyes that he was also hurting. And it just hurt Adrienne, too.

One night, they were in bed, locked in each other's arms. Adrienne stared up and found Justin staring at the ceiling.

"Are you okay?" she asked him.

He looked down at her and smiled. "Yes."

She propped up on her elbow so she could look into his eyes.

"Justin...I know it must be difficult for you. I'm sorry."

He caressed her cheek. "It's not your fault, Adrienne. It's my parents who aren't making sense to me. But if I had to make my choice, over and over again, I would still choose you."

She leaned forward and kissed his lips.

"I wish I can soothe your pain. I know you're hurting. I know this is difficult for you."

He drew her to him. "Just be with me, Adrienne. You're my source of strength. If you weren't with me now, I don't think I would find the courage to fight my doomed fate."

"I was the reason why you are breaking your parents' hearts right now."

"Time heals all wounds, honey. Maybe someday, when they see how happy I really am… they would find it in their hearts to forgive me."

And somehow Adrienne hoped that was true. She couldn't believe that Justin just gave up the most important thing to him… for her…for their love.

Tears rolled down her cheeks, but she refused to let Justin see it. She wanted to be strong for him. But deep inside, she hurt because she knew, his heart was shattered into a million pieces at this very moment.

25.
Pyeonghaeng Segye.
Korean for Parallel World

The next Friday afternoon, when Adrienne got back from work, she found Justin sitting on his balcony. He had his back to her. He seemed lost in his thoughts. He was taking deep breaths and she realized that he was silently crying.

As she watched him, she saw his pain. The pain that he refused to let her see. And her heart broke just a little bit more for him. She realized more than ever how selfish she had been. Justin had to make the tough choice because she refused to let him go. Because she had given him a choice. She fought for him. She could have made it easier for him, but she held on to her claim on him. He chose her. But it became evident that he wasn't going to be the same man she loved. His happiness would never be complete.

Tears rolled down her cheeks. She wiped them and then she went and knelt in front of him. She took his hands in hers.

His face was tear-stricken, his eyes were red.

"Justin..." she whispered.

He held her cheek and looked into her eyes. "My mother is in the hospital, Adrienne," he said.

She blinked back at him. "What?"

"She had a car accident yesterday. Apparently, she had been drinking, since the day my father asked me to move out of the house." Justin spoke in a low voice. "She'd fallen into depression. She wasn't drunk when she rammed the car into a tree. But her depression led her there. My Mom is not as tough as you are, Adrienne," he said. "She was a sheltered, rich girl who didn't go through so much in her life. After my grandfather's death, this was probably the second instance she felt like somebody she loves abandoned her. She took this worse than I thought."

"Justin...you have to go home," she said, not knowing how she found the courage to tell him this.

He blinked back at her. He shook his head. "I'm not going to leave you, Adrienne."

"Justin..." she whispered softly. "Fix this. Your parents loved you and took care of you all your life. You can't just walk out on them for a girl you met less than a year ago. If they are making you marry some other girl, then make them understand why you don't want to, why you can't. But don't just walk out on them.

"Just because you're rich enough by your own right, you'll show them that you don't need them anymore. They have been there for you when you were a kid and weren't strong enough to handle life. Now it's time you pay them back."

"Even if they're asking me to give up my own happiness? My own life?"

"Even if it hurts to be unselfish," she whispered in a weak voice.

She stared up at him, tears rolling down her cheeks.

"They're your family, Justin," she said. "I would give everything to have parents who loved me the same way your parents loved you."

"Adrienne, when I go back to them, they might not let me return to you anymore. You see this… this is emotional blackmail."

"But she's still your mother. Do you really want to risk not knowing whether she's just doing this to make you feel bad about your choice?"

He closed his eyes and they both knew what the right answer to that question was, no matter how badly it hurt.

Then he stared at her again. He took a deep breath. "I love you, Adrienne."

"And I love you, too, Justin."

"You know I would fight for you…until the end, right?"

She nodded. "I know. But this time…I don't want you to."

"Aren't you going to fight for me, too?" he asked weakly.

"I did," she replied. "But I love you too much to do this to you. I love you too much to deprive you of who you were born to be…who you really are. Maybe fate is telling us that I'm not the girl for you."

"I don't believe in fate, Adrienne."

"But I do. And I think fighting it will only make us hurt the people around us."

He cupped her face in his hands.

"I don't want to let you go. I don't want to go back to them." His voiced sounded broken. Tears welled up in his eyes.

Tears spilled from her eyes, too. "But you have to, Justin. For your family's sake."

"I won't accept this fate, Adrienne. I can't."

She stared up at him and gave him a bitter smile. She took a deep breath and mustered all the courage she could to finally do what was right. "But I am letting you go, Justin. So you would be free to take your destiny in your hands."

"Honey, don't do this," he whispered. "You said you love me."

"And I do. That's why I'm doing this. Because I don't want you to hurt anymore. I don't want to make things difficult for you anymore. I don't want you to lose the family you have before I even came into your life. I know it's a tough choice you made. And now…you don't have to make it anymore. I will make it for you." She took a deep breath. A whimper escaped from her lips. "Go back to them, Justin. I am no longer claiming you. Because this is the right thing to do."

Justin shook his head. "If this is right, then why does it feel wrong?"

"Hey." She smiled at him apologetically. "It's time you start believing in destiny, Justin. Some things are beyond your control. Don't pull against gravity. You will only end up hurting yourself and the ones around you. Let's not be selfish anymore."

"Adrienne…I don't think I can love anybody the way I love you now."

She smiled at him. "I will always love you, Justin." She whispered the words that became the most painful things she ever said. "You are Justin Adams. You cannot escape that. Deep inside you're still the same guy I fell in love with. And I know you will always be. But it's time to embrace your destiny. Even if I cannot be a part of your future."

He shook his head slightly. "Don't say that. You are my life. I will never stop loving you. I can't!" He leaned forward and crushed her lips into his. Adrienne savored that kiss. She knew…they may not have that many kisses left to share.

"But you cannot change who you are. You can't change who you were born to be. At least…not without hurting the ones you love. And you don't want that in your future, Justin. If something bad happens to your Mom, do you want to carry the burden of guilt all your life?" Adrienne shook her head slightly. "You don't. It will change you. It will break you. And I love you way too much to make you suffer for this, Justin. I want you to be happy for the rest of your life."

"Then don't let me go," he pleaded.

"No. The only way you will be happy is if you're free," she said and reached forward and wiped his cheeks with her thumbs. "Give this a chance, Justin. Maybe…maybe this is your true happiness, and you're just repelling it. Maybe she could make you happier than I could. And if she can't, then at least you tried. And you would still make your parents happy that at least you gave it a chance. If it works, then good for you. If it doesn't work, then your parents would still have been thankful that you chose them over me."

"You're asking me to make a choice that would destroy us both!" His voice became almost angry.

"I'm asking you to make a choice where you have a shot of winning both ways," she said. Those words are like knives stabbing her heart.

"And if in the end, it still didn't work?" he asked.

She smiled at him ruefully and then she reached forward and kissed his lips. "Then you come back to me, okay?"

Justin stared back at her for a while. "Are you going to wait for me?"

She nodded. "Yes."

Justin sighed. "Adrienne, why? Why can't you just be stubborn and possessive and ask me to go with you to Vegas now and marry me so my parents couldn't do anything about it anymore? Why do you have to do this?"

She cupped his face in her hands. "Because I don't want to make things difficult for you. I have nothing to offer you in return, Justin. The only thing that I can do... is make things easy for you. So now, you have two choices. Each gives you a chance to win. I think I just made this less difficult for you." She tried to smile at him brightly.

Justin shook his head. "No. You just made me realize how right I was about you. You know there's ninety-nine percent chance I choose the option that I come back to you, right?"

"But you can only do that after you've tried the other options that you have," she said.

Justin sighed in defeat. He took her hands in his and kissed her fingers.

"Adrienne..." he whispered. "You know I love you. Forever...always...you are the only woman who owns this," he said, bringing her hand to his chest, to where his heart is. Tears were welling up in his eyes again.

He stood up and pulled her up on her feet as well. Then he said, "Let's...pretend that my parents didn't take away my free will."

She nodded.

"I will ask you a question. And I want your honest answer. No conditions, no buts. Just answer me yes or no."

She nodded again.

Justin stared into her eyes and took a deep breath. "Adrienne Miller...I love you so much. With all of my heart. I want no one else in my life, in my future. I want to spend an eternity with you. I want you to be the mother of all my children." He paused and with teary eyes, he asked, "Will you marry me?"

Adrienne blinked back at him. If it was real, if they were in the world that wasn't crazy...that question would have made her jump in joy. But now...it just broke her heart a little bit more. She wanted so much to hear them from Justin and answer them for real.

She stared up at him, tears streaming on her face. "Yes, Justin. I would."

He smiled at her. But that smile was sad, too. Because they both knew that just might only happen in dreams now. He had a duty to fulfill. And she set him free. But in this hypothetical world, where he asked her a hypothetical question, they allowed themselves to savor a few moments of bliss.

He leaned forward and kissed her lips. Thoroughly. Passionately. He swept her up on her feet and carried her to bed.

Adrienne lost herself in him. Justin lost himself in her. He kissed almost every inch of her skin. He drowned himself in her scent. The room was filled with their moans and their screams. They let their passion consume them and their love to take them to oblivion. They savored these moments…which might as well be their last.

Adrienne woke up early the next day, with a heavy heart. She wrote a letter to Justin. It was the most painful one she had to write. She felt like crying but she willed herself to be strong.

> Justin,
>
> In the ideal world, first hour in the morning today, I would pick up the phone, call my friends, and scream at the top of my lungs, "I'm engaged! I'm engaged!"
>
> Then, I would take a shower, hopefully with you. And then I would go to all the magazine stands and purchase every bridal magazine I could find. Then I would sit in Starbucks and read each and every one of them, and put sticky neon flags on the pages I would find interesting.
>
> But we're not in the ideal world. We're in this crazy, parallel universe. And in this world, the first thing I did when I woke up, is stare at your handsome face…memorize it feature by feature. The second thing I did is kiss your lips. Then I savored your scent and wished I could drown in it forever. Then I put my lips close to your ear and I told you in your sleep, "I love you very much. And it is because I love you that I have to let you go. And if by some miracle you find your way back to me…then I promise you. I will hold on to you…and never let you go anymore."
>
> I want you to know that I will be okay, Justin. You don't have to worry about me not being able to get through this. You've taught me how to love myself, you taught me how to be stronger.
>
> Don't think about hurting me by embracing your destiny. If destiny wills you to be happy with her, then know this. I am the happiest person in the world for you. Because I love you, I cannot be selfish with you. And whatever makes you happy, makes me happy.
>
> And now, if by some chance, it doesn't work out for you, then please come and find me. And when you ask me that question again, you know my answer will still be the same. And I promise I will try my best to make you the happiest husband on Earth.
>
> I will not pray for either of the options to happen. I will leave it up to fate. To destiny. I will only pray for one thing, Justin. Your happiness.
>
> I love you very much, Mr. Adams. Know that you will always be in my heart. I will never forget you. Now…forever… always.
>
> Love,
> Adrienne

She left Justin's apartment with a very heavy heart but somehow, the feeling that she did something right prevented her from breaking down. She believed that the only way they could both be happy is if they set each other free, if Justin made peace with his family.

If someday, they find each other again and Justin is free of his duties, she would take him back, no questions asked. Because in her heart, she knew she could never love anybody as much as she loved him.

She meant every word she said to him. It wasn't easy for her to let him go just like that. She took a big risk. There's a great chance that Justin may not be able to convince his family that the arrangement will not work out. There's also a possibility that the girl he was promised to was really the right girl for him all along.

Whatever the case will be, she meant what she said. She would not make Justin turn his back on his parents, on his destiny as the heir of Adams Industries. And if he found his happiness without her, then she would truly be happy for him.

26.

Murka
Indonesian for Fury

$\mathcal{A}$drienne went to Yuan's house. She told him that she let Justin go.

"You must be out of your freaking mind!" Yuan said crossly.

"I have to do this, Yuan," she said sadly. "I love him."

"Then why the hell did you let him go?!"

"I don't want his mother to fall into deep depression! I don't want her to get hurt. I don't want to ruin his perfect family. I never had that! And I wanted it for him. I don't want him to feel guilty if something happened to his Mom or his Dad. He will never be happy with me this way."

"Do you think he will be happy without you?"

Adrienne sighed. She knows Justin felt devastated with her decision to let him go, too. But he had to fix things with his parents. And the only way she could do that is if she gave him up.

"Maybe someday, Yuan," she said in a sad voice. "If we were really meant for each other, he will find his way back to me."

"And you're going to wait until that happens? How long will that take? You'll hold off your life hoping he will come back?"

She shook her head. "I'm still young, Yuan. I'll just let things flow into my life. A year or two, maybe by then he will have figured out if it's working or not. If by then he's happy then I would move on."

"This is plain stupidity!" Yuan said.

"It's also called unselfishness," Adrienne argued. "And I needed to give him that chance. I love him too much to hold him back from what's really out there for him. I can't bear the burden of him being disowned by his own family because of me. He would never be happy like that."

Her phone beeped. She stared at it nervously when she saw Justin's name on the screen.

Justin: *You talked about that parallel universe. You didn't mention one thing: Reality. Because in reality, you know this isn't for good, right, Adrienne? I will use this chance you gave me to convince my parents that they have to let me go. And when they do, be ready to answer my question for real. I love you very, very much, Miss Miller. Hold on to that, while you're waiting for me to set things right.*

Tears rolled down Adrienne's cheeks. She missed him already. But she knew she couldn't turn back. She couldn't go running back to him. He wasn't strong enough to let her go. She had to be the strong and firm one. She had to be the one to stand by what is right this time. If she left it up to Justin, she knew that he would rather lock themselves in his apartment and make love to her all day.

It took all her strength not to answer Justin's message. He had to move on. She had to set him free. So she didn't answer. She brought the phone to her lips and kissed the screen, closing her eyes, thinking that it was his lips she kissed instead.

Suddenly her phone rang and she almost dropped it. She looked at the screen nervously and saw her mother's number on it.

"Hello."

"You told us that you would come home to explain yourself. Well, it's been weeks and you still haven't shown your face here!" she said in a demanding tone.

"I'm sorry Mom. I got caught up with a lot of work."

"It's Saturday. Are you working today?"

"No."

"Then I suggest you pay us a visit." Then she hung up.

Adrienne groaned. "God, kill me now!"

"Monster Mom?" Yuan asked.

Adrienne nodded.

"Go. We'll come with you. I'll call Jill. This time, you need reinforcements!" Yuan said.

"Yuan…I just…broke up with Justin!" Adrienne murmured. "I can't face my parents. It's going to be like pain after pain after pain."

"Well, Justin's off fighting his own battle. I suggest you fight yours. This might do you good for a change. You know… one pain lessens the other. The more heartaches your mother gives you, the more distracted you will be about your breakup with Justin."

Yuan did have a point. And Adrienne realized that she can't put off fixing her own life while waiting for Justin's fate to turn around. Maybe if he came back to her, they'd both be free of excess baggage and everything would flow smoothly.

"Are you sure you want to come with me?" Adrienne asked.

"Yes," Yuan replied, sending a text message to Jill. "You need us to be there. I just sharpened my nails at the salon. Who knows? Maybe Kim will need a little facial massage."

Adrienne didn't bother going back to her apartment. She still had enough clothes left in Yuan's place from the last time she crashed with him. Within half an hour, they were all in the airport checking in.

Adrienne still felt like floating in the air. She continued staring into space, barely listening to what Jill and Yuan were talking about. She was reminiscing all the good moments she had with Justin. From the first moment they met, to the times they spent together in their own world when she kept him a secret, to the time he beat up Troy for her, to their reconciliation at the beach… to the time he first told her he loved her and that last night, when he asked her to marry him.

You're a fox!

She couldn't stop thinking about those words over and over again. And now, more than ever, she longed to hear him whisper those words again.

Tears started rolling down her cheeks without her even knowing it. She wanted to call him so badly, to hear his voice again. But she knew she couldn't. She promised to make it easy for him. Calling him and taking it all back wouldn't solve his problem. And in her heart, she knew it was the right thing to do. No matter how painful.

Jill and Yuan checked in to a hotel while Adrienne went to her parents' house.

It had been months since she went home. She felt a sense of familiarity as the cab entered her neighborhood. She instructed the taxi to stop in front of a maroon colored three-floor house.

Kimberly's pretty face was the first one that greeted her when she opened the door.

"Oh, you're here," she said. She looked behind her and found that Adrienne was alone. "So, where's the hotshot boyfriend? Gone too soon?"

She gripped her bag tightly and prevented herself from swinging it on Kim's face.

"He's a busy man, Kimberly," she murmured. Somehow, she couldn't bring herself to admit to her sister that her relationship with Justin just might be over. She could hardly admit it to herself.

She stepped inside the house and immediately heard noises in the living room.

"I didn't know you were having a party," Adrienne said.

"I didn't know you were invited," Kimberly responded, giving her a fake smile.

When she stepped inside, she found that Troy and his whole family were there with his parents.

Oh shit!

Immediately, the room fell quiet. They all stared at her in surprise. Troy looked like he saw a ghost. His mother, however, looked like she saw an insect she wanted to squish with her boot.

"Hello," she greeted them.

There was silence. Then her father went to her and gave her a hug.

"I missed you, sweetheart." He may have embraced her, but Adrienne felt so unwelcome and scrutinized.

How she wished she brought Justin with her. But she didn't think she'll be bringing him to any of her family gatherings in a long while.

"I missed you too, Dad," she replied to him.

She pulled away from her father and walked over to her Mom and gave her a peck on the cheek.

Then she bravely looked at Troy's family. "Good day, Mr. and Mrs. Williams." Then she gave Troy a slight nod.

She turned to her father and told him she'll just go freshen up in her bedroom.

When she got inside her bedroom, she found that it was a mess. Almost all of her stuff was in boxes. They were marked with her name. Even her bed only had the mattress, no pillows and no bedspreads.

She wondered who did this, and why. Maybe when Troy's family left, she would ask her parents about what happened.

She took some clothes from her bag and changed into a yellow floral dress that ended nicely above her knees. Then she tied her hair in a half-pony.

She took one last look at her disastrous room before going back to the living room. She nearly entered the living room when suddenly she heard her mother and Troy's talking on the other side of the wall.

"Well, I am just so glad that Troy finally came to his senses and went after Kimberly! I mean…I don't know what he was thinking going for Adrienne." She recognized Troy's mother's voice.

"Well, I have always wanted Troy to end up with Kim. I knew Adrienne would embarrass me at one point in time. I just never imagined it would end up in a brawl between her new boyfriend and Troy."

Adrienne stood behind the wall and listened to the older women's conversation. She was concealed by the door in front of her and the two women have no idea that their conversation was no longer private.

"I cannot believe that your daughter was cheating on my boy, Marina," Mrs. Williams said.

"Well…I tried, Betty. I tried to raise her like Kim. But she really got a bad set of genes. She didn't get that from our side of the family. She's given me problems ever since."

"But you're lucky, Kimberly is such a good daughter. My boy is happy to have Kim as his girlfriend now. I was afraid Adrienne was going to be my daughter-in-law. I didn't want to say this to you before, but I was really worried. Just imagine! She was sleeping with somebody else behind my son's back?"

Tears pooled in Adrienne's eyes. How could they talk about her like that? Didn't they know that Troy and Kim were cheating on her all this time? And how could her own mother talk about her like this?

"Oh, I'm sure Kimberly will make a better wife than Adrienne would ever be. Troy and Kimberly look fantastic together. With Adrienne…I worry about the grandchildren she would give you."

"I worry, too. Well, with Adrienne I will always be worrying if I'm really looking at my own grandchildren or someone else's." Mrs. Williams gave out a shrill laugh. Adrienne expected her mother to defend her. But her mother only laughed, too.

She wasn't a slut! She wasn't sleeping around! What is wrong with Troy's mother? What lies did her mother and her sister feed her head about her?

Suddenly, Adrienne felt a hand creep around her waist and somebody pulled her from behind. She quickly spun around and found Troy looking down at her, pulling her towards him. His eyes were teary.

She pushed him away.

"Let me go, Troy!" she hissed sharply.

"Oh, my Adrienne," he said. "I'm so sorry!"

Adrienne pushed him away. But Troy was quick to pull her to him, trying to hug her.

"I'm sorry, Adrienne," he kept saying. "I know…I can't compete with your new boyfriend but if you only give me a chance…I would make you happier than he ever will."

"No, Troy! Let go!" She pushed him again, gathering all her strength.

"What are you two doing?" Adrienne heard a shrill voice behind Troy, with made her pause. It made Troy pause, too.

Adrienne looked behind Troy and found Kimberly staring at them angrily. She pushed Troy once again and he no longer forced himself on her. She gave him another slap on the face.

"I said, let me go!" she said to him angrily. "What the hell is wrong with you?!"

Suddenly, the elders rushed from the living room to the corridor to see what the commotion was about.

"What is going on here?" her mother asked, looking at her crossly.

"Troy…" his mother started.

"Mom! Adrienne was trying to seduce Troy! I saw him pushing her away but she was forcing him to kiss her," Kim said.

"What?!" Adrienne couldn't believe what Kimberly said.

She stared back at her mother and Mrs. Williams who looked at her disapprovingly.

"You believe her?" Adrienne asked them.

"Why would she lie?" her mother asked her back. "And what else could be the explanation for it?"

"Troy was forcing me!"

"Come on, Adrienne, we all know you've always been easy. Why? Is your boyfriend busy humping somebody else so you decided to steal mine this time?" Kimberly asked venomously.

She stared at Kimberly's pretty little face and all she saw was… red. Blood red.

She didn't breathe. She didn't even think! Nobody saw it coming. Nobody even thought it was possible at all.

All these years of being patient with her sister, tolerating her in making her life miserable, all the days of bottled up pain and anger just exploded in a few seconds.

Suddenly, Adrienne no longer stood on Troy's side. She was beside her sister and grabbing the thing that she had always dreamed of pulling: Kimberly's hair.

"Aaaaahh!" Kim screamed in pain. Kim started flinging her arms and Adrienne managed to get hold of one of them and she twisted it behind Kim.

Wow! My sister is a wimp!

"I am so sick and tired of your lies!" she said to her angrily. "I never did anything to you! You kept lying about me! Why don't you tell everybody how I found out about you and Troy at the beach? Huh?! Tell them how you were fucking my boyfriend behind my back! How the two of you have been cheating on me all this time!"

Her mother gasped. Then she was quick to come to Kim's rescue. "Kim is a virgin!"

"Virgin her ass!" Adrienne released her sister and pushed her to Troy. Troy caught her. Kim's face was tear-stricken and she looked positively scared of Adrienne. Adrienne turned to Troy. "What did I ever do to you? You were cheating on me! I found you having sex with my own sister…during the weekend getaway you planned for us! And when I broke up with you, you got drunk and beat me up! Did you tell them that? Did any of you know that Troy has a bad temper with women? He sliced up my lip pretty badly… after sleeping with Kimberly!"

"Is this true?" Troy's father asked him, unable to believe what she just said about their son.

Troy stared at the floor. And then he nodded.

"Oh my God," Troy's mother breathed.

"I'm not some slut like you think, Mrs. Williams," she said to Troy's mother. "I didn't love your son. And I wanted to break up with him and at least remain his friend. But would you be friends with some guy who cheated on you with your own sister and beat you up after?"

Mrs. Williams shook her head slightly.

Adrienne looked at Troy once again. "What were you thinking, forcing me just now? I pushed you away and told you to let me go! You wouldn't let go. What did you want?"

Troy took a deep breath. "A chance, Adrienne," he replied. "A chance to make things right between us. It's always been you I wanted. I made a mistake." He turned to Kim. "I'm sorry, Kim. I tried. I tried to fall in love with you. But I can't. I still love your sister."

Kim looked like she didn't know what hit her. She expected Troy to take her side on this one.

"Are you happy now?" Kim turned to Adrienne. "Are you happy making my life miserable?"

Before Adrienne could talk, the doorbell rang. Her mother opened the door and two police officers entered the house.

"Her! That girl! Get that girl!" her mother said pointing at her. "She physically assaulted my daughter. We're going to file a case against her and make sure she stays in jail!"

Adrienne stared back at her mother, in pure shock.

"Mom?"

Somehow, she remembered when she was young how she held her in her arms and sang her to sleep. She could hardly believe that this was the same woman. What did she ever do to her?

"Marina!" her father shouted. "You can't do this!"

Even Troy's parents were shocked. Sure, her mother can just reprimand her or say nasty things to her, but to have her arrested?

"Marina, she's still your daughter!" Troy's father said.

"I don't have a violent daughter! She's crazy! If she doesn't belong in jail, then maybe a mental institution would fix her."

Adrienne stared at her father. "Dad?" Tears poured from her eyes as she felt the police officers take her arms and cuffed her hands behind her.

"Marina, stop this!" her father pleaded. "My daughter cannot be jailed!"

"My daughter cannot be battered by that crazy girl! She's out of control. She shouldn't be let out in the streets!"

"Marina, you are overreacting!" her father said angrily.

Tears kept pouring from Adrienne's cheeks and she wanted to curl in a ball in one corner. She realized that her mother didn't just not love her. Her mother hated her. And she couldn't understand why. She couldn't understand what she did to make her mother loathe her with so much passion.

***

"I love you, Mommy. Happy Mothers' day!" She remembered her eight-year-old self, bringing home a bouquet of roses for her mother. She was the only one in the family who remembered that it was Mothers' Day right then.

Her mother stared at the roses for a while and then placed them on the kitchen table. "Thank you…sweetie." Then she leaned down and kissed her forehead lightly.

It wasn't special, and she barely saw the appreciation on her face, but it was one of those rare moments that Adrienne got a little bit of affection from her mother.

All her life, she was trying to win her approval. Whenever she came home, Kim would jump into her arms and she would kiss her all over the face. Then Adrienne would look at her mother expectantly and she would… just ruffle her hair.

When Kim got her period, her mother was all supportive, telling her what to do. When Adrienne got her period, her mother couldn't care less and told her to search the internet about it.

Now…her mother called the police to have her arrested. And for what? A simple hair-pulling? Kim didn't even have a scratch on her. But her mother was hell-bent on making sure she pays for this—behind bars! Her father tried to reason with her mother but she knew he would never win. Her father showed her some affection. But it always seemed like he feared what her mother would say or do to him.

Adrienne stayed in a cell for a couple of hours while her father tried to convince her mother to stop this craziness. Unless her mother came to her senses and saw how petty this was, she would drop the charges. But as of the moment, she's in for assault causing physical injuries. If Adrienne really knew Kim and her Mom, they would go for attempted homicide.

Oh God! What did I do to deserve all this? What did I do to deserve the parents that I have now?

She knew her friends were somewhere outside, trying to do what they could to convince her mother to find some sensibility or lucidity. But she knew for sure how stubborn the woman could be.

She sat on a bench and noticed that the chair had some markings on them. She saw some scribbles, some names. Maybe they were done by some kids who got to spend a day or a night in the detention cell like her. Maybe for petty crimes too. Like shoplifting. Stealing condoms and bubble gums. And now her: a completely justified and long overdue hair-pulling escapade.

She smiled in spite of herself. She wondered what Justin would say if she told him about this.

He will be mad, for sure. But he would admire her for standing up against Kim, for not allowing Kim to keep trampling on her over and over.

Kim's been doing that to me my entire life. It's high time Kim gets scared of me.

"Miller." Adrienne heard a policewoman call her.

She stood up and followed her outside.

"Somebody posted bail," the desk sergeant told her. "But your mother still seems keen on filing charges." He shook his head, and looked at her apologetically.

No surprises there!

Of course, it was her precious Kimberly she hurt. Plus, she ratted Kim out in front of Troy's parents. Her mother must be seriously pissed.

At least my father posted bail!

She found her parents waiting for her. So was Kim… also known as '*the victim.*' Her friends stood on one side throwing daggers at Kimberly. Troy and his parents sat in one corner.

"What is she doing out? Why is she out?" her mother asked upon seeing her free.

"She posted bail, ma'am."

"Bail?" her mother echoed. "We didn't post bail."

The policewoman rolled her eyes at her mother. "Well, somebody did!" Then she turned to Adrienne and asked her to sign a paper and handed over her stuff, which only included her phone and her wallet.

"Did you bail her out?" her mother asked her father.

"No," her father said. "You wouldn't let me!"

"So, who posted bail?" Kim asked, turning to her friends.

"We would have, but we didn't have enough cash on us," Yuan said in an annoyed tone.

"Marina, I'm begging you! Shut up! And stop this!" It was probably the first time she saw her father angry at her mother.

Her mother took a step closer to her and looked at her contemptuously. "How dare you hurt my little baby like that? You ungrateful snake! I raised you! I let you share my home! And this is what you do to me in return?"

Adrienne didn't recognize the woman in front of her anymore. She was so angry at Adrienne, she even looked possessed. Without warning, she raised her hand and hit Adrienne solidly across the cheek.

Adrienne didn't duck, she didn't even try to block her mother's slap. She was too broken, too confused to think about anything else. And she thought she could use the physical pain to alleviate the emotional one she felt.

She staggered backwards from the force of her mother's slap. Her father immediately grabbed her mother to prevent her from hitting Adrienne again. Only then did Adrienne realize that somebody had caught her. Somebody held her, kept her warm, and kept her away from her mother... kept her safe from further attacks.

"Let me go! Let me go!" her mother screamed.

Yuan and Jill gasped. They stood frozen on their places.

"Marina, get a hold of yourself!" her father said angrily, still struggling to restrain her. "You're in a police station for crying out loud! You can get arrested for assault!"

Adrienne finally looked up at the person who had caught her, and shielded her from her mother's attacks.

She found herself staring at a familiar pair of aquamarine eyes. Adrienne thought that his eyes were more striking than usual. She saw a hint of emotion there. It took her a moment to recognize what it was... *fury!*

27.
Xiāoshī
Mandarin for, To Vanish

"Are you all right?" Jin Starck asked Adrienne.

She nodded slowly.

Her hand went to her cheek, rubbing it to ease a little of the sting caused by her mother's palm. Jill and Yuan now stood behind her, trying to give whatever comfort they could provide at that moment, both were throwing daggers at Kim and her mother with their eyes.

Jin turned to look at her mother, her father and her sister. He stood in front of Adrienne, as if to shield her against her own family.

The charming, mischievous and seemingly innocent aura that he usually possessed seemed to have evaporated instantly. Instead, her family faced a cold, murderous and scary man that even froze her mother in her place.

Jin pointed a finger to her mother and said, "You touch her again, and you will find yourself with a sorry-ass lawsuit! And I will file a complaint with the state medical board to make sure you will never be able to practice your profession ever again!" he said in a voice that almost sounded like a growl. He turned to Adrienne. "I'm the one who posted bail."

"Is this the rich boyfriend you were talking about?" her mother asked Kim in a low voice.

Kim shook her head. "No, it's a different guy." She rolled her eyes and murmured, "What a slut!"

Unfortunately for her, Jin Starck heard that.

"Kimberly Alexis Miller!" Jin said in a booming, loud voice that turned everybody in the room silent. "Adrienne only had two boyfriends in her life and she barely even saw one of them. Is that your definition of a slut? Or is it the goody-two-shoes who lost her V-card at the age of thirteen to her college neighbor, Danny. Then slept with the whole football team in high school, including the married coach.

"Bar-hopping every weekend in med school, waking up with strangers in the morning. Sleeping with university professors to make sure she got the grades she wanted…and sleeping with somebody high up as her insurance for graduation."

Adrienne watched Kimberly's face drain of blood.

"I've got dirt on you Miss Miller. And when my people dig, they dig deep," Jin said relentlessly. "Does your mother know you were treated for sexually transmitted diseases at least six times now?" Jin tried to look innocent and then he added, "Oh! I guess you went to a different OB-GYN. Too bad, Dr. Miller. Your daughter would have made a good patient. Lots of repeat consultations and procedures."

Kim's eyes filled with tears. Her face was white. And everybody, including Troy and his parents heard what Jin Starck said to her.

"How dare you say those lies about my daughter?" Mrs. Miller asked angrily.

"How dare you lay a finger on Adrienne!" Jin barked back at her. Then he stared at Kimberly. "And they weren't lies, were they, Miss Miller?"

"Who are you anyway? Why do you say these things like you own us? Like you could buy us?" Adrienne's mother asked angrily.

Adrienne's father on the other hand was staring at Jin with narrowed eyes, like he was trying to place him.

Jin stared at Mrs. Miller and Kimberly crossly. "My name is Jin." He looked at Adrienne gently. "Jin *Adrien* Starck." Then he gave Adrienne's father a sharp look.

Adrienne's father gasped, as if the name rang a bell. And then his face turned red. He suddenly looked ghastly.

"I own Starck Hoteliers Corporation, so yes, I think I can buy you!" Jin said to Adrienne's mother. Then he turned Adrienne and gave her a rueful look. "And I'm also… your brother."

Adrienne gasped. Her hand went to her mouth.

Brother? How?

"You're Kim's brother too?" Adrienne asked softly.

"Thank God, no!" Jin replied. Then he gave her father a hard look. "You should have told her a long time ago. Now, you lost that chance!"

"What truth?" Adrienne asked, confused.

"Adrienne…" Her father started.

"Your father's real name was Henry Dennison." Jin cut him off. "When you were two years old, he changed his name to Henry Miller, with the help of Marina Miller, of course, the lady you thought was your mother."

Adrienne stared at her father in shock. "Daddy…why?"

Her father now has tears in his eyes. "Because…I didn't want your real mother to take you away from me."

"My real mother?" Adrienne echoed. She looked at Jin.

"Our mother, Adrienne," Jin said as gently as he could.

Adrienne shook her head. "How…how…I don't understand."

"Our mother was raised in the States, where she met your Dad and had you. But she didn't tell him who she was in France. She was an heiress of a hotel tycoon and her father had arranged for her to marry his business associate's son…Pierre Starck, the then heir of Starck Hoteliers Corporation, my father." Jin said.

Adrienne watched her father's reaction. He couldn't even look at Adrienne now.

"Your parents separated and after, our mother found out that her father was suffering from cancer. He was considered terminal when Mom went back to France. She couldn't tell him that she had a family in the States because she thought he would never forgive her. And she didn't want him to bring that pain to his grave. But she told my Dad about you and he still agreed to marry her nevertheless.

"Mother made arrangements for your father to keep you safe until after her wedding and she would take you to France. Your father agreed to give her custody of you...because she would be able to take better care of you. She trusted your father. But when she went back to the States, Henry Dennison disappeared, without a trace. So did you."

Adrienne's father was crying now. Finally, he looked at her with great remorse.

"All my life, my mother searched for you, Adrienne. Her heart was broken and her happiness with us never seemed complete because she thought she lost you," Jin continued. "My father hired people to look for Henry because he promised our Mom he would return you to her. But we were in vain. All we had was a picture of you, when you were two years old. Our grandfather came to know about you eventually and forgave our mother. Even on his death bed, he wished for you to be returned to us."

Then Jin stared at her father. "You changed your name and hers and erased her mother from her past. You let her grow up thinking that her own mother and sister couldn't love her. You deprived her of the maternal love she so deserved." He gave the Mr. Miller a disgusted look. "What kind of father are you?" Jin almost spat.

"If you had let her live with us, my father would have loved her as his own! She is the daughter of one of the wealthiest women in France and you deprived her of her birthright. You deprived her of the luxuries she could have lived with. She could have lived like a princess all her life! You denied her all of that. But what's unforgiveable...is that you deprived her of the joy that a loving family would give her!"

Adrienne stared at her father. She struggled to find her voice. "Dad...please...tell me it isn't true!"

Her father closed his eyes. Tears rolled down his cheeks. "I was afraid of losing you, baby. I knew how powerful your mother was and I knew she could take you away from me. I was...a struggling doctor. I had little means to fight for you. Especially not against your mother and her new husband." He took a deep breath and turned to Marina. "We had a deal," he said to her. "I will father your daughter and in return you would replace Adrienne's mother in her life, give her the motherly love she needed. But...you never loved her."

"How could I love her?" Adrienne's mother fired back. "Every time I look at your daughter...all I see is...her! Ariana Blanc! The love of your life! I was everything to you before you met her! You left me for her! And then when she left you, you came back to me! I accepted you thinking that things would go back to the way they used to be. But no! You couldn't love me the way you loved her. She meant the whole world to you! She left your life, but she never left your heart! I know it! I feel it!

"So, how could you expect me to love her daughter the way I loved my own? She reminded me of how you left me for her mother! And how you asked me to save you when she left you torn and broken. You married me after Kim's father left me…after Adrienne's mother left you. But you never stopped loving her!"

Adrienne looked at the mother she's known all her life. She wasn't just imagining it. Now, she knew the truth that she tried to deny over and over all her life: Her mother never loved her.

"Mom…I truly loved you. I was content just to have…a little bit of the love you gave Kim. And all my life I asked myself why you couldn't love us equally." Tears rolled down her cheeks. "I truly believed there was something wrong with me." She shook her head. "But there wasn't. All my life, you took out your jealousy on me."

Marina looked at Adrienne, contempt still visible on her face. But she didn't say anything. Either she had nothing to say to her, or she felt scared that if she did lash out on her, Jin Starck will retaliate, at her or at Kim's expense.

"This is so messed up!" Adrienne breathed. Then she looked at Jin. "How long have you known?"

"Not long," he replied. "When I first saw you, I thought you looked very familiar. So familiar that I found it creepy. It even gave me goosebumps. After a while, I realized why. You look like Mom when she was your age. Then I set up a meeting with you to get to know you. And to get a DNA sample from you."

"How did you do that?"

Jin sighed. "We dined in my restaurant, Adrienne. It was easy enough to sneak out the glass you used and immediately send it to a lab. My staff got briefed beforehand on what they needed to do. You didn't even realize it."

"And?"

"And they compared it to my DNA. Just as I suspected. We had the same mitochondrial DNA, which means, we have the same mother. And trust me. I made the lab run the test three times. You are my sister, Adrienne." No matter how gentle his voice was, the blow still felt the same to Adrienne. It didn't take away the fact that her parents had lied to her all her life.

Jin turned to her father. "I must admire the way you covered your tracks. We searched high and low." Then he looked at her mother. "You must know all sorts of crooks to be able to pull off what you did." Jin shook his head. "But you can't get in the way of fate, and the truth, of course. God found a way for Adrienne and I to meet. Unfortunately for you, I don't believe in coincidences. And I always follow my gut feelings."

Adrienne looked at her father. She honestly didn't know what to feel. She felt mad at him for what he did. She was angry at the fact that he forced her to live with a monstrous woman who did nothing but belittle her and destroy her self-respect. She became furious that he stole precious years she could have spent with her real mother and her real brother. Years she could never get back.

"Adrienne..." her father stated softly. "I am sorry, my child. I am so, so sorry."

Adrienne bit her lip. Tears overflowing her eyes, she said to him, "You could have at least stood up for me throughout all these years, Daddy. The mother I've known may not have a reason to love me. But you did. You could have fought for me all these years that she and Kim made my life miserable. All those years that Mom made me feel I was good for nothing. Those years that they crushed my spirit and crippled my self-worth." She couldn't help herself. She wasn't shouting at her father. But she spoke harsh words straight from her heart...finally telling her father how hard life had been for her.

She wiped the tears on her face. "But you know what's more painful, Dad?" She paused, giving him time to absorb everything she said. Then she took a deep breath and added, "Is that you just stood there and watched!"

With that, she grabbed her phone and her wallet, and turned her back on them.

She blindly walked to the exit of the station. When she stepped outside, the cold breeze greeted her and she shivered. But only for a second. Because immediately, she felt the material of Jin's leather jacket cover her bare arms.

She looked up at him—her brother.

"I'm sorry, you had to find out that way," he said to her.

She took a deep breath. "So that day we met at the bar and I passed out, you already knew you were my brother."

He nodded. "Took me all my strength not to tell you, you know. That was the same day that the DNA results came to my mail. I was so happy. But I couldn't figure out a way to tell you without breaking your heart."

Adrienne sighed. "It broke my heart either way."

"I know," he said. "There was no way to break it to you gently. So last night, I just stopped figuring things out. I thought, just rip off the bandage. When I found out you went to Boston, I flew here immediately. I was hoping to talk to your father first. Give him a chance to tell you himself. But when I learned that you were picked up and detained, I just blew my top." He reached up and touched her cheek gently. "No one hurts my sister and gets away with it."

Adrienne's heart swelled at those words. Because she knew…that would be the exact opposite of what Kimberly would say and do. She reached forward and hugged Jin. As she buried her face against his chest, she cried her heart out.

When Adrienne's tears subsided, Jin pulled away from her and wiped her face with his fingers.

"We're going home, Adrienne," he said. "Now. Not a day later. Mom has waited for you for almost half of her life. She's suffered too much already."

"Didn't you say that she was Amanda Seville? The famous writer," Adrienne asked.

Jin grinned. "Now you know where your talent came from."

A surge of happiness filled Adrienne's heart. She felt like…finally all the questions she's been asking herself all her life were answered by Jin in one night.

She nodded. She would love to meet her mother… her real mother. The one who sang songs to her and cuddled her in her sleep when she was too young to even remember.

Jin put an arm around her shoulder. Then he turned back to find Yuan and Jill standing behind them, still in shock. They were as dumbfounded as Adrienne, herself

"I'm taking Adrienne to Paris tonight. You guys wanna come?" Jin asked them.

It took a moment for Adrienne's friends to recover. Then Yuan asked, "Why? You're going to pay for our flights?" It was a sarcastic question.

"Flights, food and accommodation for a week, or however long you want to keep my sister company," Jin replied without blinking.

Yuan and Jill stared at each other in pure shock. Once they recovered, Yuan grinned and said, "Oh, Jin Starck, we're totally sold!"

28.
Xemethistos
Greek, meaning Sober

"*T*he prodigal son returns." Jordan Gibson was peering from the top of the staircase, looking down as his older cousin walked inside the house.

Justin looked at him out of the corner of his eyes. His cousin had a smirk on his face and it almost took all of his strength not to climb the twenty-step staircase and break his nose. He was usually not a violent person. But he just spent the entire flight from New York to Chicago pushing his alcohol tolerance to its limit. Patience did not rank high on his virtue list right now. "Fuck off, Jord!" he muttered instead.

Jordan received a gentle punch on the shoulder from his other cousin, Gian. They watched as Justin walked straight to his father's study on the ground floor of the twelve-bedroom mansion.

Just before Justin opened the door, Gian called out to him.

"Hey J!"

Justin turned back to Gian. He smiled at him. "I like her!"

Then Ian peered from behind her twin brother's shoulder. "Me, too! I became a fan when she slammed the door in your face. No wonder you're crazy about her." She smiled at him encouragingly.

Justin nodded at his cousins. He appreciated their support. He needed it. Especially now, since his heart bled from Adrienne's decision to give him his freedom. Freedom to embrace his destiny. Freedom to give his parents' crazy decision a chance.

No! What Adrienne did only made him love her more. He knew how broken she was and how painful it was for her to give him up to another woman. And yet, she still set him free because she didn't want him to destroy his relationship with his parents.

And because of what she did, she just proved to Justin that she was the only woman worthy of becoming Mrs. Justin Adams.

God! Let me fix this! I could use a miracle!

He opened the door of his father's study. His father looked up from the stack of papers he worked on, his eyes transfixed on his son.

"Where's Mom?" Justin asked his father.

"In the hospital," he said. "I'll take you there after I sign these papers."

Justin nodded and went to the wine counter and poured himself some whiskey. He was quiet. He felt that nothing he could say to his father would make him change his opinion of him, or his mind about making him marry the brat of their good friends. He drank the liquor, keeping his back to his father. He silently looked at the books in front of him, not really reading their titles. But he just needed something to look at to keep himself from having another verbal judo match with his father.

He felt a hand on his shoulder.

"Son..." his father started.

Justin inclined his head slightly towards his old man.

His father took a deep breath. "I'm sorry I kicked you out. But I'm glad you're back."

Justin looked at the books in front of him again. He didn't say anything.

His father removed his hand from his shoulder. "Thank you. For coming back. Your mother took it very hard."

Justin drank his whiskey straight up. Then he turned to his father. "Don't thank me," he finally said. "Thank Adrienne." Pain shot to his heart when he mentioned her name. "She set me free. Because she didn't want me to destroy my relationship with you. If she didn't beg me to come here, I wouldn't be in front of you...feeling absolutely miserable."

And then he went to the door. "Are we going to the hospital or not?"

"Justin!" his father roared at him. "Do not disrespect me."

Justin threw his hands in the air. "I'm not disrespecting you! But I hope you excuse my less-than-gallant demeanor today, Dad. I happen to be a little heartbroken! The love of my life asked me... no, begged me, to leave her so I can come back to you. I'm sure you remember what a heartbreak feels like! Or maybe you don't. Coz you've woken up to the love of your life for the last twenty-eight years."

"Son..." his father started. "When I was in your place, before I met your mother, I was exactly like this. I didn't understand why my parents forced me to marry somebody I haven't met yet. I understood the business arrangement. But at that point, I asked them, too...why it's me who needed to sacrifice for the family. We had more than we needed. I couldn't understand why we wanted more." His father looked at him wearily. "But I couldn't thank them enough for their choice. Your mother is an excellent woman."

Justin raised a brow at his father. "So is Adrienne," he said evenly.

"We want to make sure you marry well," his father said. "That the woman you will marry is marrying you not for your money or your privilege."

Justin narrowed his eyes and pretended to look thoughtful. "Gees! If I wasn't Justin Adams, she wouldn't be arranged to marry me. Isn't that considered marrying me for my money or my privilege?"

His father took a deep breath, doubtless trying to control his temper. "This conversation is pointless. You're drunk. You aren't in your proper frame of mind."

Justin grinned at his father sarcastically. "It won't make a difference, Dad," he said. "Because this is how I'm going to be for the rest of my life. Drunk and not in the proper frame of mind. So I suggest, get used to it."

"One more disrespectful word out of your mouth and your wedding will happen sooner than you can turn sober!" his father said in a booming voice.

"Sir, yes, sir," Justin murmured, turning towards the door and opening it. "I'll see you in the car. I have a feeling...and this is just a hunch...that... that I'm way over the alcohol limit. Obviously, I can't... can't drive."

He exited the room. He was a little tipsy, yes. But he had a high alcohol tolerance, he knew he couldn't entirely blame alcohol for his less than respectful words to his father.

He found Ian standing at the foot of the stairs, staring at him wearily. She has a look of sadness on her face.

"I'm sorry, Justin," she whispered. She ran to him and gave him a hug. "I'm so sorry."

It took a moment for Justin to put an arm on Ian's back.

"Don't be sorry for me just yet, Ian," Justin whispered. "Be sorry for the girl whose fate is being forced to mine."

Ian pulled away from Justin and stared at him. "Justin... what do you mean?"

Justin stared down at Ian. His eyes glittered in spite of himself. "Just wait, Ian. I would die first before I marry some other woman other than Adrienne."

"Justin...they would...disown you!" Ian whispered.

"They already did," Justin said. "And yet, I'm still here. More miserable than ever."

Gian and Jordan appeared behind Ian's back.

"We feel you, cuz," Gian said. "If you need help, you know you can count on us, right?"

Justin smiled at his cousins. "I know. But right now, I think I might be on my own."

His father emerged from his study and looked at his son and his cousins. "You guys going to visit your aunt?" he asked.

"We just came from there," Ian began. "She's doing fine. Just minor cuts and bruises. Doctor said she'll be home in a day or two." Somehow Justin knew that it was her way of telling him not to feel too guilty about his mother's condition. It wasn't anything serious.

Jac Adams looked at his son. "Let's go."

Justin didn't speak the rest of the way to the hospital. He leaned back on his seat and closed his eyes. He thought about Adrienne. The way she looked the first time he saw her. She appeared so conservative and reserved, hiding away her beautiful personality beneath her knit sweaters, plaid pants and black-rimmed glasses. She looked like a woman who had no idea how attractive she could be and couldn't care less about what others would think about her.

The first time he laid eyes on her, something in him stirred. The fact that she didn't even look up at him when he passed by the corridors of Blush made her even more attractive to him.

He never had a problem with the ladies. He didn't even have to memorize or master the use of pickup lines. He had always been confident of his looks, and the name he carried had its advantages in charming a woman to his bed. But he made it clear from the start that he was just having fun. Nothing spelled permanency. The fact that he knew he was already promised to another woman took the pressure off his back to make a woman fall in love with him. He didn't care if the woman walked out on him after they spent the night together. If she didn't, then he would.

Remembering how he used to be, Justin couldn't help thinking that Adrienne was right. He was an asshole when she first met him. But he was no longer that guy. He no longer wanted to play the field.

He played on Wall Street because he did well there. That was him. Things just seemed to come easy to him. He played the stock market and made millions on his own, because it gave him something worthwhile to do before he embraced his destiny of being the heir of Adams Industries. Just like how he played the field with women. It gave him a reprieve before he surrendered himself to his bride-to-be. The woman he would pledge his faithfulness to for the rest of his life.

But when Adrienne came to his life, he realized that he was done. It was time to start taking things seriously. He started working for his father. He only kept the stocks he thought were worth keeping. He stopped playing on Wall Street...he stopped playing the field with women. He started becoming serious. He stopped being rebellious...and hoped his family would see how this woman changed him. How she was so good for him. But nothing changed. The moment they saw him coming around, they also thought he was ready to meet his destined wife.

They didn't see that he changed because of Adrienne. Because finally, he started seeing his future with her. He started imagining himself taking the reins from his father, and then coming home every night to the woman he couldn't live without. He started believing he could be happily married to a woman... something he never saw before, knowing how he would end up marrying his parents' choice for him.

"We are here." His father interrupted his thoughts.

When Justin opened his eyes, he felt pain in his head. The effects of alcohol had started to take a toll on him. He pressed his temples with his fingers.

"Headache?" his father asked.

"Good that we're at a hospital then," Justin murmured.

His mother had the most luxurious suite in the hospital. When she saw him, she cried almost instantly.

"Oh, Justin," she said, stretching her arms out to him.

Justin went to her silently. He gave his mother a hug. When he pulled away from her, he saw that she only had a small cut on her forehead. Ian was right. She had minor injuries. But what Justin really worried about was her emotional pain.

"Sweetheart, I'm so glad you came back."

Justin still didn't say anything. He didn't want to make her feel any worse than she already did.

Then his mother stared back at him. "Have you been drinking?" she asked.

He nodded slightly. Then he finally said, "I'm glad to see that you're doing better now."

She smiled at him apologetically. "When your father said you were going to move out of the house, I thought I'd never see you again."

He gave her a reassuring smile. "You know that...won't happen, Mom. I will always find time to see you."

"I'm sorry, sweetheart," she said. "You know...you know we were only looking out for you."

Justin nodded again. He may disagree with his parents on many things, but he would always love them. Other than the fact that they were forcing him to marry somebody he didn't love, he knew that they've always been the best parents.

They were interrupted by the nurse. Justin went to stand by the glass windows and looked at the view of the hospital. Again, he lost himself in his thoughts. His heart still ached every time he thought about Adrienne and her pain when she let him go. How she made love to him the prior night. How she answered his question when they pretended he was free to ask that question at all. The letter she wrote to him, which he knew she wrote with deep sorrow.

He knew he had to play his cards right. Making his parents change their minds was a tricky business. He's played the games of life many times and didn't care if he won or lost. But this time... he knew he couldn't afford to lose. Money wasn't at stake here. This time, it's his life, his heart, his soul. And he's already decided only one woman has the right to claim them.

"Justin..." his mother called him.

Justin turned to his mother and didn't say anything.

"Are you okay, honey?" she asked.

You think?

He didn't say that out loud. His father might tolerate his attitude towards him, but he would never forgive him if he even utter one disrespectful word to his mother.

He nodded slightly. He stared out the window again. Nothing in the view in front of him seemed interesting. But he just didn't want to look at his mother and not say anything.

"Have you eaten?" she asked. "I will ask somebody to get you food."

Justin shook his head. "I'm not hungry, Mom."

Her mother nodded and smiled at him ruefully.

After a long period of silence, Justin went to his mother and kissed her forehead. "I need to get back," he said. "I could use a shower and my head feels like it's gonna split."

His mother hugged him. "I'm sorry, Justin," he heard tears in his voice. "I hope you will be able to forgive us."

Justin didn't hug his mother back, nor did he say anything. When he pulled away from her, he kissed her cheek again and then he headed for the door. His father didn't make an attempt to follow him.

Justin went out of the hospital and decided to walk to clear his head.

He looked at his phone. No calls. No messages. He stared at Adrienne's picture on his wallpaper. He missed her and his heart broke every time he thought that he couldn't be with her…at least not yet.

He dialed her number, unable to resist the urge to talk to her.

But it was off. He tried again. Still off. After two more attempts, he gave up. He took a deep breath. Maybe Adrienne was really pushing him to try his parents' way first and if it didn't work out, he could come back to her.

He didn't know how long that would take. He didn't have any intention to prolong it. He thought his best chance right now lay in his parents seeing how wrong this choice was. The next chance he has is if the girl he was arranged to… no, he would never use the word 'engaged'…would see what a monstrous, despicable guy he was. He hoped she would save herself the trouble and lifetime of misery and just let him go.

When he got home, he took a long, hot shower. He must have stayed under the water until his skin wrinkled. He sent a message to their butler to bring some food up for him. He no longer had any energy of facing any of his family members. At that time, he just wanted to be alone.

After dinner, he asked one of the maids to bring whisky and ice to his room. He drank in his room's balcony, looking at the starlit sky. There was a lover's moon in the sky and he again wished the woman he loved was in his arms, looking at it with him.

"Adrienne Miller…I love you so much. With all of my heart. I want no one else in my life, in my future. I want to spend an eternity with you. I want you to be the mother of all my children. Will you marry me?"

"Yes, Justin, I would."

He repeated that memory over and over in his head. How he wished, too…that everything was in the ideal world. That he asked her that question for real. And that she said yes.

He didn't know it, but tears started to well up in his eyes. He realized how scared he was. Scared that his parents wouldn't accept him returning to her. Scared that if he did come back, he would be too late.

Adrienne was an exquisite woman. A lot of guys were interested in her at *Blush*. Even some rich heirs seemed to have found a liking for her. It wasn't just him. And what killed Justin was the fact that he couldn't even do anything to prevent her from finding happiness with another guy... when he, himself, isn't free to give her the happiness that she deserved. And he's scared that someday, when he is finally free... she has grown tired of waiting and has given up on him.

He wiped his tears with his fingers. Then he took his glass to his lips and drank his whiskey again.

He had no idea that he was no longer alone. His father was standing behind him, watching him.

Jac Adams sat on the chair beside Justin and poured himself a glass of his whiskey. The two men sat there quietly, looking into space.

Then finally, Jac said to his son, "How do you know you're not going to fall in love with your betrothed?"

Justin sighed and in a more respectful tone he replied, "Because I only have one heart and it's no longer mine to give away."

"All the while, we thought we were only doing what's best for you."

"I did, too," Justin murmured. "Then I met her. And I realized that my love, my loyalty, my allegiance, my soul...wasn't yours to promise to some girl you see fit. The choice must be up to me. Because I'm going to be the one to decide whether I will be happy or miserable for the rest of my life. You cannot choose my happiness for me, Dad."

His father sighed. "Justin...to back out this late on this agreement would destroy the friendships we've built for generations. Her grandfather and yours were like brothers."

"So you'd rather destroy my life?" Justin couldn't help muttering.

"No. That would never be our intention."

Justin didn't answer back. Instead, he just drank his whiskey.

"Your mother was dreaming of a wedding in two months."

"And she's going to be disappointed." Justin said. His father stared at him. "You can't compel me to marry this brat earlier than three months."

His father raised a brow at him. "Why?"

Justin sighed. "I almost lived with Adrienne, Dad. And I'm sure it's no surprise to you if I say that...we've been together in bed. If I'm going to agree to this marriage, I have to at least make sure that Adrienne isn't pregnant. Because if she is, I won't care if you disown me or erase any trace of me in this family. I will not make my own child a bastard. I'm sure even you would understand that."

His father fell silent for a moment and then he nodded. "Fair enough. But in return, I want you to do something for us."

Justin sighed. "Really? Haven't you already asked me to hand in my life to a woman I've never even met?"

Jac nodded. "I want you to court your betrothed."

Justin almost fell from his seat. "You've got to be kidding me!"

Jac shook his head. "Get to know her. One year. That's what we usually do. Build a bond with her and make her like you...fall in love with you."

"Even if I'm not in love with her?" Justin asked.

"You don't know that, son. I didn't know that and yet I am still as in love with your mother now as I was when I married her. When I proposed to her, it wasn't a business arrangement anymore. I was proposing as a man...in love with the woman of his dreams."

"Really? You're really sure this woman you set me up with is the woman of my dreams? Because the last time I checked, I already found her."

"Justin...one year. And if she doesn't feel even a little bit of fondness for you...we will set you free."

Just held on to his glass tightly. Suddenly, he wanted to punch something, but he doubted his father would take that well.

He thought his father just gave him a way out of this. But one year is such a long time to wait to be with Adrienne again... one year seemed too long to make her wait.

"She will fall in love with you. Because you're Justin Adams...the guy underneath is so much more worth falling in love with."

Adrienne's faith in him made his heart swell and break at the same time. How the hell is he going to make her wait that long? And how the hell is he going to make sure that the woman his parents arranged for him to marry wouldn't like him at all?

"I think I've just given you a fair bargain," his father said. "One year, son. And in that one year, you're not allowed to see or contact your girlfriend. Give yourself a chance to be happy without her. And if by some miracle, you find it in yourself to accept your betrothed...give your girlfriend the chance to move on and find her happiness with somebody who is free to give it to her."

Justin didn't say anything. His father put his glass down on the table in front of them and stood up. He took one last look at his son. He put a hand on his shoulder and gave it a gentle squeeze. Then he silently left the room.

Justin sat alone in his balcony, thinking.

One year. One year was too long. He absolutely believed that he couldn't wait that long, even if Adrienne could. He had to find a way to expedite things...and make his misery shorter. He targeted one month as his limit. Not a day more.

But how could he turn one year eleven months shorter?

He took a deep breath. Well, his father gave him permission to see his so-called betrothed as often as possible to make sure she fell in love with him.

An idea formed in his thoughts. He would break some of his principles and values, but hell! He thought it would be worth it.

One month.

It seemed too short to make somebody fall in love. But too long to do the opposite.

Smiling now, he felt a new sense of hope and energy surging through his veins. He flipped his phone and typed a message to the only woman he would want to spend the rest of his life with.

Justin: *Where will you be in exactly forty days? Let me answer that for you. In Italy. Changing your last name to mine.*

JERILEE KAYE

29.
Stjålet
Norwegian for Stolen.

*A*drienne walked beside Jin Starck into the lavish mansion he called his home. Yuan and Jill trailed behind them.

"You still live with your parents?" Adrienne asked.

"In this house, yes," he replied. "But I have apartments of my own. This is a ten-bedroom house. It gets a little lonely for Mom sometimes so I make it a point to spend time here to keep her company. She doesn't work for our hotels. She spends a lot of time in her study. Writing."

Jin was greeted by their butler in French. He gave instructions to take Yuan and Jill to one of the waiting rooms and serve them refreshments.

Then he turned to Adrienne. "Follow me."

They ascended the stairs to the second level of the house. Adrienne couldn't help admiring how elegant and luxurious the house appeared. Never in her wildest dreams did she imagine that somebody related to her could live in a house like this.

They stopped in front of the room, situated in the corner. Jin took a deep breath and stared at her.

"Are you ready?" he asked.

"I don't think I will ever be," she replied truthfully.

Her brother reached down and squeezed her hand. "She is wonderful, Adrienne. You have no idea."

Adrienne nodded. "Let's go."

Jin gave her one last smile and then he opened the door.

The room they entered in was huge. She saw the four walls covered in shelves, all full of books. The room almost looked like a library. At the far end of the room was a huge oak desk with a white Macintosh computer and stacks of paper.

Jin pulled her towards the desk, where a woman sat, staring intently at the computer screen.

She said something in French to Jin, without looking up from her screen.

"English, Mom," Jin requested. "We have a guest from America."

The woman looked up from her screen. "Oh. I'm sorry. I expected you twenty-four hours ago. You didn't show up and left no word. And now, you're disturbing my battle scene."

Adrienne walked slower than Jin and hid behind his back.

"I doubt this can wait, Mom," Jin maintained, as he stopped in front of their mother's desk.

Finally, the woman peeled her eyes away from the computer screen to look up at his son. She immediately noticed Adrienne behind Jin's back, uncertain of what she would do or say.

No one will ever be ready to meet their real mother ten hours after learning about her. Adrienne's heart pounded loudly against her chest.

"Jin Adrien Starck!" the woman exclaimed. "Are you telling me that I'm going to be a grandmother soon?"

Adrienne blinked back for a second. Then she heard Jin laugh.

"I'm only twenty-three, Mom. And I'm not the first one in line to give you grandkids. I'm not your first-born, remember?"

Adrienne immediately saw the sadness that crossed the woman's face. "Well..." she sighed sadly. "Maybe you should then introduce me to your lady guest. I thought I taught you better manners."

Jin pulled Adrienne and made her step forward. She stood face to face now with the woman...who's been searching for her all her life. The woman whose words she lost herself to during those hours when she read her novels. The woman she didn't even know was her birth mother.

Ariana looked at Adrienne curiously. Her eyes narrowed, as if she was trying to figure out what was so familiar about her.

As Adrienne stared at the woman in front of her, she could see how Jin thought she looked familiar that first night they met. Her hair was the exact color as hers, even with the red highlights in them. Her eyes...exactly the same green of hers. She was older and looked more confident than herself. But Adrienne could see herself in this woman...the way she never saw herself in the mother she'd known all her life.

"Mom..." Jin said softly. "I'd like you to meet... Adrienne." Jin paused for a second. "Actually, we've been calling her Andrea for years."

Andrea?

In a second, her mother's eyes widened. Recognition and realization finally crossed her face, as if she finally found the final piece of the puzzle she's been trying to solve for decades.

"Adrienne..." she whispered. Then she stared at her son, "Our Andrea?"

Hearing her say those words brought tears to Adrienne's eyes. She heard the love in her voice...just by saying the name of her child. And she realized she's been waiting all her life to hear the mother she's known say her name the way this woman did just then.

"I have three DNA results that says she is," Jin disclosed.

Adrienne heard her mother gasp and put her hands on her mouth. Tears spilled from her eyes. Immediately, she moved from her desk and in a few seconds, Adrienne felt her arms around her. She was almost hysterical, hyperventilating as she hugged her.

"Oh my God! Oh my God!" Ariana cried. "My baby! My baby!"

Adrienne couldn't help crying, too. She put her own arms around the mother she never knew existed until a few hours beforehand.

Ariana pulled away and stared at her. She cupped her face in her hands and whispered, "I thought I had lost you forever. I thought I would never see you again."

Adrienne bit her lip. She couldn't stop crying. She held her mother's hands in hers.

"Where were you all these years? Was your father good to you? Did you have a good life? Where did you grow up? Did he give you everything you needed? Did he take good care of you?"

Adrienne didn't know which question to answer first. And even if she did, she couldn't find her voice. She just kept crying, finally feeling for the first time in her life the motherly affection she craved all her life.

"She lived in Boston. Your ex changed his name, his identity and hers so we wouldn't find them. He changed her name from Andrea Blanc to Adrienne Miller," Jin answered for her. "If by good life, you meant did she have a roof over her head or food to eat, or was she taken care of whenever she got sick, or was she sent to the university to finish a degree, then yes. She did. She was." Jin paused for a moment and then he added, "But if you mean did she have a mother who loved her and took care of her the way you would have? No. She didn't."

Ariana bit her lip and looked at Adrienne apologetically. She hugged Adrienne again, as if she was trying to erase all the pain that her separation from her birth mother had caused her.

"I'm so sorry, baby," Ariana whispered to her. "I am so sorry. None of this was your fault. None of this would have happened if I made the right choices from the beginning. I shouldn't have trusted your father. I am so sorry, my baby."

Adrienne cried like a little girl. She felt the comfort, security and love that her mother's embrace provided her. Now, more than ever, she wished she'd have felt her embraces whenever she got wounded or hurt all those years when she was growing up.

"I-it's not your fault," she whispered. She pulled away from her mother and looked into her eyes. "We cannot recover those years that were stolen from us. But I'm so glad I was still given a chance to meet you now."

Her mother nodded and kissed her forehead. "Yes, my baby. I never thought I would have the chance to see you again. But thank God your brother found you. A couple of weeks ago, he said he had a lead on you. I didn't really think that it would be so soon. I thought this day wouldn't come at all. I have loved you all my life. And until now, I thought I would never get a chance to say that to you at all."

Her mother pulled away from her, took her hand and led her to the couches. They sat beside each other. Then she turned to Jin. "Have somebody bring something to eat and drink here. Adrienne and I have a lot to talk about. Then have dinner prepared. We're all dining together."

Jin nodded. Adrienne looked at him and smiled in spite of the tears rolling down her cheeks. She gave her brother a smile.

Jin turned to his mother and spoke to her in French. Her mother nodded. Then Jin smiled at his sister one last time and turned to leave the room.

Ariana turned back to Adrienne and once again touched her cheek, tears brimming her eyes. "I thought I would never see you again."

Adrienne let out a small whimper. Then she said, "I... never knew you existed until after Jin came to find me in Boston."

"He erased me from your life," her mother said soberly.

Adrienne took a deep breath and told her mother everything that her father did and how she grew up all these years.

They must have talked for hours. Her mother couldn't stop crying and cursing at the same time. Adrienne understood how she felt. She felt exactly the same. They were both just victims of her father's lies and treachery. She didn't tell her much about how the mother she's known all her life had treated her. She figured that could be saved for later. Right now, her father's obvious deception seemed already too much to bear.

"When you were a baby, I wanted to name you Adrienne," her mother divulged. "Your father knew I has half-French. I didn't tell him though...that I had a family obligation I wanted to escape. My father...bless his soul...was a tyrant. What he said...must be done. He arranged for me to marry Pierre. I didn't want to. Then I met your father and fell in love with him. He thought Adrienne was too French, and named you Andrea instead." Her mother looked at her, "Then he changed your name to Adrienne? I would never have thought he would use that name. He was so much against it when you were born."

"Were you ever married to my father?"

My mother shook her head. "No. We lived together. We didn't have enough money. I was writing but it wasn't enough. Your father had just started his career and we struggled."

"Why did you separate?"

My mother took a deep breath. "Because your father was too proud," she stated. "I decided to be honest with him. He found out that I was an heiress. He was nothing. He couldn't accept that. It made him feel small. It got into his head. Plus, money remained difficult. He was hot-headed." Her mother sighed. "Then I found out that my father had become very ill, and I couldn't take the guilt. In the middle of it all, we just...decided to go our separate ways. It wasn't an ugly fight. We just both decided to give up.

"I went back to France. Upon my return, my father set everything into motion. He wanted me to marry Pierre as soon as possible. I was still heartbroken about leaving you. I know it was a mistake. And it's not a valid reason, but I wanted to fix everything here first. My father was dying...all my life, he'd provided for me. The only thing he asked in return was for me to marry Pierre so our company would become part of Starck Corporation.

"Then I finally met Pierre. He was the exact opposite of what I thought he was. He was very level-headed. I was heartbroken with your father and torn apart about losing you. I didn't know how to tell my father about you. And surprisingly, I found myself confiding in Pierre. And when I thought he would surely reject me for my past, he still accepted me and promised to help me bring you back from the States. He was the one who told my father about you. He told my father that he didn't care. He would still have me and would raise you as his own."

She looked at Adrienne wearily. "My...father wasn't pleased to know I already lived with somebody in the States...he thought at first that he had delivered... 'damaged goods' to Pierre and he felt embarrassed. But Pierre said he didn't care. We became the best of friends. Soon, I fell in love with that wonderful man. He did for me what your father didn't. He became my friend. He fought for me. He stood up for me. He was my only ally during those times.

"When Pierre told my father I had a daughter, he wanted to meet you." Her mother sighed and looked at Adrienne for a minute. Then she smiled bitterly. "In his last days, he accepted you...and wanted you to be returned to our family. But... your father had disappeared. You both vanished." Tears rolled down her mother's cheeks. "I would never forgive your father for stealing you. You have a destiny here in France. He took that away from you. He prevented you from claiming what is rightfully yours. I put down Andrea Blanc in your birth papers. You didn't even carry his name. He changed your identity...to keep you away from me." With a grave look on her face, she said, "He will pay for this!"

Tears rolled down Adrienne's cheeks. She felt her mother's pain, and her anger towards her father. Anybody would feel that way. Even she. She felt like her father stole the most important thing a person could have—an identity.

"He must have been so angry at me. When I returned to the States, Pierre came with me. I felt he was jealous of Pierre. He also knew he couldn't do anything about it. He knew Pierre was my fiancé by an arranged marriage." Her mother sighed.

"But,...maybe during that time we met him to give him money so he would have means to take care of you for a couple of months while I fix my life and my rift with my Dad...he saw that Pierre had become more than a forced fiancé. During that time, we were really together. Not because my father wanted me to. But because I was falling for him. I think I hurt your father. And his way of hurting me back...was to take away the most important thing in my life—you."

Her mother looked at her apologetically. "Oh, sweetheart. I am so sorry. I am sorry you suffered for this. This was my fault. And your father's revenge. What your father did has no valid reason, no excuse. But you shouldn't have been the one to pay. I am so sorry, child." Her mother reached out and gave her a tight hug. They both cried in each other's arms.

Then her mother pulled away from her. "It's okay, baby. You're home now. And I promise to make it all up to you. Your father is going to pay for the difficult life he put you through."

Adrienne shook her head. "Mom…he's still my father."

"No father could stomach depriving his child of the life she deserved. Just because of what? Jealousy? Revenge? Anger? None of those are reasons enough for him to take you away from me."

Adrienne knew it wasn't time to argue about this. Right now, she couldn't defend her Dad. She was also mad at him for doing what he did. Especially for…letting her stepmother and stepsister crush her and break her spirit.

Jin came back to the room and announced that dinner would begin shortly.

"Where is your father?" her mother asked Jin.

"He just got in," Jin replied. "I ensured that Adrienne's friends come dine with us, too. I figured all this hoopla will be much easier for Adrienne to handle if she had her best friends to keep her company."

"Of course," their mother responded. "They are more than welcome. And besides, I would be thankful to anybody who loved my daughter all the time that I wasn't at her side."

They went to the first floor of the house and Jin and her mother led her to the huge dining room. There was a long table in the middle of it with twenty seats.

Jill and Yuan already sat there and Adrienne introduced them to her mother. After a few minutes, a handsome man in his fifties entered the room. His hair was darker than Jin's and his eyes were aquamarine.

"Oh, we have guests," he said, smiling. His smile was warm and welcoming. Then he turned to her mother and kissed her lovingly on the lips.

"Pierre," her mother began. "Jin just brought me the most wonderful surprise. I'd like you to meet her." Ariana pulled her husband towards Adrienne.

Pierre Starck stood in front of her and took a good look at her. He blinked back twice and, immediately, recognition crossed his face. Without having to introduce them, he said, "Andrea."

Adrienne smiled at him shyly.

"But her name now is Adrienne. All the while, we were looking for Andrea, when that's not even her name."

"How?" Pierre asked his wife.

"I will tell you all about it later." Ariana whispered

Pierre looked at Adrienne again. "My God, you look like your mother."

"Jin found her," her mother announced. "Now, she's finally here, Pierre."

Pierre Starck smiled at his wife and hugged her. "Oh sweetheart. I'm so happy for you. You've waited decades for this."

"I know." Tears rolled down Ariana's cheeks again. "And you have patiently waited with me."

Pierre Starck leaned forward and kissed his wife once again and then he turned to Adrienne. He gave her a hug and then he said, "Welcome to the family, child."

Tears welled up in Adrienne's eyes and she felt happiness surge through her. She saw that Pierre Starck genuinely loved her mother and it was true what Jin said. He's accepted her existence even before they got married. And had her own father allowed her to live with them, this man would have treated her like a real daughter.

"Th-thank you, sir," Adrienne said.

"Oh, child. I have been hiring private investigators in the US to search for you for almost all your life. I think, now that I have finally met you, you should call me Papa."

Adrienne smiled shyly and nodded. "Thank you, Papa."

After dinner, Adrienne went with Jill and Yuan to the Starck's huge garden at the back of the estate.

"Wow," Yuan breathed. "Your family is really lovely." He couldn't help the tears in his eyes, too.

Jill was also crying. "Adrienne, we know how much you've wished to have a family that shows even just a little bit of affection for you. Now you do. This is some sort of a miracle!"

"I know," Adrienne admitted happily. "I mean…it's still too much to absorb at the moment, but I never ever dreamed that some people would love me enough to dedicate decades of their lives trying to find me…because they felt that I belonged with them. It's just…so surreal considering I grew up feeling out of place with the family I had then. I never felt like they accepted me. And now…I met some people who turned out to be doing everything they could just to make me one of their own."

"If this happened to me…I don't think I would be able to forgive my father at all," Yuan said.

Adrienne felt a sharp pain in her chest again. Tears welled up in her eyes and she stared down on the grass on her feet. She shook her head. "What he did…maybe he thought that was right. He didn't want to lose me. But what he did was wrong. I felt like he cheated me. He was being selfish. My real mother loved me all these years, while I was growing up thinking that motherly love didn't exist for me at all. Maybe I would be able to forgive him. But I need time to take all this in. I'm still angry at him. But yes, I think I would forgive him. In time."

"Your mother is Amanda Seville, Adrienne," Jill asserted, her voice said that she found that surreal.

"I know, right? Unbelievable."

"Well, the apple didn't fall far from the tree at all. That's where you got your talent. You always wondered how no one in your family ever knew how to write."

"Now, I don't feel out of place at all. My mother loves me. And I have a brother who genuinely cares about me, too."

"And he's bloody hot!" Jill couldn't help saying.

Adrienne narrowed her eyes on her friend. "He's my brother, Jill! How could you even talk like that about him in front of me?"

Jill giggled. "And to think I thought at first that he was interested in you. Well, he was. But not in the way I thought, not romantically. Just like you said."

"So what are you going to do now?" Yuan asked. "Will you live here in Paris?"

Adrienne sighed. "I don't know. What I do know is that I want to get to know my family a little bit more."

"Yes. You deserve that," Jill said. "Your stepmother and your stepsister hated you. Now, it's time you stay with the mother and brother…including the stepfather…who felt that your coming home today was a miracle."

Her mother called them. It had gotten late and they came from a long flight. Jill and Yuan stayed in two of the guest rooms. Adrienne said goodnight to them. She wanted to talk to her mother more, though. She felt like talking to her for hours would still not suffice for getting to know her.

"This is your room, Adrienne," her mother said, opening the door of the room opposite Jin's.

When they stepped into the huge room, Adrienne almost gasped. The luxurious queen-sized bed in the center was covered in purple and pink bedspreads, duvet and pillows. The pillows in the center of the bed had the letter A embroidered in them. There was a desk and a shelf full of books. A huge couch and center table stood on a corner opposite the bed. Luxurious violet curtains cover the glass walls and doors that led to a huge balcony. The walls were adorned with beautiful, serene paintings on canvass.

"Wow," Adrienne breathlessly stated. "This is so beautiful."

Her mother smiled. "I'm glad you like it. We decorated this room as often as we could. The sheets and curtains get washed and replaced every week."

"Is this a guest bedroom or does someone actually stay here?"

"This is not a guest room, Adrienne. We have been decorating and keeping this room ready for years…hoping this day would come…that you would finally come home to us."

Adrienne found herself overwhelmed by emotions once again. She never expected to hear what her mother just said. She remembered her bedroom in Boston, the room where she actually stayed in for years before she went to college. Her bed didn't have sheets and all her stuff got put in boxes, as if her supposed mother expected her never to return at all. And now, here in this house, her real mother made a room for her, kept it ready for the day when she would finally return to her.

She turned to the paintings on the wall. Some of them were abstract, painted in pastel colors, beautiful and elegantly feminine to match the theme of the room. These included a painting of a rainforest with a lagoon in the center and exquisite wildflowers.

Adrienne thought that the paintings matched the room so well that someone painted them for it…a room meant for the princess in the family.

"Do you like the paintings?" Her mother asked, noticing how she was admiring the canvasses on the wall.

Adrienne nodded. "They're lovely."

"Jin painted all of them," her mother said proudly.

Adrienne stared at her mother. She couldn't hide the awe on her face.

"It's his hobby," her mother revealed. "He's been painting for this room since he was fifteen, hoping that one day, his big sister would come home, see them… and admire them the way you are doing now."

Adrienne's heart swelled. Her brother painted for her, when he hasn't even met her. Kimberly never even had nice thoughts of her when she lived with her all her life.

As she stared back into the room, she couldn't help but wonder how it was possible that the Starcks have managed to make her feel like she belonged to them in a space of five hours, and the family she grew up with hadn't made her feel accepted when she'd lived with them for over twenty years.

An hour later, after she'd taken a shower in the huge elegant en-suite bathroom, she lay down on the luxurious bed that was always meant for her. She turned on her phone. So much has happened, she forgot to turn her phone back on after she took them from the police station.

She had notifications of missed calls from her father and some from Justin.

She sighed. How she wished Justin was with her in this longest day of her life. She missed him. She missed how she confided in him all her pains, her thoughts, her dreams and her ordeals. She wondered what he would say when he found out how her life had turned a sudden three-sixty in the space of sixteen hours.

Her heart pounded inside her chest when she read his message to her: *Where will you be in exactly forty days? Let me answer that for you. In Italy. Changing your last name to mine.*

She smiled bitterly. All her life she was called Adrienne Miller. But now she found out that it was a fake name. Her legal name on her real birth documents was Andrea Blanc. If her mother had it her way, she would have been Adrienne Blanc. If Pierre could have it his way, she was almost certain he would change her name to Adrienne Starck.

Now that she knew who she really was, she's confused about which name was right for her to use.

But in her heart, at that moment, she knew what name she would rather use out of all the options she had.

She would rather be Adrienne Adams.

30.
Novo življenje
Slovenian for New Life.

*O*ver the next days, Adrienne spent most of her time in the Starck mansion, getting to know her mother. It was like they both couldn't get enough of talking to each other. As gently as she could, she told her how difficult it was, growing up with Marina Miller, the woman she thought was her Mom, who provided little comfort and constant negative comparisons to her stepsister.

Yuan and Jill enjoyed Paris just as much. Jin took them around anywhere they wanted whenever Adrienne desired some alone time with her mother.

"Do you have a boyfriend, Adrienne?" Her mother asked.

Adrienne sighed. She was reminded again of the broken pieces of her heart. She hadn't heard from Justin since the last time he told her she'd be going to Italy in forty days. She reckons he was still working on convincing his parents to let him go. She had no idea how he's going to do it, but deep inside her heart, she really, really hoped he would succeed, so he could come back to her.

Adrienne looked up at her mother. "I did, but it was…complicated," she disclosed.

Her mother's eyes narrowed. She didn't miss the shadow of pain that she saw cross Adrienne's eyes.

"You loved him?"

Adrienne blinked back the tears that are threatening to pour from her eyes. Then she replied, "With all my heart, Mama."

"Then why aren't you together?"

"Because…because we can't," she replied. "His family is rich and powerful. Apparently, he needed to marry an heiress."

Her mother raised a brow. "Are you saying to me that his family couldn't accept you because you were from a middle-class family? Well, now you're not anymore! You're an heiress now, too."

Heiress.

She still has not gotten used to that word. She didn't even know what it was supposed to mean and what obligations or duties were attached to it.

"Well, his family already arranged for him to marry some girl."

"Oh. Well, I can't say I'm surprised, considering it happened to me, too. What did your boyfriend do? Didn't he fight for you?"

"He did," Adrienne replied sadly. "His parents disowned him. He still fought for me. But I couldn't make him leave them for me, Mama,"

Adrienne said. "So, I gave him up."

Tears slid down her cheeks and she wiped them as she smiled at her mother ruefully.

"You truly are a brave girl, Adrienne. I am so proud of you, sweetheart." She reached out to Adrienne and pulled her into her arms. Adrienne cried silently in her mother's arms, wishing she had this luxury when she was entering puberty and finally realizing how harsh the world really was.

Her mother pulled away from her and touched her face between her palms. She smiled at her. "Don't worry, sweetheart. You are a beautiful woman," she assured her. "Don't worry. I will introduce you to someone who is worthy enough to claim your hand. Handsome, rich, smart and powerful. You will forget your boyfriend in no time."

She was about to say that she wasn't interested in other wealthy heirs, but her mother already pulled her away into the house.

"Come quick! Let's go to the salon. Nothing beats a nice spa to heal a broken heart. And shopping of course." Her mother laughed.

Adrienne couldn't help but admire the spirit of the woman in front of her. She was contagious.

Wow! My mother rocks!

They went to a spa in one of the Starck's hotels, with Jill and Yuan. Then they had lunch with Jin in one of their restaurants. While waiting for their car to drive them to the nearest shopping mall, Jin came up behind her.

"So, is she wearing you out yet?" Jin teased.

Adrienne smiled at her brother. "Oh my God, Jin! She is wonderful."

Jin nodded. "Yes. And she's waited for you for years. So if she gets to be a little clingy or overprotective, just bear with her. She will loosen up eventually."

Adrienne shook her head. "I don't care. I've waited all my life to feel like this. Like I have a mother."

"I know. And I'm glad you're smiling genuinely these days."

"Thank you, Jin. If you didn't find me, I would have been sulking behind my desk in Manhattan instead of being here in Paris, happily getting to know my mother."

"You're wrong," Jin said and Adrienne raised a brow at him. "You wouldn't be behind your desk in Manhattan. You would probably be in Boston…behind bars." He teased and Adrienne couldn't help hitting him on the shoulder.

Then she smiled at Jin warmly. "Thank you. I mean it. I will forever be thankful to you for bringing me back home."

"And speaking of home," Jin paused. "Have you thought about what you're going to do?"

"What do you mean, what I'm going to do?"

"Adrienne, you realize you don't have to work another day of your life, right? You have a trust fund just waiting for you. We have a company of our own. You can work for one of our hotels if you really want to work. And you can pursue your love for writing."

Adrienne took a deep breath. "I have a job at *Blush*."

Jin raised a brow. "And you'd rather spend your days with your heartless editor than your family?"

Adrienne bit her lip, not really knowing what to decide. Jin did have a point.

"Come on, Yen," Jin said. "Mom has waited for you for so long. She deserves to get to know her daughter."

Adrienne nodded. Jin was right. She owed it to her mother. She needed to spend time with her to make up for what they had lost. She needed more time to bond with her new family…to feel like she belonged to a family.

And moreover…a new life, environment, new country would take her mind off Justin while she waited for him. He said he would find her after forty days. But what if he didn't come back?

She could keep herself busy learning how to live her new life…to forget that her heart had sustained irreparable damage. She would never forget Justin. But she needed help going through one step at a time.

Adrienne and her mother spent the whole afternoon shopping. Adrienne's mother insisted on getting her a new wardrobe and Yuan and Jill happily helped her pick out more than a dozen different tops, a dozen different jeans, skirts and other stylish items.

Adrienne didn't really want expensive clothes, handbags and accessories, but Jill and Yuan talked some sense into her.

"It's not for you, Yen!" Jill hissed.

"Do it for your mother!" Yuan insisted. For many reasons."

"Like what? Squander her money?"

"No. Like you're her daughter now," Yuan explained. "She has a semi-celebrity status and her family is like the crème of the crop. And since you're the latest addition to that family, people in their world will look at you, gossip about you, scrutinize you. So, why don't you give them something beautiful and good to look at? Some girl with style and finesse, as well as the sense and the brains."

"Leave your old self behind, Yen," Jill said. "Your stepmother and Kimberly can no longer hurt you. Change your image, free yourself and embrace who you really are!"

As much as she wanted to argue with them, Adrienne realized that they did have a point. She can't be the plain, simple Adrienne anymore. Because she's no longer ordinary. She's Andrea Blanc. And she will not let others criticize her for the sake of hurting her mother, her brother, or her stepfather. She would not embarrass them. If they introduced her to their world, she had to make sure that she will make them proud.

So, they raided several luxury shops. Chanel. Balenciaga. Gucci. Armani. Prada.

Her mother sat in a corner and worked on her mini laptop while the three of them shopped.

"Buy anything and everything you want, my child," she told Adrienne. "You guys dress her up and don't worry about the bill. I'm sorry I just need to finish this intense scene I was working on. I just can't concentrate on anything else."

When they finally got home that evening Adrienne probably carried more than fifty paper bags from luxury designers.

Jin shook his head when he met them at the front door. "So who's responsible for turning you into a shopaholic so soon?" He grinned.

"Mom. And these two." Adrienne pointed at Jill and Yuan.

"Come on!" Jill urged. "We just thought that now she's one of you, she has to dress the part."

"Well, you're right," Jin said. "Mom will soon introduce Adrienne to her circle of friends and sons and daughters of her friends. They would be very excited to meet you. Not because they think you're an interesting person. But because they want to know what's wrong with you and how you could stain our mother's spotless reputation."

Adrienne blinked back at her brother. "So…are these your friends, too?"

"Hell no!" Jin said. "I couldn't stand them. If they're not good for business, I don't bother to know them at all. I honestly don't know and care about ninety percent of Mom and Dad's friends. I haven't even met them. But there can only be one black sheep in the family. And unfortunately for you, I've already called dibs on the title!" He grinned. "So they don't expect anything good to come out of me. I've gotten to the point that nothing bad I do even makes it to social gossips anymore. They just don't care. When you're bad, and you do bad things, people just ignore it. But when you're good… like you my dearest sister…and you do bad, you'll be talk of the town…tabloid meat…for a whole week."

What he said actually scared Adrienne. The look of shock ran across her face. Jin laughed and put an arm around her shoulder to give her a gentle squeeze.

"Relax, Adrienne," Jin said. "Mama and Papa never really cared about what others around us thought. So you'll be all right. And I'm sure you'll be a hit among the sons of our parents' friends."

"I'm not interested," she said.

Jin smiled at her. "Hmmm…speaking of that, where's the hotshot boyfriend?"

Adrienne sighed. Yuan and Jill gave Jin a slight shake of head, as if warning him not to open a whole can of worms.

"Oooppps!" Jin whispered. "Tell you what, let's go out tonight. Take your mind off things."

After a few hours, they were at a club called Rendezvous. When they arrived, the line seemed long but, Jin led them to the beginning of the line. With only a slight nod, the bouncer let them in. Others waiting in line just groaned.

"That's not fair," Adrienne said. "I hate it when people with money and influence could just do that."

Jin grinned. "It's not money and influence that got us in. It's just plain face value." And he winked at her.

"Oh God, my brother is a first class jerk."

Jin laughed. "And I'm just getting started!"

Jin introduced her to some of his friends. There was a girl named Tara and her boyfriend Mac. There were brothers Van and Victor, who were half-French and half-Brazilian. Then there was the French guy named Jean, who looked familiar, like she's seen him in a print ad before.

"Yes, he is actually," Jin said to her.

She stared up at him. "What?"

"If you're wondering if you've seen him before and if he's a model, he is. He modeled for several perfume campaigns."

"Oh, that's why he looked familiar," Adrienne said.

Jin leaned forward to whisper against her ear. "He's a Yuan."

Adrienne stared back at her brother. It took her five seconds to figure out what he meant. And then she smiled. Already, Jean had started stealing glances at Yuan.

Hey, Yuan is a very good looking guy, too.

"You guys look too much like each other to be hooking up," Mac said to Jin, referring to Adrienne. "It's strange."

"Nope, not hooking up. But that doesn't mean any of you guys should get any ideas, okay?" Jin had pointed a warning finger at Victor and Van.

The two guys groaned. "Seriously, dude?"

"Seriously!" Jin said crossly. Then he pointed at Adrienne. "Sister."

"Oh!" the two said in unison. "Sorry."

"I didn't know you had a sister," Tara said.

"Now you do," Jin said curtly, not really wanting to explain the whole history behind it.

"Seriously, Dude," Van began to tease Jin. "Guard her with your life."

"That's what I'm doing," Jin said.

"So, where have you been all this time, Adrienne?" Mac asked.

"In New York. Writing for a magazine called *Blush*."

"Oh, she writes like your Mom." Tara smiled. "I love *Blush*. I have my copies delivered every month. Seriously, you work there?"

"Yes," Adrienne replied. "Me and Jill."

Tara, a journalism major, asked for pointers from Jill and Adrienne. Both women were happy to help her start a career, should she want it. Her family owned Rendezvous, and she didn't really have to work. Yet she didn't want to be branded a good for nothing rich brat. She wanted to make a name for herself, too.

They got home around one in the morning. Jill and Van exchanged numbers after dancing saucily together. Yuan and Jean actually couldn't take their eyes off each other. And Adrienne successfully made some more new friends.

Before she went to bed that night, she checked her phone to see her messages.

Kim: *I hope you're happy! You successfully ruined my life! Troy won't talk to me. Mom and Dad are divorcing. And Troy's family thinks so low of me now. Congratulations, Adrienne! You won again! I hope you die! Really!*

She read the messages a couple more times, and then she just hit delete.

She read Justin's last message to her again. Over and over. She tried her best not to call him. Tears rolled down her cheeks. She attempted to make it through one day at a time. Still, she felt so happy with her new family. She's happy that Jill and Yuan were both with her in Paris.

But heiress or no heiress, she still felt heartbroken that she couldn't be with Justin.

31.

Josnic

Romanian for Despicable.

*T*wo days later, Yuan and Jill had to say goodbye to Adrienne. As much as they loved their week in Paris, they had to go back to reality. They still had jobs that required them to go back to New York.

Adrienne decided to do what's right. She sent Jada her resignation letter. She figured, she'd spent years working her ass off because she didn't want to be a failure in her mother's eyes. But she was never really her mother. She's her stepmother. And her real mother would prefer she stayed in Paris, if not for good, then for a while longer.

Although he partied like a kid at night time, Jin actually wore the Starck heir coat pretty well. He made a lot of progress managing their business. Little by little, her stepfather trusted him to take the reins of their empire.

A week after Yuan and Jill left, Adrienne's mother told her she would meet her at a coffee shop in one of their hotels and she will introduce her to some of her friends and their kids, so she could make new friends. The family driver took her there.

Adrienne must have been in the coffee shop for an hour yet her mother didn't make an appearance. She received a call from her.

"Sweetheart, I'm sorry I can't make it. But Christine just might come at any minute. If she reaches there, tell her I had to rush to meet my editor. But if you could please... have coffee with her. She's just in town for a visit. She could use some company."

"Okay, Mom."

She appreciates it that her mother is slowly introducing her to her circle of friends as part of her family. She needed to meet new acquaintances to keep herself from thinking too much about Justin and to keep from getting bored.

She checked the calendar. Thirty days left. And still no word from Justin. She resisted the urge to text or call him. She couldn't. If he's doing what he could to get to know his fiancée, she didn't want to ruin it.

She badly wanted to tell him about the recent turn of events in her life. She did not want disturb his focus. She wanted him to do this on his own, with no influence coming from her. That wouldn't be fair.

She must have stayed in the coffee shop, browsing the internet through her phone, for about three hours. No one came. Her mother's friend didn't make an appearance.

She called her mother.

"So, how was it?" she asked, sounding ecstatic.

"Mama, your friend didn't show up."

There was silence on the other end of the line. Then her mother said, "Oh. Okay. She must have been caught up in something. I'll give her a call now. Meanwhile, you can call the driver to take you home."

"Mama, is your friend all right?"

Her mother sighed on the other line. "I hope so. Don't worry about it. I'll sort it out. I'll see you at dinner."

Adrienne went home. When she got to her room, she saw a box sitting on her coffee table. It was wrapped in silver wrapper with a metallic purple ribbon.

She read the card.

Boredom kills.

So maybe it's time you start writing your next bestseller.

Love,

Jin

She smiled. Her brother was so thoughtful. He was everything that Kimberly wasn't. And her heart swelled with the love that her new family offered her.

She opened the box and found a brand new Macbook Air. She couldn't stop smiling. Jin was absolutely right. Writing would be the best thing for her to do whilst she stayed in Paris. She remembered the novel she started writing. Then she remembered, she can't work on that again. She would make herself too heartbroken if she continued that story. Justin inspired that love story. But now, her love story with him faced an uncertain ending.

Her mother entered her room.

"Sweetheart, I'm sorry you had to wait in the coffee shop for nothing," she said. Adrienne could see the disappointment all over her face. "My friend's son's flight was delayed."

"Your friend's son?" Adrienne repeated. "I thought I was meeting your friend."

Her mother stared at her for a while and then she said, "Oh, yes, yes. Er… Christine was… wasn't able to make it to Paris. But her son came to town. And he wanted to see the sights."

"Mom, I cannot be a tour guide." Adrienne said. "I've been here less than two weeks."

"Yes. But he frequents Paris. He doesn't need to be shown around. He just… needed company."

Adrienne narrowed her eyes at her mother. "Why me?"

"He's from the States, too. And I wanted you to meet my friends' family. Whenever Christine's son is here, he usually didn't… have any company or friends to tour around the City."

"He's a guy. Maybe Jin would be able to show him a better time than I would."

"He's not Jin's age. And Jin…hates my circle of friends and their children. Do you know, he's met none of my friends' children? And he hasn't gone to any one of my gatherings or meetings with my friends."

"Really?"

"If it's not business-related, he's not interested."

"Maybe he can start with meeting Christine's son. He'd be a better company than me."

"Well, Pierre just sent him to Dubai to facilitate the construction of our hotel there." Her mother smiled at her. "Would you be a star and help me out then? I sort of promised Christine I'd introduce you to her son."

Adrienne raised a brow. "Mom…just a question. You're not setting me up with your friend's son, are you?"

Her mother stared back at her blankly. And then she shrugged. "Well…my friends have very good-looking kids. They're smart, too, and come from very good families. And I specifically remember that you were trying to get over some guy whose parents couldn't accept you."

Adrienne laughed. "Oh my God, Mama!" she said. "Please stop. I am not looking to jump into a rebound relationship. I just broke up with my boyfriend ten days ago. And besides, I sort of promised him I would wait."

"Wait?" her mother echoed. "Don't be absurd, Adrienne. You should not be the one doing the waiting. He should be chasing after you. His parents should be begging him to come back to you. You're my daughter and you're beautiful, smart and kind-hearted. Any guy would die to be in your boyfriend's shoes right now."

Adrienne felt happy to hear that for a change, she has a mother who is truly proud of what she is.

"Mom, don't worry about me," she asserted. "I'll be okay."

Her mother sat beside her and put an arm around her shoulder. "Can you at least promise me you will let me introduce you to my circle? Okay, you don't have to start dating right away. Just…meet new people. I don't want to see you wasting your time waiting for somebody who may not come back to you."

Adrienne sighed. She didn't want to do it. But she also wanted to make her mother feel that she's trying to fit into her world. And this is the first time that she felt that her mother actually cared about her.

"I'll meet new friends," she said firmly. "But I will not date anybody romantically, Mom. I promise I'll try my best to become friends with your friends' kids. And they have to be both boys and girls. Not exclusively boys. I'm all for making new friends. But I won't have a boyfriend. Until…" She sighed. "Until I'm ready."

Her mother smiled. "Okay. That's fair enough. By the way, I'm going to throw a party in two weeks. It's the best way to introduce you to the society. Everybody should know who you are and that you belong to this family." She kissed her forehead.

"What?" Adrienne began to protest. She thought this heiress thing was going to be easy. "Mama, no. It's not necessary."

"Of course it is!" her mother claimed. "To not make you feel awkward, I'd do it on the same night as my victory party. My book 'Clever Tales' is number one on the New York Times Bestsellers' List for six weeks now. I've sold about two million copies. It's time to celebrate. I do it all the time with my other books that hit a milestone. And on that night, we will formally introduce you to everybody."

Adrienne almost panicked.

Her mother laughed. "You will do great, Adrienne. You're my daughter. Just breathe and be yourself. Everybody will love you. And if they don't, they can just go to hell. I don't care. I'm proud of you."

Her mother stood up and headed for the door. Then she turned back to her. "I've been a romance novelist for decades, sweetheart. And I know…you meet the guy for you at the most unlikely places and situations. You never know. You just might meet someone who's really worth forgetting your ex-boyfriend for."

Adrienne just smiled at her mother. But in her mind she thought, *I sincerely doubt that, Mom. Nobody is worth forgetting Justin for.*

***

The next day, her mother told her to meet her friend, Christine's son again. She sat at the same coffee shop for more than an hour, but this friend's son was again a no-show. Honestly, she was getting infuriated. If she didn't want to please her mother, she would have left fifteen minutes ago. Obviously, this guy also didn't want to meet her. And besides, how ungentlemanly was it to stand up a girl two days in a row?

She didn't plan on dating him. Adrienne saw this as a meet and greet type of thing. She promised her mother she would try to befriend those in her circle. But she wondered if rich kids usually act like this? Do they assume that only their time matters and to hell with anyone else?

After another ten minutes, she gathered her stuff, about to leave.

Just then a guy approached her.

"Are you Andrea Blanc? Ariana Starck's daughter?" he asked in a cocky voice.

Adrienne stared up at the dark-haired guy standing in front of her. He wore a pair of shimmery black pants, long-sleeved black shirt with white tie and white suspenders. His hair was dark brown and he's wearing a pair of silver shades. His plucked brow was raised, and he looked like he was impatiently waiting for her to answer.

Adrienne nodded.

He immediately pulled the chair opposite from her and sat down. He pulled his shades up his head and revealed a pair of electric blue eyes.

She was sure he's wearing contact lenses to make his eyes appear more striking.

"I'm sorry, I'm late," he said. Then he paused for a while and laughed. "Actually, I'm not. I was…with this model and she was hot!" Then he winked at her.

He then scrolled through the menu and raised his hand and waived to the waiter. "Hey, waiter guy!" he called in a very loud voice, the coffee shop actually went quiet. Adrienne sank lower in her seat and actually used the menu in front of her to cover her face in embarrassment.

It took a while before the waiter came to their table. The guy raised a brow at him. "What? You're going to make me wait for Christmas?" he asked him. He didn't wait for the waiter to reply. "Get me a machito."

"Excuse me?" The guy blinked back at him. "Sir, what is that?"

"The coffee? Hello?" the guy said looking at the waiter as if he thought he was stupid.

The waiter stared at the guy blankly, clearly having no idea what he meant.

"Are you stu…"

"O-kay!" Adrienne interrupted, before the guy could actually continue what he was about to say. "I think he meant macchiato."

"Yeah, that's what I said. You deaf or something?" the guy asked the waiter.

The waiter bit his lip to prevent himself from either snapping back or laughing his ass off at this imbecile in front of them.

"Right away," he said and gave Adrienne a thankful smile.

"In your dreams, peasant," the guy in front of her said under his breath after seeing the waiter smile at Adrienne.

"Excuse me?" Adrienne turned back at the guy. "Who are you?"

"You don't know me?" he asked and he looked genuinely offended that she didn't recognize him. "Really? Where have you been?"

Adrienne stared at him blankly. No! She didn't know him and she wished she hadn't even laid eyes on him today.

"I'm… I'm sorry. I… I was confined in a mental institution for the last ten years. I really have no idea who you are," Adrienne said in her most innocent voice.

He grinned at her. "Justin."

"What?" Adrienne blinked back. The name still makes her heart beat a thousand times faster.

"My name is Justin. I'm Christine's son. My mother said I should meet her friend Ariana's daughter, Andy. Are you the daughter? Because I know the Starcks. And…well…you don't look half as posh as your brother."

Seriously? His name is also Justin? God, kill me now!

Bile rose to Adrienne's throat and she balled her hands in front of her. She would have hit the guy and she bet the waiter and the other patrons around them would love to help her gang up on this asshole. But she cannot embarrass her mother.

"Okay. It's nice to meet you, Justin, and now I must go." She started to stand up.

But she felt a hand on her wrist, grasping it tightly.

"Sit down, will you?" he asked in a low firm voice that Adrienne actually scared her a little.

She sat back on her seat and stared at the guy crossly.

"You know, Andy…a lot of girls would die to be in your shoes right now. Having coffee with me." He didn't even get her name right, but Adrienne felt irritated enough with him, she didn't bother correcting him.

Adrienne closed her eyes for a second. She didn't remember why she allowed him to stop her from getting up on her feet and leaving him.

"But my mother begged me to meet you. Get to know you. Make you head over heels in love, if I didn't make you fall in love at first sight. She and your mother are hoping we're a perfect match, you know."

"Oh my God! Maybe they're right! You're probably the answer to my prayers!" Adrienne said sarcastically.

The guy grinned. "Oh sweetheart. I think I am."

Adrienne groaned. Not only is this guy a total douche, he's also a moron.

The waiter reappeared with his macchiato. The way he treated him, she wouldn't be surprised if the waiter spat in his coffee. She wanted to warn him about it, but she thought, hell! He deserved it! In fact, she wished the waiter did.

"How did our mothers meet?"

The guy shrugged. "Old family friends. Then they were roommates in college," he replied. "Closer than sisters. I think they got it in their heads that they should be family. So they're hoping we start hooking up."

"Seriously?"

The guy nodded. "You up for it?" he asked and gave her a smoldering look.

Adrienne resisted the urge to vomit right then and there.

"I'm sorry…" she said. "But I think…you're *waaay* out of my league." She tried to smile sweetly.

The guy leaned back on his seat and drank his *'machito'*. When he put his cup down, he had coffee froth all over his mouth that he actually looked like he was sporting a mustache. He didn't even make an effort to wipe it off. "That's what I thought," he said. "I only date models."

"Shocking!" Adrienne said under her breath.

"So, how come I didn't know about you, Andy? We don't see you at the Starcks' events. We knew Ariana had a daughter, but we never saw you before."

"I told you, I was in a mental institution, remember?"

He blinked back at her. "Oh, that wasn't a joke?" he asked.

"I don't have a sense of humor," she replied flatly.

She thought that if he really thought she was cuckoo he would tell his mother there is no way in the world they would hook up.

"Don't worry. Girls go crazy about me, too." And he gave her a wink again. Then he stared at her with narrowed eyes, which he probably thought was sexy.

"Is something wrong with your eyes?" Adrienne asked.

"Why?" He sounded like he was panicking. "Are they still red? Damn those Visines!" he said.

"Visine?" Adrienne echoed. "You meant to tell me your eyes were red before you came to meet me? What? Are you on drugs?"

He laughed. "No. I don't really consider pot drugs. Duh!"

Pot? Is he serious?

Adrienne was interrupted by the ring of her phone. It was her mother.

"Mama."

"Hey, sweetheart," she said. "So, have you met Justin?"

"Hmmm…" she simply said.

"Isn't he wonderful? I swear if I was only your age…"

"Mama, I thought Pierre was the love of your life."

"Of course, he is!" Her mother laughed. "But I was just saying that Justin is a dreamboat!"

"Yeah…he is…out of this world." She didn't want to be rude in front of this moron.

"Treat him well. He's my oldest friend's son. He's a very nice guy once you really get to know him. I think the two of you could really become good friends."

"You don't say." Adrienne tried to put a smile on her voice.

"Talk to you later."

"Thanks, Mom."

She turned back to Justin, the moron.

"Okay so my mother asked me to take you out tonight," Justin said. "What do you say, meet me at Rendezvous bar at nine?"

"Is that really necessary?"

He raised a brow at her. "Hey. I don't like you, either," he said. "I'd rather be fucking the lingerie model I brought back to my hotel room a while ago. But as it is, it would make our mothers happy to see that we at least tried, right?"

Of all the things that came out of his mouth, the last sentence was the only thing that made sense to Adrienne. "After tonight, you could tell your mother what you said to me. That I was way out of your league. I'm pretty high maintenance."

"Really? High maintenance would be an understatement!" Adrienne rolled her eyes. "Seriously, lady. When my mother said she'd like me to hook up with Ariana's daughter, an heiress, I was actually expecting the likes of Paris Hilton or I don't know... Ivanka. You know. Posh. Sophisticated."

"And when my mother told me to try to befriend one of her friends' sons, I was expecting to meet... I don't know...Peter Parker, maybe. Smart. Funny. Interesting." Adrienne said, feigning a smile.

"Oh, lady. I am interesting—I'm just not interested in you."

"Oh, thank God! I'm saved!" Adrienne said, rolling her eyes.

"Yeah, yeah. Nine p.m., Rendezvous. Here's my business card," he said and he handed her a card.

It was black with silver letters on them. Adrienne read it.

Justin J.
Making all other men less attractive since 1989.
Email: *justinsex10xaday@gmail.com.*

Adrienne stared back at the guy. "Seriously? You call this a business card?"

He winked at her and gave her another smoldering look. This was probably the first time she encountered a guy who has a pickup business card.

Is this guy for real?

He stood up. "See you tonight, Andy." And he went off. The waiter was about to catch him but he was too fast and Adrienne was left on the table openmouthed. The waiter then gave her the bill.

"He even made you pay for his coffee?" the waiter asked her.

She sighed. "Terrible. That was the most despicable human being!"

"Well, some rich brats are like that," the waiter said. "I am sorry your date was a douche."

"He's not my date. And I am sorry I met him, too."

He handed her the bill. "I just need your signature. Mr. Starck will take care of the bill."

Adrienne shook her head. "No. It's not that much. And I don't want my brother to hunt that guy down and punch all his teeth down his throat." In her mind, she smiled. Yes. She actually has a sibling who would do that for her now.

The waiter smiled. "He'd deserve it."

Adrienne placed a couple of bills on the folder he gave her. She doubled the bill for his tip. Then she thanked the waiter and went into the Rolls Royce that her stepfather owned.

She was going to meet up with that douchebag again tonight. And she just couldn't help panicking about how she would survive another minute with him.

32.
Chịu được.
Tolerance in Vietnamese.

Her mother was ecstatic when she got back.

"So, how did it go?"

Adrienne just smiled. She wanted to be honest, but she didn't really want to quash her mother's hopes. Yes, her stepmom still had that effect on her that she couldn't help. She just couldn't stop pleasing people.

"It's…interesting. I haven't met a guy like Justin before." She tried to sound enthusiastic. But it is true. That guy was one of a kind.

Her mother's eyes widened. "Oh, sweetheart, I know. He is adorable. His parents are so proud of him. Handsome lad, too. I take it you would be having a date tonight again?"

"Mom, it's not a date," she said.

"But he asked you?" her mother insisted.

"Well…yeah, but…"

"Wonderful!" Her mother beamed.

"Mom…don't get your hopes up. I said I will try to make new friends. I'm not really up for finding a new boyfriend."

"You'll never know. Justin is one of a kind."

Adrienne laughed humorlessly. "I bet he is!" She didn't mean that in a good way. However, her mother was so pleased, she just couldn't break her heart too soon.

"Mom," she began. "You know…my boyfriend's name was Justin, too."

Her mother looked at her for a minute. Then she said, "Ex-boyfriend. And I'm sorry, sweetheart. I know you still love him. But I really hope you give yourself a chance to meet other guys. If your boyfriend doesn't come back to you…I don't want to see you miserable."

"I'm giving myself a chance to make new friends, Mom. That's all I can promise you now."

Her mother smiled. "Okay. I think once you spend more time with Christine's Justin, you two would hit it off quickly. And you will soon forget about your ex-boyfriend, Justin."

Seriously doubt it!

Then she hugged her mom and went to her room.

She dialed Jin's number.

"Hey, how's my favorite sister doing?"

"Jin, I'm your only sister," she reminded him.

"Oh! You'll never know if we have extra siblings lying around, you know," he teased. "So, what's up?"

"I think Mom is trying to set me up with one of her friends' son."

"Good luck with that," he stated. "She tried with me. Epic fail. She's a romance novelist. She can't help the match-making thing."

"Now, I met one of her friend's sons. He's awful!"

"Really? Why'd you say that?"

"He's egoistic and he's a moron!" Adrienne groaned. "He even insulted me and made me pay for his coffee."

"Wow! Douche!"

"Anyway, I don't want to break Mom's heart. I want to show her that I at least tried. I did promise her that I would try to be friends with her friends' kids."

"Okay, is this guy really that despicable you can't even be friends with him?"

"You haven't met him, Jin. You would make him eat his underwear if you did!"

Jin laughed. "Well, so what are you going to do?"

"The guy asked me to meet him at Rendezvous." Adrienne replied. "He wanted to keep up with the appearances that we're getting along just fine. Or at least we tried, but it didn't work out."

"Why? Is he blind? Wasn't he a little bit attracted to you?"

"It doesn't matter. Because I am not the least bit attracted to him. I'm not looking for romance. My life is complicated enough as it is now. I promised somebody I'd wait for him. And until I'm sure he's not coming back, I think I'll take my chances. And apparently, this guy only goes for supermodels and hot heiresses and I didn't make the cut."

"Freaking crazy! Who's this guy? I would like him to meet my fist!" Jin said crossly. "Seriously, he said that to you?"

Adrienne sighed. "Yes. But he's not worth it. I just need to get through tonight and try not to kill myself."

"All right. I'll tell Tara to meet you there so you will have company."

"Hey! That's a great idea. I seriously can't be alone with that guy."

"It's done, Yen," Jin said. "Okay, I got to get back to work."

"See you later."

That night, in spite of hating Justin J, the male whore, Adrienne refused to make him think she didn't deserve to be called Ariana Blanc's daughter. So she dressed up in a classy Christian Dior yellow cocktail dress that ended above her knees to show her flawless long legs. She tied her hair in a bun and left some tendrils flowing around her face. She went for a smoky-eyed look. Then she grabbed her new Hermes purse and slipped into a pair of yellow Jimmy Choos.

She smiled when she stared back at her reflection in the mirror. She looked classy and posh all right. That morning she wasn't even wearing any makeup. Now, that moron couldn't bring her down or ridicule her at her family's expense. But she swore, she would never see him again. Except during family gatherings where he would be on the guest list and on those occasions, she would try her best to ignore him.

Her mother was more than pleased with her look when she waved goodbye to her and got inside their chauffeur-driven Rolls Royce.

Tara met her at Rendezvous.

"Wow!" She beamed. "You look gorgeous!" She kissed her on the cheek.

They sat on the VIP lounge that has a view of the dance floor. Mac arrived a few minutes later and joined them.

"Jin told us you have a predicament," Mac said.

Adrienne sighed. "Yep. I'm meeting Neanderthal 1-9-8-9 here in a few minutes."

"Seriously? Your mother really thought you should be set up? Like hasn't she seen her daughter yet?" Tara asked.

"It's not just about setting me up with guys. She thought she's trying to help me get over my breakup with my boyfriend and at the same time hooking me up with somebody whose family is dear to her."

"You just broke up with your boyfriend?"

Adrienne nodded. She was again reminded of the fact that she hasn't heard from Justin in about ten days and she had no idea what he'd been doing. She hoped he was all right and at least his mother was doing fine. She wanted to hope that he's managing to convince his family to let him go so he could come back to her. Maybe now, when they find out who she really was, they wouldn't feel so bad about Justin marrying somebody other than his designated fiancée.

"It's complicated," she said. "He was previously engaged. I didn't know."

"He didn't tell you?" Tara asked.

"Like he cheated on his fiancée?" Mac asked.

"Not really. He was arranged to be married to some girl he hasn't met yet and then he met me. He didn't want to marry her anymore."

"So, what happened? He still married her?"

Adrienne shook her head. "No. But I let him go."

"Do you love him?"

Adrienne heaved a sigh. "Yes. In this life, even up to the next life."

"Did he let you go?" Tara asked.

Adrienne shook her head.

"Then why didn't you fight for him?"

"Sometimes, I wonder the same thing," she admitted. "But his parents disowned him after he chose me. I couldn't let him go through that. His family seemed too important to him. I can't compete with that."

"I hate it when parents do that," Tara said. She intertwined her fingers with Mac's. "Fortunately for you, my father adores you," she said to him and kissed his cheek.

They were interrupted by somebody who sat on the empty chair opposite Adrienne.

"I hate falling in line," Justin J. said. "Seriously! This place should have like a barcode for people with face value."

Tara and Mac stared at Adrienne with raised brows.

"Yep. Meet N-1-9-8-9," she said to them.

"What does the N stand for?" Justin J. asked. "Noteworthy? Naturally hot?" He grinned at Adrienne. She realized that he was no longer wearing those weird electric blue contacts and his eyes were actually gray.

"Try the French word, *nulle!*" Tara said, raising a brow at him. "It means crappy in English!"

Justin looked at her for a second then at Adrienne. "Seriously, who is this chick?"

"Careful there, chief," Adrienne said with a warning on her voice. "She actually owns the place and could have you kicked out and banned for life."

Tara smiled at him for a second then she switched it to a look of warning.

Justin dismissed Tara and looked at Adrienne. "Glad to see you dressed up for me, babe," he said. "You can be pretty hot if you make an effort, you know."

Adrienne saw Mac grip Tara's hand tighter, as if he, too, was resisting the urge to put a shiner on N-1-9-8-9's face.

A waitress went to their table to take their order.

"I don't usually drink, but what the hell, I think I need a daiquiri!" Adrienne said.

Tara ordered a margarita, and Mac said he wanted a beer.

The waitress turned to Justin J. He was ogling at her, literally staring at her big boobs and long legs. "Damn! Are you on the menu?" he asked her.

The waitress just smiled at him coyly.

Justin J. licked his upper lip and said, "Could you give me a Blow Job?"

Adrienne's eyes widened. "You pervert!" she said crossly, unable to stop herself.

Justin J. stared back at Adrienne, raising a brow. "What? I meant the shooter. You know? Irish liquor mixed drink? Haven't you heard about that before?"

Adrienne bit her lip in embarrassment. Tara turned away from Justin J. so he wouldn't see that she was suppressing her laughter.

"I sure will," the waitress said. Then she left. After a few minutes, she was back with their orders.

"Anything else?" she asked them.

"Maybe when you get off work, you and I can have some Sex on the Beach," Justin J. said to her.

The waitress just giggled and then she left.

Adrienne glared at him. "What? Don't tell me you don't know that Sex on the Beach is a mixed drink, either?" he asked her, giving her an innocent look.

"You think you're very funny, don't you, you little piece of Gorilla Fart?" she asked him angrily, trying to turn his joke on him.

Mac and Tara actually laughed this time.

N-1-9-8-9 gave her a dazzling smile. "Ahhh… she is smart," he said. "And nope, I'm not funny. I just think I'm a little too hot."

Mac took a gulp of his beer. "Left fist or right fist, Yenny. Just say the word and I'll give it to him," he offered.

Justin took his drink with him and stood up. "You are such a bore. I'm gonna find myself a good time." He stood up and left. It was only then that Adrienne noticed what he was wearing. Gold baggy pants, over very tight fitting black shirt and again… suspenders.

Seriously? Gold?

Seriously? Suspenders?

When he left Tara stared at Adrienne. "What the hell was that creature?" she asked. "Really? Your mother thought you would hook up with that?"

"Yep." Adrienne nodded. "I don't think I could even be friends with him."

"You have to get out of this," Tara said. "We'll tell Jin! We need to convince Ariana that she could not do this to her daughter."

"Guys, don't…tell every detail to Jin, okay?" Adrienne said. "This guy is an ape, I know. But Jin is becoming overprotective of me. If he finds out how this guy treated me, he might just give him a swing of his fist. And I don't want to break our parents' friendship because of that. I just came here two weeks ago."

"Yeah, we were wondering about that," Mac revealed. "Jin never mentioned you before. How come?"

Adrienne didn't know whether Jin really want to disclose the very small details about their family. "Well, Jin is my half-brother. I'm not a Starck. I lived with my Dad ever since I was a kid."

"Oh, that's why," Tara said.

They spent the night talking, listening to the music and watching the interesting patrons on the dance floor. Adrienne thought she was actually having a great time. Tara and Mac didn't leave her side. Maybe they're just afraid Neanderthal would come and harass her when she's alone. She is after all wearing a skirt! And he looked like a guy who would hit on anything that is wearing one.

Adrienne saw Justin J. on the dance floor. He was dirty dancing with a girl. She watched him grind his crotch to the girl's behind, like he was already humping her with clothes on. The girl was happily twerking her ass against him. Then he gripped her to him, pulling her by the waist and nuzzled her neck. He was even casually touching her boobs. And she seemed to be liking it.

"Unbelievable!" Tara said behind Adrienne. Obviously, she was watching him, too.

"Your mother is really thinking this ass-wipe is boyfriend material? Are you seeing what he's doing to that girl?" Mac asked.

"Yeah. And he claims he has a lingerie model locked up in his hotel room."

"Asshole!" Tara muttered. "If you don't have a ride home, we're taking you. You cannot even hitch a ride home with that guy!"

"I don't intend to," Adrienne said.

She looked at the dance floor with all the couples dancing and she remembered the first night she met Justin Adams. He didn't grope her like N-1-9-8-9 did to that girl he's dancing with. Justin flirted with her, yes. But he never disrespected her or harassed her. And he always knew the smartest things to say. He was breathtaking and swoon-worthy.

If Justin's fiancée met him, Adrienne doubted she would want to break off the engagement and let him go. Who wouldn't fall in love with him?

She stared at her phone again. Still no word from him. And in a way, she felt glad. Because she knew that the minute she heard from him, she would tell him everything that's going on in her life and that would make him turn around and take the next flight to Paris. She knew he would. No doubt about that.

But he shouldn't do that. He should be somewhere in the States, trying to get to know his fiancée better. Trying to see what his other future had in store for him. And hopefully after that, trying to convince his parents that it would never work out between the two of them. Because after all his efforts, after all the tries...his heart still belonged to her.

It was two in the morning when Tara and Mac decided to drive Adrienne home. They took her to the private entrance out to where Mac's car was.

On the way out, they saw a couple making out near the door. When Adrienne looked, she saw Justin J. with a girl wrapped around him.

"Hey! You should take this somewhere private!" Mac said crossly. "This is a high-end club. We don't tolerate public sex here."

Justin J., the Neanderthal looked up and saw Adrienne. He released the girl.

"Are you ready to go?" he asked.

"Yes. But don't bother yourself. My friends are taking me home."

"Oh, good," he said and then put his arms around the girl he was making out with. Then he turned to Adrienne again. "By the way, if your Mom asked, tell her we had a great time."

Adrienne rolled her eyes. "I'll tell her what a pervert you are!"

"Come on, babe," he said. "You don't really like me. So why not just tell her we had a great time, but wrong chemistry?" He smiled at her sweetly.

Adrienne took a deep breath. "You're probably right. Anyway, be safe." And she turned towards Mac's car.

"Oh my God! I hope your mother never insists that you see that guy again!" Tara said when they got inside the car.

"Despicable, isn't he?" Adrienne sighed.

"He's actually quite funny," Mac observed.

"Really? Then maybe you have a better sense of humor than me," Adrienne said.

"Well, you're not really willing to get together with him. You wouldn't want to like him regardless of whether he's great or not. So just laugh at his antics. He already knows you're not each other's types."

"He's right. Because apparently, he only hooks up with the easy ones," Tara agreed. "Let it go, hon. If your mother really wants you to meet boys, who come from rich families, are good-looking and smart, we could help you with that."

"No thanks," Adrienne said. "I sort of told my boyfriend... I'll wait for a while for him to set things right."

"And you believed he would?" Mac asked.

Adrienne sighed. "He would," she said. Then in a sad voice, she added, "If he could."

33.
Maskaradë
Albanian for Masquerade.

Adrienne kept herself busy by helping to organize her mother's victory party, aka, 'Adrienne's Introduction to Society'. She didn't like that bit, but her mother thought she deserved it. Her mother promised to do it subtly. No speeches, special mentions or any form of acknowledgement whatsoever.

Adrienne insisted on taking care of the venue, the decorations, the catering and the program. Her mother's assistant, Maryse took care of all the invitations and RSVPs. Most of the people on the guest list were French and Adrienne couldn't speak French to save her life.

Adrienne actually enjoyed what she did. For days, she was busy ensuring that every detail was in place, everything would be spotless and perfect.

"I could actually make you Head of Banquet Reservations and Events," her stepfather said to her, finding her in the ballroom, choosing different table linens.

"Papa." She smiled at him. She was hesitant to call him that. Pierre isn't really her flesh and blood. But then again, he's her mother's great love, and her brother's father. And he was great to her so far. So, every day, it got easier for her. "I used to review a lot of restaurants and event services in my previous job."

"I can see you really know what you were talking about." He smiled.

"Thank you."

"You know you always have a place in this company, Adrienne," her stepfather said. "When I married your mother, Starck Corp. acquired more than a dozen of your mother's family's hotel chains. This business is yours as much as it is Jin's."

She smiled at her stepfather, feeling how sincere he was in showing his affection towards her. If only, her stepmother was like this to her when she was growing up. "Thank you, Papa. But I have no idea how this works."

"I can send you to a few courses here or in the States if you want. It would help you learn more about what we do, if you decide you want to be a part of this. Jin told me you have an inclination for writing. Well, you can write on your own time. You can do something here. It's totally up to you."

Adrienne found that thought really exciting. She really had to start planning her life now. She hadn't heard from Justin and she knew…even if she didn't want to think about it, there was also the possibility that he wouldn't come back at all. What would she do if that happened? If finally, she came across a newspaper announcement that he was getting married?

She had to be ready, too.

She wanted to start thinking about her future as well. Paris would be a good start for her. She couldn't be in New York and not think about Justin. Going back to Boston to her father wasn't an option.

She hadn't forgiven her father yet. He called her once but she didn't answer him. Her heart broke over that. But she wanted to be honest with him, the way he'd been so dishonest with her all her life. She wanted him to know how painful it still was for her. By spending time with her mother, she wanted to bring back all the years that were lost between them.

"I think we should start by sending me to French language classes," Adrienne admitted to Pierre.

Pierre smiled. "You're right. Whenever you're ready, let me know."

When she got home, Adrienne was surprised to see a box on the bed. The box said Versace. She opened it and found a white cocktail dress. It was beautiful and elegant. And Adrienne loved how it wasn't screaming for attention. A matching silver Manolo Blahnik high-heeled open toe sandals also came with the box.

She sighed. She wasn't really used to this. She knew her mother's friends and colleagues would have high expectations of her. She wanted to live up to those expectations not for her own sake, but for her mother's.

Jin called her that evening. He was still in Dubai and would only return on the day of the party.

"You have to be here. You have to do some escort duties for me, please." She almost begged him. She really felt that she needed Jin to stay beside her, orient her on the norms of the French crème of the crop.

"I shall try. But I think Mom wants you be escorted by somebody else."

"Justin the Neanderthal?" she asked.

Shit, no!

"This is just a warning. She seems so keen on making this guy her son-in-law. I haven't spoken to her about it yet. But this guy does come from a pretty powerful family. And from what I heard, he's the perfect package—whatever you girls mean by that!"

"Have you met him?"

"Oh no, no. I am not in the business of socializing with Mom's friends unless they're doing business with us."

"Well, this guy feels like he's the god of awesomeness!" Adrienne said sarcastically. Apparently, Jin has not yet spoken to his friends about N-1-9-8-9.

Jin laughed. "Don't worry, Yen. If he makes a wrong move, party or no party, my fist is going to connect with his face."

Adrienne sighed. "Just be here on that day, okay?"

"I sure will," he said. "All right, got to go."

"Jin…" Adrienne said softly. "Thank you…for everything. It's the first time I actually felt I have a sibling."

Jin took a deep breath. "I've known I have a sibling all my life. And you were taken away from us. Mom never really told anybody that we lost you. For years, she's just been telling people, including her best friends that your father got custody of you and thus, you lived with him. But every day her heart broke because you weren't with us."

"I wish I could have known that when I was growing up. At least, I wouldn't have felt like something was wrong with me."

"Mom, Dad and I are thinking of filing a case against your Dad," he said.

Adrienne felt a shot of panic. "Jin…is that really necessary?"

"Mom is very furious. She just doesn't show it to you. She didn't want you to worry too soon. You just came back into our lives." Jin took a deep breath. "She wanted to raise you in Paris. She told your father that. He could visit you anytime and you could even live with him during school breaks. That was their agreement. She was furious that he chose to have you all for himself and erased her from your life.

"I get that. We celebrated your birthdays, even though you weren't with us. Every day, she feared that she would come across the obituaries in the States with your name on it. She found relief each day that she hadn't."

"I know, my Dad was wrong. What he did was unforgiveable. But honestly, Jin. I also know that he did what he did because he was afraid of losing me, too. And I don't want this to get bigger and messier than it already is." She sighed. "My father knows it's difficult for me to forgive him. His marriage to Marina is over. I haven't been talking to him or answering his text messages. Maybe he's suffered enough."

Jin was silent for a few moments. Then he said, "Not for me. Not for Mom. It would never be enough compared to the pain and ordeal he made us go through for twenty-three years, Adrienne."

"Let's talk about this as a family. Don't do anything yet, okay? If Mom tells you to push it, you tell me first, okay?"

Jin sighed. "Okay. Let's wait until after the party."

"Good. Now go back to work."

Adrienne started a group chat with Yuan and Jill. She told them about the party. She invited them to her coming-out-to-society. She offered to pay for their flights, too.

Yuan: *Sorry, Yen. I have a convention on the same day. I won't be able to come. But send me pictures, okay?*

Adrienne: *Okay. Will do. Oh my God, I'm dreading that day! My Mom is setting me up with her friend's son. And his name is Justin, too. But he is the exact opposite of my Justin!*

Jill: *Is he hot?*

Adrienne: *Maybe. Without his weird contact lenses, and absurd taste in fashion, I guess he can be cute. He has gray eyes and he's a few* inches shorter than Justin. Yeah, I guess he's not bad looking, but he is such an asshole! I don't know what my Mom was thinking!

Yuan: *I guess setting up kids is quite common in rich people's circles, huh? Welcome to Justin Adams's world, sweetie! Now, at least you have more understanding about what he must feel. And you should be proud of yourself for being unselfish enough to let him go because you didn't want to play tug-of-war with his folks."*

Jill: *By the way, I saw Justin in the office this morning, Yen. You wanna hear about it?*

Adrienne stared at her screen for a while. She didn't know what to type. Of course, she was dying to know what's going on with him. But what if she doesn't like what she finds out? She knew it would break her heart even more.

Before she knew it, she was typing: *Shoot!*

She waited anxiously for Jill's reply. After what seemed like an eternity, she heard a notification from her computer.

Jill: *He gave notice to Jada that he will no longer be working part-time for Blush. He said it was because of family obligations and he said, he would be getting married soon and would be settling down in Chicago. I'm not going to lie to you, Yen. He didn't look devastated. In fact, he was looking...chirpy. I'm sorry.*

Adrienne stared at the screen for a whole five minutes. She read what Jill wrote to her. Justin announced that he was getting married and settling down in Chicago?

She looked at the calendar. Twenty days. She still had twenty days. That's what Justin said to her. Twenty days and they'd fly to Italy.

But then... maybe he's met his fiancée and maybe he did give it a try. He made no more effort to contact her after his last message to her. Maybe his fiancée didn't turn out to be so bad after all.

Well, she wanted him to do this. She should have been ready for this ending. But then she realized, nothing could prepare anybody for the blinding pain the finality of a relationship would cause. Maybe she was in denial the whole time. Even if she did let him go, deep inside her heart, she really did believe he could convince his parents to set him free.

Tears rolled down her cheeks. She thought her heart couldn't be more broken than it already was.

She started typing: *It's okay, Jill. I wanted him to be happy, remember? I will be fine.*

Yuan: *I'm sorry, Yen. We know someday, you will find your real happiness, too. Maybe it's not your time yet. You have so many things to look forward to now. You had Justin before, but you didn't have the love of a family. And now you do.*

Jill: *I guess something's got to give sometimes. But don't worry. After your coming out to society thingy, I'm sure hundreds of eligible*

bachelors would be pining for your hand. Hang on, okay?
Adrienne: *I love you guys. Now, I have to go.*
She didn't really have to go. But she wanted some time to herself. She went to bed and hugged her pillows. She closed her eyes and didn't suppress the tears that came.

In a way, she was asking herself why she let him go. But then again, if she didn't, and later he met his fiancée, who may be his real destiny, then she would have to give him up eventually.

So maybe…just maybe…it's better this way.

***

Friday night the whole banquet in Starck Hotel Paris was in full swing. Everything was perfect. The ballroom glimmered in its full soiree decorations.

Adrienne stood on the mezzanine floor of the ballroom and looked on as the guests came pouring in. Her mother asked her not to come down and meet the guests just yet. She said she wanted her to wait at the gazebo on the second-floor garden and they will come and get her.

No announcements, huh!

But her heart had been so numb over the bad news she heard about Justin that she couldn't care about anything else anymore.

Everybody was wearing lavish clothes and Adrienne couldn't help feeling mortified as she looked at the people below her. And an hour from now, they would all meet her…put her under the microscope to see if she's worthy to be one of them.

Well, she knew she dressed the part well at least. She was wearing the white Versace gown that has a crossover-keyhole neckline and back with asymmetrical straps. The floor length skirt flowed over her perfect curves, and the slit on the thigh reveals a little glimpse of her long legs under the gown. Her hair was braided behind her and left little tendrils around her face. Her makeup was nude over her cheek and smoky on the area of her eyes, making her look like angelic and tough at the same time.

"You look lovely, my dear," her mother said to her. "Justin will not be able to take his eyes off you."

Adrienne took a deep breath. "Mom…" she started. "I hate him." There! She finally said it. No need to pretend otherwise.

Her mother blinked back at her. "What? I thought you two were hitting it off."

She shook her head. "We didn't get along from day one, Mom. And besides, I told you I wasn't looking for a boyfriend. I was just looking to befriend your friends."

"Sweetheart," her mother began. "Okay…I know how we can fix this."

"Mom, there's nothing to fix," Adrienne argued.

Tears welled up in her mother's eyes. "No, sweetheart. You don't understand. I haven't been completely honest with you." She took a deep breath. "Well...I wasn't just setting you up with Justin. I was hoping you would really fall for him...enough to get... married one day."

Adrienne's eyes widened. "What?"

Her mother sighed. "I know. It's terrible. I couldn't tell you. I made that arrangement a long time ago. When you were a baby and I just got back from Paris. My father...made me promise to return you to this family and form a strong bond with Christine's family. She was my oldest friend. Our families were always keen on becoming related to one another someday. She had a boy. I had a girl.

"Our fathers were like brothers. Your grandfather invested in Christine's father's business venture, which gave them a lot of fortune. They were keen to merge this family not just because of money...but also because of gratitude and friendship. So, we sort of...arranged for you to marry Christine's son." Her mother squeezed her hands.

"Mom!" Adrienne couldn't help the feelings that overwhelmed her. "How could you have agreed to that arrangement when all these years I was missing?"

"I know, sweetheart. It's wrong. But all these years, I never told anybody outside of this family that you were really missing... stolen by your father. We wanted to keep this a secret because... we didn't want anybody to take advantage of the situation or sensationalize it and drive your father further into hiding.

"We silently searched for you. Even Christine didn't know. I always just told her that you were in the States with your Dad. And I actually forgot about the arrangement until Christine reminded me about it a couple of weeks back. They said that Justin seemed to be ready to get into a serious relationship. Maybe it's time to introduce you to each other.

"Christine lived in the States. I didn't see her often. It was easy to make an excuse to everybody, including her, why you were not with us. To be honest with you...I had forgotten about the agreement. My focus had always been about finding you. When Christine sent me a message, reminding me about it...and to start introducing you and Justin...I meant to tell her the truth. But Jin... Jin called me and told me that he had a lead on you. So...I held it off for a while."

Adrienne couldn't believe her ears. How could this happen to her? She was a casualty of an arranged marriage herself. Now she found herself a subject of one. And to a hopeless ass-wipe!

"Mom, please...I can't even stand Christine's son." she protested.

"Okay...I'm sorry. I know...there's absolutely no reason that would justify what I did. I promise you, I have no plans of forcing it. Your grandfather forced me to Pierre, employed all means to ensure I married him. But I didn't regret it because he was a lovely man. And I fell in love with him after a few dates. So, I was hoping after spending some time with Justin, you two would hit it off and you won't find this terrible anymore. And if you really couldn't stand it…I had no intention of forcing it."

"He's terrible, Mom!" Adrienne argued. "Mama, my ex-boyfriend is going to marry the girl who was arranged for him. That's why we broke up. Until now, I was still heartbroken about it. I promised to wait for him as long as I could. Or until I know for sure that he's already accepted his fate. Please do not do this to me. I beg you." She was almost teary when she said those words to her mother.

Her mother looked at her ruefully. She cupped her hands around her face. Then she nodded.

"Okay." she said. "I love you. I will break the arrangement with Christine. It will break her heart and she may not talk to me in a few months, maybe years, but she will get over it. My father is long gone, he couldn't do anything about it. He seemed so keen about planning the future of this family. I messed up your life because of him."

Her mother took a deep breath. "I'm so sorry, Adrienne. I shouldn't have left you with your father. I should have been brave enough to face my father…instead of leaving you to your Dad. I did this to you. And I will not mess up your life even more by forcing you to marry some guy you do not want. After all these years, the one thing that I realized is that your happiness is more important to me than anything else." Her mother smiled at her apologetically. "I realized this when I got you back. I know the pain I went through when I lost you. And I am not going to lose you again. So if you say you won't marry Christine's son, then so be it."

She smiled at her mother. "Thank you, Mom."

"But maybe it's too late to back out on making Justin your escort for tonight. But after this soiree, I swear to you, you won't have to see him again."

Adrienne was still disappointed she had to spend some time with N-1-9-8-9. But if it's an assurance that he would disappear from her life forever, then one night won't be that bad.

"Okay, Mom, I guess I can live with that. Besides, Jin can just rescue me anytime I feel the urge to vomit."

Her mother smiled. "Okay, now go to the garden. Justin will fetch you when it's time."

The second floor of the hotel led to a small garden. There was a small gazebo and a wishing fountain in the center. It was filled with lights and the trees had lighted LEDs to look as if fireflies infested them. The garden was indeed magical especially at nighttime.

She stood inside the gazebo and enjoyed the spectacular view in front of her. In the sky, there was a lovers' moon and she couldn't help the tears that peered in her eyes.

She missed Justin. She felt like he was just right there. Every single day. Every single hour. When she walked, she felt like he was walking beside her. When she slept at night, she imagined being locked in his arms.

She wished that love was enough. She wished that life was not complicated. She wished that the world wasn't crazy and her life didn't come with complexities and obstacles. She wished everything was just…easy.

She couldn't believe what her mother just told her. She couldn't believe she agreed to marry her off to some guy she didn't know, and hadn't met before.

And Justin the Neanderthal? The hairs on her arms actually started to rise in disgust.

But she was thankful that she didn't have to try so hard to convince her mother to let her go…unlike her Justin, who was forced to embrace his own destiny. How she wished that Justin's fight had been easy, and that he had succeeded in fighting for her.

She stared at the moon again, then she closed her eyes and thought about Justin Adams…her Justin.

I wish you all the happiness in the world. I wish you all the smiles, laughter and love that you deserve. I wish…that finally… all your prayers will be answered…that the miracles you hoped for would be given to you.

She wished those things with all her heart. It killed her a little each day when she thought about not seeing him again, not feeling the warmth of his skin against hers, not hear him say he loved her…not see the wicked, mischievous look on his face whenever he said his usual line to her…words she wished she could hear him say again…if only for the last time.

Tears rolled down her cheeks. She gently wiped them with her fingers. Her escort would come soon and she didn't want to be caught crying. Not by him. Not by the insensitive, stupid jerk who was probably heaven's curse to all women.

Suddenly, she felt like she was no longer alone. She felt that somebody was standing behind her. And she realized in horror that Justin the Neanderthal had already come for her, finding her in a private moment, seeing the tears she didn't want to show anybody else.

She realized, too, that he stood close to her… too close he was almost touching her.

But before Adrienne could turn around to face him, she felt his breath against her ear. And then in a soothing voice, he whispered, "You're a fox."

34.
Sufletul pereche
Romanian for Soul Mate

*A*drienne quickly spun around and found herself staring at a pair of crystal blue eyes. She blinked back at him, all the muscles and bones in her body froze, including her voice.

He looked as handsome as ever, dressed in a black tux. His hair was still a little disheveled but it only added to the charm of his devilishly handsome face. His eyes though, weren't dancing, like they used to. They had a shadow of circles under them, as if he hadn't been sleeping properly in days.

Adrienne realized that she hadn't been breathing in a long time. She closed her eyes for a moment, thinking for sure that he would disappear once she opened her eyes. But when she did, he was still there, looking back at her curiously.

"Justin..." she whispered.

He didn't speak. He looked as dumbfounded as she was. Then he took a deep breath and instead of uttering a word, he reached to pull her waist and in a second, he crushed her to his arms and his lips devoured hers into one hungry kiss.

Adrienne didn't think. Her arms wound around his neck and she kissed him with the same intensity as he was kissing her. She poured all her love in that kiss. She knew that she promised to let him go, but right now, she felt that after suffering for weeks, and yearning to feel his existence again, she deserved this moment of insanity...this stolen piece of heaven.

When the kiss ended, they were both breathless. She was sure her dress was slightly crumpled, her hair probably disheveled and her makeup could be ruined, but she didn't care. Right now, all that mattered was this moment, and this man in front of her.

He leaned his forehead against hers. "Honey...." he whispered in a hoarse voice.

"Justin...what are you doing here?"

"What are *you* doing here?" he asked. "I thought you were in New York."

She pulled away from him, to look into his eyes. "Justin..." she started. She didn't even know where to begin telling him what happened to her while they were apart. "Something...big happened to me. I found out that my mom wasn't really my mom. She's my stepmom. And now...I found my real Mom. She lived here in Paris all throughout these years. I've been living with my new family for two weeks. I have a stepdad and a brother. Kim is not my sister, Justin!"

She knew they didn't have a lot of time to talk. Justin the Neanderthal just might walk in on them any minute now, and once Justin met him and he opened his mouth, she was ninety-nine percent sure the Neanderthal would get the beating he deserved for the way he'd been treating her since he met her.

Justin looked at her with a confused expression on his face, absorbing everything that she just said, trying to make sense of what little information she could provide him.

"Justin...are you okay?" she asked.

He blinked back to reality and looked at her with narrowed eyes.

"Honey..." she said.

"Adrienne..." He took a deep breath. "Your mother...your real mother..." he said. "What's her name?"

"Ariana," Adrienne replied. "Ariana Blanc-Starck."

Justin released her and took a step back from her. Adrienne suddenly felt cold once the warmth of Justin's body left hers. He continued looking at her with that dazed expression on his face, which made her curious and nervous at the same time.

"Justin..." she whispered. "Could you please say something? You're scaring me."

Justin closed his eyes for a moment. He took a deep breath. And then when he looked at her again, his eyes were suddenly teary.

"Honey...why are you crying?" she asked.

He shook his head. And then suddenly, he smiled. Then he chuckled. And then he just laughed. Adrienne stared at him as if he just completely lost his mind.

Justin wounded his arms around her waist, lifted her off her feet and spun her around while he laughed his heart out. He laughed as if he hadn't been doing that for weeks.

"Justin, what's going on?" Adrienne asked.

He settled her back on her feet. He shook his head. "Nothing, honey," he said. "I think...I've just been given the miracle I was asking for." And then his face descended towards hers and he gave her another head-spinning, sanity-disturbing kiss.

"Justin..." Adrienne whispered after the kiss. "I know we have a lot to talk about. But you should go. I should be going down to the party. My escort will come any minute to get me. And it's not advisable for you to actually meet him."

He raised a brow at her. "Why not?"

She sighed. "Because I don't want to you to go to jail for assault or...worse, murder."

Adrienne didn't expect it, but Justin actually laughed again. "He's that bad, huh? Damn! He's good," he said under his breath.

Adrienne blinked back at him. "What did you say?"

Justin shook his head again. Instead he asked, "Did your mother tell you that you're arranged to be married to this guy?"

Adrienne nodded. "Was. She's going to call it off."

Justin stared at her with a sober expression on his face. "And what if your fiancé doesn't allow her to call off the engagement?"

"He doesn't have a choice. And besides, he hates me as much as I hate him."

Justin shook his head. "He doesn't hate you, honey. In fact... he is head over heels in love with you, he wants to marry you right now." Adrienne stared back at him, her eyes widened. Then Justin added, "I don't think your fiancé will come any minute and interrupt our moment, Adrienne."

"Why?" She asked in almost a whisper, her knees getting weaker by the second.

"Because...he's already here." Justin replied in a soft voice, his face full of affection as he said those words.

"Justin..." Tears welled up in Adrienne's eyes. "How..."

He smiled at her ruefully. "The guy you met...isn't your real fiancé, Adrienne," he said. "I am."

"You? Your mother is..."

"Christine Adams," Justin supplied for her.

"You're my mother's best friend's son? But how? I met a guy, his name is Justin, too. And he's the most despicable creature to ever walk the face of the Earth."

Justin smiled at her. "Yes. Because I paid him to act that way."

"What?"

"I didn't want to go through with this engagement. There was no way in hell I would marry the girl my parents chose for me. I already knew who I wanted to spend the rest of my life with.

"My father asked me to meet this girl and make her fall in love with me. I didn't want to. So I asked somebody else to pose as me and... make sure she would hate him so she would back out of this engagement herself. Once I was sure she hated the idea of marrying me, I could meet her as myself and give her an even worse time than what the other Justin did."

"You paid somebody to pose as you? Didn't you realize that somebody might realize that he's an impostor?" Adrienne couldn't believe what Justin did.

"I counted on that, too," he replied. "I hoped her parents found out what I did and think the worst things about me, and never trust the fate of their priceless daughter in my hands. After all... what kind of a lunatic treats a girl that way?"

"Justin! That guy was a whack job!"

"He's not. He just happens to be a very good actor," he said.

"Meeting that guy was like eating my own vomit! It felt absolutely disgusting! And you did that to me?" Adrienne asked, almost in a daze.

"I'm sorry, honey. I had no idea it was you! I hadn't met my fiancée. I didn't have a picture of her. I wasn't interested. All I knew was her mother's name and which family she belonged to. How was I supposed to know you have this whole family mystery that may make you end up as my designated fiancée?"

"What if he...took advantage of me? What if he harassed me?"

Justin shook his head. "His real name is Jordan. He's my cousin. We grew up together and he almost lived with me. He may be a menace most of the time, but I know he's not capable of doing that."

Adrienne stared back at Justin. His eyes were now dancing and she didn't think she's seen him so happy before.

"You're going to pay for that!" she said to him crossly.

He grinned at her. "Now that I know who my parents wanted me to marry, I am willing to pay the price no matter how high."

Adrienne narrowed her eyes at him. Then without warning, she slapped him. He was taken back a bit. But when he turned to her again, he was still grinning. His eyes were dancing and he looked like nothing she would say or do would dampen his spirit or wipe out his happiness.

"I wanna kill you!" she said to him and a part of her really wanted to do that for putting her through the worst afternoon and evening of her life. Then she stared up at him and said, "But maybe later," she said and she pulled him to her and kissed his lips.

His arms wrapped around her waist and he pulled her to him as he deepened their kiss. When that kiss ended he took a deep breath and inhaled the scent of her. "God, I missed you."

Adrienne sighed contentedly. "I missed you, too. Just a while ago...I was praying you would be happy. I was praying that God gives you a miracle."

He chuckled. "Your prayers are powerful. God must like you the most."

She couldn't believe what just happened. A few minutes back, she thought that he lost his battle. She was heartbroken when she found out that her mother had betrothed her to somebody against her will. She wondered...if she hadn't gotten lost all throughout these years, would her mother still insist she marries her best friend's son? If she hadn't met Justin before she found out her real identity, they would be forced to like each other enough to spend the rest of their lives together...even if there was no love between them.

Justin pushed back a lock of stray hair away from her face. "You look beautiful, honey," he said. "I know now...that you're really Andrea Blanc. But you will always be Adrienne to me...my Adrienne."

Adrienne smiled bitterly. "My mother said that my real birth papers say that I'm Andrea Blanc. My passports say Adrienne Miller. But that's not my real name. It was the fake name my father picked out for me to prevent my mother from finding me. Now, I don't know what name I should really use."

Justin stared at her thoughtfully, feeling her confusion, and her pain for the way her life had been. It's never easy to know you have two different identities and you don't know which one really fits.

He smiled at her and said, "Let's do something about that, shall we?"

Adrienne didn't get what he meant by that. But then he pulled away from her. He stared at her seriously, took a deep breath and then slowly, he went down on one knee.

Adrienne sucked in a deep breath. Her heart pounded loudly inside her ribcage, she could almost hear it. She had to hold on to the rails beside her, as she no longer trusted her knees to support her weight.

Justin took something from his pocket. It was a small black box. He opened it in front of her and she saw a gleaming five carat diamond ring.

Justin took a deep breath again. "There are a million things I wanted to tell you. A hundred lines I thought I would say whenever I imagined the moment that I would finally propose to you…for real. But right now, all I can say is that I love you, Adrienne…I love you…very, very much. I said this to you before, and I'm going to say it again now…you're the one I want to spend the rest of my life with. I never want to let you go. No matter how many times you set me free. I had planned to propose to you after I convinced my folks that there was no way they could force me to take another bride. But now…by some miracle, I don't need to do that anymore.

"But I am saying these things to you not because our families arranged for this. But because this is what I want…for the rest of my life. I love you so much, I'm willing to give up everything for you…I live for you…I'm willing to die for you. You are my life…now, forever, always." There were tears in his eyes when he said those words. Then with a wistful look in his eyes, he added, "You don't have to choose which of your names you should use. Will you let me change it to the name that rightfully belongs to you…the one that suits you the best? Will you be Adrienne Adams? Will you marry me?"

Tears rolled down Adrienne's eyes. She wanted to find her voice right away but she couldn't stop crying. Justin's eyes were filled with tears, too, as he held his breath for her answer.

"Yes." she said when she finally found her voice. "You know I will!" And she knelt in front of him, throwing herself in his arms.

He caught her and wound his arms around her. He hugged her tightly, burying his face against her hair, as she buried hers against his chest.

They savored that moment. They're engaged. Not by some sort of arranged marriage. Not in the hypothetical pretend world. But for real. In this bizarre turn of events, their alternate universe, where they are betrothed to each other and planned to spend the rest of their lives together without obstacles…just came true.

Adrienne pulled away from Justin and looked into his eyes. He smiled tearfully, as he took her hand and slipped the ring on her finger. It fit her perfectly.

Justin leaned forward and slowly, kissed her lips…thoroughly…passionately. And Adrienne wished that kiss would never end. When it did, he stood up on his feet and pulled her up with him. Then he picked her up and spun her around. She was crying and giggling at the same.

When Justin put her down on her feet, she wiped the tears on her cheeks and admired the gleaming rock on her finger.

"It's beautiful," she said to him.

"So are you," Justin whispered to her. "That was my mother's engagement ring. She gave it to me before I came up here. She was really hoping that you and Justin J. had hit it off." He chuckled.

"Yes. I came so close to hitting him…with a titanium alloy bat!" Adrienne said.

Justin laughed. "And I believe that. Jordan actually told me you were quite feisty. Knowing now that it was you…you made me so proud."

"On his business card, it said Justin J." Adrienne said. "What does the J. stand for?"

"My middle name, Jeffrey," Justin answered. "My twin died a few days after he was born. My mother thought to give me his name so he would always live in our memories…through me."

"Why didn't you put your surname on the business card then?" Adrienne asked.

"Are you kidding me? If that card leaked out with my full name on it, I've just committed social suicide!" Justin said.

Adrienne laughed. "That card was a sure way to turn a girl off."

"That was Ian's idea." Justin said.

"Your cousins actually helped you out in giving me the worst hours of my life?"

"We were trying to mess up with Andrea Blanc. And it worked, right?"

Adrienne nodded. "You got me at 'machito'," she said, now giggling at the memory of her afternoon meeting with Jordan, alias N-1-9-8-9.

Justin raised a brow at her, clearly not getting what she meant by that.

"When Jordan ordered coffee at the shop, he asked for a 'machito', instead of a 'macchiato'. I thought he was such a moron."

Justin laughed. "He is good. There is absolutely no way he could mistake a 'macchiato'. Their family owns a huge coffee shop chain in the

States."

Adrienne shook her head. "I cannot believe you guys!" she said. "Your cousins are going to be the death of me."

Justin laughed. "Ian and Gian liked you—Adrienne. So they went out of their way to make Andrea Blanc pay."

"If you sent Gian, our problem would have been solved earlier."

"If you answered my calls or actually returned my messages and told me the whole thing about your real identity, we would have ended this before you even met Jordan."

"I was a mess during those times. The whole thing about my family was just overwhelming. Why didn't you call me after that then?"

"Because it was part of my agreement with my Dad. I couldn't contact you. I was supposed to be focusing all my attentions in making my fiancée fall in love with me. I didn't want to break that promise because I didn't want him to find out just exactly what I was doing. Until I accomplished my mission, of course."

"Congratulations! Mission accomplished!" Adrienne smiled. "What did you plan to do at this party now that you're showing up as yourself and without the aid of Mischief Jordan?"

"Something that would make Andrea Blanc wish she was engaged to the fake Justin instead. At least he was a little bit funny."

Adrienne narrowed her eyes at him. "Really? You'd leave the gentleman cloak behind just to make her hate you?"

"Desperate times call for desperate measures, honey." Justin grinned at her. "I'd rather live in shame than in misery for the rest of my life."

"Jill told me when she saw you at *Blush*, you were looking...rather chirpy. You didn't look miserable at all."

"Of course. Jordan fed me with news of how my designated fiancée never wanted to see me again. The plan was working. And I couldn't wait for the whole thing to be over so I could be with you."

"If you asked him to take a picture of me, we would have been out of this misery earlier."

"I didn't need a picture. I didn't need to know what she looked like. I wasn't interested."

Adrienne sighed. "I can't believe our parents did this to us."

Justin touched her cheek with his fingers. "It was hell for me, Adrienne. I could count the number of days I actually stayed sober—with one hand."

Adrienne bit her lip and her heart went out to Justin. She touched his cheek with her hand and he turned sideways to kiss the inside of her palm.

"I think I'd drink every night, too, if I didn't find out about my new family. It was painful to know the truth about myself. But I was at least thankful that it provided me a little distraction. And of course... now I understand why my sister and my mom never really liked me."

"Adrienne..."

"Hmmm..." Adrienne stared up at Justin.

"We're never going to arrange our kids' marriages," he said. "We will let them find their own happiness. Let them be free to choose the person who would make them happy."

Adrienne smiled. "I totally agree," she said. "My mother arranged my own marriage when I was two. Now that she found me again...she thought I should try to fall in love with my fiancé first. If I hadn't gone M.I.A., I wonder if she would have enforced this...the way your parents did."

"Judging by the way my mother was so adamant about this...maybe."

"Your parents are going to be so happy about this, aren't they?" Adrienne asked.

Justin stared at her for a while. Then he nodded. "They will be ecstatic. Our mothers would think that it was right to meddle with our lives. My father would be gloating in front of me and they would probably arrange the wedding of the century by tomorrow."

Adrienne's eyes widened. "Do you think they would?"

"I know my parents, Adrienne. And I think I may even know your mother more than you do. I've known her longer than you have," Justin observed. "And yes...they would be so damn proud of this! And they wouldn't even feel sorry for the hell they put us through."

"You're right. It was only because of a miracle that we fell in love ahead of the time they set to introduce us to each other... but in any other ordinary circumstance, both of us would have been devastated, wouldn't we?"

Justin nodded. "Yes," he whispered. Then he took a deep breath and pulled her to him. He planted a long kiss on her lips and then he asked, "Do you trust me, Adrienne?"

She smiled against his lips. "With all my heart, Justin."

He pulled away from her and smiled. "Good." Then he took her hand in his and pulled her towards the exits.

"Where are we going?" she asked him.

He turned back to her and smiled, "Remember my last text message to you?" he asked.

She nodded. "Of course."

"We still have two weeks," he said.

"Yes...yes we do."

Justin stepped closer to her. With a mischievous grin on his face, he said, "Well, I don't think I can wait two more weeks... Mrs. Adams." And he gave her a kiss that blew her mind and took her breath away.

35.
Rhedeg i ffwrdd.
Welsh for Running Away

*T*wo hours later, Adrienne was at the airport with Justin. She wasn't thinking. She didn't care. She knew it was wrong in some way. But she felt tired of doing everything that everybody around her expected of her. She lived with a stepmother who never saw anything good in what she did, a father who didn't know how to stand up for her, and now she had a mother who mapped out her future without even telling her. Maybe the time had come for her to think about herself. Time to follow her heart and go after what she wanted. And that's Justin.

Jin walked in to the lobby of the airport, carrying a small bag with him. She texted him that she left the party and she needed him to bring some of her stuff to the airport.

He looked at her with a sober expression on his face.

"I hope you know what you're doing, Adrienne," he said to her.

"I don't," she said to him. "But for the first time in my life, I'm just…doing what I want."

He smiled at her and looked over at the counter where Justin was, booking their flights.

"And it's him?" he asked.

Adrienne nodded. Then she asked him, "Jin…did you know that Mom arranged a marriage for me?"

Jin raised a brow. "No. If I knew, I would have done something about it. I'm against arranged marriages, Adrienne. I knew Mom played matchmaker. But I didn't know she'd already sentenced you."

Adrienne nodded. "She told me at the party."

Jin smiled. "She was so worried. She didn't know how to tell Christine that you didn't want to go through with it. But then, you didn't show up at the party and texted me that you left. Now, she feels so guilty that she scared you off."

"Oh my God, Jin." Her hand went to her mouth. "Is she okay?"

Jin grinned. "She'll be okay. Let's make her contemplate on what she's done for a while. She can't meddle with our lives like this."

"Do they know?"

"That the guy they set you up with was already your boyfriend?" Jin asked. He shook his head. "Only I know. Because when your betrothed showed up at the soiree, I immediately recognized him. I remembered him from the bar the first time I met you. I didn't know he was *the* Justin Adams, whose family had been so close to us all these years. But I wouldn't tell her that, Yen. Let's enjoy this little joke to ourselves for a while." He grinned.

"What about Justin's parents?"

Jin stared over to where Justin stood again. "I think…his phone has rung non-stop. I won't be the one to break the news to them. If you ask me, our mother and his parents all deserved to be taught a lesson." Then Jin winked at her. He handed her a small bag. "I just grabbed whatever I could. Your IDs, wallet and passport are in the pocket. Where are you going, anyway?"

Adrienne smiled at Jin uncertainly. For the first time, she didn't know where her destination was, but she had complete faith in Justin. She trusted him with her heart, and now, she's trusting him with her life.

"I don't know. I don't care. Right now, I just…wanna be with him."

"I told Mom that I thought you ran away and that I was going to come after you. I'll probably just tell her you wanted to go back to New York and think for a while. After all…all this hoopla could be overwhelming, too. I'm sure she should give you time considering she kept it from all of us how she tried to manipulate your future."

"Jin, please don't let her think that she's going to lose me again. This is just… something that I have to do. I broke up with Justin a couple of weeks ago because his family arranged for him to marry somebody else. His family disowned him. I couldn't do that to him. So I gave him up so he could get to know the girl chosen by his parents for him. And it almost tore me apart. He didn't give up on me though. He fought for me nevertheless.

"I hurt Justin when I gave him up. We've been through the worst in our lives. I need to make this up to him, now that I know his parents will no longer disown him if he chooses to be with me." Adrienne took a deep breath. "I just want us to savor this moment."

Jin nodded. "As long as you're happy, Yen." He leaned forward and gave her a hug. "I hate it that I just got you back and now he's taking you away from me," he whispered and his voice really did have a trace of sadness.

"You won't lose me, Jin," Adrienne said, tears welling up in her eyes as she hugged her brother back.

"I know. But when I see you again, I have a feeling you'll be…Adrienne Adams. Impressive ring, by the way. Congratulations."

She giggled then she pulled away from him. "Take care of Mom, okay? Don't let her get too sad. Yes, she shouldn't have meddled with my life like this. But I don't want her to be depressed. Besides, she already apologized to me and promised to call it off."

Jin nodded. "Of course. I don't agree with what she did, but she's still our Mom. She deserves to know that her plan worked out after all…well, after feeling sorry about it, of course."

Justin appeared behind them. He looked at Jin for a while and then he extended his hand to him.

"I'm Justin." he said to Jin.

Jin shook his hand. "And I'm the guy who will beat the shit out of you if you hurt my sister."

"Jin!" Adrienne hissed at her brother.

"It's okay, honey," Justin said. Then he turned back to Jin. "I will take care of her, you don't have to worry. She will be safest when she is with me."

Jin nodded. Then he turned to Adrienne. "Keep in touch. Call me if you need anything. And I mean anything!"

Adrienne nodded. Then she hugged Jin again. "I love you, Jin," she whispered to him. And she meant that. Even though, she just met her brother, she managed to build a sibling bond with him the way Kimberly never did in the twenty-five years she thought she was her sister.

"I love you too, sis. Be happy, okay?"

"You know I will be."

Jin left and Adrienne turned to Justin.

"That guy is going to be my brother-in-law?" he asked, raising a brow while staring at Jin's back.

"Justin...."

"I remember wanting to punch all his teeth down his throat when I thought he was interested in you."

Adrienne smiled. "He was. But not for the reasons you thought. He suspected I was his long, lost sister."

"Thank God, you were!" Justin smiled.

"I'm surprised you didn't recognize him."

"He probably hates going to our little family reunions as much as I do. So, we never met each other. But I've always known the girl I was supposed to marry belonged to the Starck family. Once, when I thought he was going after you, I feared an unimaginable fate for myself. You—becoming my sister-in-law."

Adrienne's eyes widened. "Oh my God! That would be really messed up, right?"

"Yup. I didn't even want to think about what I was going to do. I think I'd probably live halfway across the globe and never show up to family reunions ever."

Adrienne giggled. "Why would you do that?"

Justin's eyes narrowed at her. "Did you really think I could ever stop loving you, Adrienne?" He pushed a lock of stray hair away from her face. "I probably would want to kill myself every single day if I ended up with that fate."

Adrienne smiled. "Then let's be thankful that I was the missing sister of Jin Starck instead. So be good to him, okay?"

He pulled her to him and gave her a soft kiss on the lips. "Yes...for now. So let's get married soon so I can show him who's the boss."

Adrienne laughed. "Where are we going, anyway?"

Justin grinned at her. "We're eloping to Italy," he replied. Then he stared at her with a wistful expression on his handsome face. "Are you sure about this, honey? Because once you board that plane, there will be no turning back for you. When you go back to Paris or New York, you will be Mrs. Justin Adams." His eyes were dancing and Adrienne could see just how happy he was. And she felt exactly the same way.

"Your parents called you yet?"

"Once every five minutes in the last two hours."

"Did you answer them?"

"Nope. I did send my Mother an apology text message."

"What did you say?"

Justin shrugged. *"I'm sorry Mom. I really love my girlfriend. And I only want her in my future. Someday I hope you will understand.'* And that's it."

"Justin…she will think you went and eloped with your girlfriend," Adrienne said.

Justin grinned at her. "And I am."

"But…they don't know me."

"Yes. They don't know I'm already in love with the girl that they wanted me to marry. And right now, I'm not too excited to break the news to them just yet."

"Justin…they will be mad at us for running away."

"You think?" he asked. Then he smiled. "They will get the ending they wanted. I just don't want them to gloat just yet. I want them to pay even just a little bit of a price for it."

"That's why we're eloping to Italy?" she asked.

He grinned at her mischievously. "That's my excuse," he said. Then his face turned serious. "The real reason is that…I know what it was like to not have you in my life and face an uncertain future without even knowing for sure that you're going to be a part of it. I don't want that anymore, Adrienne. I want to wake up with you in the mornings and hold you in my arms at nights. Right now… I just don't care what anybody will think or feel. It's our time, Adrienne. This time… what matters is just the two of us. Our parents…threatened our happiness before. I just want to make sure they couldn't do anything to it again."

"They will be disappointed when they find out we got married without them. Our mothers probably planned our wedding in their heads a long time ago."

"But that's the point. They were planning the wedding of the children they arranged to marry. That's not us, Adrienne. We fell in love with each other without their help or influence. Our love story has always been about…just the two of us," Justin said. "I planned to marry you in Italy. Like this. In a romantic setting fit for two lovers who won their fight against the world. Nothing should change that just because I found out that you and the girl I was arranged to be married to are one and the same person. I'm still marrying Adrienne Miller. Not Andrea Blanc."

Adrienne smiled at him. She thought that he did have a point. She accepted her betrothal to the man she loved with all her heart. Not the person her mother thought she should marry. Sure, their parents might be disappointed and would probably get mad at them when they do not return tomorrow or the next day. But they've been through a lot in the past few weeks. She thought they deserved this little piece of heaven. And nothing changed between the two of them. Especially not their love for each other.

"Unless…you want a big wedding, honey," he said. "In that case, we're going to Italy not to get married…but to advance our honeymoon." He grinned at her.

Adrienne smiled at him. She shook her head. "I never wanted a big wedding. Just because I found out that my mother is rich and can afford the biggest wedding of the century doesn't mean it would change who I am and what I want. I am still Adrienne Miller—the girl with simple needs and desires. And right now…I only want one thing." She stared up Justin. "You."

He smiled at her. "Then I promise you, you won't regret it, Mrs. Adams."

"I'm not Mrs. Adams yet." She laughed.

He kissed her lips and pulled her towards the check-in counters. "You will be in less than a week. So better get used to that name…Mrs. Adrienne Adams." He winked at her.

As she walked beside him, she said her new name in her head.
Adrienne Adams.

"I like it very much." She said to him. "It feels like… me."

36.
Upendo ni nuru ya maisha.
Swahili for "love is the light of life"

*J*ustin and Adrienne arrived at a luxury hotel in Florence. It was more like a luxurious, sophisticated home than a hotel with its elegant townhouse façade, neo-classical furniture and centuries worth of art collections in a four-story structure.

They were greeted warmly by all the staff dressed in expensive suits and uniforms.

Adrienne blinked back at Justin, obviously in awe of the VIP treatment they received. Justin smiled and whispered to her. "I rented the whole place for the whole week. So we are their only guests."

Adrienne's eyes widened. "Justin!" she hissed. "That's too much!"

"What's the point of eloping if you cannot have some sort of privacy, right?" he asked, his eyes twinkling.

A couple approached them. Justin smiled at the sight of his cousin. Mason. The only cousin that Adrienne hasn't met yet. His wife, Abigail, accompanied him.

"Justin, my man!" Mason greeted him warmly as he approached them.

The two guys gave each other a manly hug. Justin hadn't seen Mason in almost a year and among his cousins, Mason was his best friend. Sadly…he was…not in good terms with his parents. Justin couldn't forget the day he pulled everything off so he could get their private plane to get Mason out to Italy. And since then, Mason never looked back.

In a way, Justin couldn't blame him. Mason was black and blue and being held for ransom by some poker sharks he owed a lot of money to. Half a million dollars in exchange for his life. Mason's parents refused to pay up. They didn't even believe him. They thought he was orchestrating the whole thing to get more money from them.

Justin couldn't let anything happen to Mason no matter how many mistakes he made. So, he paid the money out of his own pocket, took Mason to the hospital to have him treated, and then boarded him on their private plane to Italy to where his long-time girlfriend Abigail lived.

He felt glad to see that Mason learned his lesson. Justin gave his cousin a fresh start. He ultimately gained his own casino hotel in the city and from the looks of it, it did quite well.

Gambling didn't sit well with their family but Justin loved that Mason made good use of his talents for a change.

Justin turned to Adrienne and said, "Mason, I'd like you to meet, Adrienne. My fiancée."

Mason smiled widely. "Nice to finally meet the woman who straightened my big cousin out." He grinned. Then he turned to the woman beside her. "And this is the woman who straightened me out, Abi, my wife."

Adrienne smiled at both of them and shook their hands. "How many more of your cousins are you still hiding from me?" she asked Justin.

"He's the last one, I promise." Justin chuckled. Then he turned to Mason. "All set?"

"Three more days, cuz," Mason replied. "Your last minute requests are going to be the death of me."

"Please do everything that you can. I don't want anybody to come and put a stop to this whole thing, you know," Justin said.

"Are you scared that there's somebody more powerful than the formidable Justin Adams?" Mason joked.

"I know there is," Justin muttered. "His name is Jac Adams!"

"Oh, you're right. How's everybody at home?"

"Still crazy," Justin replied curtly. "But no one's crazier than you, of course."

Mason laughed heartily. "I refuse to relinquish the crown. Neither Jordan nor Gian seem fit to wear it."

"Considering you took mischief to extremes, you're probably right," Justin said. Even when they were growing up, Mason got into a lot of things. Pot, drinking, smoking, gambling, gangs, street fighting and some underground stuff. He made Justin, Jordan and Gian look like angels.

"So which room do you wish to stay in?" Mason asked. "They have twenty, all for your own disposal."

"Justin…this is too much," Adrienne hissed beside him.

He put an arm around her and gave her a gentle squeeze. "Just because we're eloping doesn't mean I'm going to make it a rushed, less romantic experience for you, honey," he said, looking down at her. "Come on, we need to pick a room."

They all entered the small elevator, which took them to the top floor.

There were only two rooms on this floor. And they were both elegant, covered with cream-colored wallpapers with gold trim. Both the rooms had a four poster king-sized beds, crystal chandeliers, walk-in closets, fireplaces and sitting areas with lavish couch sets. The big balconies provided astounding views of the city.

"Which one do you want to stay in, honey? I'm okay with either of them," Justin said to Adrienne.

Adrienne had her back on him. She was looking at the view of the city. Then she spun around and looked at Justin. Her eyes were twinkling and she gave him a dazzling smile. Justin had to blink back. He felt his heart skip a beat and he still wondered how she could steal his breath with just a simple glance or a sexy smile.

Justin felt that familiar feeling of desire creeping through him again, and suddenly, he had this urge to push Mason and his wife out of the room so he could have his way with his fiancée. It had been three weeks since he last made love to her…three weeks since his desires has been catered to. He didn't mind being celibate for that long. For the previous weeks, his only focus had been how to get out of the prison his parents sent him to. Funny how the thought of marrying a girl he didn't love was enough for him to stop thinking about sex at all.

"When are we getting married?" Adrienne asked him, her eyes sparkling and he could tell that she was up to something.

"Three days." Justin whispered uncertainly. He was trying to figure out what was on her mind.

Adrienne smiled at him widely. "I'll take this room. And you can take the one across the hall."

Justin didn't think he heard that right. "I'm sorry, what?"

"I said, I will take this one. And you could take the other one."

Behind him, Justin heard Mason snickering.

"Why?"

Adrienne shrugged innocently. "Because we're not yet married. Surely, we couldn't share a bedroom until then."

Justin stared at Adrienne as if she had completely lost her mind. He couldn't get why she asked for that. Wasn't she counting? It's been three weeks!

"Adrienne…" He took a deep breath, trying to keep calm. "Honey…we've slept in the same room before. In fact, we've almost been living together until…you found out what my parents set me up with!"

Adrienne gave him a small pout. She approached him and put her hands on his chest. Her touch almost burned him. He took a deep breath to calm his nerves.

"Well…you rented like twenty rooms," she said innocently and he knew she was doing this deliberately. "It's a shame if we don't maximize it as much as we can. If only you rented one room, then we wouldn't have a choice to but to share, right?"

Behind him, Mason couldn't help laughing. Justin wanted to punch something and he's climbing high up on the target list.

"Honey…" Justin took a deep breath. "This isn't funny. I'm serious."

She stared up at him. "So am I, Mr. Adams," she said. "You're going to have me for the rest of your life. That's in three days. Surely, you can wait, right?"

Justin took a deep breath. Then he inclined his head to the right. "Can you leave us, please?" he gently asked Mason. He and his wife, closed the door behind them.

Justin turned to Adrienne again. He wanted to kiss her and throw her on the bed and make her scream his name over and over. But now…she's saying to him that not only were they going to stay in different rooms, but they were going to wait until their honeymoon to do the things he wanted to do to her in bed.

Justin drew a frustrated sigh. "You're killing me," he whispered to her.

"Do you really love me or are you just after the sex?" she asked. "Because if that's the case, then let's not get married. Let's just stay in bed all day for a week and then go back home."

He pulled her to him a little too roughly that startled her a little bit. "You little minx. You know I love you. And you're not getting out of Italy until you become Adrienne Adams." He gave her a passionate kiss on the lips. He traced her lips with his tongue and invaded her mouth in a kiss that left her breathless and wanting more. When he pulled away from her, her face was flushed and she looked disoriented. Her breathing was ragged and Justin knew she was as lost in desire as he was. He grinned at her. "I lasted three weeks. Surely, I can last three more days." With a mischievous smile, he added, "But I will make sure you'll be begging for it, too."

Then he released her. Adrienne had to lean on one of the couches for support. She looked disoriented and innocent and Justin just wanted to take her right then and there. But she asked for three days. And the gentleman he is…he will give it to her. But he refused to be the only one hurting and burning every time they touched.

Adrienne looked up at him. "We won't make love until we're married," she said but her voice no longer carried much conviction. "Do we have a deal?"

Justin took a step closer to her. She took a step back, as if she feared that her defenses would crumble if he touched her.

"That's the only thing we cannot do, okay?" he confirmed. "Consummate the marriage before we say our vows."

She smiled and nodded.

Justin grinned at her. "You're playing with fire, Adrienne. It's a dangerous game." He narrowed his eyes at her and gave her a devilish smile. "Are you sure you want to play against me? I am, after all…Justin Adams. What did you use to call me? Manhattan's most notorious playboy?"

Justin didn't miss her hard intake of breath and he smiled at her. He took a step closer to her. She took a step back. He took a step towards her again, and she kept backing down, until she hit the wall behind her. Justin took a final step towards her, trapping her against the wall and his body. He caught her, wrapping his arms around her waist.

Adrienne put her hands against his chest, giving him a gentle push that wasn't convincing.

"Justin…" she whispered.

"Can you really stop me, Adrienne?" he asked her.

"Justin, please..." she whispered.

He smiled at her and then he leaned forward and took her mouth in his. She opened up to him like a flower. And Justin reveled in the fact that he had so much effect on her, the way she had so much effect on him.

Soon, they were kissing each other like they wanted to make up for all the weeks that they lost. Justin nuzzled her neck and made her moan. He felt himself completely falling. She was getting softer and softer by the second, making it easier for him to break her resolve. And Justin knew he, too, was gently drowning into that trance. One more kiss, one more pull will make it impossible for him to control himself.

There was a tap on the door. They both stopped, realizing that Mason and his wife were probably still waiting for them outside. Justin leaned his forehead against Adrienne's. He took deep breaths. Then he looked into her eyes and smiled gently.

"You're putting us both through hell, you little sadist," he said to her and gave her a kiss on the lips again. "God, it's going to be so hard to put my hands on you and then stop halfway through."

Adrienne giggled. "It's tradition, Justin," she asserted. "The bride and groom are not supposed to do it until the honeymoon, remember?"

He inhaled the scent of her. "Hmmm..." he murmured. "I'm not really one for traditions."

She laughed. "You're not the only one suffering, you know. It's hard for me, too."

"And yet, I'm not the one who made the rules!" he muttered.

She laughed and kissed him gently on the lips. "Three days, honey." she whispered. "And I'll be all yours."

He pulled her to him one last time and kissed her forehead. Then he took a deep breath and said, "I can hardly wait."

***

They had dinner with Mason and his wife in one of the garden restaurants in the hotel. They discussed the arrangements for the wedding.

Mason knew some people and used his connections to ensure they got quick approvals for their marriage license. It would be a garden wedding to be held in one of the largest estates in Tuscany. Justin used the word 'estate', but it was slightly more than that. He wanted it to be a surprise for Adrienne.

Abigail gave them all the details about the flower arrangements, venue decorations, famous photographers and videographers who will be flown in from the States. And of course, Adrienne's gown.

"Wait!" Adrienne interjected. "This sounds like a grand wedding." She turned to Justin. "I thought we were going to have an intimate and simple one."

"It's going to be intimate. With just you and me, and these two as our witnesses. But I want it to be as amazing as it could be. Like your dress… I want you to wear a wedding dress like you've always wanted. You will only get married once, Adrienne. Sure, we can renew our vows in a couple of years, but this is your wedding. And I want it to be close to what you've dreamed of."

Adrienne smiled at him and nodded. Her eyes were a little bit teary and it broke his heart just a little bit to know that she wished she could have some of her loved ones with her on this day. Justin took a deep breath and pulled her to him. He kissed the top of her head and whispered, "I love you." Right now, that was the only thing he could do to make her feel better.

"I love you," she whispered back to him.

"We're going to go look at some couture tomorrow," Abigail said. "You will have to try on some dresses, choose one and finalize everything so they could get it ready in time for the big day."

Adrienne nodded. "Okay. Anything else we need to do?" She let out a sigh. "I'm nervous now."

Justin chuckled. "I'm sure these two got it covered. They've been working on it for weeks."

Adrienne stared up at him. "Weeks?"

Justin nodded. "I've been asking them to make the preparations while I made… my arranged fiancée's life miserable enough for her to reject me."

"What happened to that anyway?" Mason asked. "How'd you successfully get out of it and sooner than you planned?"

Justin shook his head. "I didn't."

Mason's eyes widened. "Shit, man! Your parents are going to kill you! Don't get me wrong. I love this whole rebellion thing going on with you. But I worry about how Uncle Jac is going to react."

"He's going to get pissed for a while," Justin stated, smiling. "And then I'm hundred percent sure he will forgive me."

"He loves you," Mason asserted. "Wish my parents were as forgiving."

"You cannot get what you do not ask for, Maze," Justin said.

Mason just grunted. Then he asked, "How sure are you they would accept you guys?" He looked at Adrienne. "No offense, Adrienne."

But Adrienne smiled and answered for Justin. "Because our parents are going to find out that I and the girl they arranged for him to marry are one and the same."

Mason and Abigail stared at both of them for a long while, unable to believe their ears.

"Seriously?" Mason asked.

Justin nodded. He gave Adrienne as gentle squeeze. "Destiny, isn't it?"

Mason and Abigail nodded in disbelief.

"So why are you eloping? Everybody at home will be delighted to be at your wedding."

"I don't want to give our parents the satisfaction that they were right to meddle with our lives like this. It gave me hell for a long time. I just want them to know that they can't do that to me. Even if I liked how it all ended."

"That is one hell of a love story." Abigail smiled. "Then let's make the wedding as magical as possible."

"I don't understand this arranged marriage thing," Mason informed them. "When Justin first told me about it, I warned him. That's going to be his life imprisonment."

"You were almost right. During those times, I contemplated why I didn't run away with you three years ago. It was our grandfather's wish, I think. He felt that…he owed the family's fortune to Adrienne's grandfather. When he was penniless and all he had were great ideas, Adrienne's grandfather financed his first venture. And he never asked for anything in return. Our grandfather always felt indebted to him. They were like brothers. They wanted to connect our families together through marriage. But he never had a son. Neither did Adrienne's grandfather. When they learned of our existence they just decided that we'll be the ones to make their dreams come true for them."

Adrienne's head snapped back at Justin. "Learned of our existence?"

Justin shrugged. "I meant, when we were born and they knew they have a boy and a girl on either side. That meant a marriage was possible."

Adrienne let out a sharp breath. "I was my mother's daughter from her first…relationship. At first, my mother thought her father wouldn't be able to forgive her if he found out about me. I think…my mother told me that when my grandfather heard about me…that I'm a girl…he forgave her and asked her to bring me home." She sighed sadly. "And I thought he really did want me to be part of his life. Maybe he accepted me because finally…he had something to offer to your family."

Justin saw that Adrienne had suddenly gotten upset. She felt unwanted all her life. She was raised by a woman who wanted nothing to do with her. And she just realized that her grandfather accepted her because she had value. She was a bargaining tool.

Justin wanted to deny that, but he couldn't lie to her or speak for her grandfather. Maybe that really was his intention, but Justin didn't know. And the last thing he wanted was to lie to her just to make her feel better.

He pulled her to him and kissed her forehead. "Well… he didn't have to offer you to me, you know. I'd take you even if it's against his will. I'd steal you away even if he promised you to somebody else or you belonged to somebody else." He paused and said, "Wait, I think I actually did that." He smiled at her. "Because I want you to be part of my family…my life. That's how much I love you, hon."

Adrienne smiled at him. Then she leaned forward and rested her head on his shoulder.

"You said you were trying to make her miserable." Mason asked. "What did you do?"

"I actually sent Jordan to pretend to be me and be a total ass!"

Adrienne laughed. "It worked! My God, I wanted to kill him! He's…despicable!"

"But he didn't find you hateful, actually." Justin said, remembering that day that Jordan first met 'Andrea Blanc'.

Jordan called him immediately after the meeting.

"Dude, are you crazy?" Jordan asked on the other end of the line. "This girl is beautiful!"

"Don't really care," Justin said to him.

"Not just cute. Not just gorgeous. But beautiful! And she's not even wearing makeup!" Jordan said. "And she's…cool! She wasn't even rude to me, although I understand she just tried her best to be polite."

"Again, I don't care," Justin said. "Don't tell me you're backing out of this deal?"

"It's just that…" Jordan sighed. "She doesn't deserve this, man," he said. "Can't you at least get to know her? You might like her. Hell, I like her and I've just met her!"

"You like her? Then you marry her instead!" Justin snapped.

"Dude, I'm too young for that stuff! But if her folks can wait five more years, yeah, I'd take her. I am a part of this family, too. So it's basically the same thing."

"Jordan, just do what you're asked to do!" Justin said in a more authoritative voice. "Or I'm keeping my 911!"

That threat actually made Jordan work on irritating Andrea Blanc even more. And it worked. It brought Justin comfort that even if the ruse didn't work, he would still be marrying Adrienne one way or another. But he really did prefer it this way. Here. In one of the most romantic cities in the world. Just the two of them.

"I was being nasty to Jordan!" Adrienne said, bringing Justin out of his thoughts.

"Men generally like feisty girls," Mason said. "When you think you were repelling us, you are actually getting us intrigued. And when we're intrigued, we tend to come back for more."

"Oh my God. Then I should be thankful that Jordan was a fake!" Adrienne rolled her eyes.

"Did your mother tell you, you were engaged to him before you met him?" Mason asked.

Adrienne shook her head. "I told her I would try to befriend her friends and their kids. I told her I was waiting for my fiancée to set himself free." Then she stared up at Justin. He pushed a lock of stray hair away from her face. "I'm glad you still fought for us after I set you free."

Justin smiled at her. "I would never give up on us, honey. I would never take another woman for a wife. I want to be as happily married as my parents."

Adrienne sighed. "I planned to be happily married. My own parents separated even before I was old enough to remember my mother. And the mother I've known had a twisted concept of love and happiness."

Justin leaned forward and kissed her lips. "I promise you will be happy, honey. Your happiness will be my top priority. You're done being sad now. Your stepmother and your stepsister can no longer touch you...or do anything to hurt you. If they do...they will pay the price. And it's not going to be cheap."

Justin's voice held a hint of a threat. And he meant what he said. Adrienne has suffered too much at the hands of her family. They belittled her and crushed her. In becoming Adrienne Adams, no one could question her, doubt her or look down at her anymore. Well, she is an heiress by her mother's family anyway. Becoming an Adams just sealed her place in the world of the privileged.

Justin smiled at the thought. He didn't believe in destiny before. But now... he couldn't help thinking that Adrienne was born to be with him. And he was born to love her for the rest of her life. Even if they didn't meet each other at *Blush* or live next-door to each other...or even if Jin Starck didn't find her. They still would find a way to be together. They would still fall in love with each other. He would still choose to marry her and spend the rest of his life with her. Because Adrienne is and will forever be his destiny... his choice.

JERILEE KAYE

37.
Rohanás
Hungarian for Rush

The next day became hectic for Adrienne. Abigail may have looked shy and quiet at first, but hell! She ran a military rule when it came to organizing stuff. She got on the phone, putting pressure on the photographers, videographers and other suppliers. She seemed so meticulous and so strict. Adrienne no longer wondered how she managed to straighten out the old Mason.

Abigail turned to her, taking deep breaths. "Okay, I sorted out the cake! Now, let's get you to the couture house so you can pick out a dress."

Adrienne nodded. She almost got scared of her future cousin-in-law. While Abi's driver transported them to a shop, she spoke over the phone in Italian. She was almost raising her voice. Adrienne found it a little amusing now.

When she hung up the phone, she turned to Adrienne and smiled. "Sorry. That was Justin." She turned to her driver to give out instructions in Italian. Adrienne had no idea what she said.

"My Justin?"

Abi nodded. "Yeah. He speaks perfect Italian."

It was already past noon and Adrienne realized they hadn't eaten yet. Abigail kept her busy with choosing anything from ribbons, to flowers, to linen and paper. The arrangements were looking grand now and there would only be four people attending the wedding.

They stopped by a small hotel. Adrienne seemed confused because she thought they would go to look at wedding dresses.

"Abi, I thought you wanted me to pick a dress."

"Yeah, but Justin berated me for starving you." She laughed. "He said we could schedule dress-shopping after lunch."

Adrienne just nodded but deep inside she thanked Justin for rescuing her. Abi looked like she didn't know how to take a break. She was all work, work, work!

"Where is Justin?" she asked Abi.

"In the restaurant with Mason," Abi replied. "We all will have lunch together."

Abi led her up the marble staircase to the mezzanine floor to the restaurant. The door was closed. Abi turned to her and smiled.

"Smile, Adrienne," Abi said.

Adrienne didn't get what she meant. But then she opened the door to the small restaurant. Adrienne then saw Justin and Mason talking to some people seated across from them. Adrienne looked at their guests and she felt like her heart immediately went up to her throat as she looked at their familiar faces. Justin's guests were none other than…Jill and Yuan.

"Oh my God!" Adrienne breathed.

Jill let out a scream. She and Yuan stood up their seats and immediately ran to her to give her hugs and kisses.

"What are you guys doing here?" she asked them. Her eyes started to get a little bit teary. This was indeed a pleasant surprise.

"Your boyfriend…I mean… your fiancée…" Jill said, her eyes sparkling. "Contacted us last night and told us to immediately get on the next flight to Italy. No matter what the cost."

"I cannot believe you guys eloped!" Yuan said.

Adrienne waved her finger in front of them to show them her ring.

"It's wonderful!" They exclaimed.

"Heirloom?" Yuan asked.

Adrienne didn't exactly know the answer to that. Justin came to her side, wrapping an arm around her waist and giving her a kiss on the forehead. He turned to Jill and Yuan and said, "That ring originally belonged to my grandmother. She gave it to my father when he proposed to my mom. And my Mom gave it to me when she wanted me to propose to my… 'betrothed'."

Yuan's eyes widened. "You guys are so dead!"

"Maybe." Adrienne smiled at them mysteriously.

They both raised a brow at her and she laughed. "Funny how my mother arranged me to be married to someone, too."

Yuan and Jill's eyes widened. "What?"

Adrienne smiled widely at them. "What are the odds that my parents arranged me to marry somebody I was already in love with."

"You?" Jill echoed. "You were the 'brat' who had been destined to marry Justin all along?"

Adrienne laughed. "Yes. It's…surreal, really. Like, what are the chances, right?"

"The chances of that happening is not even one in a million!" Yuan said in amazement.

"Yep," Justin agreed. "But it doesn't change my decision. My parents could never force me to marry anybody else than your best friend."

"And when I saw you at *Blush* you were looking rather happy."

Justin laughed. "Maybe I was. Because I planned to scare off my designated fiancée and it was working. I had no idea then that it was Adrienne."

"Did you tell your parents?"

Adrienne shook her head. "We'll just…shock them when we get back."

"I'll bet they will be," Justin whispered staring down at Adrienne. Then he leaned forward and kissed her forehead again. He turned to Jill and

Yuan. "Let's have lunch first. There are still a lot of things to be done. And I believe I have made Abi fall behind schedule. She will order a firing squad if we don't eat fast. Don't choke on your food, okay?" He grinned teasingly at Adrienne.

Adrienne sat beside Justin. She felt very happy. She would have loved it if Jin, her Mother and Pierre were present…even her Father, but for now she's content that at least Jill and Yuan had made it. And she couldn't help falling in love with Justin even more for doing this for her.

"I love you," she whispered in his ear. "Thank you so much for getting Jill and Yuan here. I don't know how to pay you back for this."

He grinned at her. "I accept payment…in kind," he whispered. "And you already know which kind."

She laughed. "And yet you're gonna have to wait."

He let out a frustrated sigh. Then he pulled her to him and gave her a squeeze. "You're going to be the death of me."

Adrienne looked at him from under her lashes and said, "And I'm just getting started," she said in a voice full of mischief.

Justin laughed and gave her a squeeze again. "I can't wait to spend the rest of my life with you."

"And I can't wait for you to start ordering lunch," Mason said to Justin, bringing them both back to reality.

Adrienne blinked back at the other people in the table. She immediately turned red, realizing they've been oblivious of the others around them. They had whispered but Mason sat close enough to Justin that he couldn't help overhearing.

Justin shot Mason a murderous look and then he looked at the menu in front of him. Mason just laughed. It was obvious he loved taunting his cousin. And Adrienne found it adorable how Justin had so much patience for Mason. Maybe even more than he'd shown Gian.

After lunch, Abigail took Adrienne away from Justin and they went gown shopping with Jill and Yuan.

They went to a boutique that looked like it only sold expensive couture gowns. The moment they walked in, the doors closed behind them and the saleslady turned the "Closed" sign on the door.

Abigail smiled at Adrienne. "So you can shop without interruption."

The VIP treatment gave Adrienne a bit of a headache. She wasn't used to this. And she felt like Abigail would make a good principal at *"How To Be A Bitch Academy."* It's amazing how she didn't even have to open her mouth but things would just go the way she wanted them to be.

"Well, I like her," Yuan said beside her. "Besides, you're running out of time. A woman who runs military rule is exactly what you need to get everything up and running in two days."

Abigail took her to an aisle of dresses. They were all beautiful, flawlessly tailored with sparkling crystals and rich laces.

Adrienne picked out a simple gown that went all the way down to the ankles.

What could you wear in a wedding with six people, right?

"Ah-ah!" Abigail said, shaking her head. "That looks more like a cocktail dress to me, sweetheart." She took out a ball gown that had folded layers over the skirt.

"Seriously?" Adrienne asked. "For a four-guest wedding?" The dress looked too grand for such a simple occasion.

Abigail raised a brow at her. "Seriously," she stated simply. Then Abi let out a sigh. "Adrienne...Justin is Mason's go-to guy. My husband owes him a lot. If there's one thing I'm good at, it's reading people. Your fiancé feels guilty about not being able to give you a wedding that's fit for an heiress like you are. He knows that you deserve a fairy-tale wedding. But as it is...you've eloped and can't bring the whole United States of America to Italy. So apart from the lack of guests at the wedding, don't you think you should do everything else as grand as it would have been?" Abigail said, finally giving Adrienne a piece of her mind. "That would erase Justin's guilt and make him really happy!"

Adrienne blinked back at her. Then she realized Abigail she was right. Justin would want to give her a grand wedding. And he could afford it. But his desire to have an intimate, solemn and romantic ceremony prevailed. And honestly...she preferred it this way, too. But Abi made a great point. Nothing should stop them from making this wedding majestic. Their love story was a fairy-tale anyway.

She took the dress from Abi. "You should have said that earlier!"

When Adrienne finally came out of the dressing room, her friends gazed at her in awe. She turned to the mirror and almost gasped at herself.

The silk gown hugged her body to perfection. The bodice with a sweetheart neckline, was fully embroidered and lined with crystals. The flowing side draped skirt was made of folds of rich silk. Each fold ended with floral crystals and embroidery. Additionally, the dress included a detachable crystal-adorned chapel-length train that could be used during the ceremony and removed at her convenience during the reception.

"Wow!" Jill cried. "That *is* the dress, if you ask me."

Adrienne had to agree. She wanted to check out the other dresses, but she was sure this was it. She fell in love with it. She actually imagined herself getting married in it.

"See?" Abi began. "This is perfect-ion!" Her voice was full of approval.

"How could you get it right the first time?" Adrienne breathed.

"Talent, my dear." Abi giggled. "Come, you have to choose your shoes."

Adrienne looked at herself in the mirror one last time and smiled. The dress she wore looked fantastic. It was doubtlessly expensive, but she didn't care. Its beauty glowed…exactly how she felt inside. And she couldn't wait for Justin to see her in it.

Abi and Jill also chose their own gowns. Then they all chose their shoes and other accessories. In the evening, they returned to the hotel to meet Justin and Mason. Adrienne felt exhausted by the time they had dinner. It was a long day. Brides usually have at least three months to plan the wedding of their dreams. She had three days.

The whole group gathered at the poolside to have some beer. For Abi, it was the time to remind everybody of their roles for the next two days. By ten in the evening, Adrienne yawned. Justin gave her a squeeze, then he turned to the group.

"Guys, we would have to go now," he told them. "I think my bride-to-be can hardly keep her eyes open."

"No, I'm okay," Adrienne said.

Justin shook his head and stood up from his chair. Adrienne stood up after him. To her surprise, Justin scooped her up on her feet and carried her bridal style as they bid goodnight to the group.

"This is embarrassing!" she said to him. "Put me down."

Justin laughed. "I would have to carry you the same way after the wedding. I should practice not to drop you."

"I'll be wearing a big gown, I'm sure you'll have difficulty nevertheless," Adrienne warned him.

Justin looked at her for a moment and his eyes sparkled. "Really? How big?"

Adrienne smiled proudly at him. "Cinderella gown big!"

Justin smiled back at her. "Oh, I can't wait to see you in it." He walked inside the elevator. Adrienne pressed their floor number. She turned back to Justin. He smiled at her mischievously. "And of course, I can most definitely not wait to see you… out of it."

Adrienne laughed. "Justin, will you stop that? You have less than forty-eight hours to go."

They reached their floor and Justin walked towards Adrienne's bedroom. Adrienne swiped her access card and the door opened. Justin kicked the door closed behind him and put Adrienne down on the bed.

"Forty-eight hours is torture, honey," he whispered to her. He leaned forward and touched his lips with hers.

She kissed him back. Then Justin deepened the kiss. He wrapped his arms around her waist and pulled her to him.

"Justin…" she moaned.

"Adrienne…" he whispered coarsely. He nuzzled her neck and she almost squirmed in his arms.

He pushed her towards the bed. She landed on her back and he landed on top of her. His hands and lips claimed her and she felt completely and insanely lost. She could feel him between her thighs. Desire was evident in every part of his body. Her arms wrapped around his neck and she pulled her to him.

It had been too long since she held him like this and she forgot that this one man could undo her in ways she never thought possible. His touch electrified her and his kisses made her forget anything…everything.

She felt desire completely overtake her. She pushed his jacket off him. She felt Justin's hands underneath her shirt, touching her… skin to skin, feeling the pounding of her heart inside her rib cage.

"Oh God!" she moaned as she felt the urgency overtake her. She felt him suck at her neck and she let out a moan of pleasure. "Justin… please!" She moaned although she wasn't aware that she spoke at all.

His lips returned to hers and he kissed her savagely, biting at her lips, invading her mouth with his tongue. Then he kissed her more gently… and he suddenly stopped moving.

She gently opened her eyes to stare back at him in confusion. He looked at her with a smile of triumph on his devilishly handsome face.

Finally, she remembered the rule she made. They cannot make love until they're married.

"Now, don't you wish you didn't make those damn rules at all?" he asked with a slight smirk on his face.

She playfully hit him in the shoulder.

"I told you…you'd be begging for it, too," he teased her.

"I didn't beg for it," she protested.

He narrowed her eyes at her. "Oh, right! You just said… what was it you said? '*Justin… please*'?" He shook his head. "Sounds like begging to me, honey."

She laughed and pinched his shoulder.

He leaned forward and kissed her lips gently. "You can break the rules, Adrienne," he said. "If you ask me nicely again… I just might have mercy." He continued taunting her.

She punched his shoulder again. "That's it! Get off me and get out of my room, you conceited prick!" she said in between giggles.

Justin laughed and kissed her gently on the lips. "Really? You're not going to change your mind about this?"

Adrienne gave him a push. She shook her head. "Nope. Let's torture ourselves some more."

Justin lied on his back and gathered Adrienne in his arms. She rested her head on his shoulder.

"You better have plenty of energy drinks prepared on our wedding night," he said, chuckling.

She stared up at him. "A lot of people say that newly-married couples usually don't have sex on their wedding night. You know…because they'd be too exhausted they would just sleep. Do you think that would happen to us?"

"Are you kidding me?" Justin asked. "I can barely keep my hands off you now. Do you really think I would let the wedding night pass? Besides...there's only one wedding night. We could sleep any other night but that night deserves a celebration. Why did you think I opted for a very small wedding? You could put your energy to better use than smiling all night and entertaining a lot of people you barely even know."

Adrienne laughed. "You're probably right. Where are we getting married anyway?"

"If you can torture me about not being able to make love to you before the wedding day, then I can torture you about not knowing where exactly we're getting married."

Adrienne stared up at him. "You think you're very clever, huh?"

He laughed. "I don't think I am. I know I am."

"Come on, Justin!" she insisted. "Where?"

He pulled her to him. "No. I want it to be a surprise. Patience, okay?"

She sighed in frustration. She couldn't understand, but she suddenly felt really angry about it. She felt like she didn't have a say in anything about their wedding when in normal weddings the most involvement grooms have is to just actually show up on the wedding day. But on hers, she was the one tagging along and being pushed over. Everything came as a surprise...or a shock. She didn't understand why, but normally she wouldn't make a big deal out of these things. She might actually feel it's sweet how Justin got so involved with their wedding preparations. But right now, she couldn't help feeling...angry.

She pulled away from Justin and turned her back on him. She stood up from the bed to head for the bathroom. She suddenly felt queasy. She ran to the bathroom, hoping she would make it to the sink. It only took a second for Justin to run after her. Adrienne threw up almost everything she ate that evening. When she finished, she washed the sink. Then she washed her face and gargled mouthwash.

Justin leaned on the sink beside her, carefully studying her. She caught his eye in the mirror in front of her. She still felt nauseated, her pulse was hammering visibly at the base of her neck.

He narrowed his eyes at her and couldn't help the grin that was slowly forming on his face.

"Justin..." she began. "Why are you smiling?"

Tears welled up in Justin's eyes and he pulled her to him in a tight hug. Then he said, "I'm just...very happy, honey. I think my insurance just came through."

JERILEE KAYE

38.

Vznešený
Czech for Sublime

*A*drienne didn't want to feel emotional, but feeling Justin's tight embrace on her, and seeing the tears in his eyes also made her want to cry.

At first, she thought it could be something that she ate. It could be fatigue catching up with her. It could even be Abi. But looking at Justin's teary eyes and hearing him say that his insurance just came through… Adrienne remembered that amidst all the chaos that happened to her in the last few weeks, she forgot that she didn't have her period at all. And that night when Justin first told her that he loved her…he made love to her without protection…without reservation. And the following nights after that, they were both caught up in his problem with his parents, and the thought that their days together were numbered, they just didn't bother much on using protection.

Adrienne pulled away from him. "Justin…" she whispered. "Did you…plan this?" An accusation hung in her voice.

For the first time, she saw Justin actually unsure of himself. Like he suddenly got scared of her.

"Not really plan…like 'hatching-an-evil-plan' kind of plan," he said, uncertainty was all over his voice.

She raised a brow at him. "So what kind of plan is this plan?"

He took a deep breath. "More like… 'counting-on-it' kind of plan." He tried to smile at her, as if hoping she would find him cute, she wouldn't actually get mad.

She groaned. "Justin!" She pushed him away from her. But he held on to her, refusing to let her go.

"Hit me. Slap me. Punch me." he said. "Do you think I care right now?" He still smiled this huge, stupid grin. "Nothing can wipe this smile off my face, honey. Nor take away the joy that I feel right now!"

"Really?" she asked in a challenging tone. "What if I say that the wedding is off?"

His face immediately turned sober. "Except for that." He shook his head. "Don't say that. Please…don't say that."

She pushed him away and walked into the bedroom. He was on her heels right away.

"Adrienne…honey…"

She sat on the bed, refusing to look at him. She didn't know whether to be mad or happy. Sure, she would really feel ecstatic if it were true.

She's twenty-five years old. She may be too young to be a mother.

She may be too young to be a wife. But she never grew up with a mother who nurtured her or gave her love. The only way she could truly replace those memories... is if she created new ones... good ones. If she nurtured her own child and gave it the love she never had.

She wasn't sure whether she was really pregnant. She might not be.

The thought that she might not be... actually made her sad. That's when she realized that she wanted to be.

Then she looked at Justin, who was kneeling in front of her, looking at her pleadingly. Suddenly, she had this sudden desire to slap him on the face... just for the thought that he could have planned this all along without telling her.

She groaned. That's like three different emotions in a space of one minute.

I am so pregnant!

And she realized, she was happy.

"Insurance?" she asked him. "This baby is just an insurance to you?"

He groaned. "No! No! No!"

"But you said it is!"

"I didn't mean it like that," he said. "At the time...I was so desperate to stay with you. I sought all sorts of reasons to marry you. Reasons that not only you would accept...but also my parents. I wanted this, Adrienne. I wanted this more than anything I've ever wanted in my life. I wanted a family with you. And back then, when I thought my parents might take this dream away from me, I just...wanted to...fast forward time...I would give anything and everything just to be...where we are now. Pregnant and getting married." His eyes were pleading now.

"What about me?" She asked him. "What if I wasn't ready?"

He looked down and kissed both of her hands. When he looked up at her, his eyes were full of emotions. "I fell in love with you because you have a big heart, Adrienne. You give yourself completely to the ones that you love, and I am so lucky you fell in love with me. When you first told me you love me...I knew that if heaven wills that we get pregnant...you will give your heart and soul into starting a family with me.

"The last nights we were together, we both weren't trying to be safe. We knew you could get pregnant. I knew that you wanted this as much as I did. I knew that you would be ready. And even if you weren't... I was. I was always ready. And I will take care of you." He reached forward and touched her abdomen gently. "Both of you. Just...leave it all to me."

Adrienne couldn't help the tears that ran down her cheeks. She stared at Justin's teary eyes and smiled. "I love you, too," she said. "I wanna kill you for planning this without me. But I still love you!"

Justin laughed. He sat on the bed and pulled her so she could sit on his lap. "Okay...then you can punish me for the rest of our lives," he said.

"The wedding is still on, right? What you said back there…you were only kidding, right?"

"I meant it," she replied, a mischievous smile pasted on her face. His eyes widened. "But now…it's on again." Then she shrugged. "Too bad. We had this rule of no sleeping with each other because we were actually getting married. If we weren't, then…we could…make love, right? But now…the wedding is on again. So the no-sex-before-marriage rule is also back on. I'm sorry you missed your five-minute window." She batted her eyelashes, curved her lips downward and tried to look sorry for him.

Justin looked shocked, as if he didn't know what hit him. Then he groaned. "You are so unfair! Come on! Let's call it off again. Sixty minutes and then I'll propose to you again!"

Adrienne laughed. "Sorry, chief. That ship has sailed. It's bad luck to break the engagement twice."

"Third time's a charm, remember?" he argued.

She shook her head. "It's now or never. And besides… I'm the one who could be carrying your baby in my tummy. So, I'll be making the rules."

Justin narrowed his eyes at her. "I've been letting you make the rules since the first night we met, honey," he whispered, wrapping his arms around her waist.

Adrienne blinked back at him. "That's not true!"

"Is too," he said, hugging her to him again. "And it's okay. I like it. For once…there's one person in this world who has complete power over me."

Adrienne laughed. "Now there could be…two."

Justin sighed, contentment and happiness were evident in his voice. "Yes. Now there are two of you."

"Justin…" Adrienne whispered. "We aren't sure yet. Let's check tomorrow, okay?"

"I would do it now if it wasn't too late," Justin stated.

Justin insisted on sleeping in Adrienne's room that night. "I don't care about the rules, honey. I will not attempt to make love to you until the wedding night. But I will stay here with you. If only to make sure your needs are taken care of. And that you'll be safe. And tomorrow, first thing in the morning, I'll get some of those kits we could use to test."

The next day, when Adrienne woke up, Justin was no longer in bed with her. Sunlight came into the room from the windows. Adrienne didn't feel like getting up yet. Like her body wanted to remain in bed some more. But she knew Abi would be breathing down her neck if she didn't head downstairs in an hour so she willed herself to get up.

The door opened and Justin came inside the room.

"Good morning," he said, leaning down and giving her a peck on the lips. "Slept well?"

She nodded. "Where were you?"

He waved a bag in front of her. "I got you some things. You want to confirm what we already know?"

Adrienne smiled excitedly at him. She grabbed the bag from him and went into the bathroom. Justin gave her a few minutes of privacy before he went inside the bathroom. He sat on the edge of the tub and she sat on his leg while they waited for three minutes to go to the sink to check the results.

"You know there's a huge chance that we are, right?" Justin asked her.

"I know," she replied. "Do we tell the guys?"

"I wanna tell everybody!" Justin said, his eyes dancing.

Adrienne remembered her family. She would have loved to share this information with her mother first. "Justin…our parents…"

"Would be ecstatic about the news."

"I know. I just wish…" she trailed off. "They would be mad at us if they find out we did all this without them."

"I know. My father's been calling me non-stop. He's sent me about a thousand *'Where are yous?'* but so far no, *'I'm sorry I tried to control your life.'*"

"Is that what you wanted to hear from them?"

"I wanted them to say that they will accept you and love you as a daughter-in-law…before they found out who you really are. And before they find out you are carrying the fourth-generation heir of Adams Industries. I want them to accept you… simply because I chose you. Because I love you."

Adrienne nodded. "If I am pregnant… I want my family to be the first to know."

Justin nodded. "Okay," he replied. "Let's not tell anybody yet until we tell our parents. It's bad enough they're not going to be at the wedding."

Adrienne's phone beeped, signaling that the three minutes of waiting had passed.

They were about to stand up and look but Adrienne stopped Justin. "Wait." She looked at him nervously. "What if…I'm not?"

Justin grinned at her impishly. "Then you probably will be…by the end of next month."

"You're keen on starting a family quite early, aren't you?"

"Keen on starting a big family," he admitted. "I was an only child. It got a bit lonely sometimes."

Adrienne smiled. "My God, I'm going to grow big."

Justin chuckled. "And you'll always be a fox to me, honey." He kissed the tip of her nose. "Shall we?"

Adrienne stood up. Justin stood behind her and wrapped his arms around her waist. He gently pushed her towards the sink and they stared at the three different tests… all saying the same thing.

They stood still for a moment. Then Adrienne felt Justin gently turn her around so she could face him. He let out what sounded like a howl of triumph before he lifted her off her feet and spun her around.

"Justin, put me down!" Adrienne said, giggling. Tears ran down her cheeks.

When Justin settled her down on her feet, she reached up and hugged him.

"Happy now?" she asked him.

He leaned down and when his lips were an inch away from hers, he said, "Bliss."

***

Adrienne sat inside the limousine nervously. It was four in the afternoon. She had spent probably the whole day with Jill and Yuan, getting all dolled up.

Her gown appeared impeccable. She found it absolutely stunning. A stylist tied her hair at the top of her head in a bun. Tendrils were cascading all the way to her shoulders with little white flowers clipped into her hair, making her look like a garden deity. Her makeup was light but it seemed to make her glow. Well…she knew what else caused at least some of that glow, too.

Photographers and videographers surrounded her, documenting her every movement.

The road they were travelling were surrounded with tall trees, as if they were going further into the woods. Justin, Mason and Abi were already at the venue a few hours earlier. Adrienne learned it was about an hour's drive from their hotel.

"We're in the middle of nowhere," Yuan remarked. "Didn't know Justin could be creepy."

Adrienne raised a brow at him. She knew she may come off as moody to her friends lately, but she hadn't told them she was pregnant and that her patience over the following months would grow really short.

Finally, they stopped in front of a wall covered with green grass. Adrienne was now more curious about what lay behind the very high wall that no thief would actually attempt to climb.

Finally, the vine-covered steel gate opened slowly and their limousine went in. Tall pots with white and pink roses formed dual lines from the gate up to the entrance of the most magnificent façade that Adrienne had ever seen in her life.

"Holy crap!" Yuan shouted. "You're getting married in a freaking… castle?"

Adrienne almost forgot to breathe. The structure they approached looked like a well-restored historic medieval Tuscan castle. Now, she was glad she let Abi change her mind about her dress. Her original choice would not fit this venue at all. She suddenly felt like Cinderella, about to meet her Prince at the altar.

Their limousine stopped at the separate entrance near the side of the castle. Jill and Yuan came out and Abi instantly greeted them, giving out instructions, not even letting the two breathe and enjoy the scenery before them.

It took only about five minutes and booms and camera equipment were set up on standby in front of them, waiting for Abi to signal Adrienne to come out of the vehicle.

Adrienne clutched her bouquet with one hand, and she caressed her tummy with her other hand. Since yesterday, when she confirmed her pregnancy, she started developing this habit of touching her tummy gently, as if imagining holding her baby in her arms.

Soon, Abi approached her limousine and she knew it was time for her to come out.

"This is it, Baby J," she whispered. "Mommy's going to make Daddy a very happy man."

Abi slowly opened the door of the car and Adrienne felt the camera flashes around her. She took a deep breath.

This is it! I'm going to be Adrienne Adams in an hour!

With that thought in mind, a permanent smile slowly carved itself on her face.

Yuan took her hand and Jill quickly picked up her train as she walked into the private garden entrance at the side of the castle. The path seemed to be covered with pink and white roses. It led them to a steel gate where Adrienne could hear music playing. Her heart pounded inside her ribcage wildly.

On Abi's cue, Jill stepped in front of Adrienne. Adrienne thought she looked beautiful.

"Well, it's an honor to give you away to your Prince Charming, sweetheart," Yuan said to her.

Adrienne blinked back the tears that were starting to form in her eyes.

"I love you guys," she whispered.

"We both love you, too." Yuan responded.

The gate in front of them opened, revealing the picturesque garden where their ceremony was going to be held. There was a veiling curtain in front of them. It was probably placed there to obscure the view of the bride. Adrienne could still clearly see what came in front of her.

Pillars and walls covered with green vines enclosed the garden. Paths formed by small white stones were accented with well-trimmed bushes that formed shapes of hearts and squares along its four walls. Grass covered the center space and white linen-covered chairs dotted the area on both sides.

The center aisle featured a white carpet with the initials J&A

inscribed in a golden, medieval script. The carpet ended in the canopy situated at the end of the garden. Its four pillars were wrapped in white and pink roses. Inside the canopy sat a makeshift altar and two gold-accented chairs before it. On both sides of the canopy an orchestra sat and played Pachelbel's Canon.

At the entrance of the canopy, Adrienne saw him. He stood there dressed in a magnificent white tux. His hair looked like it was gelled at first but then he didn't like the hairstyle so he decided to comb it with his fingers instead. And on him, it looked sexy. Behind him stood Mason, whose every hair appeared to be in place, shining from a wet gel. Adrienne had to suppress her laughter. She thought she knew exactly what happened there. Abi must have been giving instructions even on hairstyles.

Finally, the curtain partially opened and Abi cued Jill to walk to the front. Jill took her time in the spotlight. She was, after all, the Maid of Honor, and no bridesmaid.

Finally, Abi signaled that it was Adrienne's turn to come out.

The music suddenly changed to the familiar tune of "Here Comes the Bride." Then the veil curtain in front of them completely opened, finally revealing Adrienne to her groom.

Adrienne held on to Yuan's arm as they slowly walked towards the altar. She felt giddy...everything seemed surreal.

A couple of months ago... she was unpacking her stuff in an apartment she bought to impress her parents and sister. And now...she was walking into a fairy-tale wedding with her Prince Charming in a Tuscan castle. Her wildest dreams couldn't even reach this far!

She slowly walked towards the altar, still clutching Yuan's arm tightly.

She felt the weight of Justin's gaze on her. He looked at her intensely. When she finally stood in front of him, she looked up and saw his eyes had become watery, just like hers.

"You're a fox," he mouthed and she couldn't help giggling at that.

Justin finally took her hand from Yuan and then he led her to the chairs in front of the priest.

They intertwined their fingers all throughout the ceremony.

Justin chose a pair of Cartier platinum wedding bands with the signature screw motif, studded with tiny diamonds. Their names were engraved on the outside of the band in the center.

Her ring said "Justin's." His ring said "Adrienne's."

"Adrienne...I love you. I think from the very first moment I laid my eyes on you...the universe started leading me to you...my soul mate, my kismet, my other half. I hope you remember what I have been trying to tell you and show you since the day I met you... from the very first days I spent with you...you...are worth fighting for. And I will never stop fighting for you...I will never stop protecting you...taking care of you...most importantly... I will never stop loving you. Forever, and always...you are the only woman for me. Today. Tomorrow. Until eternity. In this life and all the others after."

Adrienne couldn't help crying when she heard those words from Justin. Her fingers shook when he put the ring on her finger.

"Justin...I didn't know how much my life would change the night I met you. Even now...when I look back, I still can't believe that all this is happening to me. That you are happening to me. Thank you. Because you showed me a side of myself that I never knew existed before. Because you taught me how to appreciate myself, how to love myself, how to fight for myself. Until I met you...I never knew that love could be worth a million fights...and a thousand prayers. I promise I will take care of you...and all the children that we will bring together in this world. I will nurture you and our family with love, affection, appreciation, trust and respect. I will stand with you, support you and love you...for richer or poorer, in sickness and in health...in this life...and all the others after this."

"I love you," Justin mouthed at her when she finished speaking her vows. She slipped his ring on his finger.

"I now pronounce you husband and wife. You may kiss the bride."

Justin slowly lifted her veil. His eyes were teary when he smiled down at her.

"Mrs. Adrienne Adams," he whispered.

She giggled in spite of her tears. Her heart warmed at the first mention of her new name.

Justin's face descended towards hers. He kissed her gently. One kiss and it felt like it lasted forever. Justin pulled away and looked into her face again.

"I love you," he whispered. "Mrs. Adams."

She laughed. "I love you, too, Mr. Adams."

He leaned forward and kissed her again. This time, he kissed her more passionately. He wrapped his arms around her waist and pulled her to him tightly.

The people cheered around them and they reluctantly pulled away from each other.

All of their friends hugged them and congratulated them one by one. They posed for pictures with the priest and then with all five of their guests.

A new guy there that Adrienne hadn't seen before approached them. He was good-looking, with dark blond hair and startling green eyes. Adrienne remembered seeing two guys behind Justin as he waited for her at the altar. She just didn't give it much thought because all her attention was focused on Justin.

"Honey, I'd like you meet one of my closest friends, River Jefferson," Justin said. "We are friends since Harvard."

River extended his hand to hers and grinned at her widely. "When Justin said he was getting married, I thought I was getting Punk'd. Seriously, I was waiting for Ashton Kutcher to come out anytime. But when you came out and walked down the aisle, I realized he wasn't joking. And why would he? If I find a beauty like you, I'd also rush you to the altar." With that, he bent forward and kissed Adrienne's hand.

River turned to Justin. "I understand why you had to wait until the last minute to introduce us, huh?" Justin actually hit River playfully in the stomach. River laughed. "Kidding!" he added.

They were interrupted by Abi who said that it was time for their wedding photos around the venue. It was also time for Adrienne to take a tour of the castle.

"I can't believe we got married in a castle," she sighed dreamily.

He grinned at her. "Did you like the surprise?"

She laughed. "I do! Justin…this is wonderful! I never imagined I'd get married like a princess."

He leaned forward and kissed her lips. All around them, the cameras never ceased to take footage of their time together. They documented their every move.

Adrienne looked at Abi with a raised brow.

She smiled at them reassuringly. "Go ahead. Pretend they're not even around you. You guys are in love. You don't have to act. Just be yourselves, talk, laugh, hug, kiss. We'll be catching everything on video and photos. Trust me! One day, you will thank me for this!"

Justin grinned at Adrienne. He leaned forward and nipped her earlobe. "I can't wait for tonight," he whispered to her. And Adrienne couldn't help giggling. She knew exactly what he was talking about. "It's been too long!"

"I know. And the waiting ends tonight," she said.

"I'd be making royal love to you," he teased. "Might as well make our wedding night historic, don't you think?"

"What if I got be too tired after all the wedding hoopla," she teased back.

He shook his head. "Nope. No excuses this time." He leaned forward and whispered to her ear. "I seem to remember you were a vixen in bed."

Her eyes widened at what he just said. She pinched him on the side. He let out a yelp and then he laughed, pulling her to him. His face descended towards hers and he kissed her thoroughly, Adrienne almost forgot they weren't alone.

When she pulled away from him, she thought for sure that her face was crimson. She walked ahead of him, smiling widely, and biting her lower lip, trying to contain all the giddy feelings inside her.

They toured the estate, well, at least half of it. It had a rose garden, a mini labyrinth, an orchard, another garden featuring four huge fountains and a vineyard at the back.

After an hour, Justin told Abi that Adrienne needed to rest. "I think you took more than enough pictures. My bride is exhausted," he said in a firm voice. Abi didn't argue.

"Justin, I'm okay," Adrienne asserted. She felt so happy that she didn't even feel a bit tired.

He hugged her to him so he could whisper in her ear. "Baby in tummy, remember?" he said gently. Then he added, "Besides, I would rather you save your energy today, so you can spend it well tonight." He grinned.

"You're not going to stop with the teasing, are you?" she asked shaking her head.

"It's been too long, honey," he said. "Can't really blame me, can you?"

She laughed. "Oh, my poor baby." She faked concern in her voice. She gently caressed his hair. "I am so sorry."

He raised a brow and stared at her evenly, "Sorry doesn't even count anymore. You have to pay up…big time."

She laughed and then caressed her abdomen. "Baby in tummy, remember?" she whispered to him.

"Don't worry. I won't forget. But that does not mean you're off the hook," he said and she laughed again. He pulled her to him and gave her a kiss on the lips again. "I love you, Adrienne."

She closed her eyes and breathed in the scent of him. "I love you, Justin."

Suddenly, Abi told them that their guests are ready for them. They needed to head to their reception.

It was a good one-hundred-meter walk to the next garden where the reception would take place. Justin bent down and scooped Adrienne up into his arms.

"Justin, put me down. I can walk."

"Sure, you can," he said. "But you will get tired. And remember, you can't get tired."

She raised a brow at him. "For tonight?"

He stared at her, faking a pained expression on her face. "For the baby, of course," he said. "Do you really think that making love to you is on my mind all the time?"

He sounded so hurt she started to feel guilty. But she knew him. Justin loves to make love to her and sometimes, it was difficult to keep their hands off each other. Adrienne couldn't explain it sometimes. They both have this pull, like magnets of opposite poles, they couldn't stay away from the other no matter how much they tried. In bed, they were like fireworks exploding into a million different colors. And yet…they trusted each other more than anybody else. They found comfort in each other's arms. They also had this bond of friendship that stood strong on its own... completely separate from their desire for each other. More than that...they both knew they loved each other very much, and could not, would not live without the other.

She stared up at her husband. "Actually...yes. I think making love to me is on your mind all the time," she whispered to him in a challenging tone.

Justin stared at her for a moment, his eyes dancing as he carried her in his arms. Then he grinned. "Then you know me too well, my wife."

She laughed and rested her head on his shoulder as he carried her effortlessly towards the venue of the reception. Even with her big, heavy dress, it seemed like Justin found her light as a feather.

"My father called me last night," he whispered.

Adrienne looked up at him with wide eyes, anxiously waiting for him to continue.

He smiled at her. "He finally apologized. He told me that he realized that my happiness is in fact more important to them. He promised that if we come home, they will meet you and accept you as my wife...no matter who you are. In fact... he said that you would be no one else to them, but my fiancée."

Adrienne smiled at him. She was truly happy. Justin had to go through hell just to make his parents understand that he wouldn't bend to their will. That even if the nametag of being Adams Industries' heir has been bestowed upon him, his heart is still his own and he still controlled his life.

They reached the gates of the garden. Abi signaled them to wait outside and only enter when the gates open for their grand entrance as Mr. and Mrs. Justin Adams.

Justin settled Adrienne down on her feet and they both straightened up their clothes. Music played on the other side and Adrienne could hear cheers of people. To her, it sounded like more than five people had come to the reception.

She stared up at Justin and he grinned at her.

"I told my parents, by the way, that they shouldn't accept you as my fiancée...they should actually love you as their daughter-in-law."

"And?" Adrienne asked anxiously.

Justin shrugged. "They said as long as I am happy...they will be happy." Then Justin added, "With that, I didn't really see the point of not inviting them to the wedding. But with the late notice, they could only make it to the reception.

Adrienne's eyes widened. "What?"

But before Justin could answer the door in front of them opened, revealing them to everyone. Justin took her arm and led her into the garden that held a huge canopy with three impeccably set tables which included tall centerpieces made of roses. Around the canopy stood more pots full of roses that made the scene look from afar like they stood in a sea of roses. Jeweled butterflies flew over them, too, making the setup even more surreal.

The music continued playing and their guests clapped. Adrienne realized that there were more people in the reception than in the ceremony. River sat with Mason and Abi along with Mike and James, Justin's friends from New York.

Yuan and Jill sat at another table with Jada and her date. Beside them, Adrienne saw a familiar man, who looked at Adrienne with tears in his eyes. She gasped as tears rolled down her cheeks.

Justin saw her tears and instead of heading towards their seats, he led his wife to his father-in-law.

"Sir," he greeted Mr. Miller and extended his hand to his.

Adrienne's father shook his hand. Then he looked at his daughter and smiled.

"Daddy," Adrienne whispered. She lunged forward and hugged her father tightly. She knew she hadn't yet forgiven him for what he did. Her mother probably still considered suing him. But none of that mattered now to Adrienne. She knew she wouldn't have it any other way. She was still glad that her father had come to be with her…on her wedding day.

"I'm so proud of you, Yen," he said. "I'm sorry I wasn't able to make it to the wedding. Justin contacted me a couple of days ago and sent me tickets so I could come today. The flight, unfortunately, got delayed. Otherwise, I would have walked you down the aisle myself."

Adrienne nodded and wiped the tears in her eyes careful not smear her makeup. "It's okay, Daddy," she said. "I'm still glad you got here."

Her father turned to Justin. "Take care of her, okay?"

Justin extended his hand to the older man again. "Yes, sir," he said in a serious voice.

Then Justin took her arm again. Adrienne thought he would lead her towards their table in the front center. But he led her to the table beside it where Justin's parents sat.

"Mom, Dad, may I present, Adrienne Adams, my wife," he said.

Adrienne stared at them nervously. Christine Adams had tears in her eyes when she lunged forward and hugged Adrienne. Then she looked into her eyes and smiled at her. "I'm sorry it took us a long time to meet you, dear. But thank you for loving my son, and making him happy."

Adrienne couldn't find her voice. She just nodded and smiled at Justin's Mom. Justin's Dad shook her hand, gave her a nod of approval and said, "Welcome to the family, child."

"Thank you," Adrienne said.

As if Justin found contentment that his parents had become genuinely happy for him, he said, "Mom…Dad…" he started. "Do you know Adrienne's maiden name?"

Her parents looked at him blankly.

Justin grinned. "When I met her, she was called Adrienne Miller," he said. "But the name on her birth certificate is actually 'Andrea… Andrea Blanc.'"

His parents stared at him for a moment, wide-eyed with disbelief. Then they blinked back and looked at Adrienne and then back at Justin again.

"But that's…" his mother started saying.

They were interrupted by a couple who just arrived, heading straight towards Justin's parents, shaking their hands, and kissing their cheeks.

"Congratulations. We're sorry we're late. There were some delays in our flights," Adrienne's mother said to Christine. Then she turned to Justin and shook his hand.

Her eyes caught Adrienne's and she stopped short on her tracks, her mouth dropping open.

"Adrienne?" she asked.

Adrienne didn't know whether to laugh or cry as she looked at her mother.

"Hi, Mom…" Adrienne whispered.

Her mother opened her mouth to ask her something but at that moment, Abi announced on the microphone, "Ladies and gentlemen. Let's give a round of applause to the new Mr. and Mrs. Adams as they dance for the first time as husband and wife!"

Trust Abi to either have the best or the worst timing on Earth.

Justin turned to their parents, who still looked like they didn't know what hit them. "We'll explain later. Just have a seat… and have fun knowing that we're all one happy family now…just like the way you planned it," he said. "Meanwhile, I need to dance with my lovely wife." Then he took Adrienne's arm and led her to the dance floor, leaving their parents at their table, still staring at them in shock, with their mouths hanging wide open.

Ang Huling Kabanata
Filipino for The Last Chapter

*A*drienne's heart pounded loudly. She could almost not contain the happiness inside her, but somehow a part of her felt terrified about facing their parents, her mother, most especially. Their parents couldn't be happier about this, but she also knew that they must have been planning their wedding long before she and Justin had met. And somehow, a part of her felt guilty about taking that dream away from them.

She felt Justin tilt her chin up. "Are you okay, honey?" he asked gently.

She smiled and nodded. "Nervous, though."

He smiled at her reassuringly. "They're gonna be fine. They probably got the shock of their lives, but I'm sure they are happy nonetheless."

"They must be disappointed that they weren't part of the whole wedding preparations."

Justin tightened his arms around her and gave her a kiss on the forehead. "Come to think of it, so were you. And only your opinion really matters to me."

"You know, in most weddings, the brides plan everything. All the groom needs to do is to show up."

"We're not like most couples. And you must know now, I'm not like most guys."

Adrienne couldn't help reaching inside Justin's coat to give him a pinch on the side of abdomen. "Conceited," she whispered lovingly. But she knew it was true. Justin was one of a kind. When she thought he was a typical rich, pretty boy who didn't believe in fairy tales, Justin was actually Prince Charming in real life.

She stole a glance at their parents' table. They were talking to each other and looking at their direction, doubtlessly, talking about them.

Just then, Justin slowly pulled away from her. Her father stood next to him, cutting in for the traditional father and daughter dance.

The minute she stepped into her fathers' arms, tears welled up in her eyes. And she knew, no matter what happened between them, he remained her father. And she understood that maybe he did what he did for the wrong reasons, but it didn't take away the fact that he also did it because he loved her a lot and couldn't bear the thought of losing her. And that was more than enough for her to forgive him.

"How are you Dad?" she asked.

He took a deep breath before he responded. "Finally, after more than twenty-years, I am fixing my life," he replied. He stared at her for a long moment. "I filed for a divorce."

Adrienne shook her head. "Dad…it's okay. I forgive you. Mo…" She stopped short when she realized she didn't know what to call her mother…her stepmom. She grew up calling her Mom, but now, it didn't seem right knowing that she wasn't really her mother… and she didn't deserve to be called the same name she would call the woman who gave birth to her… the woman who searched for her and loved her all these years.

"Marina," her father stated, sensing her hesitation. "You should call her Marina, now that you know who your real mother is."

Adrienne nodded. "Dad, you don't have to divorce her for me. She can't hurt me anymore. I will not let you feel guilty about being happy with her."

Her father shook her head. "It's not about guilt. It's about doing what's right. And finally, I am doing what I should have done a long time ago. I should have divorced her years ago, and not just because she treated you badly. But somehow, I couldn't bear to take her away from you, knowing what I did to keep your real mother from finding you. But it's all over now. There is no point in staying together."

"Kim…" Adrienne whispered. She knew that Kim might be devastated. He was the only father she knew.

"Kim is old enough to live her own life. I will still be there for her if she needs me. But this won't affect her as much as it would have if I divorced her mother fifteen years ago. And she had always known, anyway."

"I…I will support your decision, Dad. And I'll always be there for you. I promise you will never lose me."

Tears welled up in her father's eyes. "Thank you, Adrienne." He gave her a kiss on the forehead again and then he hugged her. "Be happy for the rest of your life," he whispered. "That would make me happiest."

The song ended and Adrienne was back in Justin's arms again. He wiped a tear from her cheek with his thumb and smiled at her. He didn't say anything, but Adrienne knew that he knew what was in her heart at that moment. And she felt thankful that he gave her father a chance to be a part of their wedding…that he gave her a chance to realize the full contents of her heart no matter how difficult things had been because of what her father did to her.

Soon Abi announced that it was time for dinner. Justin led Adrienne away from the crowd and into the entrance of a sitting room inside the manor.

"What are we doing here?" she asked him.

"I know you're starving." He chuckled.

"Well, I should be eating for two now."

He laughed. "I know, honey. But our most important guests will not be able to enjoy their dinner until they get something off of their chests, so I figured let's not prolong the agony any longer. And we have to do it in private."

Before Adrienne could say anything more, the door opened again and she watched her parents and Justin's parents step inside, followed by Adrienne's father.

Her mother immediately went to her and gave her a hug. "My baby! How...how could this happen? You said you wanted to call off the arrangement. That you hated Justin. How could you have eloped with him?"

"Okay, I think you better sit down, hon," Justin said, leading her to one of the sofas in the middle of the room.

Adrienne sat down and took a couple of deep breaths before turning to her mother. "Mom, remember when I told you that I had a boyfriend...who was arranged to be married to some heiress?" Her mother nodded. "Well, it turned out, I was that heiress. And Justin was also the boyfriend I told you about."

"Oh, God," her mother breathed. Then she smiled widely. "Thank God! I thought you would never forgive me for this arrangement."

"And I thought Justin will forever curse us for making him miserable for the rest of his life," Christine Adams said. "How...surreal!"

"Wow. The chances of that happening were as good as...zero," Pierre said.

Justin's father went to him and squeezed his shoulder. "Well, nevertheless, when you disappeared, we all realized that we were wrong to meddle in your lives. I know...this became just a lucky break that you two were already in love with each other. Otherwise, we were just forcing you to turn your backs away from your true loves because of some pact your grandfathers made to each other."

"So, before you found out who Adrienne really was, you meant what you said about accepting her into the family?" Justin asked.

His father nodded. "Every word. Your happiness does come first, we realized, and it is more important to us than any promise your grandfather may have made."

"Why didn't you tell us?" Adrienne's mother asked. "At the ball when you found out we had betrothed you to each other, why didn't you come to tell us? Why did you elope?"

Justin sighed. "Because I had already planned this wedding weeks before that night. It's not about what you wanted. I wanted Adrienne to feel that I'd still marry her because it's what I want more than anything in this life. And nothing has changed just because I found out she was your daughter."

Adrienne bit her lip, trying her best not to cry when she heard what Justin said. Even though she'd known Justin loved her more than anything, she still couldn't help the tears in her eyes when she heard him say those words again...here in front of their parents who wanted nothing less than what's best for them, even if it meant meddling with their marital choices.

Just then, they heard Adrienne's father say, "You…you arranged my daughter's marriage?"

Everybody in the room turned to him. After a few seconds, her mother had recovered from the shock of hearing his voice in the room. Adrienne realized that she was not aware that he just stood in the back listening to them.

"You!" her mother said in a sharp voice. "You have the balls to show up here after all the misery you have caused me and my daughter?" She started walking towards him. "You should be lucky the police is not yet on their way here to chain you and lock you up for the rest of your sorry life!" Then she swung her arm and slapped her father on the face.

Adrienne gasped. Nobody saw it coming. Maybe only her father did, but he did nothing to prevent that slap from hitting his cheek.

"Mrs. Starck!" Justin exclaimed at the same time that Pierre yelled, "Jesus Christ, sweetheart!"

Pierre rushed to her mother's side in an instant, restraining her.

"If it weren't for you, Adrienne would have had a better life than what you gave her! Your wife would not have laid a finger on her!" her mother cried angrily, trying her best to get away from Pierre's restraining arms.

"If it weren't for me, you would have arranged Adrienne's wedding a long time ago." Surprisingly, her father sounded calm. "It was just a sheer stroke of luck that she already fell in love with Justin when she found out about you."

"Oh, please don't you dare change the subject! This has nothing to do with the arranged marriage. I'm talking about the hell you put my daughter through when you kidnapped her! I would never have agreed for her to marry Justin if I didn't know his family, if I didn't know what kind of a man he is. But you…you made my daughter live with those bitches! You erased me from her life! You punished her for our mistakes! She suffered at your hands!" There was no stopping Ariana's wrath. Adrienne knew that her father deserved it. But she couldn't take it. This was not how she wanted her wedding to be.

Tears rolled down her cheeks and she suddenly felt weak. She leaned on Justin, who caught her firmly in his arms.

"Please!" Justin said in a calm, albeit, loud and authoritative voice. Everybody stopped and turned to him. "With all due respect… this is hardly the time and place for you to discuss your past or what you intend to do with each other in the future. This is our wedding. And I don't want my wife to remember the most important day of our lives like this. We wanted to share this moment with you because you are all equally important to us."

Nobody spoke after that. Pierre nodded apologetically at Justin. Adrienne's mother gave her father one last murderous look before looking at

Adrienne.

"I'm sorry. I'm so sorry. I shouldn't have done that," Adrienne's mother said. "And you are right, Justin. This is not how you or Adrienne should remember your wedding day." She turned to Justin's parents and said, "I'm sorry you had to witness that."

Christine Adams waved her hand slightly. "You don't have to apologize. We're one big happy family now. We're bound to know each other's secrets and fight occasionally with each other." She was positively beaming, like there was nothing in the world could ruin this day for her.

"Okay so now that we are all in agreement, we have one more announcement to make," Justin began. Everybody fell silent once again. They were staring at Justin and Adrienne, eager to know what they had to say. Justin took a deep breath and said, "You're all going to be grandparents soon."

The silence that followed was thick. It was like they all stopped breathing as they absorbed what Justin just said. Then finally, Adrienne's mother walked towards her and gave her a hug. "Oh my God, my baby!"

Soon, their parents were on their sides, congratulating them. Their mothers couldn't stop crying, tears of happiness rolled down their cheeks. They were ecstatic about the news. Even Adrienne's father looked excited. They surrounded the newlyweds, putting all their issues aside, like nothing happened at all.

Justin's parents began arguing if they preferred a boy or a girl. Adrienne's mother already considered moving temporarily to the States so she could be with Adrienne throughout the pregnancy. Pierre considered how to juggle his work load between him and Jin so both of them could visit Adrienne and Justin frequently. Even Adrienne's father suggested the best hospitals in Chicago that they should consider.

Adrienne looked up at her husband and smiled happily. It seemed like their families may have missed planning their wedding, but they sure would not miss out on her pregnancy or her delivery. They finally found their common ground, enough to give them peace throughout the reception.

It lasted for four more hours. Finally, Justin approached Adrienne and told her that it was time to leave.

"Time to go where?" she asked.

He grinned and then he leaned forward and whispered in her ear. "To our honeymoon. You've kept me waiting far too long,"

She laughed. "And our guests?"

"Abi will give them their room assignments later. They're welcome to stay here for a couple more days, if they wish. But in any case, that is not your problem. Let's leave them be. And they should leave us be." When Adrienne stared up at him, he grinned mischievously at her. "Your chariot awaits, my queen."

True enough, a Cinderella chariot awaited them at the foot of the stairs of the main entrance. Their guests lined up to bid them goodbye. Their mothers gave each of them a hug, awash in tears while doing so. Adrienne's father and stepfather shook Justin's hand and told him to take good care of her. Their friends and family cheered and threw rose petal confetti in the air.

The carriage took the path that led to a smaller castle structure. It seemed secluded, more private. Once they set foot by the door, the carriage left, leaving them to themselves.

"Welcome to your honeymoon, Mrs. Adams," Justin said. He bent and swept her off her feet. Adrienne shrieked and laughed, afraid that Justin may not be able to hold her with her big Cinderella gown.

"Easy, tiger," she said, giggling. "Remember, you're carrying two now."

Justin smiled. "I will never forget that, honey. The two most precious people in my life are right here in my arms. I will never drop you, honey. Always remember that."

They entered the castle. The outer façade looked old and medieval, but from the inside, it appeared quite modern. There were glass walls on one side, giving a perfect view of the lake. Adrienne saw crystal chandeliers hanging from the ceiling. The furniture inside included various woods and fine white textiles with gold trimmings.

Justin climbed up the white staircase that led to the second floor. No door existed. The top step immediately revealed the huge majestic bedroom. The walls were all white. Off-white sheets covered the king-sized bed along with white, tassel-edged pillows.

Justin settled Adrienne at the foot of the bed. "This is going to be your home for the rest of the week, Mrs. Adams. We will have complete privacy. Everything we need already sits in the fridge and the cabinets downstairs. People still will bring food over whenever we wish. There is a private pool, too, should you wish to go for a swim. There's also the lake. And yes, we can swim naked if we want, since no one else will see us."

Adrienne walked over to the glass windows to take a look at the veranda overlooking the lake. The moon looked big and full and the stars were shining brightly in the sky. It was a magical night indeed. Justin couldn't have picked a better night to get married.

She felt his arms around her as he nuzzled her neck. She felt a tingle in her spine and the hairs on her body seemed to rise up. Electricity seemed to flow from his lips to her skin. Her husband has always had this effect on her. "Justin," she moaned.

She felt a tug on the strings of the corset closure of her gown. She turned around and her lips met his in long, passionate kisses. Her dress slowly slipped off her body. It fell heavily into a pile on her feet. She stood before him in a white chemise and glass-like slippers. Justin bent and swept her into his arms and carried her to bed. Then he gently untied the laces on her bodice. He leaned forward and planted soft kisses on her knee, moving upward to her thighs.

Her heart pounded inside her chest. Slowly, she felt herself slipping, getting lost into the abyss. He pushed her gently up towards the head of the bed as he slowly took off his jacket, loosened his tie and unbuttoned his shirt. She held her breath as he revealed his magnificent body before her eyes.

When he took his shirt off and revealed his six-pack abs and muscled chest, she almost forgot to breathe, although she'd seen his body a hundred times before. He grinned at her, knowing so well the effect he had on her. He leaned forward, gently putting his weight on her, he claimed her lips once again.

"Justin…" she breathed as he nuzzled her neck. She felt overpowered by desire, more than she thought she could handle.

"My wife…" he whispered to her. "I love you." And he kissed her lips once again.

She smiled against his lips. "I love you, too…my husband." She felt good saying those words. To know that finally, there was nothing standing between them. He was hers now and nobody could take them away from each other.

She felt the snap of her bra as he took it off her. And then he felt his wet kisses on the peak of her breasts. "Oh my God…" She couldn't help breathing heavily. It had been too long since they were together. She remembered just how much she missed his lips on her.

He pulled away from her to unbuckle his belt and remove his pants. When he landed on top of her again, she felt the solid evidence of his desire for her. When she touched his most intimate part, he almost screamed. He felt her fingers on her. She couldn't hide the wet evidence of her own arousal. When he teased her sensitive button, she almost fell over the edge. Almost…but not quite. Because Justin Adams was the one man who knew her body more than she did. He knew how to undo her, send her to the brink of passion, push her to the edge of oblivion.

"Justin…" she murmured while he teased her, holding off the one thing she craved the most at that moment.

The smile that he gave her was as charming as it was wicked. And she knew, he punished her, too, for making up the no-sex-before-marriage rule, making him suffer for days. He held true to his promise. He would make her beg for him, too.

He nuzzled her neck as he put pressure on her body with his, touching her sensitive cleft with his rock-hard manhood. He moved a little, adding more sensation to her already burning core.

"Oh my God, Justin…" she breathed. "How are you enduring this?"

He smiled at her mischievously, "I lasted weeks begging for this. I can wait a few seconds more," he traced her lips with his tongue. "Until you give me what I want."

She kissed him back, refusing to give in, prolonging both their agonies, trying to stay in the game she started since they came to Italy.

She felt him at her entrance. She took a deep breath, preparing herself for the intense sensation that would follow, anticipating their union after weeks of agony and celibacy. But instead of fully going in, he slipped past her entrance, rubbing his underside against her slit as he thrust upward.

"Oh God, Justin!" she said in a hoarse voice.

"Fuuuck!" he cursed silently and she could tell that he barely held on, too.

One of them would have to give in to the call of their passion. One of them would have to lose…give up their pride and beg to consummate their marriage.

He pulled away again and once more, he was at her entrance. He wouldn't give in. She barely held on. He rubbed his tip against her folds, teasing her to no end, hitting her in all the right spots. When he pushed upward and hit her sensitive bud, she lost hold of all control.

She screamed, "Justin, please!!!"

At the same time, he cursed, "Fuck it! I'm done waiting!"

And within a split second, they were one. She was screaming his name in ecstasy, as he rode her throughout her climax.

It lasted a couple of seconds, but to Adrienne, it felt like an eternity before she came down from the height of her passion. Justin looked at her intensely, as if he was in a trance.

"Justin…" she whispered.

He smiled slowly at her. "You… are absolutely beautiful," he whispered. "I've never seen a more beautiful sight than you right now."

In response, she pulled him towards her, kissing him passionately. He began moving in her again. Each thrust he took drilled her down, touched her in all the right places and pushed her back again to the cliff of no return.

"Oh my God, Justin. Please! Faster!" she begged. She was meeting his trusts with the same intensity. "Harder!"

He buried his face against the mass of her hair and breathed in the scent of her. "Honey…God, I can't! I can't be rough!"

She knew he was lost in his own ecstasy, but he tried to hold it back. He feared he could harm the baby growing inside her tummy. "We're stronger than you give us credit for, hon. You can let it go."

With an assuring look on her face, he unleashed the beast within him. He speared through her, hitting her most sensitive spots inside and out. His eyes turned a darker shade of blue as he allowed his desire to fully take over him, the beast to control him. He took Adrienne to a new height of euphoria. A few more deep thrusts and she screamed his name again, allowing herself to get lost in paradise.

When she let go of herself the second time around, so did he. He carried her to the highest peak of pleasure and then he jumped off the cliff with her, screaming her name as he entered Nirvana with her.

"I love you, Adrienne Adams!"

When it was over, he looked down at her. He gazed gently at her face while his eyes were dancing. He had sweat beads on his forehead and a triumphant grin on his face, like he had just conquered the world.

"I think if you weren't already pregnant, you would be by the end of this honeymoon," he said.

Adrienne laughed. "Was that part of your plan, too, when you asked Mason and Abi to prepare this wedding?"

"I think we both know I planned the pregnancy long before that," he said, giving her a naughty grin. Adrienne pinched him on the side. "Owww!" he whimpered.

He slowly pulled out of her. Then he lay on his back and gathered her in his arms.

"Are you okay? Are you sure I didn't hurt the baby?" he asked, concern all over his voice.

Adrienne looked up and kissed his jaw, assuring him. "We're fine. The baby's strong."

They lay in silence for a while and then he asked, "Are you okay with everything? Moving to Chicago with me? I mean, you just found your real family in Paris."

"You heard my Mom. She's thinking of temporarily moving to Chicago, too."

"I'm sure my mother is thrilled about that," Justin said. "You know they've been planning this all our lives?"

"I know. They must be over the moon right now."

"They are. Except for your brother, of course."

"Jin? Why?"

"He wanted to be here. He wanted to be the one to walk you down the aisle, actually. We had our arguments over the phone. I told him that privilege still belonged to your birth father. I think he won't be pleased when he finds out that your father's flight got delayed and Yuan gave you away. I changed my mind at the last minute and invited both our parents. Your stepfather asked him to stay behind, to look after important matters. I think he's pissed that he couldn't tell them they were actually coming to our wedding and that he deserved to be here as well."

"Oh my God," Adrienne said sadly. "He will not be pleased. Jin is so much different from Kimberly. He actually wants to be part of my life."

"We'll renew our vows after five years. He can come to that one. He can walk you down the aisle, if he wants."

"Good luck telling him that. Jin Starck doesn't like to be bossed around, either, you know."

"He doesn't have a choice. Since I married you, I have officially become his big brother." Justin laughed.

"Good luck convincing him of that, too." Adrienne also laughed. Although inside, she couldn't be happier. She knew that Justin and Jin would get along just fine. They both loved her very much.

"Have you thought about what you're gonna do with your apartment in New York?"

"Actually, not yet," she replied. "I haven't paid the mortgage in full yet. And I'm out of a job. Now, I'm a wife and soon I'll be a mom. A lot has happened recently. Thinking about the apartment wasn't on my priority list."

"You know you don't have to worry about the mortgage anymore," he said. "I'll take care of it."

She shook her head. "Justin, that's my obligation." She propped up on her elbow so she could look him in the eye.

"You married me. Your obligations have become mine, too," he said.

Her eyes widened. She didn't like that idea. "Justin, no! I won't allow that. I have money saved up. Or I can sell it to somebody who will be willing to continue the mortgage. But I won't let you take over the payments! I won't!"

Justin wrapped his arms around her. "Ssshhh…okay, okay," he whispered. "Don't get stressed out over such a small thing. Hear me out first."

"Justin, you own a similar apartment. You know how much that costs. It's not a small thing."

"Compared to you, it's nothing. Look, I know what that apartment meant to you. It was not just a home or a mortgage. It was your declaration of independence. You bought that to show your parents that you had done just fine on your own. And I feel like I'm taking you away from that place. Forcing you to marry me so soon, and asking you to leave your life behind in New York and live with me in Chicago." He kissed the top of her head.

Adrienne sighed. Her husband knew her very well. He *listened* to her. He heard even the things she didn't say out loud. And yes, she didn't want to give up the apartment that was the embodiment of all she worked hard for…the apartment that was the reason why she met her husband in the first place.

"I'll think about it. But you're right. I don't want to give it up," she admitted.

He hugged her tightly. "I knew that's what you were going to say." He reached for the drawer in the bedside table and pulled out an envelope and gave it to her. "Please don't get mad. Consider it a wedding gift."

Adrienne propped up on her elbow again and took the envelope from him. Inside, she saw two property titles. She read the plot numbers and recognized one as her own apartment. The other one was on the same building, on the same floor, opposite hers. That was Justin's apartment. Both properties were named to her.

"Justin, what is this?"

He took a deep breath. "I settled your mortgage directly with the real estate. They transferred the property to you completely." He looked nervous, like he was waiting for her to shout at him.

"You can't do that? Can you?"

"Well, I have the best lawyers in the country dealing with this, plus I know who owns the building."

"And your apartment?"

He shrugged, "We both know how sentimental those properties have become to us, right? We would never give them up."

"Why did you transfer your apartment to my name?"

"Because I don't see the point of keeping two separate apartments. We're not separating...*ever,* so we don't need to make provisions for such an occasion. I'm superstitious that way." He smiled lovingly at his wife. "So, I'm having a plan drawn up to rebuild both apartments, to make it into one. It would have been easier if we lived beside each other rather than opposite each other. But I hired brilliant architects to work on the design. I'm sure they'll come up with something amazing."

"And the real estate broker and building owner agree?"

"Well, did the real estate company that manages the building agree? Of course not. But since my friend, River, owns the building, they couldn't refuse my requests."

"River owns the whole building?"

"Yep," he replied. "Now, he's scratching his head how he'll explain to the other tenants the major renovations that will be done on our floor."

"And he's okay with that?"

Justin shrugged. "Consider that a part of his wedding gift to us."

"Really, Justin Adams. You have a way of bossing your friends around."

He laughed. "I'm not bossy. I'm just persuasive...and charming. I charmed you, didn't I?"

"Yeah, you were pretty hard to resist," Adrienne said, laughing.

She meant that. She tried to resist this...to resist him. To fight his charms, and not to let them affect her. She tried to think of all the reasons why they could possibly not be together. Little did she know, they were fated to be together, they were made for each other...perhaps even before they were born.

She could reason that they were so far apart in financial and social stature they could not possibly be destined for each other. Whatever reason she could have thought of, that wouldn't stop them from being together in the end. This had nothing to do with their parents. Yes, we do make our own choices and that will make all the difference in the world. But some things are meant to be happen one way or another. You just have to believe that in the end, all is fair in love and war, and things will work out the way they were supposed to. Like destiny, like fate.

"Thank you, honey," she whispered to him.

"For what?"

"For you. For everything that you are. For everything that you do."

He smiled down at her. "I'm sorry that some of our family couldn't make it to our wedding."

She leaned up and kissed him gently on the lips. "They might have missed this. But I will be delivering our baby in less than nine months. Let's get a big hospital room. They can all be there then."

"And then two years later when you deliver our second baby. Then three years later for the third. And four…"

"Justin!" Adrienne laughed. "I can't give birth every year. How many kids do you want?"

He shrugged. "Four."

"Four?" she looked at him, wide-eyed.

"At least."

"Are you serious?"

He nodded. "I told you. I was an only kid. It got a bit lonely for me."

"You had your cousins, didn't you?"

"Yeah. But you only have one brother and I'm an only child. And as it is, your brother doesn't look like he'll settle down anytime soon and have kids of his own. So, we're the only chance this baby has of ever having a big, happy and loud house."

Adrienne sighed happily. "I would like that. A big, loud and happy house."

She felt Justin move and he was on top of her once again. He looked at her lovingly and then he whispered, "I love you so much."

"I love you, too. Promise you won't get tired of me?"

He grinned at her. "How could I ever get tired of you? You're a fox!" Then he leaned forward to kiss her deeply, taking her to an endless rollercoaster ride full of passion all over again.

About the Author

Jerilee Kaye was born under the sign of Leo in the year 1979. She graduated with a Bachelor's Degree in Legal Management from De La Salle University. She has post-graduate qualifications in the fields of Product Management, Project Management and Procurement. She is a Certified Senior Professional in Supply Management from NLPA, Pennsylvania and is currently working her way to an MCIPS certification from CIPS UK.

She manages a global supplier portfolio for multi-national and government entities in Dubai and Abu Dhabi. She is also an entrepreneur, managing a photography and fine art printing company with her husband.

She is married to her first love, Sam, who she's been dating since she was 16. They are blessed with two beautiful angels, MarQuise Justine Jerilee and Sir Alfred IV.

When she's not buried under stacks of paper at work, or engrossed with her writing, she spends some down time playing golf, kicking her husband's butt on a judo match and learning to play the piano.

Trivia: Jerilee Kaye named her daughter MarQuise Justine after her favorite male character Justin Adams.

Other Books by Jerilee Kaye:

Knight in Shining Suit:
Get up. Get Even. Get a Better Man.

Intertwined:
A relationship so beautiful, you can't risk it, not even for love itself.

Coming Soon:

All the Wrong Places
Spin-off to All the Wrong Reasons

Wingless and Beautiful
Extraordinary love can be found in the most unexpected places, with the most unlikely people.

Brother After Dark
When love ventures into the forbidden, is there hope for happily ever after?

Turning Princess Charming
Love can change anything: opinions, preferences, even gender orientations.

Taming a Princess
Sequel to Knight in Shining Suit

**Stories by Jerilee Kaye
available on the Chapters Interactive Stories App**

*Knight in Shining Suit
All the Wrong Reasons
Intertwined*

Connect with Jerilee Kaye:

Send Jerilee Kaye a shout-out, feedback, comment, suggestion, photo, snapshot or screenshot of your copy of All the Wrong Reasons through:

Email: jerileekaye@gmail.com
Twitter: @iamjerileekaye
Facebook: www.facebook.com/jerileekaye

Printed in Great Britain
by Amazon